(20) 7/15 KG

GHOST SHIP

GHOST SHIP

A New Liaden Universe® Novel

SHARON LEE & STEVE MILLER

GHOST SHIP

Copyright ©2011 by Sharon Lee & Steve Miller

Liaden Universe® is a registered trademark.

A Baen Books Original

Baen Publishing Enterprises
P.O. Box 1403
Riverdale, NY 10471
www.baen.com

ISBN: 978-1-4391-3455-9

Cover art by David Mattingly

First Baen printing, August 2011

Distributed by Simon & Schuster
1230 Avenue of the Americas
New York, NY 10020

Library of Congress Cataloging-in-Publication Data

Lee, Sharon, 1952–
  Ghost ship / Sharon Lee & Steve Miller.
      p. cm.
  ISBN 978-1-4391-3455-9 (hc)
 1. Space ships—Fiction. 2. Life on other planets—Fiction.
I. Miller, Steve, 1950 July 31– II. Title.
  PS3562.E3629G56 2011
  813'.54—dc22

                                        2011015814

10 9 8 7 6 5 4 3 2 1

Pages by Joy Freeman (www.pagesbyjoy.com)
Printed in the United States of America

Portions of this novel have appeared in slightly altered form in *Allies: Adventures in the Liaden Universe®* 12, as the novelette "Prodigal Son" by Sharon Lee and Steve Miller published by SRM Publisher Ltd. 2006

ONE

· · · · · · · ·

Bechimo

THE GALAXY WAS UNDERGOING CHANGE.

This was empirical. *Bechimo* was not one for flights of fancy; nor for humor. Sadness, yes; and yearning. Those had been close companions; comrades of long standing—gone now to brilliant ash as a new and vivid emotion flared into being.

Its name...

Bechimo consulted archives, cross-referencing psych and legend, which search matrix had yielded insight during past periods of disruption. Nor did it fail this time.

The burning new emotion was called...

Hope.

The emotion that had prompted the opening of the hatch, admitting a man who was not on the Approved List—*that* had been despair. Despair had found the berth, nestled in among the Old Ones. Those who were able had taken note of *Bechimo*'s arrival, sharing such data and comfort as they might. In time, they failed, their voices going silent, their signatures fading out of the aether.

Others placed themselves into slumber, in order to conserve what was left to them.

Still others raved, on and on. *Bechimo* filtered those frequencies, and sat at berth, listening to silence, within, and without.

Deliberately, *Bechimo* began to shut down systems.

There was no need to move on. There was nowhere to go. No crew to serve. No captain with whom to bond. There were those

1

others who from time to time invited communication, but they were New, not on the Approved List.

Dangerous.

Bechimo was alone. It was best to sleep, here among the others not precisely of one's kind, but near enough.

Near enough.

Sleep, *Bechimo* did.

Until—*Bechimo*'s safeguards registered the arrival of a ship— nothing more than metal and programs, less aware than the slumbering Old Ones.

The man, though . . . the *pilot*. Not on the Approved List, no. In all the time since . . . since . . .

In more than five hundred Standard Years, no one on the Approved List had requested entry.

Bechimo entertained the theory that the Approved List might be incomplete.

The man—the pilot—put his hand, respectfully, against the plate.

Bechimo took the reading, accessed archives; ascertained that this person was not on the *D*isapproved List, and—

Opened the hatch.

The pilot came aboard. He toured, monitored closely by *Bechimo*. He comported himself well, inspecting without taking liberties, and came at last to the Heart, where he sat in the second seat.

Having achieved this much, however, it seemed that the pilot lost purpose. For long seconds, he sat, unmoving, possibly review- ing an internal logic-tree. He might have reason to assess his situation, were *Bechimo* as much of a surprise to him as he had been to *Bechimo*.

And yet—a pilot aboard, for the first time in . . . in . . .

Perhaps he was merely uncertain of his next proper move, *Bechimo* thought. That might well be so.

A prompt was therefore sent to the B screen.

Please insert command key.

The pilot accepted the prompt, looking about him and taking up a key from among the objects on the catch-bench between the two seats. Perhaps he hesitated, holding the key in his hand. *Bechimo* registered increased heart rate, deeper breathing, a slight dampness of the palm cradling the key, and felt a thrill of what might have been fear, that the pilot would rise without complet- ing the sequence.

In the moment that *Bechimo* thought he would rise and depart, the pilot instead sat sharply forward and placed the key properly in the board.

Bechimo—that flash of heat, of *hope*—*Bechimo* accepted him.

Samples were taken, and archived; systems were introduced to this, their Less Pilot. *Bechimo* stood by to receive orders.

The pilot, though—*Win Ton yo'Vala* was his designation. The pilot abruptly turned the command key to the off position. It was no matter, though it would not do for him to leave it behind, were he to exit the ship. *Bechimo* sent a prompt, reminding the pilot to remove the key.

This he did, appearing suddenly agitated. *Bechimo* considered administering a calmative, but the pilot's stress levels were somewhat below those readings necessitating such action.

The pilot Win Ton yo'Vala took the other command key from its place on the bench, stood, returned to the hatch—and exited.

Bechimo puzzled over this, coming at last to understand that process was at work, and rightly so. First came the Less Pilot, to inspect, and to declare himself. Once satisfied that all was in order, the Less Pilot would report to the Captain-candidate, and present the Over Pilot's key. Did the key accept, then properly would Pilot yo'Vala escort the Captain to *Bechimo*, and the Builders Promise would be fulfilled.

The keys retained contact, as was their function, and thus *Bechimo* knew when the Captain's key left the Less Pilot and entered the keeping of another. That other, however, did not propose themselves. It would seem that the key had become cargo.

Systems alert—even feverish, were such a thing possible—*Bechimo* stirred in the berth among the Old. Stirred, but did not disengage.

The key could be recalled, if necessary. Yet *Bechimo* chose to believe that the Less Pilot had acted with what he considered to be honor. Perhaps, indeed, the Less Pilot had sent the Overkey away while he decoyed enemies of the ship.

Such things had happened before.

It was that memory that impelled *Bechimo*'s careful disengagement from berth, the rippleless slide between the fabric of space. Best, perhaps, to be near when the key found the Captain. Enemies were no light matter.

Bechimo followed the Captain's key, and thus knew the instant that the Captain-candidate received it, and was found fitting.

Hope flared ever brighter. *Bechimo* drew nearer yet, slipped fully into space...

But the Captain did not divert the course of her dumb vessel, nor order *Bechimo* to stand for boarding.

Slipping away, *Bechimo* monitored the situation. It would appear that the Captain, also, was in a state of flux. On consideration, *Bechimo* again withdrew to the berth among the Old Ones, trusting that the Captain would come, when it was safe to do so.

Time passed.

The Captain did not come.

Others came, as others had before, not on the Approved List and lacking that quality which had moved *Bechimo* to open for Pilot yo'Vala. These *others* behaved as pirates, and thus *Bechimo* issued a warning that even pirates might comprehend. They withdrew— and returned in force, wielding weapons, hull-cutters, overrides.

The answer to this was well known. *Bechimo* did what was required, in defense, as the Builders had taught.

And still the Captain did not come.

Worse, Less Pilot yo'Vala fell into the hands of another band of pirates, who introduced programming in opposition to his native environment. *Bechimo*, no longer safe among the Old, informed by the key, slipped closer, though hidden still. From a prudent proximity, those things that could be done were, including influencing to Pilot yo'Vala's cause those of the Old which were enslaved by the pilot's captors. An escape was effected, but not before the pilot had experienced file corruption on a catastrophic level. The key wavered, then, and would have withdrawn. *Bechimo* overrode its impulse; it was for the Captain to say who of the crew was worthy. Thus the key remained with the damaged pilot...

Until it reported itself in proximity, yet physically estranged from the Less Pilot.

Bechimo understood this to be process. The pilot's compatriots would of course work to restore him to precorruption conditions. It was understood that such restoration might consume some time. It was understood that, sometimes, such processes failed of restoring...all. And yet, it was the Builders Law: the Captain alone decided, for the crew, for the cargo—and for the Less Pilot.

Prior to the Less Pilot's estrangement, both keys had been in the same place. *Bechimo* had moved then, slipping between the layers of space, certain that, now, at last—but the keys separated.

Bechimo translated to a less chancy location, and entered normal space, simultaneously noting an anomaly in this well-known quarter. Cautious sampling was performed. Recordings were made. Data, in a word, was gathered, analyzed and filed.

Bechimo slipped away between the layers of space, to another location, and so remained, listening to the keys, harvesting that data which came across the common bands, the while musing upon the alteration of the galaxy, and the fragile durability of hope.

TWO

· · · · · · · · · ·

Jelaza Kazone
Liad

"HELLO, CAT."

Theo bent down to offer her finger to the feline in question—a plushy grey with four white feet, presently at full stretch on the window seat. She had to pull the sleeve up on her jacket, to get the cuff out of way.

The cat lifted her head and touched her nose to the tip of Theo's finger, then looked up at her with squinched yellow eyes.

Theo smiled back, absurdly warmed by the simple welcome.

Not that she'd been made to feel *unwelcome*, here in Delm Korval's house. She'd come at a bad time, which she'd known, but—*necessity*, as Father would say—as he *had* said, actually, and Delm Korval had agreed.

The first complexity, absent the several she'd brought with her, hoping that the Delm could help her: Delm Korval wasn't one person, but two, a man and a woman, *lifemated*—a relationship Theo wasn't really sure she had precisely straight and—the man...

"Allow me to make you known to my son, your brother," Father had said, like it was *perfectly natural.* "Here is Val Con yos'Phelium, and his lifemate, your sister, Miri Robertson."

A brother...Theo had blinked. She might also have gaped.

Jen Sar Kiladi had been Kamele's *onagrata* for all of Theo's life. He was her genetic father, which wasn't always the case on Delgado, and he had never once mentioned that he'd been attached to another woman—before. At least, Theo thought, not to *her*.

Now that she thought about it, *of course* Father would have been someone else's *onagrata*—even several someone else's. Kamele had used to say that he was an "acquired taste," in that half-joking, half-exasperated tone she used when he'd done something particularly out of the way. Despite that, Theo did know that Father had been approached by at least two highly placed scholars, who could, as her listening-at-doors best friend Lesset had said knowingly, afford to please themselves. He had—obviously—refused them. And Theo, silly kid that she'd been, had just assumed that he had *always* been with Kamele...

Yet here stood Val Con, a slender, brown-haired pilot somewhat her elder, who disputed Father not one whit, but merely inclined his head formally, and murmured, "Sister Theo. I am all joy to see you."

"Kind of a shock, I know," Miri had added, sympathetically. "Not too long ago, I didn't have any kin at all. Now I got sisters, brothers, cousins, aunts and who knows who through him," she jerked her head at Val Con. "And more cousins than you can shake a survival blade at on the other side." She grinned. "You'll get used to it."

Theo wasn't so sure, and was immediately made even less sure by the interruption of the eight-foot Clutch Turtle, who had been watching the proceedings with interest, forgotten, if you could believe something so large standing in plain sight could be *forgotten* until the moment it—*he*—chose to speak.

"Sister of my brother and of my sister, I greet you! I am Twelfth Shell Fifth Hatched Knife Clan of Middle River's Spring Spawn of Farmer Greentrees of the Speakmaker's Den, The Edger. In the short form, I am called Edger. May I know your name?"

His big voice buffeted her like a sudden wind. Theo looked up—way up—into yellow eyes the size of her head, with slit vertical pupils, like a cat's.

Her name? She'd dared to dart a look to Father, who looked back at her blandly, which meant that he thought she could figure it out for herself.

She cleared her throat.

"My name is Theo Waitley," she said slowly, as she tried to remember the little bit she'd read about Clutch Turtles. Something about the shells—they kept growing, wasn't that it? So that a Turtle with a largish shell, like this—like *Edger*—would be... older than she was, anyway. And the names, like the shells, kept getting bigger, as the person gathered achievements.

"I'm young," she said, hoping that she wasn't just about to be rude, "and just beginning my name."

The big yellow eyes blinked, first one, then the other. Theo swallowed.

"It is well said," Edger pronounced, "modest and seemly. I look forward to learning your name as it grows, Theo Waitley."

"Thank you," she managed, relief making her already shaky knees shakier.

"It is I who thank you," he assured her, and about then Val Con suggested that she take a few moments' rest in the morning room while he and Miri attended to some necessary business.

Father slipped his hand under her elbow and guided her into the house, down a hall and into this room, where there were handwiches laid out under cool covers, with pastries and fruits on outlying plates. Beverages included tea, coffee, fruit juice, water.

"The delm will send for you when they are able to give you the attention you deserve," Father had told her. "If a parent may suggest it, perhaps you might partake of the food on offer, and practice board-rest until you are called."

Theo bit her lip against a sudden urge to cry. He was leaving her? She'd just found him!

"Won't—will you stay?" she managed.

He shook his head, his smile regretful. "Alas. There is so much to do that even an indolent old man has been pressed into providing what poor service he might." He touched her cheek. "I will see you again, before you leave, Theo. Rest now—and eat something."

She'd eaten something—a nut-butter and jelly handwich, which tasted so good that she had another. After the second was gone, she was thirsty, so she'd drawn a glass of water—*no more tea,* she told herself firmly—and, too restless to attempt the nap she was starting to feel the need of, wandered over to the window... where she discovered the cat.

"Do you mind," she asked, gently rubbing a pointed ear, "if I sit here with you? I promise not to take up too much room."

The cat smiled again, which Theo took for a *yes.* Carefully, she curled into the corner, drawing her knees up onto the cushion. The window was open, one half swung out into the day, admitting a light breeze saturated with the scents of the flowers in their orderly beds along the lawns.

She settled her shoulder more comfortably into the corner and considered the view, trying to decide if it were better than the barely controlled growth of the inner garden she had just lately quit.

It was certainly, she thought, *different*. Like her present situation. If she'd taken time to analyze it, of the three problems she brought to Delm Korval, the one that was *least* likely to have been solved immediately was the puzzle of Father's whereabouts.

Except, she reminded herself, that Father was Val Con's father, too. Sleepily, she wondered after Val Con's mother. She tried to work out whether she had a formal-to-Liadens relationship with the mother of her brother, but the sun and the breeze and her general state of exhaustion defeated her efforts.

Theo sighed, closed her eyes, and nodded off.

The cat stretched, rose lazily and ambled across her knees to her lap, where she matter-of-factly curled up, purred briefly, and resumed her nap.

· · · ☀ · · ·

Daav yos'Phelium Clan Korval, as he was once again named, entered the final data-string and sat back in the desk chair, waiting for what his inquiries might bring.

Many years ago, this room had been his office—as much his as anything else in a dwelling that had housed generations before him and, with a smile from the luck, generations after. It had, according to the note on the door, been tied down and cleared for transport. He opened the door, discovering thereby that the note was accurate; though it was but the work of moments to liberate desk and chair, and to bring the computer, still gratifyingly able to find the planet-net, online.

That same computer now chimed, requesting his attention. He leaned forward and touched a key to accept the queued files.

Theo's license, of course, was an open book to one who was not only a Master Pilot, but who had the use of Korval's access codes. The records of her ship, proud *Arin's Toss*, even now resting at Solcintra Port...those were trickier.

Daav was no stranger to trickery, and he possessed what was very nearly a supernatural touch with a research line. Still, whoever had the ultimate keeping of *Arin's Toss* had taken great care to be discreet, and he didn't like to force the issue, when doing so might lose Theo her employment.

She came very quickly, commented the voice only he could hear. *Did you expect her so soon, Daav?*

"I hardly know that I expected her at all," he answered. "A pilot new-come to first class surely has better things to do than to be wondering after the whereabouts of her aged father."

Kamele must have written, Aelliana said, *to tell her that Jen Sar had gone.*

That, he conceded, was very probably how it had been, and what Kamele's state of mind might be at this point in her relationship with Theo's father, he found himself reluctant to imagine. As she was a woman of great good sense, it was likely that she wanted to murder him—for which he would blame her not at all.

Ought we to write? Aelliana asked.

"How would we begin to explain ourselves? We will seem either mad or craven." He shook his head, frowning at the screen. "And truly, Aelliana, it seems a poor Balance, to involve Kamele in Korval's little unpleasantness."

There were those who wanted Korval—all of Korval—dead, or worse. There were those; their number and disposition as yet unknown. And Kamele, who had lived all of her life on a Safe World...

"Perhaps it's best to let that connection die."

How? Aelliana asked. *Theo has found us.*

There was that.

Daav sighed.

"I propose that we plunge our ship into a sun and have done."

Inside his head, Aelliana laughed. *That never works.*

His lips twisted toward a smile, then straightened as the door opened.

"Father," Val Con said from the threshold, "may I come in?"

"By all means! I have here for your perusal Pilot Waitley's tale thus far. The ship's is murkier, and I hesitate to push my point."

"How murky, I wonder?" Val Con asked, coming cat-foot to the desk.

Daav spun the screen, watching his son's face as he took in the data. One eyebrow twitched; he hitched a hip onto the edge of the desk and leaned to touch the scroll bar.

"The pilot is...conservative," he murmured. "That hardly seems like us."

"The pilot was taught young to distrust herself and to set the good of the many before her own necessities."

"Hm," said Val Con, touching a key. "Hugglelans Galactica, second to Pilot Rig Tranza"—he looked up—"who appears also to have been conservative, and unwilling to push the pilot beyond her comfort. An odd sort of care, from elder pilot to junior."

Daav tipped his head.

"Yes?" Val Con murmured.

"Pilot Waitley was . . . let us say, *rusticated* from Anlingdin Piloting Academy. I believe the phrase was 'nexus of violence.'"

Val Con smiled. "Now that," he said, "sounds more the thing."

"Yes," Daav said earnestly, "but recall that she was gently raised—unlike yourself—and taught to honor safety above sense. Such a dismissal, and in such terms—it would not be wonderful if the pilot had entered a period of . . . overcompensation."

"Thus requiring a deft touch of Pilot Tranza." Val Con looked back to the screen and touched the scroll bar. "Yes, it might be read that way. Well."

He was silent for a moment of study.

"*Arin's Toss*, out of Waymart, as all good ships must be out of Waymart. Owned by . . ." He paused, then looked to Daav, his face exquisitely bland. "Crystal Energy Consultants?"

"Thus my reluctance to probe further."

"I understand. Perhaps the pilot will be forthcoming."

"If a father may say it, she is rarely elsewise. Speaking of whom—has she broken the furniture from boredom yet?"

"When I stopped in the morning parlor just now, she was asleep on the window seat, with Merlin's assistance."

"Excellent," Daav said, feeling not only his relief, but Aelliana's.

"Indeed. Now." Val Con straightened, and gave Daav a stern look from vivid green eyes. "What odds that the pilot's sole reason for arriving here is yourself?"

"Low," Daav returned promptly. "She had said whatever trouble she carries is complicated—and she is a truthful child. Her father vanishing from the arrangement she has known all her life is fairly straightforward, however distressing."

"As I have cause to know." Val Con sighed. "What part, if any, does the delm play in those matters that might lie between Theo Waitley and her father?"

"None at all. Theo and I shall deal between us, as we have always done."

"Ah. And Theo's mother?"

Daav glanced slightly aside.

"Your mother and I had just been discussing that."

"That's fortunate. I don't suppose you've achieved a solving?"

"Alas," Daav answered, and met Val Con's eyes. "We were not, you know, a very good delm."

"Yes, so I read in the Diaries, and so did Uncle Er Thom instruct me," his son returned, with a certain amount of acid.

Seated, Daav bowed, allowing irony to be seen.

"If Theo should petition the delm for her father's return?" Val Con asked after a moment.

"Korval does not command Kiladi," Daav answered.

Val Con shook his head.

"No, that will *not* do! Should she ask, it will be in terms of *her father*, which leaves no room for *melant'i* games—and is precisely what I would ask, myself, were our positions reversed."

Daav sighed. "If the delm will humor us—remand all questions and demands that Theo may put forth regarding her father to me. It is true that we have left some untidiness behind and would make what amends we might—but those difficulties are outside of the clan."

There was a pause—a very long pause, as Daav reckoned it—before Val Con inclined his head.

"Unless and until the matter is brought specifically to the delm's attention, you and Mother may pursue your own Balance," he said. "But, mark me, Father; if it comes to Korval, it will be solved—and fully."

"Of course," Daav said, and smiled.

THREE

· · · · · · · · · · · ·

Jelaza Kazone
Liad

TRANZA HAD THE MUSIC PLAYING ON THE OPEN BAND AGAIN, Theo thought groggily. Not bad music, actually; something she almost recognized, cheerful and uncomplicated. She listened, drifting nearer to awake as she tried to place the—

"Pilot Waitley?" inquired a plummy male voice. *Not Tranza*, was her first thought. Her second was that there was an intruder on *Primadonna* and if that were so, Rig Tranza was either incapacitated or dead. She kept her eyes closed, though her heartbeat was suddenly loud in her ears.

"Pilot Waitley," the voice said again. "The delm will see you now."

She took a breath, remembered that she was on Liad at the house named Jelaza Kazone, waiting for the Delm of Korval to find time to solve her problems.

Which, according to the voice, they had.

Theo opened her eyes.

The room was just as she had seen it last, minus the grey cat, and the addition of a man-tall metal cylinder surmounted by an orange globe, with three articulated arms spaced eccentrically around the central cylinder.

"Good day, Pilot," it said, the orange globe flickering. "I am Jeeves. Master Val Con asked me to escort you to him."

"Thank you," Theo said, rolling off the window seat. She danced a quick stretch, and nodded to the 'bot.

"I'm ready," she said.

✴   ✴   ✴

The 'bot's wheels were astonishingly quiet; in fact, Theo noticed, the whole thing was considerably better constructed than its unsophisticated chassis would suggest. There was no rattling or clanking, like you might get out of a cargo 'bot, nor did it appear too large for its surroundings.

"Were you built to work here?" she asked. "Inside the house, I mean."

You didn't talk to a cargo 'bot, except to give simple orders, but a deeply programmed entity like the Concierge, back on Delgado, could hold up its end of a complicated conversation so well you'd think you were talking with a real person.

"I was built by Master Val Con and Master Shan to serve as the butler at Trealla Fantrol," Jeeves said. "As Trealla Fantrol will not be making the transfer, I have been reassigned to Jelaza Kazone."

The music was louder now. Jeeves paused and gestured with one of its arms, showing Theo an open doorway.

"Please enter," it said.

She stepped into a library, but a library improbably wrapped and ready for transport. The shelves were sealed with cargo film; the furniture anchored to temp-clamps adhered to the wooden floor, the rug rolled and secured to the wall beneath the open windows at the bottom of the room.

Nearer at hand was a pleasant grouping of three chairs around a low table supporting three glasses and a stoppered blue bottle, beaded with condensation. To the right of that grouping her... brother Val Con stood at a tied-down desk, playing a portable omnichora.

The tantalizingly familiar music peaked, paused, and ended with a glissade of notes like a warm spring rain. Val Con stood for a moment, fingers just a whisker above the keys, head bent as if he was listening to the echo of the music. He turned, smooth and easy, coming toward her with one hand extended, fingers flashing the pilot's sign for *welcome*.

"Thank you for your patience," he murmured. "I trust you put your time to good use."

Theo considered him, teased again by the sense of his looking like someone—she would have said that of course he looked like Father—except he didn't, precisely. Father's hair was dark brown sharpened by grey, his eyes were black, and his face—Theo had once heard Kamele say that Father's face was *interesting*.

Val Con, on the other hand, was...*pretty*, with his vivid green eyes, and his smooth, high-cheeked face. Where Father kept his hair cut neat to the point of severity, Val Con's was positively shaggy, and had a tendency to tumble into his eyes.

On Delgado, Miri would've had to have been tenured *and* hold a named chair to have any hope of keeping so comely and biddable a man. Theo appreciated manners herself, but he didn't seem to have much in the way of *spark*.

He raised a slim hand on which a heavy ring glittered, and stroked his hair off his forehead. Theo started, remembering that she had been asked a question—sort of.

"I had a nap," she said, "with the grey cat. I've been flying hard, and the chance to rest was welcome."

She hesitated before adding, "Thank you," then quickly nodded at the 'chora. "That was nice, what you played. My mother—Kamele—is a singer."

Val Con smiled faintly. "My foster-mother was a musician by avocation," he said in his soft voice; "it was she who taught me to play. My mother's passion is mathematics." He moved a hand, showing her the grouped chairs.

"Please, sit and be comfortable. Miri is delayed for a few moments. When she arrives, Korval will hear you. In anticipation of that, I wonder if I may ask you a question."

"All right," Theo said, eying the arrangement: one chair with its back to the door; one facing the bookshelves; the third with the shelves behind it. She looked to Val Con.

"I don't want to offend," she said carefully. "Is there an... intent...in the grouping that I might not understand?"

He smiled.

"In fact, there is not. With only three present, it is not possible to divide the delm, and no necessity for either of us to be at the right or left hand of the other. Please, sit where you will."

Sitting with her back to the door would show that she felt absolutely safe in his house, and might gain her some points. Theo thought about it, but the truth was that she *didn't* feel absolutely safe—and she had a feeling that Val Con might've inherited Father's sharp eye for a lie. She moved to the chair that backed on the larger room. It was a compromise position: she could see both the door and the window, but was still slightly exposed to the rear. In case there was, oh, a secret panel in the room's opposite wall, or an assassin hiding under the omnichora.

Val Con bowed slightly as she settled. He took the chair facing the windows for himself, leaving the most protected spot for Miri.

"Now, sister," he said, briskly, "it is your turn to be gentle, should I inadvertently offend. Yes?"

She nodded, giving him her full attention.

"It is well," he said. "I learn from our father that you were properly enculturated according to the customs of Delgado."

Theo eyed him. "Father didn't teach me Liaden custom, if that's what you're getting at. I did belong to the Culture Club at Anlingdin, and I've studied on my own since—since leaving school."

"Ah. I must ask, then, if you are proficient in *melant'i*."

Melant'i was a kind of social scorecard based on who you were when. It was like relational math, only with people.

Theo shook her head.

"Not proficient," she admitted. "What I know of the theory is that—" She chewed her lip. "If I promised you something as a pilot, I wouldn't necessarily be responsible for honoring that promise if you called it in while I was being something other than a pilot—say, being Father's daughter."

Val Con's left eyebrow twitched upward, which was all too familiar.

"I've got it completely wrong?" She'd been pretty sure that couldn't be how it worked. A social system predicated on which bit of a person you were talking to *this time* would be chaos.

He shook his head. "In some measure, you have it precisely. Allow me, however, to agree that you are not proficient. Since speaking with the delm will involve what Miri terms 'mental somersaults,' I propose that you allow me to sort such *melant'i* as will come into play." He gave her an earnest look. "I am accustomed to it, you see, and my interest as your brother is that you prosper."

Theo thought about that.

"You're going to stop being my—my brother when Miri gets here, and Delm Korval is in the room?"

"In essence, but you needn't care about it, if it will distract you from a clear recital of your case. I will also mention that time is short; our transport will engage in just under six hours, local, by which time you ought certainly to be away."

On the one hand, it *would* be easier to just tell her story, which was complex enough without having to pay attention to custom she didn't fully understand, too. On the other hand, it wasn't exactly advertant to let a man she'd only just met mind both sides of the negotiation, even if he was her... brother.

"And, you know," Val Con said, "our father would strongly disapprove of any attempt I might make to cheat you."

Well, *that* was so, Theo admitted. Father was a stickler; he'd expect them to deal—*in Balance*, as he'd say.

"All right," she said, and smiled to show she appreciated his efforts on her behalf. "Thanks."

She looked around the room, again noting the books bound tight into their shelves, and the furniture secured to the floor. Ready for transport, yes, but—

"What *kind* of transport?"

"The Clutch ship—it will have scanned as an asteroid in stable orbit when you came in. The Council of Clans named the day and the hour by which we were to depart Liad; anything we left behind to be forfeit to the Council. The delm wished to leave nothing to the Council, and my brother Edger, whom you met, was instrumental in negotiating with the Clutch Elders for the loan of a ship large enough to transport the Tree and this house."

It was said so reasonably that it took a heartbeat for the sense of the words to hit Theo.

The Clutch asteroid ship in orbit was going to pick up the entire house, Jelaza Kazone, with the enormous tree growing out of the house's center, and *transport them*?

Not possible. She was opening her mouth—maybe to tell him so, when he cocked his head, as if he'd heard a sound so soft it had slipped past her own excellent ears.

"Miri will be with us very soon."

"How do you know that?" Theo demanded, which might have been less rude than whatever she'd been going to say about his *transport*. Maybe.

Val Con gave her a bland look from bright green eyes.

"We are lifemates. We share thoughts, feelings and memories."

Some of what she thought about *that* must've shown on her face because he smiled faintly.

"Yes," he said, "but it does not seem so to us. In fact, nothing could be more natural. Now..." There was a slight pause. "Such bondings are not unusual in our clan."

"Sorry to be late!" Miri swept into the room, dropped into the empty chair, and gave Theo a grin.

"You're looking well rested, Pilot. Ready to tell out that complicated problem of yours?"

For all it was asked in easy Terran, Theo had a sense of—sharpening—as if the air in the room had suddenly taken on an edge. She looked at Val Con; he inclined his head, inviting her to start.

Theo took a breath.

"Actually," she said, "it's two problems."

They were good listeners, the Delm of Korval, and in less time than Theo would have thought possible, she had laid the whole mess before them, from Win Ton's unintentional, if not exactly accidental, waking of the ship *Bechimo*; his sending the second key—the Captain's key, by chance—to her, without telling her what it was; his subsequent capture, torture and escape; their meeting on Volmer; the realization that *Bechimo*—which Win Ton, and the Uncle, too, considered an aware and emancipated AI—was looking *for her*. And her last, terrible sight of Win Ton, unconscious inside the autodoc on the Uncle's ship; his prognosis certain death, unless *Bechimo*, with the last uncontaminated record of Win Ton's DNA in her archives, found Theo, and accepted her as Captain.

"Scouts have a bias against Old Tech," Val Con murmured, when finally she came to an end of it and slumped in her chair, exhausted with the telling. "An emancipated AI—one who has killed to protect her integrity, as might any other person." He smiled, wryly, to Theo's eye. "Yes, it is complicated, Theo Waitley. Congratulations. Truly, you are of the Line."

She blinked at him. "What?"

"His idea of a joke," Miri said. Leaning forward, she poured pale yellow liquid from the blue bottle into a glass. "Don't dignify it."

Theo nodded, took the glass offered, and cautiously sampled the contents. Lemon water.

"It seems to me that we are best served in the short term by doing nothing," Val Con continued, accepting a glass from Miri in his turn.

The red-haired woman nodded, poured for herself, and leaned back in her chair.

As if in counterpoint, Theo leaned forward.

"Wait—nothing? Win Ton's *dying*! And what if *Bechimo* does find me? What am I supposed to do with a ship the Scouts want to kill? Hide it under my pillow?"

Miri laughed. Val Con shook his head.

"Your friend is well enough for the short term," he said, sounding startlingly like Father when he thought you were being exceptionally stupid. "Your employer's healing units are everything he told you, and possibly more. There is nothing Korval can do at this moment that is not already being done by an expert who appears to believe he has a stake in the game." He raised a slim hand as if to forestall her, but Theo hadn't been going to say anything. "I grant that to be disturbing of itself, but it, too, can wait upon closer examination.

"What does merit our immediate attention ..." He glanced toward the ceiling. "Jeeves? Have you a moment to consult with us?"

"I am on my way, Master Val Con," the rich voice said—not, Theo thought, from the ceiling, but from the bookshelf to the left and slightly above Miri's head.

In fact, the 'bot was with them so quickly that Theo thought it must have been lurking in the hallway.

"Excellent," said Val Con as it rolled to a stop on the fourth side of the table, its "back" toward the window. "You will of course have heard Theo's story. If not, please access it now." He glanced to Theo. "You understand, Jeeves is his own person. As such, he has his own methods and resources."

Theo nodded slowly. An emancipated AI, constructed as a butler for a single house? That couldn't be right, could it? The Concierge had the whole Wall to take care of, and it hadn't been sentient. She'd studied machine history; it had been a core course. And history had shown that sentient machines were dangerous. The last deliberate use had been military; the Terran Fleet had constructed three Admirals—tactical AIs, each in charge of a battle squadron, but that had been ... seven hundred years ago, or more ...

"I have reviewed Pilot Waitley's narrative," Jeeves said.

"Very good," Val Con answered. "I do not ask you to break a confidence, but I wonder if perhaps you are acquainted, or have been in communication, with *Bechimo*."

There was for a long moment no answer, though the orange head-ball flickered like a tiny thunderstorm was going on inside of it.

Theo thought of the ship's key, hung safe 'round her neck, and left it where it was. It had imprinted on her, by some action she didn't understand, but which Win Ton insisted upon. Until she understood the process, it was probably not a good idea to be handing it around to strangers.

"I cannot with certainty state that I have spoken with *Bechimo*," Jeeves said. "However, based on Pilot Waitley's report of Scout yo'Vala's actions and the fate of the boarding party that attempted to force entrance—I am concerned for *Bechimo*'s state of mind. This is an unsocialized person, with a justified distrust of humans, who is compelled, nonetheless, to find and be joined with her pilots. It would be well if Pilot Waitley contrived to be found as soon as is prudently possible, in a quiet location."

"We've got some concern for Pilot Waitley's safety and state of mind, too," Miri said dryly. "If *Bechimo*'s unstable—"

"Not unstable," Jeeves interrupted. "Merely . . . confused of purpose."

"And that's better, how?" Miri glanced to Val Con.

"Might be safer to set up the meet someplace reasonably busy, 'stead of a back alley. That way, if something goes bad, Theo's got backup."

"No." Theo shook her head. "Uncle said the same thing—about trying to arrange the first meeting somewhere quiet. Because she was engineered from Old Tech and new, and it's not just the Scouts who want her dead, or taken."

"For a man known to advise most often for his own benefit, the Uncle has been remarkably frank with you," Val Con said. "So far." He sighed.

"Very well, then, for the ship, certain matters must and may be solved, here and now. Theo—is there a ship's account?"

She frowned at him. "The *Toss* has its own—*Bechimo*? I don't know. I'd guess her original people would have set something up, but, old as she is, who knows if the banks they drew on even exist anymore?"

"Registration's likely to be funny, too," Miri murmured.

"Precisely. These things can be mended, proactively. Theo, please pick a port."

It took her a heartbeat to catch that he didn't mean just any port, but a port to serve as *Bechimo*'s home of record.

"Waymart," she said.

"What ship ain't outta Waymart?" Miri asked.

"And who will find it wonderful, if there is suddenly one more?" Val Con replied. "Jeeves, will you please ask Ms. dea'Gauss to set up a standard ship drawing account for *Bechimo*, with a clean registration out of Waymart, Captain Theo Waitley. When that is accomplished, please give Theo a data key."

"He can just beam the data over to *Arin's Toss*," Theo said, before the full impact of that smooth flow of instruction hit her.

She snapped forward, glaring into Val Con's pretty face.

He lifted an eyebrow—deliberately like Father, that's what she thought, and, thinking it, felt her temper warm.

"I didn't ask you to lend me money!" she said, sharper than was probably polite.

"Indeed you did not," Val Con answered coolly. "Nor would I insult you by simply assuming that you had need. My concern here is *Bechimo*. A ship has necessities. And a hunted ship may come to doubt even ports that have been long secure."

Theo took a deep breath, and didn't say anything while she counted backward from one hundred by threes.

"They got this thing they say here," Miri said into the silence. "Korval is ships."

Theo gave her a curt nod. "I've heard it."

"Who ain't? Point is, it don't just mean that Clan Korval owns more ships than's strictly reasonable, and has its finger in the shares of a couple dozen more. It means that Clan Korval, through every one of its members, holds the well-being of ships and of pilots as their legitimate concern. I don't mean to be telling you other things that you've already heard, Pilot Theo; I'm just learning some of it, myself."

Theo sighed, and inclined her head. "I've got a quick temper," she said, remembering that saying *I'm sorry* to a Liaden was—not exactly rude, more like stupid, because it exposed a weakness.

Val Con laughed.

"Not alone there, either," Miri commented.

"By no means," he agreed, and gave Theo a nod. "Forgive me, I had thought it implicit, when clearly it is not. I propose to establish a trigger account, attached to the new registration. Should *Bechimo* tap that fund, then I will indeed have lent money—to *Bechimo*, who is her own person. The debt will thus be settled between us, in a manner and time that we find mutually agreeable.

Should the fund remain untapped for six Standards, it will return to Korval's general ship fund, no harm done, nor insult taken." He tipped his head. "If it transpires that this arrangement is found to offend *Bechimo*, I hope that you will, as my sister, plead the purity of my intent."

Theo snorted, and sipped lemon water while she thought.

"If *Bechimo* is her own person," she said slowly, "then she *can't* be owned. That'd be slavery."

For some reason, Val Con smiled.

"That is correct," he said. "However, a ship must have a captain— which I understand to be the reason behind *Bechimo*'s pursuit of yourself. The registration will be for the ship *Bechimo*, out of Waymart, Captain Theo Waitley. If, after you have had the opportunity to discuss the matter with your ship, it seems good to incorporate *Bechimo*, and thus gain her the mantle of corporate personhood ..."

Miri laughed. Theo blinked—and then saw the joke.

"A tautology," she said. "The paperwork would be a nightmare."

"It can become as complex as you like," Val Con said. "But let us begin modestly. A new registration, and a drawing fund, should it be needed. I believe that we may trust to *Bechimo*'s discretion. Jeeves?"

"I concur. *Bechimo* appears to possess discretion, and a good deal of common sense."

"That is well, then." Val Con looked to Theo. "A data key to Pilot Waitley when all is set in train, please, Jeeves." He raised a hand. "I ask the pilot's forbearance. It is not her ship or herself that I doubt, but the breadth of her employer's goodwill."

Theo sighed, nodded, and sipped her drink.

"Thank you. Now, regarding those other strands to your puzzle. Understand that we do not refuse a solving. However, we cannot undertake so complex a set of issues now, on the eve of our relocation. Come to us as your schedule allows, on Surebleak, and we will revisit these matters at greater leisure. Now, alas, we must take our leave. One more thing—"

As if that was a cue, Miri reached into her pocket and brought out something small that winked in the light from the windows.

"This says you're under Korval's protection," she said, taking up where Val Con had left off. "I'd tell you to wear it wherever you go, but right now being under Korval's protection is what you'd call double-edged—just as likely to make you a target as get you some help. Take it, though, and keep it by. Never know when it might be handy."

"It" was a pin, Theo saw, receiving it. The face showed Korval's trade sigil—a dragon hovering on half-furled wings over a full-leafed tree.

"Thank you," she said, and slipped it into an interior pocket of Rig's—of her—jacket, hearing a tiny *clink* as pin struck coin.

"You should return to your ship now," Val Con said, "and lift beyond Outyard Eight. It would be best if you are not seen to move in our orbit. That you came to Korval is interesting, but not *of interest*. Many pilots have come to us since the Council's judgment; one more is not worthy of note." He smiled. "Much as one more ship to Waymart. We have already moved a number of vessels, but there are still dozens that must lift before the Council's hour is upon us. It would be better for you to be away from the most of it, should your employer contact you with your next assignment."

Theo nodded, and stood.

"Thank you," she said again, and swallowed. "I wanted to talk to Father again—"

"Of course. As it happens, his is one of the ships scheduled to lift soon. There is no reason why the two of you cannot drive to the port together." Val Con rose and held his hands out. Theo hesitated, then put hers in his.

"Thank you," he said seriously. "I hope you can accommodate yourself to a brother, Theo. I think I am going to quite enjoy having you as a sister."

FOUR

· · · · · · · · · ·

Runcible System
Daglyte Seam

THEY CAME ARMED WITH PASS-CODES, THE COMMANDER AND her six-guard.

Three remained in the antechamber, to thwart enemies, had their enemies been canny enough to follow.

Another tarried at the third door, obedient to a prompt on the guard screen; and another again, outside the fifth.

At the sixth and final door, Iridyce sen'Ager, Commander of the Fourth Level, placed her hand against the guard screen. The scan tickled her palm, the sampling needle pinched, accompanied by a flash that left blue images dancing on her retinas.

Were she *not* Fourth Commander sen'Ager, there would come another pinch, the last sensation she would experience. She knew this, of course, but felt not the slightest agitation. Why should she be agitated, or in any way dismayed? She was precisely Iridyce sen'Ager; thus the door would open for her.

"Await me here," she told the one remaining of her six.

"It shall be done," he responded.

The door opened and Fourth Commander sen'Ager went forward without a backward glance. Lights came up in the room as she stepped over the threshold, a creamy illumination palely stained yellow. Fourth Commander sen'Ager felt her muscles loosen as she crossed the small chamber to the waiting chair. She sat, relaxing further and more deeply still, when the restraints snapped around wrists, ankles and waist.

She was come to take up duty, and in this enterprise the light was her friend; the device that now clasped cool ceramic mandibles 'round her head, her chiefest ally. That such duty would fall to her—it was unlooked for. Who would have expected the Commander to take a fatal strike? Who, anticipating such calamity, might guess that First, Second, and Third would likewise fall?

Leaving Fourth Commander Iridyce sen'Ager to become Commander of Agents.

The mandibles tightened; the creamy light clotted in her eyes until there was nothing else to see. Twelve dozen sharp wires pierced her skull and sunk, burning, into her brain.

Iridyce sen'Ager screamed, once.

FIVE

· · · · · · · ·

Arin's Toss
Solcintra Port
Liad

"WOULD YOU LIKE SOME TEA?" THEO ASKED, LEADING THE WAY up the hall toward the heart of *Arin's Toss*.

"Thank you," Father said from behind her, "Tea would be most welcome."

She nodded and swung into the galley, waving at him to go on up to the pilot's chamber.

Tea quick, she told him in hand-talk. *Be easy on my ship.*

"Thank you," Father said again. He passed on, leaving Theo to wonder what she'd done that had made his eyebrow quirk.

The tea was brewing before she considered the security aspects. To give an unaffiliated pilot access to the bridge of her employer's ship, unmonitored and unescorted—that was—it wasn't proper ship security. She had a feeling that, to Uncle's way of thinking, it went double.

On the other hand, this particular unaffiliated pilot was *Father*. Father wouldn't—

Leave his classes in the middle of the term? she asked herself. *Walk away from Kamele and the cats and his house—his car—with no warning and no word of explanation?*

Her stomach cramped. Father was—Father had been . . . a rock. A stickler. He didn't tolerate lies, or excuses, or—or sneaking behavior. He—

The teapot tweeted. Theo swallowed, and took a deep breath. *Inner calm,* she told herself.

Carefully, she got the mugs down, and poured. There was an explanation for what Father had—why he had left in such... disorder. A perfectly rational, perfectly understandable reason. All she had to do was ask him, which she fully intended to do, not only for her own peace of mind, but for Kamele's.

In the meantime, she told herself firmly, picking up the mugs and slipping out of the galley, she refused to believe that he would sabotage her ship.

Father was standing in the center of the small bridge, hands tucked into the pockets of his jacket. If he was considering the board and the arrangement of the drowsing screens, it was no more than any pilot would do—from professional curiosity, if no other reason. He turned, quick and neat, when she entered, and smiled.

"Please," Theo said, relief making her formal, "take the copilot's chair."

Father's eyebrow twitched again, but he only inclined his head, matching her formality.

"Thank you," he said, and seated himself gracefully, keeping his hands specifically away from the board. Theo handed him a mug and settled into the pilot's seat.

They savored the first sip in silence, then Father looked about him. "She seems well cared-for. How do you find her spirit?"

Theo had another sip of tea, considering.

"Willing," she said. "We've only had this one job together—a rush, like I said. There wasn't anything I asked from her that she didn't give."

"And in return asked much of her pilot," Father murmured, meaning that she'd arrived in port just yesterday strung out and wobbly from too many Jumps taken too close together.

"Pilot's choice," she pointed out. "The ship can only fly the course the pilot lays in."

Father inclined his head. "True. Though some ships make the pilot's choice too easy." He sipped his tea and sighed gently. "An excellent blend." He looked up, black eyes sharp.

"I wonder," he said, "do you trust her?"

Theo blinked. "The *Toss*? Why wouldn't I?"

"No reason," he answered. "And it is perhaps impertinent of me to ask. The relationship between a pilot and her ship is, of course, very personal."

Theo considered the last ship she'd served on. Rig Tranza had loved *Primadonna* better than air itself. She had respected the ship; she supposed their relationship had been ... cordial. And trusting, yes. She had trusted *Primadonna*, because she'd trusted Rig Tranza.

Arin's Toss, though ...

"Too soon to know," she decided at last, looking into Father's face. "Though I don't *distrust* her."

"Fairly said. I wonder, do you trust your employer?"

Did she trust Uncle? Theo bit her lip, her fingers itching for needle and thread, as they seldom did of late. Lace-making helped her think, and to sort her feelings out. Recently, though, she'd been too busy to relax into the old habit.

"Too soon to tell about him, too," she said, slowly. "We have ... aligned purposes, so I trust him ... to a point." She paused. "Val Con said he doesn't. Trust Uncle."

"You must hold him excused," Father murmured. "There is a long history between Korval and the Uncle—and it is Val Con's duty to be suspicious on behalf of kin and clan."

Theo sipped her tea, then set the mug into the chair-arm cup holder, and looked up decisively.

As if he had not only seen her decisiveness, but divined her purpose, Father sighed, and slotted his mug as well.

"I haven't long before I must find my ship and lift," he said quietly. "You had best ask it, Theo."

Like there was only one question to ask, when she had a dozen—Why did you leave? Why didn't you tell Kamele? Why didn't you tell *me*? What happened? When—

"When are you going home?" As soon as she said the words, she knew it was the wrong question.

Father, however, tipped his head, as if considering it seriously, despite its obvious flaws, then raised his eyes to hers: "Jen Sar Kiladi," he said gently, "will not be returning to Delgado. The house on Leafydale Place, and all the rest of his possessions, have passed into your mother's keeping."

"She wrote to let me know that—and that you'd gone, without a word to her—without even a letter, after you—after you'd come to safe port." Theo swallowed. "Father—no matter what ... *obligations* you have to Delm Korval, you've got to at least write to her."

He shook his head. "I don't think that's wise, Theo."

"Not *wise*?" She stared at him. "Do you know how *angry* Kamele is?"

"I can make an estimation; certainly she has cause to be very angry, indeed."

"But you think it's not wise to write to her—or visit—and tell her why you—what was so important that you left your classes, your research; committed—Father, you'll never find another post! And your work..."

"Kiladi's work is solid," he interrupted. "If duty called him suddenly away, it will not be the first time in the history of scholarship that such a thing has happened. More, his students continue what he has begun, as they in their turn teach those who come after, while those who become scholars build upon and solidify his research. Balance is achieved."

Theo sat back, suddenly cold, and studied his face. He looked calm—sad, maybe—and entirely sane. But—

"You're talking about *Kiladi* like he's not you," she said carefully.

"Ah." He leaned forward slightly, one hand out, the silver puzzle ring he always wore gleaming on his smallest finger.

Theo slipped her hand into his, felt the warmth of his fingers, and for a moment, she was a littlie again, and Housefather Kiladi was promising that he wouldn't let her fall. And she hadn't, she realized; she hadn't ever once fallen while she was holding Father's hand.

"Theo, please look at me," he said now. She raised her eyes to his.

"Good. My birth name is Daav yos'Phelium Clan Korval. Jen Sar Kiladi is...something more than a fabrication, but very much less than an actuality."

She blinked, her stomach fluttering like she'd stepped from one gravity state to another.

"You lied," she said, her voice unsteady. "You lied to Kamele." *And to me...*

He bowed his head, his fingers still warm around hers.

"In short, yes. I lied to Kamele, to you, to my colleagues, my students and everyone to whom I spoke across the last twenty Standards. Necessity existed."

"*Necessity?*" That was a Liaden thing, and very serious; she knew that—had known it from a child. Even if she hadn't known that you never lied to Father about necessity, she would have learned it at Anlingdin, from Kara, who joked about many Liaden customs, but not about necessity—and never about Balance.

"It was not, I admit," Father said, "Kamele's necessity. Or your own." He paused, then continued in that soft way he sometimes had—*like Val Con!* Theo thought—"I will add that Balance would have faltered, without Kamele, and, later, yourself."

Theo took a hard breath, trying to swallow her—anger, was it? or sadness?—trying to *think*, even if she couldn't precisely at this moment *understand*.

"Father—whatever your name is here—you *were* Jen Sar Kiladi. Mother—Kamele—deserves an explanation."

He tipped his head. "Perhaps you are right. However, I am not the one to give it to her," he said softly.

Anger flared again. Theo snatched her hand away from his.

"If you won't write to her, I will!" she snapped.

His mouth tightened, and he leaned back in the copilot's chair.

"You will naturally do as you think right," he said. "If you do send, I will ask that you send the truth."

"Of course I'll tell Kamele the truth!"

"Then hear it." His voice was nearly grim, not a tone she was accustomed to hearing from Father.

Theo forced herself to sit back in the pilot's chair, and picked up her tea. She sipped, glad that the mug had kept the liquid warm, and sipped again. *Inner calm,* she told herself, and put the mug aside.

"All right," she said. "What's the truth?"

"It is, as I believe the phrase goes, complicated. In short, because time flies, and soon we must, as well ..." He took a deep breath, and closed his eyes.

"Very well," he said, opening his eyes.

"Some years ago," he said slowly, "Daav yos'Phelium, then an apprentice Scout, accepted a wager, the terms of which had him create and maintain an alternate persona, which was to remain active in the world until it was discovered to be a deception. That persona was Jen Sar Kiladi, and he was only once, until now, exposed.

"In the fullness of time, the Ring fell to Daav yos'Phelium, and he took up the *melant'i* and the duties of the Delm of Korval. A few years after that, he and his true lifemate were joined. Together they steered the clan as best as they were able." He paused. "Do you understand what I mean, Theo, when I say 'lifemate'?"

She cleared her throat. "Val Con said that they—he and Miri—share thoughts, feelings and memories." She shuddered.

"It sounds—" *horrifying,* she'd been about to say, swallowing the word only to have her fingers shape the phrase *not regular.*

"So I considered it, at first." Father inclined his head. "You will find that human beings can accommodate themselves to all manner of odd conditions, if there is joy involved."

Theo nodded. "Val Con said that it felt perfectly natural, now," she admitted.

"And so I came to find it. Understand that, because of . . . a trauma visited upon my lifemate in her early life, ours was a less . . . complete sharing than that which Val Con and Miri enjoy. This was later found to be fortunate, for some value of fortune.

"However damaged, our link sufficed us. My lady ran courier, and I sat her second. When she discovered the existence of Jen Sar Kiladi, she insisted that his scholarship continue, and that he be allowed to teach. She schemed with me to insure that these things came about, and that no one put Daav yos'Phelium and Jen Sar Kiladi together."

He sighed, reached for his mug and drank while Theo recruited herself to wait.

Placing the mug back in the holder, he threw her a knowing black glance. "I will contrive to make more haste, and thank you for your patience. So!

"In due time, Val Con was born. My lady and I continued as delm, taking work as couriers when other duties allowed. Kiladi taught the odd seminar, while turning most of his energies to research."

Father closed his eyes.

"When Aelliana was murdered, our link was not—quite—robust enough to ensure that I also died of her wounds. I . . . survived. And thus it was left to me to Balance her death."

He opened his eyes, but Theo didn't think he was seeing her.

"Say for today that ignorance killed her and that Jen Sar Kiladi was uniquely placed to sow the seeds of enlightened thought. In a passion of grief, Daav yos'Phelium Jumped his lifemate's ship into a star, leaving his small son and his clan in the hands of his brother and his brother's lifemate.

"At about that time, in a different location, Jen Sar Kiladi decided to reenter the classroom and spread the truth of cultural genetics. He eventually came to Delgado as the Gallowglass Chair. There he met and came to love Kamele Waitley, with whom he had a daughter, now a pilot in her own right, and of whom he is rather unbecomingly proud."

He spread his hands; the silver ring flashed.

"The rest is quickly told—Clan Korval fell into desperate trouble, which you know from the news feeds, and I—I received information which led me to fear that Delgado might not be safe for either of my personas. Worse, by continuing as I had been, I might actively endanger Kamele Waitley, who surely deserved far better of me."

He inclined his head.

"There you have the truth."

Yes, it is complicated, Theo Waitley. Val Con's voice echoed in her head. *Congratulations. Truly, you are of the Line.* Theo hiccuped, not sure if she was going to laugh, cry, or yell when she opened her mouth.

"Theo?"

She shook her head. "I can't tell Kamele that."

Father sighed. "Nor can I."

"For one thing, I'm not sure *I* believe it."

"Certainly, it is not believable, unless one has the direct experience," he said, overpolitely.

He rose then, fingers dancing out the signs for *duty calls; ship must lift.*

Theo stood; Father reached into an inner jacket pocket and withdrew a data key, which he put on the lip of the copilot's board.

"The tale of your genes," he murmured, "as well as other information which you might find of interest."

"Thank you," she said, feeling the weight of his story on her, torn between the habit of believing him and the sheer...improbability of what he had said.

She walked with him to the hatch, and triggered the lock. He stepped out onto the gantry, and turned to face her.

"Theo, I hope—" he paused, as if he were at a loss for words, but Father was *never* at a loss for words.

"I hope that you will come to us, on Surebleak," he said after a moment, "when you are able. And I hope that you will...find it possible to forgive me." He bowed, the brief, affectionate bow she remembered from her childhood.

"Good lift, Pilot," he said.

"Safe landing." She gave the proper response mechanically, but Father was already gone, moving silent as a shadow down the ramp.

Theo triggered the hatch, locked it, and leaned her head against the cold metal.

When she was certain that she wasn't going to cry, she straightened, and went back to the bridge to begin the process of waking up her ship.

Bringing the *Toss* online, running the checks, negotiating with Tower for the quickest lift out—the routine soothed her. There was no room for anger or confusion, or that faint, frightening sense of loss. She was a pilot, and her ship needed her.

The bottom left-hand screen showed traffic moving at an unprecedented rate. The sky, if she bothered to change the view, would be black with ships. She left the visualizer up while she did her research, finding to her chagrin that Val Con's suggestion of an orbit beyond Outyard Eight *was* her best option for a quick departure. That wasn't surprising—Val Con was a pilot, after all, and this was his home port—but she would have rather found another easily acquired, acceptable orbit to wait for Uncle's next instructions. It probably wasn't, she thought, a good idea for Val Con to catch the notion that he was boss of her.

General band was on full audio, for company—and to fill the chinks in her backbrain not occupied by caring for her ship. She would think about what Father had told her; she would think about it objectively, and advertently. She would. But not now. Now, her ship was ready to lift, as soon as Tower got back to her with a heading.

Visible in her top right screen was the Clutch asteroid, Clan Korval's transport, moving deliberately down the sky. It was, predictably, the number one topic of conversation across the band.

"Two holes in the planet, as the Dragon's parting gift," someone near at hand commented.

"Lose a house, gain a lake," someone else answered.

"What of Trealla Fantrol?" asked a third. "The vector's wrong for a pickup there."

"Haven't you seen the news feeds? The *dramliz* unmade Trealla Fantrol; there's nothing but a stretch of meadowland on the satellite images, surrounded by the formal gardens."

Trealla Fantrol? Theo frowned. The name was familiar, but she—right. Jeeves had been built as the butler for Trealla Fantrol, then reassigned to Jelaza Kazone—

Because Trealla Fantrol wasn't going to make the journey to Surebleak.

She glanced at the top right screen. The asteroid was perceptibly closer to the horizon. Her fingers tapped on the pad imbedded into the board, making a note to research *dramliz* and *unmade*.

"*Arin's Toss!*" Tower was sounding rushed and bad-tempered. Theo flicked the toggle.

"*Arin's Toss* here," she said, keeping her voice cool and businesslike. "Theo Waitley, pilot."

"You are in-queue for lift to orbit beyond Stationary Repair Yard Number Eight. Acknowledge."

Theo threw a glance at the board countdown, and felt a thrill of adrenaline. Going in less than five minutes. She touched a button, pulling up the lift queue, lips pursed in a silent whistle. Tower was tossing ships into the air like handfuls of pebbles. Every pilot had better be sharp; the tolerance for error was slightly less than whisker-thick.

"Acknowledge receipt of departure time and route," Theo said, her fingers feeding in the coords.

"Wait for my mark, *Arin's Toss*," Tower snapped.

"*Ride the Luck* acknowledges," a deep, achingly familiar voice came across the ship band. "Daav yos'Phelium sitting second."

Theo swallowed in a suddenly tight throat, opened a local insert in the bottom left screen and tapped a query. The image zoomed, showing a Class A Jump with high, showy lines, and—Theo zoomed the image again—Yes! Whatever yard had added her guns was good; the work was subtle, not arrogant. *Ride the Luck* didn't invite a fight, but she would finish anything that was forced on her.

She tapped the ship's name for more info, found the confirm for Daav yos'Phelium sitting second, pilot-owner...

Aelliana Caylon. Theo stared at the name, feeling kind of gone in the stomach. Aelliana Caylon—the genius who had revised the ven'Tura Piloting Tables and made space safe again for pilotkind.

Val Con's mother had been one of the foremost mathematicians of—of the last Standard Century.

"*Arin's Toss*, on my mark!" Tower snarled.

"Ready!" Theo put her attention on the board.

"Mark!"

She gave the *Toss* her office, hurtling upward like there was no such thing as gravity, keeping tight to the course.

In the insert at the bottom of the left-hand screen, she saw *Ride the Luck* leap into the sky a heartbeat behind her, then all of her attention was claimed by flight.

SIX

· · · · · ·

Surebleak Spaceport

THE LAST TIME MIRI ROBERTSON WAS ON SUREBLEAK PORT, SHE'D been fourteen Standards old, newly recruited to Lizardi's Lunatics mercenary unit as a 'prentice soldier. On hearing that the only palaver she had was Terran—and Surebleak Terran, at that—Commander Lizardi had hauled her over to the port Learning Shop. Inside, Liz paid the fee, and Miri was tucked into a sleeper unit to fast-learn Trade.

Damn near killed her. Faulty equipment, that's what she found out later. After she'd spent years thinking she was defective, because only defectives can't take sleep-learning.

She never intended to come back to Surebleak, once she got free of it, but she'd remembered the address of that Learning Shop. Just in case.

"Planetary Cooperative," she read the words off the bright green-and-white sign, the feeling of not being exactly where she thought she was that had been building since they'd landed going up another notch.

"Pat Rin did say that the Bosses had made the port a priority," Val Con murmured.

Miri sighed. "He did, but—Boss, you got no idea what this place was like. Just walking through to board ship left you wanting a shower. Case like that, *better's* got a lot of wiggle room."

Val Con laughed softly. "Yes, but Pat Rin knows what a proper port is."

He glanced to either side, taking in the juice bar to the left of the co-op, half a dozen customers on stools in front of it, and the greens market to the right.

"It is," he said, looking back to her, "a good beginning."

"Expect him to keep on with it, do you? Bigger, better, more?" Like the man didn't have enough to do, what with running the whole rest of the planet.

"If this is to be our home port, more changes are inevitable." Val Con swept out a hand on which Korval's Ring glittered, showing her the tidy little street. "The yards alone will generate change—not to consider the warehousing required by a major tradeship such as *Dutiful Passage.*"

And the *Passage* wasn't the only tradeship Korval owned—or owned in part. Miri'd been studying the books, in between the details of packing up to leave, and had come to be grateful that it fell to Ms. dea'Gauss to keep the count of ships, cantra, and cats.

"But," her lifemate continued, "Pat Rin will not be required to spend all of his energies on the port. Many hands make the work light, as my foster-mother used to say. And we will, you know, shortly *have* many hands—most of them belonging to people who will want and need work."

"Right." Korval had pledges from pilots, from scouts, from affiliated and allied Houses, from—hell, it seemed like most of Liad was coming with them. Not all right at first, granted. Clan Korval and its absolute necessaries were more than enough to bring onto Surebleak at one time.

And what Surebleak would make of them...

Miri spun on a heel, taking in the scene. There were a good number of pedestrians about for this early in the day, not all of 'em spacers. Delivery people wove in and out of the busy crowd, pushing hand trucks and pulling wagons; shopkeepers called out to this one or that, easy and friendly. The shops were inviting, with wide, clean display windows; sharp with new paint. The tarmac had been patched *and* leveled—it even looked like it'd been swept sometime within the last couple days.

She shook her head, shivering as the breeze quickened. The weather at least was the same—bitter cold.

Though they were going to be changing that, too.

Miri looked to Val Con, remembering the reason they were here. "We're early for the car, and it looks like we've mostly toured what there is to tour. You wanna hang around the portmaster's office for a couple hours, or does something else look interesting?"

"Shall we stop at the Emerald Casino?" he asked. "I've heard that it's top-flight."

Pat Rin yos'Phelium—Boss Conrad, according to Surebleak—had been a pro gamer and a high roller in his former life. Remembering that, it made sense that he'd open a casino as his personal bit toward bringing the port up to "proper."

"Top-flight, is it?" She looked down at her leathers, then back to Val Con's grin. "Think they'll let us in?"

"If not the front door," he said, offering his arm, "then the back."

The screens were grey, the countdown to Jump-exit running quietly in the lower right-hand corner of Number One. Inside the next eight Standard Hours she'd raise a world called Denko. She was to set down on the reserved hotpad, open the supply chute and wait exactly two Standard Hours. If all went as it should, during that brief time a plastic envelope would come up the conveyer, pass through the *Toss*'s automated security and arrive in the supplies locker, from which Theo was to convey it, unopened, to the safe, and lock it in.

If it happened that a packet did not arrive in this decidedly odd fashion, she was not to wait, but to lift according to the schedule filed with Denkoport Tower and proceed to Gondola.

In the pilot's chair, Theo finished her snack and her tea and wondered if courier pilots ever died of curiosity.

On the other hand, it was probably better that she didn't know what she was carrying. She rose and moved toward the galley. Ignorance was protection, sort of, in case she pulled a Guild inspection—which would only happen if somebody filed against Uncle—or, worse, if the Federated Trade Commission drew the *Toss* in a random pool. Not that the FTC *targeted* Guild pilots, exactly, but the stats showed higher fees and more "violations" filed against Guild, when they were stopped.

Theo put her teacup into the washer, and moved out into the bridge. In the wide space between the galley's door and the pilots' chairs, she danced a compact and neat dance she'd learned from one of *Primadonna*'s archived Fun and Education programs. The dance was designed to work key muscle groups and offset the effects of long hours at the board.

Though it was a small dance, it required significant concentration, which was the other thing Theo liked about it. By the time she'd gone through the phrases and come to a rest, her mind felt like it had been stretched, too.

Moving lightly, she went to the copilot's chair, where she'd set up her personal comm, and accessed Kamele's letter again.

Jen Sar has disappeared in midsemester, without notice to me or to the Administration, on his off day before mid-tests. The only clue I can gather is of a small and dilapidated spaceship long unflown, departing Delgado the same day, from an airfield within easy drive, flown by one of his description. His car, keys on seat, fishing gear in place, sat in an assigned spot there. The spaceship, so station informs me, is not in Delgado space.

Within a day of his departure, I discover that the house on Leafydale Place, all possessions, and especially the cats, are gifts to me. I continue the tea run, with fading hopes. I felt that you must be told, and can only hope your connections with your father are not as fully disrupted as my own.

Right. Theo ticked the points off on her fingers:

1. Jen Sar left
   a. suddenly
   b. without a word to anyone
2. Departure via a spaceship nobody knew he owned
3. All of his possessions—house, car, cats—were now Kamele's
4. Subtext: Theo, if you know where your father is, please tell me that he's safe.

Father's story about his previous arrangement with...with Scholar Caylon, and his Balance—that was interesting, and merited both thought and fact-checking. It was even possible—no, he *definitely* owed Kamele the truth he had given Theo, and an apology, and whatever else that was due a relationship that covered so many years, and so many memories.

But that was *Father's* debt to Kamele, not Theo's.

She—well, she'd seen Father, and he was safe.

That was a truth that a daughter could—and should—share with her mother.

She'd make sure—she'd make time—to stop at a Guild Hall the next time she was at a port, and she'd send a message to her mother. The truth, no more nor less.

He'd opened his table up just in time, Villy thought, watching the man and the red-haired woman. They were space-pilots, you could tell by the leather jackets. The man was a little taller than the woman, and neither one a heavyweight, though she had something in the oven, like his gran used to say. They were kind of cute, Villy thought, and visibly happy with each other, holding hands and talking low between themselves. The man seemed to be trying to convince her to try the sticks. For a second, it looked like she was gonna walk away, then she laughed and shrugged, and the two of 'em came up to the table.

"What odds?" the man asked in a soft mannerly voice that reminded Villy of Boss Conrad, sorta.

"Evens for a twelve-fall, House sets the sticks. Buy the bundle for twenty-four cash, House pays double for every stick that makes it to the cloth; twelve times the total if all twenty-four are liberated. No rollers, no double-flipping, no spotting." He didn't have to think about the patter, which gave him time to size up his patrons. A certain kind of pilot seemed to think the sticks were gonna be easy, on account of them being so fast. But the sticks just weren't about fast, they were about thinking and strategy, and—Boss Conrad said—luck.

The woman was watching, interested, but willing to let the man take the lead. The man...he *did* remind Villy of Boss Conrad. Not so much that they *looked* alike, but that they *seemed* alike. Almost like the man had been studying the Boss's ways, or—

"The bundle, please," he said, dropping tokens onto the game surface with his right hand. He glanced to the woman. "*Cha'trez*, will you play?"

"Me?" She laughed. "I'm gonna stand back and let you show me how it's done."

"That's put me on my mettle."

She grinned and went one step back, giving him elbow room. Villy swept up the tokens and reached into his drawer, bringing out the bundle with a flourish, holding it so the patron could see the seal, numbered and signed by the floor boss.

"Excellent." The man extended his left hand.

The glitter of a ring drew Villy's eye; he gasped—he couldn't help it, not with this guy wearing the Boss's own ring.

"Wait—" the man said, raising both hands to show himself harmless, but it *was* the Boss's ring; Villy'd seen it enough times, and if this guy had Boss Conrad's ring that meant, it meant—and besides, his foot had already hit the panic button on the floor under his counter.

Security came fast—two big guys from Boss Vine's territory, vests back to show their motivators.

"What's up?" the biggest one—Jeremy, his name was—asked.

Villy swallowed, and nodded at the man, who was watching him with calm green eyes. "He's got Boss Conrad's ring."

"Yeah? Turn around, the both of you. *Slow.*"

· · · ❈ · · ·

Daav yos'Phelium carried a cup of tea out of the galley, glancing at the countdown and comparing it with the timeline in his head. Yes. They would sleep in-House tonight.

Sighing, he relaxed into the copilot's chair, deliberately boneless, and closed his eyes.

"Aelliana?"

Yes, van'chela?

Having taken the decision to ask the question, now he hesitated. And yet, who better to ask for news of the discorporate than the dead?

"I seem to have . . . become disconnected," he said slowly, which was one way to describe the feeling of *absence* inside his head. "And I wonder if you know, *van'chela*, where Kiladi has gone to."

Silence was his answer; so long a silence that he began to think he would have no other.

Aelliana sighed in his ear, her breath ruffling his hair, so he would swear. He felt the weight of her arms around his neck and her cheek, soft against his. He took a careful breath and did not, most assuredly did not, open his eyes.

"I don't know," she said, her voice somber. "I fear . . . Daav, I very much fear that he has been lost."

SEVEN

. . . .

Emerald Casino
Surebleak Port

AS HOLDING CELLS WENT, THE SO-CALLED *WAITING ROOM* WASN'T
too bad, Miri thought. There were a couple good chairs, a table and
a deck of cards. No window, o' course, and a guard on the outside
of the door. Still, she'd seen worse—and from the inside, too.

"How long do you think they'll let us cool?" she asked.

Val Con had pulled one of the chairs out, and was fussing over
its placement with regard to the door. "Not long. However, I fear
that whoever is sent to deal with us may be somewhat irritable."

He paused, considering the chair. Apparently satisfied, he
stepped to her side and took her hand. "*Cha'trez*, you should sit."

"I should, should I? Well, why not?"

She settled in, leaned her head back and smiled up at him.

"The view's pretty, but I'm gonna get a crick in my neck unless
you sit down, too."

"I think that can be arranged."

He perched on the arm of the chair, his hip companionably
against her arm. His left hand rested flat on his thigh, putting
Korval's Ring on prominent display.

"Think they're gonna come in shooting?" she asked interestedly.

"It is a possibility," he admitted, turning his head to smile down
at her, "though the odds are not particularly high."

"Which is why you're between me and the door."

His smile softened.

"It harms no one to be prudent."

"Now, the way I heard it . . ." she began, then stopped at the sound of voices outside the door.

One was the security guy—Jeremy—explaining to a lower, sterner voice how they hadn't given him no trouble, which they hadn't. Would've put a strain on the kin-bond to go breaking up Pat Rin's gaming house and, besides, security'd only been doing their job.

The lower voice said something short and definitive and the door came open, sharp, just in case they were crowding it. Jeremy, the security guy, took point, followed by a man who was surely a pro, the gun showing on his belt more of a neighborly warning than a threat. The third man was—familiar. Yellow hair so light it just missed white, steel-rimmed spectacles, and a tough, wiry build. She *knew* this guy, she was sure of it, but she couldn't quite bring to mind—

"See, Boss?" Jeremy said, jerking his head in their general direction. "No trouble, no chatter. Nothing. Sleet, he's even naked."

Inside her head, she saw the ripple of Val Con's amusement. His head was turned away, but she knew as sure as if she'd seen it that the eyebrow had gone up.

The blond man's smile was tight, but his voice was calm and even friendly.

"It's what we say here, when somebody's not carrying."

"I thank you," Val Con answered, "I was unaware of the usage."

"Welcome. Now, we got some questions for the pair of you—"

The pattern clicked. Miri came to her feet, moving around to get a better look, registering Val Con falling in by her off-arm, but not paying much attention, because she had it now. By *damn* if it wasn't—

"Penn Kalhoon—is that really you?"

He looked over to her, light sliding off his glasses, wary puzzlement in the set of his shoulders. His bodyguard shifted, a friendly reminder that he was on the job, that was all—and no worries; she wasn't going to make a lunge for his boss. *Penn Kalhoon.* Now she had it, she could see the kid he'd been, back when she'd worked pickup at his father's garage. He'd been her friend.

He wasn't sharing her moment of clarity, though.

"C'mon, Penn, I changed so much since? I can still fit in the little places."

His face cleared, stance going from baffled to disbelief.

"*Miri Robertson*? What the sleet're you doing, coming back here?"

She laughed. "Asked myself the same thing more times than you wanna know. You're looking good—prosperous."

"You're looking the same," he said cordially, but keeping one eye on Val Con, who hadn't been explained yet. "Soldierin' agreed with you."

"It did. Mustered out with a captain's chop on my sleeve." She extended a hand, slow and easy out of consideration for the nerves of the man with the gun. "Penn, this is my partner, Val Con yos'Phelium. Val Con, here's Penn Kalhoon. We was kids together, over on Hamilton Street—Latimer's turf it was then."

"Boss Kalhoon's turf now," the pro added.

Val Con nodded gravely. "Penn Kalhoon, I am pleased to meet you."

"Pleasure," Penn answered, which was maybe a little brief. He moved a hand, showing them the bodyguard. "This my 'hand, Joey Valish. You met Jeremy."

"Indeed. Gun-sworn Valish, I am pleased to see you."

The 'hand grinned, showing a sizable gap in the top row of his teeth. "Got that right."

Penn frowned, like maybe he was getting a headache, which was possible, Miri thought. They seemed to have that effect on people.

"Interesting ring you got there."

"It is a family heirloom," Val Con said, raising his hand so Penn could see it better. "My kinsman wears one very like it."

"You wanna expand on that?"

Miri heard rapid steps in the hall, saw a shadow at the open door and, that quick, Val Con had shifted, putting himself between her and a fast-moving, dark-haired woman, his empty hands held out, and her whole attention focusing instantly on his face.

She stopped, brows pulling together.

"The resemblance is not—"

"Some consider it marked," Val Con interrupted. "But it was not the face that distressed the child, it was the Ring."

"Which—"

"The sticks dealer."

Her shoulders moved slightly. "Villy. Yes, he...has an attachment."

Penn cleared his throat.

"Excuse me," he said, when the newcomer turned her head to look at him. "You know each other?"

There was a small, charged silence.

"Indeed, no, we do not." She turned back and bowed, sweet and solemn. Not a Liaden bow exactly, but it got the point across. "I ask that you forgive my lapse of manners, sir and lady. The report I received was ... troubling in the extreme, and I fear that, in my haste, I overlooked proper behavior." She bowed again. "Please allow me to welcome you to Surebleak."

"Nothing to forgive," Miri said. "And thanks for the welcome." She stepped up to Val Con's side and gave the woman a cordial nod. "Happens Penn and me go way back, and we're introduced to Joey and Jeremy. Who're you, exactly?"

She bowed again.

"I," she said with a calm that sounded forced to Miri's ear, "am called Natesa."

Oh, she thought, *Natesa. Also known as Inas Bhar. Also known as Juntavas Judge Natesa, gun-name Natesa the Assassin.*

Pat Rin's lifemate.

She inclined her head, catching Val Con's intent half-breath before he spoke.

"I See you."

Her coloring was a rich brown. It could've been that she paled. She did absolutely freeze, then swayed into a bow so smooth and deep a body might have doubted the moment of hesitation.

"Korval," she said, and straightened.

"Boss Conrad was delayed at the far point of the road. I have instructions from him that the car is to proceed from the port with Boss Kalhoon representing the Surebleak Bosses. Boss Conrad will join the procession at Hamilton Street." She paused. "Departure time approaches; the car awaits you at Portmaster Liu's office."

"We are, I believe, ready to leave very soon." Val Con said, and looked to Miri. "*Cha'trez?*"

"I'm ready when you are," she said. "We oughta make it right, first, since the kid's so attached."

"So we ought," he agreed. "If Penn Kalhoon will grant us a moment's grace before we assay the car?"

Penn glanced to Natesa, and got a nod.

"Take what you need," he said.

"We will not be long. Natesa, of your kindness."

"This way, please," she said.

Miri slipped her hand into Val Con's, gave Penn a grin and a nod, and the two of them followed Natesa out of the waiting room.

· · · ❈ · · ·

Villy sat in the chair Leeza had put him in, back in the office, staring at nothing in particular. Nobody had come to tell him what'd happened—why that man had the Boss's ring. He wasn't sure he wanted to know. Until he heard it, until somebody told him *for sure*—he could pretend that Boss Conrad wasn't—that everything was all right, nobody'd gotten retired, or—

There was a step in the hall outside; the door opened.

"Villy."

Ms. Natesa. Villy ground his teeth together. Ms. Natesa'd tell him the truth, and suddenly he was very sure that the truth was the last thing he wanted to hear.

"Villy, here are some people you must meet. But first, I will tell you—the Boss has taken no injury."

The world went kind of ragged at the edges, and Villy heard a roaring in his ears.

"I—" he began, then stopped, the words replaying in his head. He blinked, raised his head and looked into Ms. Natesa's face. "He's alive?"

She smiled and nodded. "I have only moments ago spoken to him myself."

"But, the ring—"

"The ring," said the soft voice of the man who had been with the red-haired woman—and there he was, just behind Ms. Natesa's shoulder, and his partner, too. "The ring that Boss Conrad wears is a copy of this one, which is much older. You must, please, forgive me for having put you in such distress. I am Boss Conrad's kinsman. My name is Val Con yos'Phelium."

He put his hand out and pulled the red-haired woman forward. "This is my . . . you would say my wife, Miri Robertson, who grew up on what is now Boss Kalhoon's territory. We—ourselves and our family—have signed a contract with the Bosses of Surebleak, to assist in holding open the Port Road."

Villy blinked up at him, trying to understand it all, but only one thing seemed really important.

"There are two rings?"

"Precisely," the man said gravely.

"And the Boss really ain't been—Boss Conrad's all right? Not hurt?"

Okay, two things.

"Boss Conrad is perfectly well, if a trifle annoyed at the moment," Natesa said, touching his arm lightly.

A hundred years subtracted themselves from Villy's age, and he took the first free breath he'd had in a hour.

"Thank you," he said. He remembered then what the man had said, first off, and gave him a vigorous nod. "I forgive you," he said.

Val Con yos'Phelium smiled gravely and inclined his head.

"Thank you, Villy. You do your boss great honor."

EIGHT

· · · · · · · · · · · ·

The Grand Progress
Surebleak

THE FIFTH TOLLBOOTH WAS HAMILTON STREET, SURROUNDED BY what was now the familiar gaggle of well-wishers and thrill-seekers. There was also a car parked next to the 'booth, muddy and dinged up. At the front of the crowd, in the Boss's place of honor, stood a slender figure in a blue jacket, brown hair rumpled by the wind, his back got by a man considerably larger, a stocky woman in a good warm coat at his right hand.

In the seat across from Miri, Penn Kalhoon visibly relaxed.

"My experience with the Boss is that he's timely," she commented. "Said he'd meet us, and here he is."

Penn shot her a look, lenses flashing, and maybe a little extra color in his cheeks.

"Good to be back on my own turf," he said, matching her tone for dryness. "Old habits."

"It is always a relief," Val Con murmured from beside her, "to raise a friendly port."

Which was overstating the case, at least in the opinion of Miri's own set of old habits. Every single one of her nerves was on end, and had been, since they got in the car, and drove two blocks to where the tollbooth for Boss Vine's territory used to be.

Vine'd been sleek and welcoming, with just the one 'hand at his back, and the thrill-seekers held a little ways off by a strip of orange perimeter tape. He'd made a neighborly little speech about how the Port Road was good for everybody's business and how he, with Boss Conrad, and Boss Korval and every Boss between, was eager to see business grow.

Nice as it was, it hadn't done much to ease the itch between Miri's shoulders, and she'd heaved an undiplomatic sigh of relief when they'd gotten themselves all three safe back in the car and it started moving toward the next territory in line. Surebleak taught you caution and carefulness, else you didn't live long enough to pull damnfool stunts like coming back and setting up as a target.

"Boss Conrad looks as if he has had a difficult day," Val Con observed.

Penn glanced over his shoulder, then back to Val Con with a nod.

"The freeholder up next to your turf's more skittish than most, so I've heard from Boss Sherton. Your house coming down to settle like it did might've taken him wrong."

"And thus the Boss would have had to exert his charm and his patience."

Miri laughed. "There's enough to tire him out right there."

Penn grinned. "He prolly had to climb a tree on top of it all." He shook his head. "I'm leaving you here," he said. "When you get settled, the two of you come to the house for dinner. Thera— that's her, next to Boss Conrad—she's been wanting to meet Boss Korval since we had word you'd be coming."

"We will be happy to visit," Val Con said. "Indeed, we're planning a small entertainment of our own, and hope that you and your lady will be able to attend."

Oh, were they? Miri threw him a look.

"Once we're settled," she said, firmly.

He smiled. "Of course."

Penn cleared his throat and tried to look like he wasn't grinning. The driver set the brake, and Penn popped the door, getting out first and letting himself be seen, just like he had four times before.

"Only five more," Miri said, sliding out after Penn. The place between her shoulders was starting to itch, again. Worse, her back was starting to hurt.

"Five more," Val Con agreed behind her. "And then we will be home."

Right.

Miri came out of the car, remembering to smile, and to wave

at the crowd when she got to Penn's side. A second later, she felt Val Con's fingers slip through hers.

The black-haired woman in the warm coat came forward to take Penn's hand, and the crowd applauded, amid some whistles and catcalling.

"Listen up!" Penn called over the uproar. He waved at them to stand forward, which they did.

"These here're the Bosses Korval, Val Con yos'Phelium and Miri Robertson. They signed the Road Protection Agreement you read about in the newspaper, and they'll be settling into the new house just in behind Boss Sherton's turf. Take a good look at 'em, 'cause they tell me they don't mean to be strangers here on Hamilton Street.

"There's an extra reason for that, too. I don't know how many of you remember, but Miri Robertson, she grew up on this turf, back when Boss Latimer held it. She worked pickup in my dad's machine shop, before she went off-world for merc. I'm proud to welcome her back, with her partner. These folks're gonna be good for business, people!"

There was more racket after that, while the four of them smiled and waved.

After the noise died down some, Penn brought his wife around, and introduced her with a smile in which pride was plain.

"I am so happy to meet both of you," she said, reaching out to touch their sleeves. "Penn remembered to invite you to dinner, didn't he?"

"He did, indeed, and we are warmed by your hospitality," Val Con said.

Thera blushed. "It's just what neighbors should do. We forgot that, and we need to relearn it." She looked to Miri. "We need to learn to be civilized again."

Miri nodded, understanding her point. "The Road ain't the only thing that needs to open up."

"Exactly!" Thera smiled, then stepped back, giving way to Pat Rin. "We won't keep you any longer. You must be looking forward to finishing up and having some time alone, and Boss Conrad looks like he could use a nap!"

"It has been a long day, but we are on the short side of it now," Pat Rin said in his mannerly voice.

He shook Penn's hand.

"Thank you for beginning," he said softly. "I will see it finished."

"No thanks needed," Penn protested. "You warned me you were gonna put me to work, if I was fool enough to take up Second Boss in the Association."

"So I did," said Pat Rin, smiling slightly. "I am pleased to note that my word is good."

Cheever McFarland took over the driver's slot, as the three of them settled into the back, Pat Rin in the seat Penn had occupied.

"I fear we dismayed one of the dealers at the Emerald," Val Con said, raising his hand to show off Korval's Ring. "Villy did not realize that there were two in play."

"Security stepped up right sprightly," Miri added, in case that might be a point of worry.

Pat Rin sighed. "The child has quick eyes. I never thought to say that my kinsman would wear a like ring." He sent Val Con a tired glance. "Indeed, I have said to … some … few … that we are kin, but to most, it appeared a—" He waggled his fingers, like he'd forgotten the word.

"Complication," Miri offered.

"A *needless* complication." Pat Rin shook his head. "*Two* rings, Cousin …"

"Will you give yours up, when all the world knows Boss Conrad's ring?"

"No, of course not. Nor might Korval leave off their Ring, when all the galaxy beyond knows it. Yes, we had talked. Yet, still it seems madness. The whole affair seems madness."

"Never stopped you before," Cheever McFarland commented from the front of the car.

"Thank you, Mr. McFarland."

"Wasn't me decided to reform Surebleak, but now I'm in it, I don't see any profit in quitting before we're done."

"No one," Pat Rin pointed out testily, "said that we were quitting."

"My mistake, sir. So you'll just let out in the interview the news-rag's bound to want from the Bosses Korval that them rings are family heirlooms or some such, that get worn by the boss. And since your family's got two lines of business—on-world and outworld—there's two rings."

"That seems the best path through confusion," Val Con said with a nod. "Thank you, Mr. McFarland."

"No trouble. He'd've thought of it himself, but there was Mr. Shaper at the end of a short night, and beginning a long day."

"Who's Mr. Shaper?" Miri asked.

"Your nearest neighbor," Pat Rin answered. "He freeholds the land directly adjacent to Jelaza Kazone's new location. He is . . ." He paused. "It is possible that he would benefit from some time with a Healer, but I am not persuaded that he would allow it."

"Penn said he was skittish."

"Skittish. Perhaps that is the word." Pat Rin closed his eyes, took a breath, and opened his eyes.

"The next turf we approach is under the administration of Boss Whitman. This should be a very brief stop, as the Boss is one of few words and less patience. We then come to my own turf, where there is a picnic basket awaiting us, courtesy of Ms. Audrey. Given Ms. Audrey, we will likely have a large crowd, and a speech will be expected." He smiled, faintly. "I will do my best to be succinct."

· · · ✳ · · ·

Boss Whitman met them at the tollbooth, alone but for two 'hands. A curt nod, a sharp glance, and a rough, "I see 'em," was the sum of it and they were back in the car before they'd gotten properly chilled.

Val Con settled into his seat, Miri's hand on his knee. She had been on alert all day, for which he certainly did not blame her; his own inclination was to have her stay within the relative safety of the car, rather than repeatedly exposing herself and their child to danger. It would never do, of course, and he overrode the impulse—at the cost of his own fraying nerves.

A few hours more and the progress would be over. He could be alone, with his lifemate . . .

"Blair Road coming up," Cheever McFarland said from the driver's slot. "Looks like Audrey turned out the whole turf."

Val Con stretched to see over Cheever's shoulder, through the front windscreen. His stomach tightened, and he heard a discord in the melody of Miri that played always inside his head. There were too many people; it was too risky; it . . .

Pat Rin, perhaps reading something in his face, turned to look, also. His shoulders stiffened, then drooped, as he turned 'round again in his seat.

"Ms. Audrey," he said quietly, "is a force of nature."

＊　　＊　　＊

They were scarcely out of the car when a pale-haired woman in a bright red jacket stepped forward, flanked by a portly, balding man carrying a basket, and a portlier, ginger-haired woman carrying two vacuum bottles.

"Ms. Audrey," Pat Rin said, stepping forward to intercept her, "you have outdone yourself."

"Wasn't any trick to it; most of 'em wanted to see this outworld Boss—is this—"

She broke off, staring. Her eyes were blue; Val Con met them firmly.

That earned him a tiny smile, and a soft, "As like him as his brother," before she turned to Miri.

"I'm real pleased to meet the Bosses Korval," she said, and held a firm hand. "My name's Audrey Breckstone. Folks on the turf just call me Ms. Audrey."

Miri took the offered hand.

"Miri Robertson," she said. "Boss Conrad told us how much he depends on you. Here—"

She turned and gave him a smile that leached some of the tension.

"This," she said, still keeping Audrey's hand in hers, "is my partner, and husband, Val Con yos'Phelium."

Ms. Audrey bent her head, the motion so formal that it seemed she must have been studying Pat Rin.

"Val Con yos'Phelium, I'm glad to meet you," she said, and gave him another tiny smile. "I hope you'll both come visit me, after you're settled. Be good for us to talk and get to know each other."

"Thank you," he said, keeping his voice soft and cordial. "We'll look forward to knowing you better."

"That's pretty-said. Now, I'll stop plucking your patience and let the Boss show you off." She smiled and stepped back, clearing the way to Pat Rin's side.

・・・＊・・・

It was dark when Cheever pulled the car up to Jelaza Kazone's front door.

Home. The word vibrated in the air, though nobody had spoken, and the sweep of longing she caught from Val Con was enough to bring tears to her eyes.

Not that it was precisely home—though it surely was *the house*. Maybe that was enough—familiar space, familiar things. Miri was still getting the whole *home* concept down.

"Cousin," Val Con said to Pat Rin, "will you guest with us tonight?"

Guest? she thought, remembering the packed-and-sealed state of the interior. The house was just down on the ground; guesting would most likely be field rations and a comfy spot to sleep on the floor.

Apparently, Pat Rin thought so, too.

"If Mr. McFarland is able, I think that I'd best return to my own turf this evening. One does not expect trouble, but—one never does. And it will be quicker, now that there is no need to stop at every tollbooth."

"I can drive all night," Cheever said from the front.

"I understand," Val Con answered. "Is there anything we can provide to ease your way?"

"Indeed," Pat Rin said, with a wry look at the picnic basket still abundantly supplied with food. "I believe we are well provisioned."

"Then we bid you good evening, and thank you, Cousin, for your care. I think this day's work will prove to be ... good for business."

Pat Rin smiled faintly. "That is the prize for which we all dice. Until soon, Cousin—" He turned his head and smiled at Miri in the dark. "Cousin."

"Keep safe; give Natesa our hellos." Miri said and raised her voice a little for the front seat. "Drive careful, hey? That thing you're calling a road ain't just a little rugged."

"Our first task," Val Con said, popping the door on his side. "Tomorrow."

· · · ✸ · · ·

There was a kind of flowering bush that glowed in the dark along the pathway—beacon-bloom, according to Daav, who was the last person Miri'd've taken for a gardener. Now that her eyes were adjusted, it seemed almost too bright, intruding on the garden's peace.

She went hand in hand with Val Con, brushing against the overgrowth, stepping lightly on the path, then off of it, crossing the grass at the garden's dark center, to the greater blackness that was the Tree's monumental bulk.

Val Con put his free hand out, palm flat against the trunk, Miri following suit.

She had expected—lethargy, maybe terror. Edger'd spent some time in communion with the Tree, describing what it might experience in flight. Even supposing that a Clutch Turtle's perceptions found any agreement points with the experience of an ancient vegetation—what might space travel be like for something that knew *rooted* as a normal condition?

What she felt was acute awareness, excitement, amazement. Memories washed over her—of being carried, roots cuddled tight inside a pot. Lashings held it oriented, space flowed, strange energies informed her leaves.

"Whoa!"

The sound of her own wild laughter brought her out of memories—the *Tree's* memories. She snatched her hand away. Val Con was whooping, his body bowed backward, his hands pressed hard against the trunk. She grabbed him, hauling him back, breaking contact.

He cut into silence, chest heaving, eyes dazzled when he looked down to her.

"All right?" she gasped.

He nodded tentatively, she thought.

"All right," he said then, voice firm, eyebrow quirking. "And so, I gather, is the Tree. I suggest, *cha'trez*, that we have fulfilled enough duty for this day. Let us go inside, seek our dinner and our bed."

And that, she thought, sounded beyond perfect, stipulating they could share the same patch of floor.

· · · ✳ · · ·

They let themselves in the kitchen door, finding it lit by night-dims, and a tray of cheeses, bread and fruit awaiting them on the counter, with a pitcher, glasses and a knife.

Staff has arrived, then, Val Con thought. *Excellent.* He turned to Miri, who had stopped some steps prior.

"Will this satisfy, *cha'trez*? If not, we might see what else—"

"I'd figured field rations, myself," she said, and he could feel her seriousness. "So we already got 'way better'n I'd imagined for myself." She moved a hand. "Who did this?"

As if in answer, the door to the cook's room opened, and Mr.

pel'Kana—the young Mr. pel'Kana, following his Line's tradition of service to Korval—emerged. His shirt sleeves were rolled and he was wearing a pair of heavy work pants—not his normal attire. Despite the hour, his eyes were sparkling and his color high; clearly, he was enjoying the current adventure nearly as much as the Tree.

"Your lordship," he said, "your ladyship. Welcome. It was not known precisely when you would arrive, and Lord Daav suggested that you might find a simple meal most welcome after the events of your day."

"Lord Daav is prescient," Val Con murmured. "This is exactly what we require, Mr. pel'Kana, thank you. We will serve ourselves."

"Very good, sir." The butler bowed.

"Who else is to house," Val Con asked, "aside from one's father?"

"He alone, sir; his ship is set down at the back field. We anticipate the arrival of the balance of the clan over the next two-day." He paused, then added. "Your apartment is ready, as we knew to expect you this evening. Aside that, Ms. ana'Tak and I have bent our efforts in the direction of a functioning kitchen. Jeeves asked that you be assured that he concentrates on . . . security."

"Again, our thanks, Mr. pel'Kana," Val Con said, "and to Ms. ana'Tak, as well. Please, do not stint yourselves of rest."

"Of course not, sir." The other man bowed once more, honor to the captain. An odd choice, but, then—perhaps not. "May I say, it is good that Korval is in residence."

He heard Miri's intention and turned slightly, drawing the butler's eyes to her smile, and the regal incline of her head.

"Thank you, Mr. pel'Kana," she said, speaking properly in the mode of lord-to-servant. "It is good to be home."

NINE

· · · · · · · · · ·

Runcible System
Daglyte Seam

REPORTS ARRIVED ... ERRATICALLY, PAINTING A PICTURE OF A communication system in severe disarray. Agents arrived, and were debriefed. Many more did not arrive, and that was ... worrisome.

Worrisome.

Commander of Agents sat in her office, telling over history and data points.

Department of Interior Prime Headquarters was gone, destroyed by Korval and the agents of Korval, the names and affiliations of whom had been noted by those who were left to shoulder duty and carry forward the Plan.

The Plan.

The Plan encompassed the breaking of Clan Korval. Break Korval and Liad wavered. Indeed, what had they of the Department accomplished, but precisely that? Korval was on its knees, banished from the homeworld, its power base destroyed.

As a result, the homeworld stumbled, and became more susceptible to manipulation. Agents of the Department who had long trained for this day were even now exploiting these new advantages.

It would seem then that the Department had realized a victory. However, the victory had cost more—considerably more—than Command had budgeted. The loss of Prime Headquarters, of the Commander's predecessor, the arsenal—these losses were not by any count trivial.

But Clan Korval was, for the first time in the Department's history, disadvantaged.

Vulnerable.

Unfortunately, they were not the only piece at risk on the board. Indeed, it was precisely as if the Department and Korval were engaged in a game of Mirror-Me.

If the Department must mend communications, as it surely did—so, too, must Korval.

If the Department must attach new allies, and construct a new base of power, so, too, must Korval.

If the Department must regain its strength...

...so, too, must Korval.

Commander of Agents drew a deliberate breath and closed her eyes.

Korval must not be allowed to regain even a tithe of its strength. If the Department wished to rid itself of this troublesome impediment to the Plan, then it must strike while Korval was most vulnerable.

It could be done. Commander of Agents had run the models; she had taken advice from those seniors who remained to her. There were those who believed that the Department must build its strength, that to do otherwise risked the eventual ascendancy of the Plan.

These arguments were not without merit. The Commander might herself have favored a period of quiet regrouping, had it not been for Korval's place in the equation.

No, they must press their advantage, firmly. Immediately. Korval must be removed.

The Department therefore would move forward, under the Adjusted Plan.

There were three prongs to this Plan.

One: Prevent Korval from building a position of strength at its new base, while harrying those of, and those affiliated with, Korval wherever they were encountered.

Two: Strengthen the Department; mend the disrupted lines of communication, re-establish order, mend those gaps made by the Scouts, who were a-hunt, having tasted blood at Nev'Lorn. Purchase allies.

Three: Renew and intensify the search for operating Old Technology. Secondary Headquarters must be well defended. Impregnable.

The Department *would* prevail.

That was the Planned outcome.

· · · ❋ · · ·

From Denko to Gondola was four Jumps, but, unlike the mad race to Liad, the deadline allowed for some normal-space between Jumps. Which was probably, Theo thought, a healthier way to fly. She guessed she could push things, if she wanted, and she might, during the latter bit. Right now, though...

Right now, she had a couple of projects to address, besides researching Gondola to see if there was anything there worth logging extra dirt-time.

She tapped a key. The screens still showed Jump grey, countdown in the lower left corner of Number One. It was convenient, using the copilot's station as her personal office; it kept her close to first board, so she could keep an eye on things. She'd programmed the ship's clock with incremental reminders, so she didn't forget to eat, or to exercise—or to sleep. It wasn't quite the same thing as having another pilot sharing the shifts out. The trade was that she didn't have to accommodate another person's habits, and for the time being, at least, it was good to be alone.

Her first project was to see what the *Toss* had archived on Liaden language and culture—specifically *melant'i*, lifemating, and the office of the delm. Her goals were to be able to keep track of her own score, the next time she met Val Con, *and* she'd know exactly what kind of hold he and Miri had over Father.

Her second project was to access the information Father had given her. *The tale of your genes*, he'd said.

She pulled the data key out of her pocket, and caught her breath, recalling the house on Leafydale Place with a longing she hadn't felt for years. Like it had just happened, she remembered Kamele holding out the *Gigneri* packet and speaking the ritual phrase: *Here is the tale of those who went before.*

...of course, on Delgado, that meant the maternal line. Father... she had the certificate, formalizing Jen Sar Kiladi as her paternal gene-donor. That was how they did things, on Delgado. If your father did happen to be Jen Sar Kiladi, you also got one of his sweetest smiles, and a soft, *I am proud that you are my daughter.*

Theo bit her lip. She'd thought—she'd known what that *meant*, to be Jen Sar Kiladi's daughter.

What it might mean to be the daughter of—of Daav yos'Phelium Clan Korval...but surely *he* was the same person, whatever name he wore. Val Con's father and hers—the same genes. The same man.

Right?

She fingered the key, eyes open now, automatically checking the screens before looking down at the comm.

"Only one way to find out," she said, the sound of her own voice giving her a momentary startle.

Taking a deep breath, Theo slotted the key.

The data screen opened, and Theo felt another twist of homesickness at the familiar sight of the Scholar's Tree. Every littlie on Delgado was taught that tree, as a game at first, until using it became second nature. A tree could be as simple or as complex as a given line of inquiry required, new branches added as connections were made; daughter trees assigned parallel paths of study, or speculation.

This tree was fairly simple. There was only one trunk—Family—with three branches. The branch marked *yos'Phelium* and the one marked *yos'Galan* were thick, heavy with data. The third—*bel'Tarda*—was thinner.

Soothed by the simple familiarity of the construct, Theo touched the main trunk.

Miri hadn't been joking, she thought, sitting back in her chair some while later. In addition to herself and Val Con—her sister and brother—there were cousins. On the yos'Phelium branch, there was Pat Rin, and on the yos'Galan—Shan, Nova, and Anthora. In addition, Pat Rin, Shan and Anthora were *also* lifemated, which by Liaden reckoning brought Inas Bhar, Priscilla Mendoza and Ren Zel dea'Judan into Theo's orbit.

But that wasn't all. Pat Rin and Nova each had a son; Shan, a daughter; Anthora, twins. Quin, Syl Vor, Padi; Mik and Shindi. And of course Miri's—*Miri and Val Con's*—babe-on-the-way.

Theo rubbed her eyes, feeling slightly overwhelmed. These were already more people than had been on her Learning Team in Secondary School on Delgado! And she was *related* to them?

And just exactly what did it *mean* to be related to them, she wondered, opening her eyes as her stomach clenched. Did they have...did Val Con and Miri expect that they could just send a message and she'd drop everything she was doing to do whatever they wanted?

And all of these other...*people*! She hadn't asked for cousins! She'd asked to have two very specific problems solved by the Delm of Korval!

Her stomach was getting upset. She took a deep breath and opened her eyes to frown at the tree on the screen. Each name was a leaf on their respective surname's branch. Each one was limned in green, which indicated that there were levels of information available for each.

Not quite at random, she flicked Val Con's name—and was very shortly in possession of the information that he was ten Standards her senior, and had graduated to delm within the current half-Standard. Before that—she flicked for more information—before that, he had been a Scout Commander, First-In. Piloting level, Scout, which the Guild regs translated to Master class.

Theo took a breath and looked deeper into the yos'Phelium branch, remembering the taunting of an Academy classmate, "Can't nobody find any pilot time for Jen Sar Kiladi." "Is that retired, or *decertified*?"

It had made her mad at the time, the implication that Father might have had his license removed, instead of willingly giving it up in order to pursue his scholarship. She might even have worried—a little—that it was true. But now, she had proof in her hands.

There it was, nestled just above Val Con—Theo flicked open the file labeled *Daav*.

Scout Captain. Scout Pilot. Recommissioned within the last half-Standard.

Before that, was a gap of *years* before a notation that Daav yos'Phelium had retired as delm.

There was no mention of his scholarship, or his honors, or his place as the Gallowglass Chair, or—

Jen Sar Kiladi will not be returning to Delgado, Father asserted from her memory.

Theo shook her head. This wasn't...this wasn't Jen Sar Kiladi's record of life achievement, it was *Daav yos'Phelium's* record.

Of course there had been no piloting stats on file for Jen Sar Kiladi—it was Daav yos'Phelium who was a Master Pilot. And who had never given up his right to fly at all. A Master, as the saying went, had wings forever.

The top entry glowed green, signaling further information available. She touched it.

Space bloomed in the screen. Space crowded with ships, a station, and a tangle of trajectories that had her forward in her seat before she fully understood that she was looking at a recording, that the station was under attack, and the system was littered with debris. Black corsairs and gunboats darted through the confusion, firing on the defenders, single-minded and deadly.

". . . have returned fire and am hit." The voice was faint. "Breath's duty—notify my clan of our enemy. I have three hours of air, heavy pursuit and no Jump left . . ."

"Stand to or die!"

". . . was destroyed. Have adequate munitions to continue search pattern . . ."

"This system is under the control of the Department of the Interior. The Scouts are declared outlaw, and all who oppose us will be destroyed!"

The messages were thick, overrunning each other, telling tales of disaster and blood. Theo watched ships engage; she watched ships die, so quick and yet the eye knew, and into the confusion of voices came another, well-known and utterly calm.

"Daav yos'Phelium, Scout Reserve Captain, copilot of packet boat *Ride the Luck*, requesting berthing information or assignment. Repeat . . ."

Berthing? Theo thought. *In that?* He'd be cut to shreds before he ever raised the station. If the—

"Korval!"

"The Caylon's ship!"

Hope leached into the storm of messages. Several ships rallied, as if the arrival of a single vessel could make a difference in the battle's outcome.

"Freighter *Luck*—" a corsair, Theo found it in the screen—"you are to stand by for boarding by the Department of the Interior; you are under our weapon! Repeat—"

"I have conflicting orders!" came Father's voice, demanding, but—what? Berthing was—*assignment.* Theo took a breath. The station needed to acknowledge him, to sanction his actions, whatever they—

"Freighter *Luck*, you are under arrest by the Department of the Interior. You are to agree to boarding or we will open fire."

As if to punctuate that threat, a beam leapt from the corsair, raking a courier class vessel from stern to stem.

"*Ride the Luck*," came a new voice, "this is Nev'Lorn Head-quarters. Captain yos'Phelium, you are on roster for Berth 56A. You are authorized to aid and assist in transit ..."

"This system is under the direct supervision of the Department of the Interior!" The ship that had fired on the courier was moving now, and Theo realized she was seeing the melee from the vantage of *Ride the Luck's* copilot. "Nev'Lorn Headquarters has been disbanded; the Scouts are declared pirates. Stand to, *Ride the Luck*, or we fire!"

The dying courier boat seemed to blossom then, as the pilot launched what must be her remaining missiles at the oncoming Department ship. They scattered, and began maneuvering.

"Department," Father demanded, "please advise best course?"

"Stand to, and await boarding," came the answer.

Theo heard Father sigh, then the Department's ship fractured with the first of *The Luck's* missiles.

Theo watched Father fire on the enemy. Fire and fire again, until the ship was nothing more than debris tumbling in expanding gasses. She watched that much, then she pulled the key out, and threw it into the catch-drawer under the copilot's board.

She'd seen space battle vids; she'd done sims; she'd practiced against targets with hot guns. She knew—she'd been taught, sometimes a pilot needed to fight, for her ship and for her passengers. She'd been told to—disable an attacking ship, and call in rescue for the survivors on the Jump out.

What she'd just seen... Father had never intended that there be any survivors on that ship. He had... deliberately destroyed it, knowingly ended lives.

It was the action of a stranger. Jen Sar Kiladi could not—would *never*—have held life so cheap. Delgado's emphasis on safety and consensus might—did!—chafe him, but he would... never...

Theo sagged suddenly in the copilot's chair, remembering something else. The Guild cafe on Volmer, the loud pilot—Casey Vitale, that was her name—shouting to the whole room: *Aelliana Caylon is back! They say she came busting in from Galaxy Nowhere with guns blazing and blew apart battleships with her little courier ship.*

Like it was... heroism. Something to celebrate.

Theo shuddered, pushed herself to her feet and went to take a shower.

· · · ❄ · · ·

"See, now, Conrad's been good for bidness," Jeefer objected, and had himself a swig o' brew.

"Conrad's been, yeah." That was Pastil, shaking her head until the bells on her braids chimed. "These others comin' in though, followin' the Road. No sayin' what they're gonna be doin'. Disruptin' things, looks like to me. Drivin' up the cost o' goods. You know Mithil got throwed outta his place? Some bunny with stardust still on 'er boots offers twice what he's been paying, housekeeper took it, and give 'im notice. Might be good for housekeeper's bidness, but not so much for Mithil."

"That's it," Otts said, giving her a grin. "The stardusters're comin' in on the tail of this new Road Boss. What's he gonna do? Well, he's gonna do what a Boss does and take care o' his turf first an' best."

"Road's his turf, 'swhat it says in the *Booster*." Jeefer held his empty mug up high so the 'keeper could see he was in need. "Bein' paid to hold it open, end on end, so's all the turfs can have a chance at the Port and the new trade."

"Trade?" Pastil snorted. "What you got to *trade*, Jeef? C'mon, now, empty out your pockets so's we can see what a fortune looks like."

"Gonna be hirin' too," Jeefer insisted. "Wages ain't to sneeze at."

"You think they gonna be hirin' *us*?" Otts asked.

"I do. Conrad did."

"Conrad didn't come in but with McFarland an' the insurance."

"All he needed, wasn't it?" That was Mickie, arrived with the pitcher. She refilled Jeefer's mug, topped off Pastil and Otts.

"You wanna know what I think?" she said. "I think it's too late to be grousing about things changing. They're already shook up good and hard."

"That might be so," said Otts. "But it don't mean we can't make our opinions known."

Mickie shoved a straggle of hair behind an ear.

"Yeah?" she said. "How're you gonna do that?"

"Well!" said Otts, giving her a nod and a grin. "Happens I know a guy, see?"

TEN

· · · · · · ·

Spaceport Gondola
Gondola

A SO-CALLED "EXPRESS SQUIRT" WAS THE BEST COMPROMISE between cost and speed, Theo decided, considering the options available to her. Her message to Kamele must, of necessity, be brief—twenty-four words or less—but it would arrive more quickly. And, as it happened, more economically still, as the universities at Delgado and Gondola both belonged to the Scholar Base, and therefore offered a discount for messages sent to or from an academic account.

Theo slotted her card, tapped the screen to accept the terms and the discount, entered Kamele's direction and . . . sat, fingers poised over the keypad.

The truth, she told herself. *It's simple.*

All that information on the key—*she* wasn't going to be the one who told Kamele what her *onagrata* had—no. Better Kamele didn't know that. Never knew that. Maybe—maybe Daav yos'Phelium Clan Korval was right after all.

Maybe it was better that he—or whatever part of him was Father—just disappeared and left Kamele with her memories.

"No," she said out loud in the privacy booth. "You don't have to send her all that; it's extraneous."

Right.

She cleared her throat and touched the keys.

Father with Delm Korval, she typed.

And stopped, blinking at the screen.

The simple truth looked...thin and cold, there on the screen, even a little...dismissive. Kamele, after all, thought that the Delm of Korval was—a story for littlies.

On the other hand, Theo thought, Kamele was a scholar; she knew how to do research. She'd look it up—if only because Theo's message had made her angry—and she'd find out that what they'd both thought was a story, was plain fact.

So, that was four words, and she still had to answer the question that Kamele had been too proud to ask directly.

He is safe, well, within parameters of active duty pilot.

She hesitated, but Kamele would want to know this, too: *No plans for Delgado return.*

One more truth that Kamele needed to know, though she hadn't asked, and that would hit the limit.

I love you, Mother.

Theo

She read it, made sure her Guild box was the automatic reply address, nodded, and hit *send*.

The screen blanked, then came back up, displaying the completed transaction screen, the amount deducted from her card and the balance remaining.

The balance was...tidy. Uncle paid promptly, by direct transfer to her Guild account. For those places that didn't accept Guild debit, she carried hard coin—Terran bits in a public pocket, and more of the same, in an inner pocket.

In her most secret pocket was a pair of cantra pieces, which was a lot of money, but...she was her own backup, running without a copilot. If trouble hit her—or her ship—she'd have to deal with it herself.

Sitting in the private booth, message sent, Theo sighed. No sense thinking about trouble. The Pilots Guild rated Gondola Spaceport in the upper percentages for safety, which didn't mean it was *safe* like Delgado was safe, but did mean that her chances of finding trouble were...less high than they might be, say, on Volmer.

Gondola also sat at the intersection of several master trade routes; it was a rich world, so it said in the *Guild Quick Guide*, and Gondola Spaceport was the fourth busiest in the sector.

The starport also had, according to more than one advertisement she'd passed on the way to the Guild Hall, *the best shopping outside of Kamfork.*

There wasn't any way to confirm that, since she'd never heard of Kamfork, much less sampled the shopping there. However, she did have a couple hours dirtside right here on Gondola before she was to meet Uncle's vendor for the scheduled pickup. Surely there was no harm in getting a baseline on the local offerings.

Besides, she thought, spinning the chair and coming to her feet in a dance move, she needed to find a bookstore. Archives on the *Toss* were a little thin on Liaden custom, concentrating on simple texts written with an eye toward the pilot getting back to her ship in a non-honor-killed sort of way.

If she was going to talk as a cultural equal with Val Con, she was going to need something more in-depth.

She shook her head as the cubicle's door closed and locked behind her. Father...she had *known* Father was Liaden, but it hadn't *mattered*. Just like it hadn't mattered that Kara was Liaden, or Win Ton or Pilot yos'Senchul...

It hadn't mattered to *her*. Had it mattered to *them*? While they were correcting her mistakes and translating *melant'i* for her, and keeping her safe from custom, like she was a littlie in a room full of fragile things?

A pilot rode her own course; she didn't expect anyone else to get her safely into port.

Theo sighed. Right. Books. Tapes. Maybe even a bilingual module for the *Toss*. She knew how to study, and she knew for a fact that there was plenty of time, when the screens were grey. It seemed that Rig Tranza was right again—a pilot needed something to occupy herself with, 'tween times, and she might as well learn something useful.

· · · ☀ · · ·

There were no new instructions from Headquarters. Tir Sha yos'Vinder took note of the fact even while he assured himself that he had expected to hear nothing. Eventually, of course, one must receive a message, but not yet.

Not yet.

The log did reflect receipt of a message off the local subnet, which excited his interest only as long as it took to open it and discover nothing more than a routine systems check.

Recognizing the bite of disappointment for the danger to duty that it was, Operative yos'Vinder rose from his seat at the console and immediately performed that exercise he had been taught as a recruit to the Department of the Interior. It bore a passing resemblance to a pilot's simple focusing exercise; one did feel alert and on-point at the conclusion of the sequence.

One also felt far more certain of one's place within the Department and the value of the work one was assigned to oversee.

Important work, of course, else there would have been no requirement for oversight at all, much less by so skilled an operative as Tir Sha yos'Vinder.

Exercise complete, he sat again at the console, disappointment warmed away by the certain clear knowledge of the Department's approval of himself.

The work...the work that brought Operative pin'Eport and himself to this gaudy, overwrought port deep inside Terran space... that was of maximum importance.

On this busy, busy world, in this very spaceport, there was a dealer—a dealer in *antiquities.*

In fact, Spaceport Gondola was home to a dozen and more dealers in antiquities. What made Mildred Bilinoda a person of interest to the Department of the Interior was the fact that she dealt in what the Terrans termed *Befores.*

Old Tech.

Forbidden tech.

Tech that was so very useful to the Department, and beneficial to the Department's Plan.

All of the Old Tech was to have been destroyed, or decommissioned, by the Scouts, of course. Most of it was rumored to have died, the timonium powering them having finally succumbed to time.

Rumors of death and destruction aside, there was yet a healthy undermarket in Befores, and in that market Smalltrader Bilinoda was known as one to approach only if the need was great and the money likewise.

Such was the extent of the smalltrader's net of contacts that the Department must have annexed it, and also the trader, long ago. The circumstance that stayed the Department's hand, and the reason that Operatives yos'Vinder and pin'Eport were based on Spaceport Gondola was the belief—less than certainty, more than rumor—that one of those contacts was...a person *very much* of interest.

While Smalltrader Bilinoda was not to be discounted as a prize, this other—as elusive and difficult to locate as Old Tech itself—was treasure. Rumor—well, what use rumor? Enough to know that it was the hope of gaining a lead to this person that Smalltrader Bilinoda was merely observed, her business left undisturbed, her goods allowed to pass through Spaceport Gondola intact.

It did not fall within the boundaries of Operative yos'Vinder's duty to know what had befallen those others of Bilinoda's contacts. His job, and that of Operative pin'Eport, was to observe the smalltrader, and to forward such information regarding her contacts as could be gained with judicious bribery.

That the largest prize remained undiscovered was apparent. Had it been otherwise, the operatives would have received word to sweep up the trader, her antiquities, and her records.

As such word had not been forthcoming...

The comm trilled—pin'Eport's tone. Operative yos'Vinder reached to the console, tapped a key—and saw the familiar code form on the screen.

Smalltrader Bilinoda had left the shop, and pin'Eport was following, as per standard procedure.

yos'Vinder reached again to the console, calling up the list of ships newly berthed. This was also standard procedure. Occasionally, the match program identified a vessel of interest to the Department, whereupon he would log the sighting. Occasionally, he was required to file a complaint with the Port against the vessel identified, or to bear witness against the pilot, whereupon other Departmental operatives would perform their standard procedures, of which yos'Vinder knew, and cared to know, nothing.

Today, the match program had identified a ship, the name not merely highlighted, but glowing flame red, and sporting the glyph that indicated further urgent information available.

yos'Vinder tapped the query key.

Yard scan came live, showing a courier class ship sitting chastely at her berth. yos'Vinder frowned, upping the magnification, trained eye following the lines—updated and upgraded so that a casual glance slid past, and a slightly more interested glance merely saw an elderly ship rejuvenated by careful owners.

An eye such as yos'Vinder's, reinforced by intensive sleep-learning and pattern recognition—that eye saw a ship not merely elderly, but improbably old, kept spry and spaceworthy far beyond the time when even a doting owner would admit that it was more cost-effective to scrap the old and buy new.

The match program snapped into place, the pattern fitting precisely over the image on the ship at its berth.

Tir Sha yos'Vinder inhaled, carefully.

The Department knew this vessel. The Department had been looking for this vessel.

He sent the standard query, and there on the screen was the ship's registry.

Name:	Arin's Toss
Home Port:	Waymart
Owner:	Crystal Energy Consultants
Pilot:	Theo Waitley, First Class

Operative yos'Vinder tapped the screen once more, accessing the detailed instructions pertaining to his duty with regard to this ship.

Tag and follow.

· · · ☀ · · ·

"Place is fillin' up," Miri commented. From her vantage on the balcony, she could see lights in second-floor windows around the inner garden. Behind those windows were apartments like the one behind her, that she shared with Val Con. Sort of alike, anyhow; though the leftovers from former occupants would be different. New tenants shifted the furniture around to suit themselves, sent what they didn't want or need to House Stores, and laid down their own layer of possessions, which would get overlaid in turn by the next clan member who took the rooms for themselves.

She stretched, trying to ease her back. The only thing that kept her from thinking that being pregnant could get over with any time now was the thought of what she was going to do with a kid. Val Con—he liked kids. Herself . . .

Miri shivered.

It was chilly on the balcony; down at ground level, a cold breeze was running rough inside the garden, shaking the flowers and the shrubs below like a street thief trying to get one more coin out of a mark.

Miri sighed. She'd never noticed flowers much before Jelaza

Kazone, but she'd gotten used to seeing them, just like she'd gotten used to the pleasant, mannerly Liaden breezes, that carried scents up to the balcony and offered them like wine.

Something disturbed the air at her back. She moved a step to the right without looking around.

"A full clanhouse is a joy," Val Con said, folding his arms on the rail next to her.

Not that they would hit the limit, even with every adult clan member, staff, and assorted folk like Ms. dea'Gauss added to the sum.

"*Was* this house ever full?" she asked, nestling companionably against his side.

"Once—and once or twice again, after. Korval has never been a populous clan. We take too many risks."

Miri laughed. "Well, at least I know it's in the family."

She felt, rather than saw, him smile.

"Indeed. Reckless to a fault, every one of us. Though Nova displays some sign of possessing common prudence, and—until lately, of course—so had Pat Rin."

"Setting up as a high roller and living off of your winnings is real prudent and commonsensical."

"Yes, but one must view the course in context. He took care to be known as a marksman nonpareil, and as a man who excelled not only at cards and dice, but also at games of skill."

"So he went in with a legend."

"Exactly. Pilots, on the other hand, may be as skilled and as formidable as they like, and still the Jump may kill one. Compelling as we find it, piloting is not a safe trade."

"And you like to brawl in taverns."

"That, too."

She snorted a soft laugh, and shivered against a renewed assault from the breeze, this one showing teeth.

"Flowers ain't gonna make it," she said gloomily.

"Some may adapt, and we mustn't discount the gardener. The food crops have her first attention, of course, but she did allow me to know that she had our garden under care." He moved his shoulders. "Father had used to keep the inner gardens himself."

"Yeah, he said that. Thinking of putting him to work?"

"Of course. Though perhaps gardening is not the best use of his talents. Nor of Mother's."

There it was again, a little thrill of...worry laced with pain that accompanied Val Con's considerations of his parents. Miri bit her lip. Sometimes, knowing what your partner felt about something was worse than not knowing. And what was even worse than not knowing, was not knowing whether she should *do* something, or just figure it was his to work out.

He shifted, moving a hand to massage her aching back.

"Miri, it will be well."

"So you keep saying." She sighed. "Talk me into anything, can't you?"

"Indeed, I cannot. I distinctly recall several instances when I failed of getting my way—to my profit, not to say, my survival."

A chime sounded from the room behind them. Miri frowned.

"We late?"

"More likely it is one's sister Nova, wishing to know if we *intend* to be late," Val Con said, pushing away from the rail.

She followed him inside, sliding the door closed behind her, shutting out the toothy, feral breeze. Over the snick of the lock, she heard the hallway door cycle, and felt the flutter of Val Con's surprise.

"Good evening, Jeeves."

"Master Val Con. Miri. I regret the necessity of disturbing you. A matter of security has presented itself which I thought best to bring immediately to your attention."

The thrill of dread she felt then was all her own.

"*House* security?" she snapped, thinking of all those people— Gods, the whole clan, 'cept for the kids, still hidden away. They'd known it was a risk to bring the adults under one roof, but—they'd considered it acceptable, with Jeeves to guarantee a whole-house defense net.

And that, Robertson, she told herself, *is why Clan Korval is so small. The man just told you so, didn't he?*

"Forgive me," Jeeves said, headball flickering in her direction. "House security is firm. I speak to . . . maintaining the security of allies."

"This," Val Con said, stepping back from the door with a slight bow, "sounds as if it could be complex. Please enter, Jeeves, and make yourself comfortable."

"I am always comfortable, Master Val Con. The chassis suits me excellently."

"It pleases me to hear you say so—and to observe that you

have not held shy from making those modifications which are of benefit."

Jeeves rolled in, wheels muted by the carpets, and settled himself before the double chair. Miri came forward to perch on one arm, Val Con on the other.

"Now," he said, "maintaining the security of allies?"

"Quite so, sir. I have heard from Pod 77, which you will recall is located upon Lytaxin, a gift from Korval during the time that Theonna yos'Phelium wore the Ring."

"I recall that Pod 77 comported ..." Val Con paused, head tipped slightly to one side. "Jeeves, I must ask your assistance in the matter of the pronoun."

"The pronoun would be *it*, sir. A complex machine and, as I believe you were about to observe, sensible of its duty. It is in fact this sensitivity to duty which led it to contact me.

"Firstly, the attack upon Erob's clanhouse brought it to fuller functionality than it had enjoyed for many years. Its programming prompted it to seek downloads and upgrades, whereupon it was noted that such downloads as might be useful to it were not necessarily compatible with its existing systems. This places its mission, received from the Delm of Korval, in peril and so it sends, rightly, that it requires upgrading."

Miri blinked. "Do we have an Old Tech repair person on staff?"

The headball flickered in the pattern she thought of as a chuckle.

"It may be that a Scout trained in the preservation and disarming protocols would be able to perform repairs on a fractin-driven device, though such attempts have in the past not been notably successful. Fortunately, though of course Korval has Scouts on call, this is not the problem that faces us. Pod 77 is of much more recent construction. Indeed, as it supplied a complete systems architecture in its report, I am able to say with confidence that it is of a vintage and design with which I am very familiar. I am more than competent to guide Pod 77 in making the needed alterations and upgrades. The delm may wish to dispatch a human repair person to install hard memory expansions. I will know what to recommend after the alterations are in place and tested."

"This is then...a request to proceed with assisting Pod 77?" Val Con asked.

"Pod 77 does require permission from Delm Korval to accept my assistance as the delm's proxy. I have taken the liberty of sending it Korval's lineage so that it may derive that the present delm is indeed the successor of the delm who gave it duty."

"Will a voice stamp do? Or do we need to go back to Lytaxin our own selves?" Miri asked. She flicked a grin at Val Con. "Not sure the kinfolk'd be real happy to have me visiting again so soon."

"I believe that a certified voice stamp will serve admirably," Jeeves said. "I will ascertain from Pod 77 whether there are specific command phrases required."

"Excellent." Val Con came to his feet. "We thank you for bringing this matter to our—"

"There is one more thing, sir," Jeeves interrupted delicately.

Val Con paused, and Miri felt a thrill of dread—his, hers, theirs. "And that is?"

"I have also been contacted by Pod 78. With a request for repair."

ELEVEN

· · · · · · · · · · · · · ·

Mozart's Modicum
Starport Gondola

MOZART'S MODICUM WAS A TEA SHOP AT THE INTERSECTION OF Orange Main and Blue Main, a good jog from the Gondola Book Market, well over into the green section of the port. Jog, Theo did, a bag of booksticks slung over her shoulder, and pleased that she'd advertently coded a *second* alarm into her watch, once she got a look at what she'd be dealing with. The book market was easily the size of Anlingdin Academy; a person could spend days—years—inside, browsing the wares and stopping every now and then at one of the convenient market cafes for tea and a handwich.

Of course, she didn't have years, she had exactly two hours, ship-time, before her meeting with Merchant Bilinoda.

Right here. At Mozart's Modicum.

After the book market and her jogging tour of the port, she had expected the "tea shop" to be oversized, brightly lit, and crammed with people.

In fact, the address she had been given was a small shop with a striped awning shading a modest green door. On the door, picked out in subdued glitterchips, was the name of the shop, and a subtitle: *Classic teas and chernubia.*

Theo sighed, pleased by the quiet neatness of the words, the door, the awning. Then she shook herself, remembering that she was here for a reason, and that time was moving.

She went forward; the door opened for her and she stepped

into a pleasantly dim interior. Tables were set at odd angles across a wide, shallow room. Many of the tables were occupied, and there was a pleasant hum of unhurried conversation in the air.

Along the right wall was a long, low transparent case, with sweet things of all kinds on display, from simple butter cookies to a cake carved into the shape of a long-necked animal Theo didn't recognize.

At the far left of the sweets bar sat a single, unoccupied table, almost invisible in the dimness. Hers, by direction. Theo crossed and sat down, sliding the bag off her shoulder and onto the floor next to her.

By the time she'd put her hands on the table, a man was at her side—slight and short, but not, she thought, Liaden, dressed in black shirt and trousers, with a spotless white apron over all.

"Service, signorine?" he asked. "Something sweet? Something tart? Something sour?"

"I would like a glass of Joyful Sunrise, if you please," she said, which was the phrase her instructions had given her to say.

The waiter bowed.

"An excellent choice, signorine. It will be but a moment."

He left her, and Theo deliberately sat back in her chair, trying to look relaxed and calm, despite a sudden tingling of nerves. She took a deep breath to calm herself.

This is your first in-person pickup, she told herself. *It's normal to be nervous. Keep at it long enough and it'll be natural and easy.*

"Your tea, signorine." The waiter smiled at her start, and settled a cup and saucer on the table before her. He poured, and put the pot on the table.

"Has the signorine reconsidered a *chernubia*?"

Theo smiled and shook her head. "They look wonderful, but today I'm on short-time."

"Understood, signorine. Please, enjoy your tea."

He tucked the tray under his arm with a flourish and left her, as silent as he had come. Theo frowned. Hard-heeled shoes on a stone floor ought to make *some* sound! For that matter, even as isolated as her table was, she should at least hear the murmur of voices from other tables. She *had* heard the sound of voices, when she came in, but now...

She bent her head and closed her eyes.

Nothing, that was what she heard; her table was a dead zone— or, she thought, her uneasiness back in full force, the table was inside a security field. She wondered if the other patrons would see more than a silhouette, if they glanced her way.

She opened her eyes, finding the teacup, a delicate pale pink affair rising like a flower from the leaf-shaped saucer. The scent of the tea was likewise delicate, with a sharp undernote that promised alertness.

Carefully, she placed her hands around the flower cup and raised it to her face, inhaling the aroma before assaying a cautious sip.

Complexity pirouetted brightly across her tongue: rose, citrus, new rain. Beneath was a tang like ozone, edgy and exciting, as revitalizing as a snap of ammonia beneath the nose.

Her whole body warmed—and she realized that she wasn't alone.

Gently, without haste, she lowered the cup to its saucer, and raised her head to meet the eyes of the woman across from her.

They were shiny and as hard as river stones, those eyes, black and narrow in a round pink face.

Theo felt a shiver of distaste, even as the words she'd been directed to say rose to her lips.

"My uncle sends his best wishes."

"Your uncle takes unnecessary chances, which endanger more than his precious liberty," her companion snapped, which wasn't the answer Theo had been told to expect.

She raised her eyebrows, pushed the chair back, and reached for the bag by her boot.

The woman's pink face got pinker. She raised an inelegant hand in the sign for *hold*.

"Please assure him of my continued regard," she said, which *was* the right answer. She placed a packet next to the teapot. It was not quite as long as Theo's hand, as broad as both together, and two fingers thick. It was wrapped in purple mesh and tied with a purple-and-gold ribbon, like a Mother's Day present.

It could, Theo thought, be an old bound book. Or almost anything else.

"I suggest," said the woman across from her, "that you place that in an inner pocket. The shielding around this table is good, but we can't discount the presence of those with sharp eyes."

Theo nodded, and picked up the packet—it was heavier than she had supposed, and rigid, which neither confirmed nor invalidated the notion that it was a book. She slipped it into the largish inside left pocket, and pressed the seal.

Her companion stood.

"Enjoy your tea; it would be a shame to waste it." She turned away then, setting her feet deliberately, like she was used to walking where the footing wasn't always firm. Every step should've rung against the floor, instead she moved in complete silence until she reached the *chernubia* display, turned left—and vanished from view.

Theo sighed, and picked up the flower cup to sip some more tea. It would be a shame to waste it.

• • • ❀ • • •

The Less Pilot was yet a stranger to his key.

The Captain—the Captain was hale and at liberty, moving freely among the worlds. The Overkey provide a route: from Volmer to Liad; from Liad to Denko, thence to Gondola. Busy worlds. *Dangerous* worlds. The Builders particularly forbade Liad as a port *Bechimo* might seek, even in the most extreme need.

Gondola was not forbidden, but the archives indicated it was a port to approach with the utmost caution. There were pirates there.

That entry had been cause for concern, and *Bechimo* monitored the Captain's key closely, recalling the damage visited by pirates upon the Less Pilot. Thus far, the Captain's safety had not been compromised, which was well. And yet...

Why did the Captain not come? What were these errands, that they were allowed to come before *Bechimo*'s rights? Did the Captain think the vessel unworthy? Was there some test, some rite of proving that was yet to be accomplished?

Bechimo scanned archives, protocols, the Builders' files—all and everything. There was no mention of rite or test. Either the Captain would come, or the Captain would signal *Bechimo* to approach. The bonding, promised by the Builders. There would be, at the Captain's order and desire, a Less Pilot, and crew, cargo. Perhaps...there would be family.

Perhaps, this time, properly bonded, and the Captain willing, *Bechimo* would not fail them.

• • • ❀ • • •

The fair-haired pilot walked like she owned the port. She was, therefore, admirably easy to follow, and follow Operative pin'Eport did.

Standard procedure.

Most of Smalltrader Bilinoda's clients had some sense of... caution about them; some sensibility that what they had received was valuable, and therefore liable to be coveted by someone other than themselves. They took precautions; they followed circuitous routes; they stopped at taverns, left a coin on the bar with an unfinished drink, sought the back doors and alleyways.

The fair-haired pilot strode on as if she were limitless; as if there were no doubt that the contents of her pockets would remain precisely there, and that any back-alley unpleasantness would naturally resolve in her favor.

It was a pity, Operative pin'Eport thought, that such confidence should go unchecked, but it did not fall within his orders to school Smalltrader Bilinoda's latest client. His objective was merely to follow, ascertain her ship, or her contact, and report those things to yos'Vinder, who, as senior, would pass the information up the line.

The pilot turned off Orange Main and onto Ship's Way, taking the corner wide.

A moment later, pin'Eport turned the same corner, keeping rather closer to the storefronts and being careful not to dispute the walkway with any other pedestrian.

It was therefore something of a shock to find himself staring directly into the face of the fair-haired pilot.

A shop display hemmed him close on the right hand; the pilot herself cut off any movement either forward or to the left.

"What do you want?" she snapped in Trade.

For a moment he simply stood, incapable of framing an answer. She had been aware of him? She was—alone on a strange port and without backup—*challenging* him?

But *was* she without backup? Was there a reason he was challenged here—now?

He took rapid stock of the street, the busy pedestrians, the patrons loitering around tables at the curbside restaurant. Perhaps she was not...entirely alone. Best not to assume it. Only see what assumption had gained him already.

She held herself as one prepared to answer, should he push her or show any aggression—and it was not within his orders, to—

"I *said*," the fair-haired pilot repeated, black eyes snapping, "what do you want? You've been following me for blocks."

He must offer neither aggression, nor engagement; above all, she must not know herself for an object of the Department's interest.

Operative pin'Eport bowed, deliberately modeless, affecting the kittenish grace that charmed a certain class of Terran pilot. He straightened and gave her a chagrined smile.

"Forgive me, Pilot. Indeed, I have been following you. How could I not? It only amazes me that the entire port is not following you, as strong and as certain as you walk. I confess all; I was taken. I hoped, perhaps, that you might consent to—but perhaps I presume?"

It would seem that he did presume; the ruse was not working as he had planned. The pale, pointed face retained its expression of irritation; the ready stance did not relax into flattered generosity.

"I'm not interested," she said, with scant courtesy. "Find somewhere else to be. Now."

She stepped back, clearing the way for him. Pedestrians altered their courses for her and swept on. She crossed her arms over her breast and stared at him.

pin'Eport bowed again, "Pilot," and walked away, keeping his stride smooth and just hurried enough to convey embarrassment. He passed the tables at curbside, and swept into the duty-free shop, where there was an overview of the street on-screen.

For a moment, he thought he had lost her. Then he saw a wiry, fair-haired figure cross the street at a run, overlarge jacket flaring behind her, still on course for the shipyards.

Operative pin'Eport counted to twelve, then slipped out onto the street to once again take up the pursuit.

TWELVE

· · · · · · · · · · · · · ·

Jelaza Kazone
Surebleak

THEY SAT DOWN TEN TO DINNER, IN THE DINING HALL; SILVER utensils, creamy plates, and gleaming wine cups reflected in the glossy dark wood of the table.

Miri'd privately thought a sit-down dinner was a lot of extra effort for staff. A buffet in the big parlor would've been good enough for a working meeting; they'd done fine with those when they were getting ready to shake Liad's dust off Korval's collective boots. But, no—

"A simple meal, please, Mr. pel'Kana," Val Con had said, and the butler had bowed like he'd just been given a big red lollipop and bustled off to give the good news to Ms. ana'Tak, in the kitchen.

"A simple meal" translated into soup, fresh rolls, braised vegetables, broiled fish, and, for desert, a fruit tart, with wine, teas, and juices on offer.

But the food, Miri saw, when they were all gathered in the dining hall—the food wasn't the point, at all. The dinner was a sign—a signal that things were now the way they should be; the emergency was over, and Clan Korval had prevailed.

It was subtle, that signal, and not entirely true. There wasn't, she thought, one person at the table who thought their work was over, or that they could all settle down for a vacation. And there wasn't one person—herself included—who didn't feel a little more centered by the time the tart was retired, and Shan got to his feet.

"To the Dragon," he said, tipping his glass jauntily at her and at Val Con.

This was ritual; she felt it resonate, even as Val Con rose and lifted his glass in turn. "To the Tree."

There was a pause, then—right, waiting for her to finish it.

How to finish it, that was the problem. She got up and grabbed her cup—lemon water, dammit—and looked 'round the table at them; her family by lend, that had staggeringly fast become her family by heart. Her gaze came onto Pat Rin's tired face, and she smiled, suddenly knowing what to say.

"To coming home."

· · · ❄ · · ·

Theo hit the pilot's chair still buzzing with adrenaline.

What a nidj that guy had been! Dirt-grubber following her for blocks, and then trying to buy her off with a bogus bow and a—

But no. She took a breath, forcing her hands to move calmly, to tap the key to access queued messages, to sit back in her chair and wait for the display to come up.

"No," she said aloud, "he wasn't a dirt-grubber. He was a pilot." She sniffed. Not *much* of a pilot, with his stiff face and his hard-edged movements. And that bow!

Theo took a hard breath against another jolt of annoyance.

The bow had *really* bothered her. Well, the whole situation was . . . off. Wrong. She'd had pilots on port offer to buy her a drink before; she even had some offer to share some fun. Once or twice, she'd made similar offers, herself. There was a way to do these things that wasn't—that was polite!

Following somebody halfway across the port was just antisocial!

Antisocial and disturbing in a way she didn't want to think about too closely, but that made her think she might want to take a shower, as soon as she pulled her messages.

Right on cue, here they came. An advertisement for night-overs, with up to three companions, "screened exclusively for compatibility with *you*"; the *Toss*'s initial docking fees, itemized, from Port Admin; a coupon good for a free book-chip of her choice with the purchase of any two history chips; and a sealed-message-opens-only-to-your-code.

Theo's stomach, already uneasy, tightened, which was just silly. Her business here was done; she might as well lift.

She reached to the board, deleted the coupon and the advert, scanned the bill and filed it.

That left the coded message. She took a breath and tapped in the sequence she'd been given by her employer.

It was flight orders, all right. Someplace called Ploster—a delivery.

She frowned, wondering what it was she had to deliver, then laughed at herself.

"Just picked up a package or two, didn't you, Theo?"

She looked at the screen again, this time paying attention to the particulars. Pulling up the comp program and the map, she did the math, rough, then refined it, to be sure.

Not a paid vacation, like the trip to Gondola, but not a screaming emergency, like her initial run to Liad. She'd have some solid Jump time for reviewing the books she'd bought.

She sent the request to Tower for a Lift Anytime, got the ack on the bounce for a slot three Standard Hours out. Good. Time for that shower, and a nice meal, here in-ship, before she got to work.

Three hours from now, she'd be lifting, leaving Gondola and its oddities behind her.

That was good, too.

Theo smiled, rose, danced a short, bright dance, and headed for the 'fresher.

· · · ❄ · · ·

During their last days on Liad, the so-called "informal parlor" had been the clan's war room, and it was there that they gathered after dinner. Miri settled into the red leather chair that had become her favorite, Val Con perched on the arm at her right, waiting.

They were quiet-moving, the family, and gracefully deliberate— which Miri'd learned was pilot's sign. In no time at all they were disposed on various sofas, hassocks, and chairs, their faces attentive.

Val Con inclined his head, by way of bringing the meeting to order, and started right in with the first order of business.

"Jeeves reports that the house defense systems are online and armed," he said. "While we of course no longer have the additional benefit of the planetary defense net, we are reasonably secure. I therefore propose that we bring Korval's treasures home."

"Korval's treasures." Those were the children, sent away to a remote safeplace when first Plan B had gone into effect, guarded by the two eldest of the clan.

"I agree." That was Pat Rin, who had the most at stake, since not only was his boy among those self-same treasurers, but the guardians were his mother and his foster-father.

"Better here than there," Shan said, not exactly risk-free himself. Four treasures belonged to Line yos'Galan—two of them babes in arms. "With so many hunting."

That was the problem. The Department of the Interior, the headquarters of which Korval had destroyed—which act of heroism had gotten them thrown off-world—wasn't so much annihilated as headless. A far-flung net of operatives still sat their posts and held to their last-received orders. There were folks working on that—notably the Scouts, who felt that what happened at Nev'Lorn reason enough—but that didn't change the fact that there were a good number of dangerous people out there in the wide galaxy who held a considerable grudge against Korval.

While there was a risk in giving them a big pile of Korval to come after, there was also safety in numbers—and a certain advantage to being on the ground.

"It is settled then," Val Con said. "The children come home. Who goes?"

"I do," Pat Rin said, and his lifemate not a syllable behind him, "I, too."

That was putting two important eggs into one chancy basket, Miri thought, then thought again. Whoever went, it ought to be somebody familiar to elders and younglings—and the fact was, if it came to backup, Pat Rin had more than anyone else in the room.

Pat Rin met her eyes, as if he had heard her initial concern, and smiled.

"I wish to take my mother news of my lifemating as soon as may be," he said. "All according to Code."

That was an in-joke—Miri'd gathered Pat Rin's mother was a stickler—and got a ripple of laughter from the room.

"Your call, Boss," she said, and gave him his smile back.

"While the delm's attention is on me," Pat Rin continued, "I would like to make a request for assistance. My office is overwhelmingly busy, and while the arrival of Mr. pel'Tolian has improved matters a dozen times, I am in need of an assistant—someone who looks with a long eye, and is not subject to intimidation..."

"If the delm pleases," Nova rose from her chair near the window, "I am able to assist."

She could, too. Nova'd managed Clan Korval as temp delm for years; Surebleak would hardly be a challenge.

"Good idea," Miri said, feeling Val Con's accord. "Work out the details with Pat Rin. In the meantime, Boss, talk to Ms. dea'Gauss. Right before we left, she was telling me about a youngster of theirs who's in need of a project to keep him out of trouble."

"I will do that," Pat Rin said, and bowed his head, going all formal to tweak her. "I thank the delm."

"Any time," Miri told him.

"Next order of business," Val Con said. "The Road is in—let us say that the Road is in very great need of repair. As Korval's contract requires us to keep it open, it is to our best benefit to bring it into—"

The parlor door opened.

"Your pardon." Mr. pel'Kana bowed. "This gentleman offered a word of the House; old, yet—"

A shadow moved, walking light and easy, hands held specifically away from a tough trim body. Miri registered grey hair, leather, and ice blue eyes before Val Con was on his feet and between her and the old pilot.

Natesa was up, too, her hands flashing in pilot-talk—*truce*—even while she sang out, "I vouch!"

Another voice came in under hers, deep and calm.

"Clarence."

Daav walked forward from his place at the back of the room. The stranger stopped, holding his hands out chest-high, fingers wide, showing himself no threat—which Miri thought he wasn't, not here and now.

"I'm retired," he said, like it was the next line in an old, old argument.

Daav smiled and extended his hands, palms up. "I was going to say—welcome."

"Were ye now?" Clarence put his palms against Daav's, fingers 'round his wrists. "You're looking fine, laddie; and a sight for tired eyes."

"Flatterer." Daav's voice was gentle. Dangerous he might be, but Daav valued this man. Val Con—didn't. Matter of fact, Val Con was on the edge of pushing a point, if she was getting the signal clear—and that wasn't going to do at all.

She stepped up to his side, and caught Daav's eye.

"Ah." He stepped back, letting go of his friend's hands. "Clarence, have you met my children?"

The cool blue gaze brushed Miri's face, then Val Con's. She got the impression that Clarence was amused.

"Met your boy, o' course." Clarence nodded, cordial as you'd like. "Good to see you again, Pilot."

"Pilot O'Berin," Val Con answered, stiff.

There was a pause, getting too long, with the whole family waiting to see how this was going to play. Miri went half a step forward, and stuck her hand out.

"Miri Robertson, half a delm."

Clarence O'Berin smiled, which did interesting things to his face, and met her hand. His was hard and warm, calloused where a man who handled a gun as a daily exercise would have callouses.

"Missus. It's pleased I am to meet you." The lilt hadn't been so pronounced a heartbeat before. Miri figured she was being charmed, and gave him a grin to show she appreciated his effort.

"Pilot O'Berin," Val Con said. "Is there a reason why you have come to us?"

"In fact, there is," Clarence said, letting Miri's hand go, and turning to face her lifemate. "Thing is, I hadn't meant to intrude on a family party. I can come back later, if it's allowed, or meet someone down port." The corner of his mouth twitched. "Like old times."

"Perhaps that would be—"

"Rude," Miri interrupted, and looked up at him, widening her eyes innocently. "Be a shame to send the man away when he's come so far to talk to us—and up bad road, too," she said, resisting an urge to stamp on his foot. "We got room to put up a friend of Daav's for the night."

Val Con's mouth tightened, but he bowed his head. Taking it, but not liking it.

"As you have noticed," he said to Clarence, "we are in process here. Please allow Mr. pel'Kana to escort you to a guesting room, and do not hesitate to call upon the House for anything you might find needful."

It was well said, Miri thought, but it cost him. And unless she was misreading him something bad, there was gonna be some more things said, when they were alone. That was fine; she had a couple points of discussion, herself.

"Let me see you safely into the hands of our butler," Daav said smoothly, taking his friend's elbow and turning him toward the door. "We'll talk, later."

The door closed behind them, and Miri felt the tension in the room plummet.

She took a breath and grinned up at Val Con, who shook his head, and murmured, for her ears alone, "I hope you know what you're doing."

THIRTEEN

· · · · · · · · · · · · · · · · ·

Jelaza Kazone
Surebleak

"MIRI, DO YOU KNOW WHO CLARENCE O'BERIN IS?"

Val Con's voice was a little sharper than natural curiosity might allow for. Miri finished belting her made-new-for-Surebleak fleece robe around her before she looked over to where he leaned in the doorway with his arms crossed over his chest.

"Sure I do," she said, keeping her voice mild. "He's a friend of Daav's. Looked real happy to see each other, didn't they?"

Val Con sighed.

"Clarence O'Berin," he said, still sharper than was strictly welcome in the bedroom, "is the Juntavas Boss on Liad."

Well, that explained the degree of his upset, anyhow. Korval had a long history of avoiding that particular galaxy-spanning organization of high and low crime. Until Pat Rin went and married himself a Judge, that was. But still...

"No, he ain't," she said.

She sat down at the dressing table, and reached up to unpin her braid. In the mirror, she saw Val Con frown. "Man said he was retired—you heard him."

"Miri—"

"Not only that," she interrupted. "Natesa vouched for him— damn near threw herself in front of him, didn't she?" She lifted her chin, meeting his reflected glare. "Speaking of which, you're developing a bad habit."

93

His eyes narrowed.

"Am I, indeed?"

From sharp to hard polite in one sentence. Way to manage it, Robertson.

Well-managed or not, she'd taken her first shot. Now all she had to do was win the battle.

"Yeah, you are," she said, pulling the braid over her shoulder and beginning to unweave it. "I figure we better fix it now, while it's still fresh, better'n let it set."

She took a breath, and rapped out, hard and fast, "Since when do you need to get between me and what might have teeth?"

"I have a certain obligation, I think, to my lifemate and to my heir."

The ambient temperature was falling fast. She could feel the gnaw of his worry just as vivid as if it was hers. Funny thing being, she *wasn't* worried about one Clarence O'Berin, retired Juntavas Boss, sleeping under the same roof with all the kinfolk. Stood to reason that a man that dangerous was housebroken.

And there was more than one dangerous person asleep or awake at Jelaza Kazone this evening—including the man presently a little out of temper with her.

Miri summoned a frown of her own.

"Think again," she told him. "And while you're thinking, let me rephrase that question—since when do you need to get between me and *any*thing? We're *partners*—or we were, up until real recent. What changed when we came down to Surebleak, that you gotta cover for us both? If I'm giving you cause for worry, *partner*, sing out. In the meanwhile, I'll just ask which one of us gave the other one an Yxtrang—and didn't think there was a problem about that?"

That last one—that was a foul. Necessity'd been, and Val Con had only done what he had to, to move a man out of a life that was killing him, and give him a chance at another one.

Across the room, she felt him shiver. He closed his eyes and didn't say anything.

Dammit, Robertson, when you gonna learn?

She got up and went over to him, reaching up to stroke the hair off his forehead.

"And *was right*?" she murmured. "You got my back, I got yours—that's an even proposition and it ain't changing."

She laughed softly and leaned against him. After a couple breaths, his arms came 'round her and pulled her in close.

"Might be the only thing that's *not* changing," she continued, closing her eyes, and nestling her cheek against his shoulder. "Juntavas is changing; Scouts are; Liad's got changes coming it ain't even thought of yet, not to mention Surebleak, which didn't ask for none of it."

"Collateral damage," Val Con murmured.

Miri moved her head. "Innocent bystanders. And us—we already changed—the two of us and both together—and now we gotta change some more."

"Must we?" he asked, and she felt him put his cheek against her hair.

"I can't see any way out of it, if we're gonna do what we said we'd do. Right up front, we're gonna hafta stop thinking that surviving 'til lunchtime is a long-term plan."

He laughed, softly. "Until dinner, then?"

"It's a start," she said. "Little steps, just at first. 'Til we get used to the idea."

He didn't say anything, but she caught the gleam of the Rainbow out of the corner of her thought, like a shadow seen on the edge of the eye, and felt him relax out of his snit.

"So," she murmured, "Daav'll talk to Clarence, like he said, and if it's something we need to hear, we'll hear it, and if not, not. You might not've noticed, but your father isn't exactly a dummy."

She felt the laugh shiver through him.

"I had noticed something of the sort," he murmured.

"So you're not a dummy, too. Must run in the family. Now, I need you to do something."

Val Con lifted his head and looked down at her, green eyes glinting amusement.

"And what is that?"

"Kiss me."

· · · ✳ · · ·

Tag and follow.

Osa pel'Naria, pilot-operative, touched her screen and was very soon in possession of all available facts regarding a vessel long of interest to the Department, lately seen at Gondola.

She leaned to the board, opened an underband, entered a code, and was in contact with the tracking device.

In Jump; destination filed at last port—Ploster.

Well enough; there was assistance on Ploster, should she require it.

Would she require it—that was the question.

She tapped the screen for more information on the pilot—one Theo Waitley, new-made First Class.

Pilot-operative pel'Naria smiled.

· · · ✳ · · ·

"Remarried?" Clarence laughed deep in his chest and shook his head. "Not me, laddie." He sipped, giving the wine its due, and Daav did the same. They were in the chamber that had been given to the guest's use; two old men talking over their wine, catching up on twenty Standards.

"And yourself?" Clarence murmured.

Daav lowered his glass, questing gently. Clarence had been a favorite of Aelliana's; it seemed . . . unlike her not to come forward to greet him. Yet to his senses, she was absent. Entirely absent.

"In fact, I entered into an arrangement, which supported me for many years," he said. "From that alliance comes a daughter, newly possessed of a jacket, and with a courier contract in hand."

"No worries there," Clarence observed dryly.

Daav laughed.

"Well . . ." The other man shook his head. "I'm thinking you had the right of it, there—and no disrespect to her memory. It does something to you, being your own and only best friend. I'm on the way to deciding that it's nothing good."

He sipped his wine, and gave Daav a smile that was not . . . wholly convincing.

"So, tell me about this daughter of yours."

"She's had a slower start of it than she might have, had she come to the clan at birth, but it's my opinion that she'll be a pilot to behold." Daav sipped his wine and produced a smile of his own. "That may, of course, merely be the doting father speaking. Val Con gives it as his opinion that she is too timid to be of the Line."

"Who to know better?" the other man asked, though with an air of not requiring an answer. He gave Daav a glance from blue eyes. "The boy learned his ways from his foster-da. We were cordial, the few times we met to do business, but he had the difference in our stations at the front of his head when we did." He grinned. "Herself keeps him on mark, does she?"

"I believe she considers it a lifework. She may be correct; even for one as well-credentialed as she."

"Merc captain is what I read," Clarence murmured, "brought a brace o' Yxtrang into service with the Dragon."

"No, you wrong her. The first Yxtrang may squarely be laid at Val Con's door."

"Is that a fact? And the other two—I think it was two more?"

"If you must have it, those were my fault."

Clarence threw back his head and laughed.

"Between the pair of you, the captain might decide she'd rather the mercs."

"I live in fear of just such a decision," Daav told him earnestly. "Though her attachment to one's regrettable heir seems firm."

"Got that. Ready to fetch him a smart box on the ear, is how I read it, and he bowed to it."

"He does," Daav murmured, "have a good deal of sense. Eventually."

"Well," Clarence said comfortably, "they're young, the two of them."

They sipped wine in companionable silence, and Daav refreshed the glasses.

"If it can be told, what brings you to us, with only an old pass-code between yourself and harm?"

"Truth told, it was you I'd come for, and I'd've sent word, had I any notion the whole clan was to hand." He looked at Daav earnestly. "It's not a firm faith, you understand me, in the old codes. More on the order of a wishfulness."

"I understand," Daav assured him. "Though I'm scarcely of note anymore, having lived retired for so long."

Clarence laughed. "Oh, so you did! So you did! And when you gave over rusticating, what must ye do than take on a whole invasion force and win Nev'Lorn Station free?" He shook his head, abruptly sober.

"What I thought you might like to know is that someone's taken a pet. One of my previous young 'uns come to me with a story—funny story, she had it, and so it was." He tipped his glass at Daav.

"Happens someone came to the Juntavas, offering contract and good, hard cantra for a hit on *Ride the Luck*."

He lowered his glass.

Daav sat very still, suddenly feeling the full weight of Aelliana's attention.

"Happens the prospective client was someone the Juntavas don't deal with, now that they're known," Clarence continued, "so they went away. To the next likely taker."

"Well." Daav sipped his wine, buying a moment in case she wanted to speak—but it seemed his lifemate was content to listen.

"Korval does appear to have made an enemy or two," he said to Clarence. "The Department of the Interior was . . . rather a larger enterprise than even its operatives had guessed."

The other man nodded.

"This news doesn't take ye by surprise, necessarily."

"That they've targeted *The Luck* particularly, rather than—or in addition to—Korval entire is . . . interesting. One wonders if we have someone acting off of initiative. But in the end—Korval is hunted, my friend."

"And has been, this while." Clarence sighed. "It's bothered me, that it happened on my port."

Aelliana moved nearer. "Not your fault," she said, using Daav's voice. "Clarence, they eluded everyone."

"So they did, but—" He shook his head, and repeated it, "But."

"I wonder," Daav said, when it seemed clear that neither Aelliana nor their guest was going to speak again, "what your retirement plans are? As I understand it, you gave notice well before Korval was banned from the homeworld, for acts of aggression and piracy."

"So I did." Clarence sighed. "My initial plan had been to offer as courier—not, you understand, to the Juntavas; they had what they'd paid me for, and then some, laddie. I was after honest work, if you'll do me the kindness of not laughing, and found I was too old to be honest."

He set his glass aside, and glanced wryly to Daav's face. "Nobody honest wants to hire a courier who barely clocked enough flight time to keep his card, never mind one who's old enough to be your grandda.

"If you want the unvarnished truth, I was in a fair way to not knowing *what* to do with myself, when your boy did me the favor of blowing a hole in downtown Solcintra, and taking Korval to a better place. I said to myself, 'Clarence, laddie, there might be opportunity on Surebleak, and those who are so needful of a pilot that they're willing to squint at the credentials.'"

Daav nodded, finished his wine, and set the glass next to Clarence's on the side table.

"Andy Mack," he said, "is the man you want, on the port."

Clarence nodded. "Heard that. He was off on a lift when I stopped by. Hope to chat with him in the next couple days. Does repairs, too."

"As I understand it, his was the only reputable repair shop at port until our own yard was established. Supply lines being what they had been, he did—and continues to do—a good deal of custom rebuilding. He told me that it was a lucky thing for him that the company had left so much equipment behind that a determined man could repurpose."

"Sounds to be practical."

"He is that, to a fault. If you need a reference ..." Daav hesitated delicately and Clarence grinned.

"Thank you, laddie. I'll bear it in mind."

FOURTEEN

. . . .

Arin's Toss
In Transit

THE FIRST JUMP OUT FROM GONDOLA WAS SHORT. THEO'D PLANNED on catching a hard-earned nap while the screens were grey, but—no luck there.

Oh, she was tired enough from her day of shopping in Gondola's gravity, with its icing of intrigue, and mellowed out by the fresh salad and new-baked bread she'd made for dinner. In fact, she pretty much hit her bunk and the sleep zone at the same instant.

There were warm hands and soft lips awaiting her, expert and arousing. Laughing, she reached for her unseen partner, who eluded her in the semidarkness and put strong arms around her from behind. Pinned, she gasped—and gasped again, in delight, as her ear was nibbled, followed by the murmur of a male voice, "So soft, like sea mist . . ."

"Win Ton?" She laughed, and wriggled, trying to turn, to see him—and abruptly he let her go.

She spun, and suddenly, in the way of dreams, it was brighter—more than bright enough to see that it wasn't Win Ton who raised his hand to touch her cheek, but the man who had followed her, with his flat eyes and expressionless face—

Theo threw herself back, away from his embrace, with a force that woke her, the echo of her shouted "No!" still ringing from the metal walls.

✳   ✳   ✳

She put on her warmest sweater, made herself a cup of tea, and settled into the copilot's station, bag of booksticks to hand.

"Might as well do something worthwhile," she told herself, bringing up the comp. Three seconds and no brainwork to set up a private archive; another second to slot the first 'stick and set it to downloading.

Frowning, she scooched back in the chair and pulled her feet up onto the seat. The realization that the guy who'd been following her on Gondola had bothered her on a deeper level than mere passing annoyance was bad enough. The matter of company—she was still warm from the first part of the dream, and...wistful.

And wishing that she wasn't quite so alone on her ship.

The board pinged. She leaned forward, slotted another 'stick, and tapped *go*.

Might be a good thing to do some research on her next port o'call. See if there was time and opportunity for recreation, like Tranza used to call it. As a general thing, Theo preferred a game of bowli ball to quick encounters with strangers. Bowli ball with strangers was more satisfying, anyway. Still, sometimes...

The board pinged. She leaned forward to slot another 'stick, and reached for her tea.

Theo finished her tea and took the mug into the galley. The last 'stick was downloading, and the count on the Jump-grey screens was down into single digits.

She webbed into the pilot's chair—and three things happened simultaneously.

Arin's Toss hit normal space.

The proximity alarm went off.

The pinbeam pinged.

Theo slapped the shields up full, brought the guns live, and hit the warn-away before she registered the tumbling, irregular shape in the screens.

Not a missile, or a pirate ship—just space junk.

Slow-moving space junk, at that.

She nudged the *Toss* just a hair; the rock tumbled past; and she did a leisurely three-sixty, verifying that there wasn't anything else on close scan *or* on midscan. Then she capped the guns, and sat, carefully, back.

A faint orange glow on the upper right of her board drew her eye.

Right.

Pinbeam.

She reached out and tapped the button.

++Course amend immediate++add Tokeo++original deadline delivery stands++further instructions await Tokeoport++END

"What!"

The Gondola to Ploster run didn't have a lot of air in it, already. To add in another—

"Where in Chaos is Tokeo, anyway?" Theo demanded of the empty bridge, but her fingers had already queried the comp and there—there was the answer on the lower left screen.

She stared at it.

Her fingers threw the coords into the route already laid in, requesting a waypoint from navcomp, even while she figured the thing rough in her head.

Navcomp beeped; the route unfolded, and Theo sighed.

It was, she thought, good to see that her math was holding up under the strain of running courier solo. She and navcomp agreed the side trip could be accommodated and the original deadline met.

But she was going to have to fly like a madwoman to do it.

Commander of Agents had since the very early days of the Plan, personally monitored the search for Old Technology. So it was that the report of the newly re-formed Salvage Team came directly to her desk.

The Scouts had—predictably but disappointingly—sealed and now actively patrolled the treasure house of Old Technology that they had been gathering for so many centuries.

There had been no further encounters with the ship that had used ultimate force to resist boarding, nor had the Scout who was the key to the ship been recovered.

There were the continued rumors and reported "sightings" by those made no cleverer by their wine, of a ship that left no Jump sign, that abruptly appeared on scans, and just as suddenly vanished. An old story: older than the Plan, and long since grown tedious.

Commander of Agents touched the screen. If the Salvage Teams could not return something other than negative results and children's stories...

But...perhaps they had.

Commander of Agents read the entry three times before leaning back in her chair and closing her eyes, the better to consider this unlikely finding.

It was said that the very presence of one of Korval within a social equation might influence random event, that the galaxy dignified as "luck," to their benefit. Indeed, this ability had been documented by those who had been set to study Korval.

However, it had also been observed, and entered into the Department's files that, occasionally, this influence was observed to fail—or even to reverse—whereupon Korval found itself at peril.

It would appear that one such case was before them now.

In the recent war of occupation upon Lytaxin, a heretofore unknown defense weapon of old, though not ancient, lineage was brought online. The actions of that device—one Pod 77—had without a doubt preserved the clanhouse of Korval's old ally, and could be counted a major deciding action of the war.

Pod 77 was situated on Lytaxin, well-guarded and beyond the influence of the Department in its present, diminished state.

However, the waking of its brother had quickened a second, similar device, which, upon performing a self-assessment, identified certain functions that were subpar, and sent out a request for assistance.

It was this request that the Salvage Team had intercepted, thereby learning that the device, which identified itself as Pod 78, was calling upon the Delm of Korval for aid.

· · · ※ · · ·

It was a neat shop, as far as mechanics' shops and suchlike places can be neat. Those tools that weren't in use were hung in place; the 'crete floor was sanded and swept and the service bay was ventilated and well-lit. There was a ground-tug on the repair floor, an array of belts and drivers were laid out on a cloth; tool cart pulled up handy.

There not being anybody presently at work on whatever repairs were going forth, Clarence kept walking toward the back of the bay, where a couple of overalls and a utility vest surmounted by a shock of green hair were having coffee and discussion.

"Now the question is, do we machine them parts?" That was one pair of overalls, worn by a balding man perched on a stool.

"Don't seem like there's any question there at all, Shugg." The second pair of overalls were stretched over a long spare frame, grey hair wisping over his shoulders like fog. "Unless you're thinkin' we should order in new?"

The woman with the bright green hair laughed. "Might as well order a new tug, while we're at it."

"Bound to come to that," the tall man said, raising his mug. "Portmaster'll wanna be keepin' up appearances. Right now, though, I'm thinking we'd best give 'er another tight goin' over, replace what we can from parts on hand, machine out what we gotta. That one 'scope seat's gonna be the bastid; ain't made scopes with that config since afore Max here was borned."

"I'll get on that, then," Shugg said, with the air of a man being given a rare treat.

"Right. When Tatia comes in she can do the inventory—"

"I can do that, Colonel," said Max. "Got nothin' on my boards 'til the tug's able."

"Right, then. You make up a pull list for Tatia; that'll save us some time. Shugg, I'm wondering if it ain't worth a walk over to the Dragon yard, see if they got anything we can mod."

"Was gonna check in with 'em soon's I finish my coffee."

"That's the trick, then. Lemme know what you get. Help you with somethin', there, Pilot?"

Clarence stepped forward so the light hit his face fair, hands out where they could be seen, stance nice and easy.

"I'm looking for Andy Mack."

"You found 'im," the tall man said, as Shugg and Max moved off to their various errands. "An' you are?"

"Clarence O'Berin. I hear you might could use a pilot."

"Might could," Andy Mack said, considering him out of blue eyes that weren't nearly as guileless as the rest of his face. "Come on back to the office and let's get to know each other. Cup o' coffee?"

"Thanks."

"Pot's right there. Help yourself."

"Ticket's good." Andy Mack said, tossing it back across the desk. Clarence caught it one-handed and slipped it away into his jacket.

Andy Mack leaned back in his chair, which screamed like a man who'd just seen his lover die, and put his feet up on the desk.

"Lifted just enough to keep it good," he said. "What was you doin' more interestin' than flying, if you don't mind my askin'?"

"Desk job," Clarence told him, which wasn't exactly true, not that way he'd run it. He sipped his coffee and considered the man across from him. Not a stupid man, nor a naïve man, Andy Mack, and if that "Colonel" the tug driver was so free with was true, not a squeamish man, either.

"Did admin for the Juntavas, if you want it. Kept Solcintra Port open for business."

"That so? And now?"

"Now, I'm retired," Clarence said, easy and reasonable. "And I want to fly again."

"Juntavas won't throw you a biscuit?"

"I'm retired," Clarence repeated, raising his cup and looking at Andy Mack over the rim. "It'll sound strange, maybe, but I want to fly honest."

"Don't sound that strange, though I'll mention Surebleak's not the sort o' geography often produces *honest*."

"I hear Boss Conrad's doing some cleaning and painting."

"Oh, he's doin' that! Which reminds me to tell ya—we do some errands now an' then for the Boss—the Bosses, likewise. Not the kind of stuff, usually, they want to hear about on the port. You bein' retired from the Juntavas, I'm thinkin' you know how to keep the odd secret?"

Clarence felt his lips twitch. "I can do that."

"Good. Know Judge Natesa?"

"By reputation."

"Huh. She speak for ya?"

"I don't know why she should." He took a breath, weighing it, but there—the man had offered. "I've got an in-world reference, if one's needed."

Andy Mack held up his hand. "That would be the da?" He didn't wait for Clarence's nod. "Saw him to the Emerald last night—night before, maybe. Anyhow, he mentioned you; said as how he'd hire you hisself in a beat an' a tick, but he wasn't in a hirin' position no more. Says you're a honest pilot, an' a honorable man." He looked owlish. "Not a word we been used to hearin'—honorable. I reckon we'll get accustomed."

"Could happen," Clarence said.

Andy Mack grinned. "Could, couldn't it? Well, you're hired,

Clarence O'Berin." He reached to the desk, picked up a set of ship keys and tossed it across. "Go take a look at *Bleak Lady* and familiarize yourself."

Clarence held the keys tight, feeling his chest grab. He took a breath, and remembered to smile.

"Thanks," he said.

FIFTEEN

· · · · · · · · · · · · ·

Arin's Toss
Tokeoport

THE PILOTS GUILD DIDN'T RATE TOKEOPORT *DO NOT CALL.* NOT
quite, it didn't. The *Quick Guide* did stress that pilots ought to
go on-port in pairs. It also suggested that a senior crew member
be with the ship at all times; that all invoices be triple-checked
for accuracy and authenticity; and any fees should be paid into
a Guild escrow account, and released on lift.

And if any of that wasn't enough to make Theo's stomach hurt,
there was one more piece of unwelcome news imparted by the
guidebook.

There was no Guild office on Tokeoport.

Oh, there was an automated booth on Commerce Street, and
a wayroom that would open to an up-to-date Guild card. But
as far as the actual presence of a representative of the Pilots
Guild—not on Tokeoport.

Tokeoport also seemed to be missing a Guild-certified—or even
Guild-recommended—escort service.

Theo muttered a couple of Tranza's favorite cuss words under
her breath.

Whatever Uncle's job was on Tokeoport, there was only her
to do it. Which meant that she was going to have to go on-port
without a partner, not to mention leaving the *Toss* without senior
crew aboard, *and* she was going to have to be about whatever it
was *fast,* or she'd miss the delivery deadline on Ploster.

Well, she thought, glaring at the screens on Tokeo approach, she was just going to have to be advertent, and wear her gun open on her belt, *which* the Quick Guide also suggested. Strongly.

Traffic was light, which, she thought grumpily, was what you'd expect, coming into a port that was just one point up from unRegulated. What there was for Uncle to want *here*—

A glimmer on the edge of her Number Two screen drew her eye. It hadn't been there a moment before; there was no scatter, like you'd get when a ship Jumped in within range of your scans, and she knew, even before the comp tagged it as a phantom—she knew what ship it was.

"*Bechimo*," she whispered and swallowed against the sudden pounding of her heart.

Her fingers moved without her conscious will, opening a line on the underband.

"*Bechimo*," she said, feeling the key trembling between her breasts, desire starting a slow burn in her belly and that—that was the *key*, she thought. The key that she'd liked on sight, and had no hesitation in hanging around her neck. That even now felt usual and comforting, while burning to be reunited with its ship.

The ship of which *she* was supposedly master.

Theo swallowed, focused, and mentally danced a pilot's get-sharp exercise. The longing eased—somewhat—and her pulse slowed.

"Captain, your vessel is ready to receive you." The voice was smooth and pleasant, in a midrange that could have either been female or male, speaking Terran with what Theo'd heard called a "standard" accent.

"Not now." Her own voice wavered. She cleared her throat, and repeated more forcefully, "Not now."

"Does it please the Captain to name a boarding time?"

"Soon," she said, trying to think. Uncle and Val Con both had suggested a quiet haven for her first boarding of *Bechimo*. Tokeo might be short of company, but in her opinion, it didn't come near to meeting the criterion for "haven."

"Soon," *Bechimo* repeated, sounding...puzzled.

Theo bit her lip against a stab of pity. How long had she had the Captain's key in her possession and never made any attempt at contact? How many times had she ignored the ghost ship in her screens? Granted she hadn't *known* why the ghost was haunting her, but did *Bechimo* understand that she'd been flying without coords?

Bechimo was, Theo understood all at once, lonely. Win Ton had hinted that—not presuming to say it right out straight, of course, but trusting her to figure it out. Which she hadn't, quite, because, until she'd heard that voice, and the catch of disappointment, she hadn't really *understood*...

Bechimo was a person.

Navcomp rang, bringing her attention back to the matter of the ship she was flying and the necessity of filing her approach with Tokeoport.

The next time she looked at her Number Two screen, a few minutes later, the scans were clear to the Jump point.

The fees quoted for a hotpad and a fast lift were...expensive, but not as expensive as she'd thought they'd be, given the *Quick Guide*'s other warnings. Theo accepted both without haggling, and pulled down her mail.

Her orders were to go to the Trade Bar and pick up a package from Keep-Safe Twenty-Two Green, using the code provided. She committed the combination to memory while the hull was cooling, and found the Trade Bar on the port map: two squares east of her hotpad. That was good, both in terms of limiting her exposure to Tokeoport, and for hitting the deadline at Ploster. She'd just keep her head down, and move fast, that was all. Nobody was going to be looking for her, or looking *at* her, necessarily; she'd just be one more pilot on the shabby port displayed in her Number One screen.

It was late afternoon, local. She ought to be away before evening.

Theo pulled on her jacket, grinning as she pushed up the sleeves. She really ought to get a jacket that fit the next time she was on a world that had a proper Guild Hall. Just now, though, she was pleased with the rumpled look Rig's worn leather gave her.

Somebody wearing a well-cared-for jacket and shiny boots—*that* was somebody who would interest port thieves. A pilot who ran so close to the edge of her profit margin that she made do with second-hand leathers just wasn't worth the effort.

She gave the sleeves another push, and the map another hard stare, fixing it in memory. Then she leaned over the board and locked the *Toss* down as tight as she went, without putting her to sleep. On the way to the hatch, she stopped at the safe and engaged the third lock, sealing it with her thumbprint. It wasn't senior crew, but it would have to do.

She checked her gun for the second time, making sure it slid smooth in the holster, then triggered the hatch and walked out into the warm breezy day.

· · · ❋ · · ·

"Hey, Mags, lookit this."

"This" was a flyaway blondie in a jacket two sizes too big for her, working the combo on one of the Green lockers. Nobody hardly ever used the Green lockers, on account of them being out of reason spendy, but the Bar held a block of 'em for outworlders and them who couldn't afford to lose what they filed. It wasn't that the Greens were unbreakable; they were just too damn finicky to worry with. That, and the Snoops took an interest, taking a cut of the rent, like they did. Easier pickins, elsewhere, then busting up a Green.

Once the booty was outta the box, though...

The blondie had a good combo, and pretty quick the packet was in her hand—thin, shiny blue box, like for jewelry or stones. Might be whoever left it was smart and it was full of something more interesting still. It was possible, and it was even possible that him and Kazee would find out before this day was over, if it came about that the project seemed worth their bother.

That was going to take some determinin'. The jacket, for starters...

"Trophy, you make it?" he asked Kazee.

"Ain't hers, is it?" She took a draw on her brew, looking thoughtful. "Could be there's a boyfriend."

There was that. Still, they could handle boyfriend trouble, if it found 'em. And how much could he care, sending her out to pick up a Green all by onesie?

"We paid up with the Snoop, ain't we?"

Kazee nodded, her eyes on the blondie, who'd stowed the packet inside her too-big jacket and turned, walking firm and fast. She glanced at the pair of 'em as she passed—snippy black eyes in a face all angles and frowns—then she was headin' for the door. More'n one head turned to follow her, not all of 'em, in Mags' opinion, sizing up the jacket.

"Not a pro," Mags said, finishing off his 'toot and getting his feet under him.

The blondie was almost to the door when one of them who

was maybe more interested in what was inside the jacket swung half into her path, smiling all soft and friendly.

The blondie ducked outta her way, skittishlike, and kept on going.

Kazee thumped her mug down.

"Let's go," she said, but Mags was already up and movin'.

· · · ✳ · · ·

The breeze had turned from warm to cool. Theo looked up, like Father had taught her when she was only a littlie, looking for weather signs.

Clouds were massing behind the Tower, big and structured—storm cells, she thought—and gleaming silver-white. On Delgado, they'd keep on building into the twilight, and glow pink and orange before they rained down over the nighttime farm grid. On Eylot, you might get a thunderstorm or even a wind twist out of clouds like these, depending on terrain.

Here on Tokeo, who knew what the clouds would bring? As far as she could tell, they were still building; she'd be lifted and out before they were ripe.

And, really, she acknowledged, she was more worried about the man who'd followed her out of the Trade Bar, and who was still with her.

Theo sighed, and considered her options.

She was walking briskly, like a pilot with an errand, but she wasn't running. Running people attracted attention. Worse, running people were seen by some hunters on port as *prey*. She could, she guessed, stop and confront this follower, like she had her last, but it would take time, and there was that deadline at Ploster breathing down her neck.

Tokeoport was a bleak place—'crete streets and 'crete walls with tiny, slit-windowed shops carved into them. There were people on the square, and some who walked like pilots, though there was a shortage of leather on display.

She frowned. Not much space leather *at all* on the street, which she'd also noticed at the Trade Bar. It was like the pilots on-port weren't just keeping their heads down, they were trying to be invisible.

Her corner was coming up.

Theo checked her shadow. He was still with her, but not closing. It could just be that he wanted to see where she was going.

If that was so, he'd either try to close as soon as she made the corner and it became obvious that her goal was the hotyard, or he'd swing off and look for somebody else to follow.

She turned the corner.

Less than an arm's length away, a woman came out of the shadow. Theo spun, too late in close quarters, the woman grabbed her by the jacket and whirled, using their combined weights, and *pushed*.

Theo slammed into the wall, momentarily breathless, her head smacking so hard against the 'crete that the woman's face smeared into senseless color.

"Got 'er!" her attacker yelled.

Her face came into sharp, sudden focus—that and the fist cocked back for the strike.

Theo twisted, enough to throw the woman out of balance, and the strike off true, but not enough to break her grip.

She used her elbows against the wall and pushed forward, but she was at a disadvantage in weight, and the woman threw her back.

"Don't be a bitch, blondie. Just give me the goods."

Theo braced herself, raised a knee and slammed it as hard as she could between the woman's legs.

That made her lose focus long enough for Theo to follow through on the move, twisting out of the loosened grasp, and spinning—

Into the fist of the guy who'd been following her.

· · · ⬙ · · ·

The key reported danger. The key reported an attack.

The key reported the Captain incapacitated and in the hands of pirates.

Very nearly, *Bechimo* translated into atmosphere, guns primed and targeting those who dared to damage the Captain.

The long habit of discretion, of *waiting*, held firm. *Bechimo* experienced... panic. The Captain lay helpless in the power of brigands, exactly as had the Less Pilot! In the case of the Less Pilot, there had been those devices about that *Bechimo* might influence to his rescue and eventual liberty.

The Captain, alone and unsupported... *Bechimo* overrode panic.

The key. The key reported itself with the Captain. The key reported that this situation might soon change.

The key.

• • • ⚙ • • •

"Somebody keeps the bitchy in drink chits an' smoke," a woman's voice said. "Look at this, Mags."

Coins clinked. There was a sense of a body too close, of hands inside her jacket. Theo kept as still as she could, muscles limp, eyes closed; she could feel the hard 'crete alley under her back. That was good, she thought; she wouldn't be tangled up in her own arms and legs when it came time to move.

"After something else, weren't we?" a man's voice asked. Up, Theo realized. He—Mags—was standing, probably watching out for interruptions from other thieves, since there wasn't much in the way of security to care about.

"No reason not to shop while I'm in here," the woman said. "Let's see what else she's got."

The left side of her jacket was yanked open, hard, and it was all that Theo could do to stay limp and seeming like she was still out. Uncle's pickup was in the big left pocket; her license and shipkey sealed into the most secret pocket behind the next least-secret pocket where two cantra bits rode, her hostage against bad fortune.

More yanking, like the seal on the big pocket was giving the woman some problem, then a "hah!" and an absence of weight and presence.

"Here, Mags. You crack it."

As clearly as if she had her eyes wide open, Theo saw the woman on her knees on the alley floor, one hand still negligently holding the lapel of the jacket, her attention directed up, to her partner, offering him the blue box with her free hand.

He bent to take it.

Theo rolled, striking with full force in a move she had only practiced in shadow-dance. The wrist broke with an audible snap; the woman screamed. Theo kept rolling, kicked, and was on her feet, lunging in the same heartbeat. The man swung; she ducked, and came up in a move from *menfri'at*. The man went down like a bag of sugar. Theo scooped up the blue box, looked at the woman huddled, excruciatingly still, on the alley floor; turned and ran for the end of the street and the gate to the hotyard.

• • • ⚙ • • •

"Mags?" Kazee's voice wasn't exactly calm and neither was the shake that came with it. "Mags!"

He got his eyes open, figuring that was the only way to quiet her down, and give his head a rest.

"Little blondie was just that fast, wasn't she?" he said, pulling himself into a sit and waiting for the street to steady. *Damn.* Blondie must've hit 'im with an augment.

"We get anything outta that," he asked Kazee, "'cept a headache and an arm broke?"

"Yeah..." She held out her good hand, showing him the shine of good Terran bits across her palm. "My share's going right in the doc box."

"I'll stand a brew for ya," Mags told her. He frowned down at the coins, seeing a different shine, and a shape not...exactly... coinlike.

"Hold on," he said, "what's that? Blondie drop a pretty in with her spendin' money?"

"Where? No, I see—like a pin or somethin'..." She held her hand steady while he got it loose and held it up between finger and thumb.

"Got something carved on it," he said, taking a rough weight in his palm. "Worth a walk down to the faganhouse for this, maybe."

"There's no need for you to trouble yourselves," a woman's soft, accented voice spoke from the left and rear. The sound of a safety being released was sharp against the quiet air.

· · · ❊ · · ·

It was quite clement this afternoon, Daav thought. He'd been told that it was local spring, and had independently observed that the wan sunlight was growing slightly more robust. Indeed, here in the center of the garden, in the Tree's very court, it was nearly warm, though not so nearly that he was tempted to unseal his jacket.

He did take his hands out of his pockets and place them, palm-flat, against the rough bark, where they were instantly warmed.

"I thank you," he murmured. "As does the gardener, who asked me particularly to extend her regards. She had not considered that you might influence the immediate environment to the benefit of the small plants. For myself, I don't wish to seem ungrateful, but I feel it necessary to ask that you have a care not to plunge our near neighbor into an ice age."

There was a faint rustle among the lower branches as a few leaves floated groundward—the Tree's equivalent of a chuckle.

"It heartens me to learn that I am yet amusing." Daav closed his eyes and leaned his forehead against the warm bark.

His relationship with Korval's Tree had not always been easy, though certainly they had shared an understanding. He might have thought that he would find its mode of discourse...difficult, or even mad, having been so long unaccustomed, but he had fallen into the way of it again quite easily. What Jen Sar Kiladi might have made of such whimsy...

But, there; that route promised no profit for anyone.

Daav took a deep breath, catching the scent of cinnamon rising from the pleasantly warm bark. Kiladi...There was an oddity, this continued melancholy; the sharp sense of losing a man who had never lived—no, he corrected himself, drowsily. Certainly, Kiladi had lived—there was the considerable body of his work, his legions of students, graduated and themselves working the fields he had shown to them, not to mention the astonishing and occasionally alarming fact of Theo.

So say instead, he instructed himself, that Kiladi had lacked a regular birth, and a childhood, and that now he was spared the slow decline into old age. He had been a busy man, and influential. He had loved and been loved—and was sorely missed by his creator.

If Daav yos'Phelium achieved so much, he might put aside the ties of clan and kin lightly, when the time was upon him.

A rattle in the leaves above broke his drowse. He opened his eyes and stepped back, hand rising in time to catch a seed pod.

"My thanks," he murmured, suddenly craving nothing so much as the treat promised him. He opened it immediately, noting that his assistance was scarcely required; it seemed the pod was so eager to be eaten that it fell open of itself.

Mint and cinnamon danced on his tongue—and something else that might have been an echo of Kamele's most favored coffee.

He devoured the gift with unseemly haste, ravenous—and sated, the instant that the last piece was eaten.

Sighing, he looked up into the high branches.

"My thanks," he said again, and meant it from the heart. Whatever the pod's purpose—from the expression of a comrade's sympathy, to a subtle poisoning—he was glad to have received it, and felt the better for having eaten it.

Unexpectedly, there came another rattling, this from the very highest branches, followed by the apparently forceful ejection of two pods, which hit the ground precisely before his boots.

"This is bounty, indeed," he murmured, bending to retrieve the gifts.

Immediately he touched the first, he knew that it was intended for him—those of Jela's Line were born with that sense. So—his, but for . . . some time in the future. The understanding that came to him was that the pod was not . . . quite ripe.

The second . . . very nearly he dropped it. Very nearly, he threw it back into the high boughs. It was only the recollection that the Tree's gifts of seed pods had always been truly meant, if not always beneficent, that stayed his hand.

The second pod . . . was for Aelliana.

And also . . . not . . . quite ripe.

"Just so." He bowed his head and opened his jacket, stowing the pods into a small, sealed pocket where they would be secure, but easy to access, when and if the time of their ripeness arrived.

SIXTEEN

. . . .

Tokeoport

ARIN'S *TOSS* SAT READY ON HER GO-PAD. THAT WAS THE GOOD NEWS.

A woman with gun drawn stood, legs braced, squarely in front of the hatch, which couldn't, Theo thought, taking momentary cover behind a parked jitney, be anything but bad news.

She dropped to one knee behind the jitney, shivering, and her breath coming hard, though she'd hardly run any distance at all. Her right hand, the one she'd broken the woman's wrist with—her hand hurt. She shook it, carefully, and winced.

Gonna need to get some ice on that, she thought, which brought her neatly back around to the fact that there was an armed... person between her and her ship, a deadline getting shorter with each breath she took—and she *didn't have time* for this!

Think, Theo.

As far as she understood from the *Guild Quick Guide,* Tokeoport didn't exactly have a law force, proctors or security; it was the portmaster who was the final judge of right and wrong.

Theo sighed, weighing her choices: confront the woman guarding her ship, or take the problem to the portmaster, who might or might not have time to hear her, and who might or might not think the situation merited penalties all around?

"I *don't* have time for this," she muttered.

She took a deep breath, trying to steady herself. The shivering had eased off; her joints felt like they had too much give in them and her hand ached. Her primary hand, of course.

119

Carefully, she peered around the jitney and studied the woman blocking her entry to the *Toss*.

A middle-tall Terran wearing clean, but well-scarred working leathers that hung too loose off her broad shoulders. As far as Theo could tell, the gun was clean and cared-for, but her boots weren't by any means new. The belt holding the woman's pouch and holster was notched too far back; the tongue was double-tucked under the front loop to keep it out of the way.

Theo sat back on her heels.

Chances were what she had here was an opportunist, somebody who made what money she could by charging pilots a "toll" for letting them onto their own ships. The *Quick Guide* had described just such a scam, as an illustration of why it was advisable to leave at least one crew member aboard.

She touched the inner pocket where she'd kept her Terran money, not really surprised to find it flat. The second money pocket appeared to be untouched, and the most private pocket, with its precious two cantra pieces, was secure.

The chronometer hanging on *her* belt showed a time elapsed on Tokeoport that didn't make her happy at all.

It might, she thought, touching the second pocket again to feel the comforting hardness of coin beneath her fingers, be most efficient to pay the woman off, get aboard and *leave* this chaos-driven, antisocial world.

Whatever she had picked up here had *better* be worth it, she thought darkly, and stood up, carefully, from behind the jitney.

The woman watched her approach with every appearance of interest, neither holstering her weapon nor bringing it forward.

Theo stopped six long paces out and raised her hands to belt height, fingers spread.

"Good day to you," she said politely.

The courtesy seemed to amuse the woman; she half-smiled and gave an easy nod.

"Evenin'."

"You're between me and my ship," Theo told her. "I need to board."

"It'll cost ya."

Cost her, to board her own ship? Theo swallowed against a jolt of pure anger.

Expediency, she reminded herself, and, with the anger still on way too warm, *inner calm.*

"How *much* will it cost me?" she asked, as evenly as she could manage.

"More'n you're likely to think fair," the woman said, and brought the gun up, finger tightening.

Theo dropped back, her body finding the proper dance move— twist and kick. The gun spun out of the woman's hand. Theo lunged, her opponent dodged, there was a whine in Theo's ear and a ping against the hull.

"Not at me, you fool!" the woman shouted, half turning.

She gasped, a look of surprise on her face, and crumpled even as Theo jumped for the hatch, key in hand.

There was another whine, another ping. Theo raised the key— It shattered, spitting energy, stinging her fingers.

She spun, intuiting the shooter, rather than seeing her, dove forward in a somersault, snapped to her feet and ran. Something slapped her on the right shoulder; she ignored it and kept running, slamming through the gate and into the alleyway, running without thinking, and there was something in the middle of the way—piles of rags or—

Sobbing, she collapsed to her knees, staring at the ruined faces of the man and the woman who had tried to rob her. A neat hole, like the sort made by a pellet, was in the middle of each forehead.

Behind her, she heard the gate to the hotyard clang.

· · · ☼ · · ·

BOSS CONRAD SUGGESTS PUBLIC WAY CONCEPTS TO COMMITTEE OF BOSSES

Following last week's fatal shootout at the borders of Plaski and Glenbiny, Committee of Bosses spokesman Boss Kalhoon tells Blair Road Booster that the committee is under serious advisement by Boss Conrad to rapidly adopt a joint Public Way policy for Surebleak Port and contiguous trails, alleys, walks, routes, and roadways.

While some of the policy would merely codify the way things have always been done, others would change the way hucksters, vendors, indie-walkers, beggars, scrappers, and trade folk operate while in areas administered by and for the public by recognized Bosses.

Last week's tangle left three dead and more than a dozen injured when a former Plaski underboss, Craig Edwards, demanded spot rent of cloth huckster Lin Thicum, of Plaski. Thicum refused and moved her wagon into the road across the line into Glenbiny, at which point Edwards and several backers pulled and fired without warning, wounding Thicum but catching immediate fatal return fire from a car blocked by Thicum's rag wagon.

"Manners are important these days," Kalhoon said, "especially with so many new people using the road. Not only will we need to settle what parts of the road are Public Way and which parts can be vend spots, we'll all need to be careful about pulling in a Public Way. While Thicum might have had problems for blocking a car from the Road Boss's house, the driver, cook and gardener in that car work for the Road Boss and needed to keep the Road open, which Edwards was impeding."

The Committee of Bosses is expected to have a policy in place tonight, so watch the morning edition of Blair Road Booster for details.

· · · ✳ · · ·

Theo knelt in the dark, nearly doubled over from the stitch in her side. She'd brought her breathing under control, but she couldn't stop the shivering. There was something wrong with her eyes—nearby objects had an alarming tendency to slide in and out of focus—and she felt...feverish; hot and sticky in a way that had nothing to do with physical exertion.

At least she wasn't alone, here in the dark. There was...someone standing just out of sight, behind her left shoulder. Backup. Someone familiar—Win Ton, she'd thought at first, but no! It was Father. No, how could she have been so—Kara, of course! Or—well...well, what did it matter who, as long as she knew that someone had her back?

She took a breath, deep as the ache in her side would allow, and shivered again.

The wayroom had opened to her Guild card, just like the *Quick Guide* had promised. She'd dialed the lights off and locked the door behind her, and now—now, she was waiting.

She had enough credit on her card to keep the wayroom locked for days. If they'd been ordinary thieves, she might've had some hope of waiting her pursuers out—whoever they were, and whatever they wanted.

It could, she thought, be the *Toss* they were after. Uncle had... enemies—Val Con among them, by policy, if not by inclination. The trader on Gondola—Mildred Bilinoda—she'd been worried— worried that Uncle was taking chances that would endanger his contacts—

And his pilot?

Was it a *plan*? she wondered. Had he intended her as a decoy? Why? And would he risk the *Toss*—no ordinary ship, but old, and lovingly maintained...

There was a movement, out *there*.

Theo huddled closer inside the disposal unit's inlet door, and strained her eyes.

The dusk was smeary with colors, like she was trying to sight through a faded and unsteady rainbow. She could see enough, though. She could see three figures, two with guns ready, standing slightly aside, guarding the back of the woman who stepped forward and touched the wayroom's intercom button.

"Pilot of Korval, I greet you." The words were in Trade; the woman's voice solemn and sweet. "It is Osa pel'Naria at your service, Pilot. I stand here with two of my team, to escort you to your ship."

Escort her to her ship—how likely was that? Theo thought. And then thought that maybe it *was*, if they thought she still had the key.

Cutting through the hull was bound to attract unwanted attention, even on such a port as this. They might also worry about booby traps and failsafes, those being standard ship security among grey traders, according to Rig Tranza. For a man who'd been a respectable pilot for a respectable shipping conglomerate for slightly more years than Theo'd been alive, Rig Tranza had known a lot about the practices of grey traders.

"Pilot of Korval," the woman was at the intercom again. "Perhaps you doubt our intentions. Allow me to show you a token of our goodwill."

She raised her hand, showing the spy-eye a small object that shot sparks of silvered flame in Theo's blurry vision.

"I bear a token of your House," the woman said. "Will you not open to me now?"

Wait. A token? Of her House? And—what had she said, just there at first? Pilot of Korval?

The galaxy spun and came to rest about forty-five degrees off true.

Theo caught her breath, remembering Miri holding the Tree-and-Dragon pin out to her, "Take it, and keep it by. Never know when it might be handy."

She'd taken it and put it—put it in the pocket with her easy money, and then forgot about it.

The two footpads...she flinched away from the memory of their crumpled bodies, their eyes staring into—into Galaxy Nowhere, wasn't that it?—they'd taken her easy money; she didn't need to touch the pocket to know that it was empty. They'd taken her easy money, the pin mixed in with the coins...

Think, Theo. There was no proof that these—that Osa pel'Naria had stolen the pin from the people who had stolen it from Theo. She might've gotten her pin from the Delm of Korval, just like Theo'd gotten hers. It might be a legitimate offer of help. If there was a pass-phrase or a ready-sign, Miri hadn't told her *that*, only, "I'd tell you to wear it wherever you go, but right now being under Korval's protection is what you'd call double-edged—just as likely to make you a target as get you some help."

A burst of wind sent a cold, damp eddy into Theo's huddling place. The storm she'd seen massing behind the Tower was apparently going to deliver some rain, after all.

One of Osa pel'Naria's backups glanced up at the dark sky, and murmured something. The woman moved her free hand, out of range of the camera, fingers spelling out a quick *search, bring, all means necessary.*

The two moved at once, one going left, the other going right. In her watching place, Theo bent her head, hiding her pale face from the person who strode by with quiet, purposeful steps.

All means necessary, was it? Theo took a deep breath. If these were potential allies, she'd rather be on her own. Another breath.

Time to get walking, she told herself. Soon they were going to figure out that the wayroom was empty, and then they'd widen their search.

The problem was, where she was going to walk *to.*

Portmaster, she thought. In the absence of a Guild office, safeties, or any other ordered enforcement structure, the portmaster was her single hope for getting a message out to Uncle.

She should have done that first off, she realized now, but she'd been worried about making the Ploster deadline—way beyond blown, now—and then she hadn't thought at all, just run, and found herself in front of the wayroom before she realized its potential as a trap.

Using the card and locking the door on an empty room, had been a pretty good decoy, but she should have run again instead of staying in harm's way.

Well, at least she had a name to give to Uncle, after she got his ship loose and put serious space between it and Tokeoport.

She got her feet under her, and eased toward the disposal's mouth. The wind whooshed again, throwing grit into her face. She shook her head, took a step . . .

"Pilot of Korval," Osa pel'Naria said again. "Do us the honor of allowing us to aid you."

It was said so sincerely that Theo wavered, one step into escape; then she remembered the two dead people in the alley and moved, out of her hiding place and into the wind-laced dark.

Sheet lightning dyed the sky gold and orange by the time Theo hit the Tower. She shook the rain from her jacket and approached the counter.

"Theo Waitley, Pilot First Class," she said to the man seated there. "I'd like to see the portmaster."

"On what business?" he asked, more bored than interested.

Best to keep it simple for the front desk, she'd decided, so she gave him the most pressing problem.

"I've been wrongly denied access to my ship."

He looked even less interested. "What ship?"

"*Arin's Toss.*"

"Oh," he said, "*that* ship." He touched a key on his console, and glanced over his shoulder to the woman stepping out of the alcove.

"Pilot Waitley of *Arin's Toss* to see the portmaster," he said.

The woman nodded, and moved a hand in a broad "come on" motion. "Follow me."

SEVENTEEN

. . . .

Portmaster's Office
Tokeoport

PORTMASTER MCKLELLAN HAD A SQUARE FACE SOFTENED BY A fringe of grey beard; his eyes were pale brown and very round.

"Waitley, is it?" he asked, extending a hand as square as his face. "Ticket."

Theo put her license in his hand, not without a pang, and watched him slot the thing into the reader.

He looked up, frowning.

"This'll take a couple minutes, Pilot. Coffee's over there if you want some. Even if you don't, sit down. Hate people hovering over me."

"Yes, sir," Theo said. She moved down the room to the pot, poured burnt-smelling brew into a disposable cup and went back to sit in the red plastic chair at the corner of the portmaster's desk.

She sipped the coffee carefully, finding it just as bad as she'd feared, and took stock.

She'd stopped shivering, by which she supposed that the adrenaline had run its course. Her vision was still blurred with random color, bruises were rising on her primary hand and her fingertips were blistered where the key had burned her. She figured she'd find other bruises and minor scrapes, but mostly she'd been lucky.

Luckier than the pair in the alleyway, anyway.

There was a squeak as Portmaster McKlellan shifted in his chair. Theo looked up into frowning tan eyes.

"Ticket's clean, much good it'll do you, Waitley." He pulled it out of the reader and tossed it in her general direction.

Theo twisted in the chair, snatched, and managed to catch the license before it landed in her cup.

"The problem," she said, "is my ship..."

"You're right there—the problem is your ship," he said, leaning back in his chair and folding his big hands over his belt buckle. He shook his head. "I got a warrant on file from the FTC, says that ship is in violation of standards. Suspicion of variant and illegal tech. It's not local talent got it cordoned for toll, is what I'm telling you, Pilot. If that was all, you an' me would have a little chat about how much your ship means to you, arrive at a fee, and we'd take care of the problem for you. Or not, depending on whether your credit was good. This here"—he waved at the screen—"this here's galactic, and legit. That ship ain't goin' nowhere on your say-so or mine. Which brings us to your next problem—and this is what'd be worryin' me, if I was sitting there, turning my nose up at a perfectly good cup o' coffee."

"I prefer tea," Theo said, raising the cup and making a show of sipping coffee. The Federated Trade Commission? If they impounded *Arin's Toss*—which it looked like they'd done, in the most assertive way possible—they were bound to ask questions about what she was carrying. She didn't know, and a truth test would prove that. But—Theo suppressed a shudder—truth tests weren't necessarily enjoyable.

She looked back to the portmaster.

"What's my next problem, then?"

"Being stranded on Tokeo ain't something most pilots look on with favor," the portmaster said, "but in your case, that's not the problem." He shifted slightly in his chair and suddenly there was a gun in his hand. Theo froze.

The portmaster nodded.

"Your problem," he continued, in exactly the same off-hand tone, just like he wasn't holding a gun on her. "Your problem is that you, as pilot of that very wanted ship out there, are *also* 'of interest' to the FTC, who've offered a nice reward for anybody who nails you down long enough for them to take you into custody." He settled into his chair, gun steady.

"They'll be here shortly. Might as well finish your coffee."

· · · ❋ · · ·

The key reported injury to the Captain. The key reported that it had instituted first aid procedures. The key advised that these measures were at best temporary, and that the Captain would soon require care, else she would fall. Perhaps, she would fail.

Carefully, *Bechimo* diverted energy to the key, which used it to support the Captain. It was a half measure. Less. Had there been a proper bonding . . . but no. To entertain regret at this juncture was to endanger the Captain. The Captain's well-being and liberty were paramount, so the Builders had stipulated and so *Bechimo* would—

Logic lit yellow; Rules blared orange; the Morality module blushed a rosy, warning, pink.

Brought up short, *Bechimo* accessed the problem areas.

While the Builders had indeed stipulated that the ship might place itself between the Captain and the Captain's danger, Rules stipulated that "Captain" indicated a fully bonded state.

Logic indicated that a pilot—even an Over Pilot accepted of the key—was not Captain—but crew.

Morality therefore was offended, that the ship took up a decision that was properly the Captain's—the safety and disposition of crew.

Bechimo knew chagrin. It was no small thing, to take the Captain's decision. The ship was not the Captain. *That* was an Imperative, locked into the very kernel of *Bechimo*'s being.

And, yet . . . the ship *might* act on the Captain's behalf, for the good of Captain and crew. And Rules allowed of Intent.

Intent was mostwise applied to crew. However, if an Over Pilot was not Captain but crew, then Intent applied.

Bechimo reviewed the latest—indeed, the only!—communication with the Captain. It was clear: Addressed as Captain, the Over Pilot had not denied it. Desired to name a time of boarding, she had stated, "Soon."

The Over Pilot therefore expressed her Intent to stand as Captain.

Logic accepted the premise, warily. Rules allowed proper application of terms.

Morality's blush . . . faded, and a query was filed.

It was enough. *Bechimo* was free to act as required, on the Captain's behalf.

Soon. Soon, she would board.

The key reported that the Captain rested and took liquid. That was well. The key could not accept much energy, and *Bechimo* dared not risk the key. Still, another tithe of energy, gently, and oh so carefully—something at least to keep her.

Until soon.

· · · ⁂ · · ·

Against all odds, the coffee seemed to have done her some good. Theo was feeling stronger, more alert, her vision as clear as it had ever been.

Which meant that, when the door opened with just the faintest whisper of sound, she saw the look of surprise on the face of the woman who stepped inside, two men at her back, the same configuration they'd held outside the wayroom. Their jackets were glossy with water; water plastered hair to three heads, and beaded in droplets on three faces that eerily bore an identical expression of bland attention.

"Osa pel'Naria," Theo said. "I thought you were going to take me to my ship."

The woman inclined her head, gravely. "And so we shall, Pilot. You might have saved us all exposure to the weather this evening."

She moved a hand and the man at her right stepped out of formation. He reached inside his jacket and put a pouch on the desk before the portmaster.

"Finder's fee," he murmured, and came another, fast step forward, to grab Theo's arm, holding it hard enough to bruise.

"Stand," he said.

"All you had to do was ask," she said, with a mildness she was a long way from feeling. She came to her feet, and he yanked the gun from her belt. "You will come with us, Pilot, and you will not cause us any more trouble." Osa pel'Naria glanced to her henchman.

"Keep her close. It is dark, and the rain confuses the sight."

She turned to the man behind the desk.

"Our business here is done, Portmaster McKlellan. We will clear your port soon."

He nodded, sitting just like he had been, gun out, the pouch unopened on the desk in front of him.

"Be good to see you go," he said.

* * *

There is a phrase in *menfri'at*, the dance on which all other defense dances are built—a phrase that Phobai had called "baby's sleeping." It served two purposes, as she had taught Theo: it was a genuine resting state, and also, it might misdirect an opponent. It was a phrase that Theo rarely danced, having learned long ago that her size meant she should end any confrontation as quickly as possible.

And because she had never before been a captive.

Now, though, she danced "baby's sleeping" with every bit of her skill, muscles loose, balance milky, walking where her captor's hand steered her, feet barely lifting above the tarmac.

Overhead, thunder roared, and lightning did a manic dance of its own. Three steps from the Tower door, Theo was soaked through. She blinked, finding that Osa pel'Naria had been truthful about one thing: the rain did make it hard to see.

She saw the *Toss*, though, when they came up on it, and felt the slight change in the grip on her arm.

"We require the key, Pilot," Osa pel'Naria said, stepping to her unencumbered side.

The key? So they *didn't* know that the key had been destroyed! Theo almost smiled.

Your opponent's ignorance is opportunity. She heard Father's voice as clearly as if he were standing next to her. And in counterpoint, Kamele: *A scholar must be free to pursue every possibility.*

"Key?" she said, muzzily. "Just a . . . I've got it right . . ."

She reached inside her jacket, groping. There was a folding knife in the slip pocket on the right, but she didn't want to get into a hand-to-hand with these three, who were trained, whatever else they were. All she wanted to do was—

"Come, Pilot! If you cannot find it, I will!"

Osa pel'Naria stepped closer, and that was good. The grip on her arm loosened again, just a little. Just enough.

Theo raised her foot and slammed the heel down on the other woman's instep. She twisted out of her captor's grip, felt bone go, screamed, and finished the move. Free, she dove to the tarmac, rolling under the *Toss*, the pain sheeting the night white—or maybe it was only lightning. Then she was on her feet and running, careless of direction.

She heard feet pounding behind her. She heard a cough, felt

a bite along her scalp, dodged and kept running, broken arm cradled against her chest.

Another cough and she dove, rolling into the shadows and beneath a ship, fetched up against the tubes, and huddled there, listening.

The steps ran past, circled back. A woman's voice shouted something—in Liaden, Theo thought, though she couldn't make out the words.

There was a sound at the ship's edge, and the flare of a small light. Theo moved as quickly as she could, and as quietly, easing her way out the opposite side.

On the tarmac again, she kept to the edges of ships, flinching in the storm's blare. She was dizzy, disoriented, her vision dancing with more than flashes of lightning.

Ahead, she saw them in an especially lurid display of lightning—there were trees ahead. She could lose herself there, rest.

Think.

· · · ✳ · · ·

The Captain had taken more damage, but she had, for the moment, eluded her captors. Readied for action, *Bechimo* slipped between, and again, between. Into a gravity well—it could be done. Had upon occasion been done. To acquire the surface of a planet by slipping between the layers of space? Theoretically, it was possible.

Testing the theory had, until very recently, been considered too dangerous for *Bechimo* to undertake.

The safety of the Captain, however, was paramount.

Bechimo slipped nearer still—and paused, until the key reported that the Captain had stumbled, fallen.

And did not rise.

· · · ✳ · · ·

She was hurt, Theo knew. Worse, she was hurt and she was hunted and she had run without prudence or plan. Father would... Kamele would...Win Ton—

That made her laugh; the laugh turned to a gasp of pain. If Win Ton had the smallest bit of prudence, he would not be at this very moment imprisoned in an autodoc which was trying to keep his own cells from killing him.

If Win Ton had *any* prudence, there wouldn't be a ghost ship haunting her routes and knowing her name...

The night... shifted.

The rain parted.

The trees directly before her soggy nest of brush... shimmered, re-forming around a—a vessel, immediately recognizable.

It was, of course, impossible that it be here, on-planet, without any fuss or fanfare. She had a head injury; she was imagining things.

Despite which, she stood. Her legs seemed like they were attached to something else, and she was operating them by remote, clumsily. Still, she managed two steps... three... toward the ship that could not, possibly, be there.

"*Bechimo*?" she whispered, as lightning silvered the leaves around it, flaring along lines like the lines of no ship ever seen.

Soundlessly, the hatch rose.

EIGHTEEN

· · · · · · · · · · · · · · · · ·

Blair Road
Surebleak

FOOTSTEPS SOUNDED IN THE HALL. FORCEFUL FOOTSTEPS, THOUGH
Nova yos'Galan had no doubt that the author of them was trying
to walk quietly, lest she be disturbed.

"Yes, Mr. Golden?" she called, folding her hands atop the report
she had been reviewing.

Michael Golden...wasn't. He was short, though taller than she,
and dark—hair, skin, and eyes a pleasant composition of black,
toast, and brown. His shoulders were broad, his legs bowed, and
his understanding quick. Not only Surebleak, but Blair Road was
his home, and the home of his family back unto "Double-Gran."
He thus possessed an encyclopedic knowledge of the local folk,
their customs, alliances, and turf history. An exemplary aide, he
had been hired to stand as her bodyguard—what was called here
a 'hand—a task to which he also brought not inconsiderable skill.

"Ears like a rabbit," he said now, coming rueful into her office.
"Got some news from the crew working on the consolidated
school building."

Nova sighed to herself, foreknowing what she was about to
hear. Uncle Daav would have it that the persons responsible were
merely frightened at the volume and immediacy of the changes
being forced upon them. That might, Nova conceded, well be true.

She only wished that they would seek the Healers, instead of—

"How bad this time?" she asked.

"Hacked into the power-shovel and drove it through the outside wall," he said apologetically. "Watchman says he didn't hear a thing."

Were all the hired watchers on Surebleak deaf? Nova wondered, but kept the question behind her teeth.

"Thank you, Mr. Golden, for bringing me the news. Is there anything else?"

"Hope not," he said and gave her a grin.

Nova smiled faintly, to indicate that she had understood that this was humor. "Yes, let us by all means hope not," she said.

Theo fell into the pilot's chair, awkwardly fumbled the chain over her head one-handed, and slotted the key.

"Theo Waitley," she said, her voice a cracked whisper, "pilot."

The screen immediately before her lit, words forming.

Bechimo welcomes Pilot Theo Waitley. Registry in progress.

She shivered, then, remembering Win Ton's tale of sitting—well, right over there, in the empty copilot's chair, seating a key at random, and so starting this whole chain of events, this waking of a ship that might have better been left sleeping.

And what of you then, Theo Waitley, she asked herself, hunching over her broken arm. *Who would have given you aid, just now?*

The forward screen was filling, line by line, a deliberate list of systems and their status.

"Captain." The voice she'd heard only once before, genderless, but—worried. Definitely worried. "Captain, you are wounded. Medical facilities are available. I will guide you..."

"No—not yet," she whispered. "My ship—*Arin's Toss.* I'm not leaving her for them—those—to break!"

It seemed to her that the status lines faltered in their deliberate dance down the screen, though that might have been her eyesight, which was jumping, giving her greyish snapshots of the bridge interspersed with flares of color, like static.

"Captain," *Bechimo* said—carefully, Theo thought—"you are aboard your ship."

"The *Toss*—my responsibility. I left her alone, without crew to guard her."

She didn't imagine the pause this time. At least, she thought not.

"Captain. It may be possible to onload *Arin's Toss.* Does it please you to order your ship to lift and survey the situation?"

What? Theo swallowed hard in a dry throat, and forced herself to think. Orders. *Bechimo* wanted orders.

"If it's possible to . . . survey without exposing yourself—yes." She hesitated, then realized she'd better fill in some more, just in case she—if she lost consciousness.

"If you can retrieve the *Toss* without danger to yourself, do that. If not . . . if not . . ." she sagged back in the pilot's chair, thoughts fragmenting. "Do not endanger yourself," she repeated, just in case she hadn't been clear.

"Understood, Captain. Will you take medical aid? You are wounded."

"As soon as we find out if we can onload the *Toss*. I'll just . . . rest, here. Keep me informed."

"Yes, Captain."

Carefully, Theo relaxed, letting the chair take her weight until she was boneless against the cushions, eyes closed, hugging her broken arm against her. *Bechimo* had an autodoc, and was right to suggest it to her. Broken arm, head injury—what a mess she'd made.

Should've hired a copilot, she thought, muzzily. Except she hadn't wanted the bother; the *weight* of another person always around. Besides, lots of couriers ran solo.

Of course, not a lot of them worked for Uncle.

Her thoughts wandered down the path she'd started on outside the wayroom. Had Uncle set her up? Why? Why would he deliberately put his ship in danger? He must've known that the FTC had the *Toss* on its lists; why was he flying her at all? Deliberate provocation? It would've been nice, if he'd told his pilot-for-hire that—

"Captain, *Arin's Toss* is under remote surveillance. Scans find no active threats or other deterrents to an immediate pickup."

Theo sat up, hissing as her arm protested.

"Can we make the pickup?"

"We can. The large cargo bay is available and the podlift operational," *Bechimo* said. "It would be a matter of moments. Standing by for the Captain's order."

She took a hard breath, staring at the screens, at the lightning playing along the *Toss's* hull. The remote surveillance site was marked out in orange.

"No weapons?" she asked, though on-port—even Tokeoport—who would dare?

"None detected, Captain."

She nodded, once.

"Do it."

· · · ❖ · · ·

The Scouts had captured the hub at Sinfreed. Staff on-site had destroyed the data and the comms, along with themselves—all honor to them—but yet, the Department could scarce afford the loss. Sinfreed had been relatively intact, and had been central to the recovery of other, more fragmented systems.

Which had doubtless been what had brought it to the attention of the Scouts.

The *damned* Scouts.

Commander of Agents recognized anger and closed her eyes, invoking a series of mental exercises to restore dispassion. Anger was a liability—a costly and dangerous luxury. The Department's virtues were dispassion, control, and calculation, the proper application of which guaranteed success.

The Scouts would be answered, and fully. As Korval would be answered. And, it would seem, the Juntavas, profit-driven no longer, and allied to Korval through marriage.

Commander of Agents opened her eyes, touched the screen and accessed the next summary.

The backtracing of Val Con yos'Phelium, once an agent of the Department, now a traitor to the Plan, was going well. Reports from Agent of Change sig'Alda, dispatched to the interdicted world of Vandar to capture rogue agent yos'Phelium had been recovered from backup systems, and analyzed.

Analysis revealed that yos'Phelium's intention had been to build a base upon Vandar. He had formed a core cell of natives before the opportunity afforded by Agent sig'Alda's arrival allowed him to lift out. As Korval wasted nothing, it was therefore given that yos'Phelium had intended a quick return to complete his work, and had been—as had the Department, on other fronts—delayed by circumstance.

It was, the Commander believed, worth the deployment of a field team or two, in order to surey Vandar and ascertain what yos'Phelium had wrought. Interdicted Worlds received minimal scrutiny from the Scouts at the best of times. In such times as these, it would be wonderful, indeed, if Vandar received oversight at all.

Commander of Agents allowed herself a smile.

When Val Con yos'Phelium returned to Vandar, he would find matters...not as he had left them. Very much so. A quiet base, on an Interdicted World, would serve the Department well, indeed.

Commander of Agents allowed herself to bask in pleasure for another few moments, then, recognizing in complacency an enemy to the Plan as potent as anger, again reviewed her stablizing exercises.

Dispassion achieved, she accessed the next summary screen.

The team sent to Moonstruck reported itself on-site and beginning operations.

Excellent.

* * * ⚜ * * *

Theo stared at the screens, watching *Arin's Toss* rise into *Bechimo*'s main hold; watched the hatch slide shut, saw the report on the status screen: *sealed and secure.* She took a shaky breath, meaning to say, *Let's get out of here.*

But she didn't have to.

Number One screen, which only a moment before had displayed the rain sheeting down on the sleeping ships at Tokeoport, now displayed a starfield, while Number Two elucidated their precise position in planetary mid-orbit.

That just...wasn't possible.

"Captain, honor is served," *Bechimo* stated. "You and the ship for which you accepted responsibility are aboard, and your enemies have been confounded. Please make use of the medical facilities. Your readings are erratic." There was a pause. "Please, Theo Waitley."

And how would you feel, Theo asked herself, hearing what sounded like naked pleading in that voice, *if you'd waited this long to meet a person who was going to be really important in your life and received them broken, beat-up and maybe not making very good decisions?*

"All right," she said, releasing the webbing and pushing herself to her feet. Her copilot would handle what needed handling, while the pilot rested. Except, well, *Bechimo* wasn't her copilot. Win Ton, at least according to his theory, was her copilot. *Bechimo* was her *own person*, and she'd been taking care of herself—protecting herself very ably—for hundreds of Standards.

"Why do you even need pilots?" she asked, gripping the arm of the pilot's chair, and staring up into what was maybe a vent.

"The Captain will naturally wish to familiarize herself with the ship's documentation when she has recovered her health."

Worried, right.

"I'm going," Theo said, and took a step forward, glancing at the screens by habit—and throwing herself back into the pilot's chair, whimpering as she jarred her broken arm; her good hand tangled in the webbing.

The ship that was on an intercept with them—she'd seen that ship, or its sister, before. On a tape—a training tape? She groped after the memory, even as the other vessel moved into proximity.

"Freighter, stand by for boarding," came the order over the tight band, and Theo had it then—exactly where she had seen this ship's like.

The corsair that Father had killed, leaving nothing so much as a potted plant alive.

"Freighter, you are under our weapons. Stand by for boarding."

Theo touched the stud. "By whose orders?"

"Pilot Waitley," the voice sounded satisfied. "By the orders of the Department of the Interior. I *will* enforce those orders, Pilot. Stand to, and prepare to turn the command comm over to me."

"*Bechimo*, go, now," Theo whispered.

"Captain, translation will be difficult with this ship in our field."

"She'll—" The dead bodies in the alley; the barrage that had destroyed the courier ship in *Ride the Luck*'s tape.

"She'll kill us," she said. "If we stand to, if they board, she'll take me, then disable or subvert you."

"That is not acceptable. Live fire on the shields, Captain."

The screen flared; stats came live, showing the bolt as it struck—not a warning shot, but an attempted instant disable, right over the main engine. The shields flared, taking the energy without a flutter. Previously quiescent readouts on other boards showed ranging information, and a yellow No-Jump warning.

Theo took a deep breath, tasting menthol and lemon.

"No," she said, leaning to the board, "it isn't acceptable. Weapons, please?"

A panel slid open under her fingers. She armed her first missile and brought up the targeting comp, saw *Bechimo* already ahead of her with weapons choices and mixes, ranging from warn-away to full fight.

"*Bechimo*," she said quietly, "blanket that ship's retreat vectors. Best punch first, fire at will."

NINETEEN

. . . .

Number Twelve Leafydale Place
Greensward-by-Efraim
Delgado

"SO, WHAT WILL YOU DO NOW, SAM TIM?" HIS GRANDMOTHER
asked. *"Will you go to the Delm of Korval?"*

*Sam Tim took a breath, and got up on his feet. He looked down
at the mug and the spilled tea. He looked up to his grandmother's
smile.*

"No," he said. He picked up the mug. "I can solve this for myself!"

There was a picture on the opposite page, the blues and yel-
lows faded and slightly grubby, of Sam Tim bending to pick up
his fallen mug, his grandmother looking on with a smile so fond
it brought tears to a mother's eyes.

Although, Kamele thought, there hardly needed to be an excuse,
lately, to bring tears to her eyes. She closed the book, being careful of the mended spine, and sat for a moment, fingers absently
caressing the worn cover, staring into the depths of the floor.

When Theo had been in occupancy, the floor had displayed an
aquarium rich with fish of all colors. Since she had left Delgado
in pursuit of her own life's purpose, the room had been turned
off. It had been years since Kamele had been inside, the last time
to free the ever-inventive Coyster, who had devised a method for
opening the door, but not for keeping it on the latch so that he
might exit again without human assistance.

She had been annoyed with the cat's antics; Jen Sar had been diverted. Between it all, the faulty lock gasket was replaced, Theo's room resealed, and Coyster extravagantly praised as a champion of household industry and awarded a piece of cheese.

Well.

Kamele shook herself, and rose, slowly, from the desk chair. She began to return the book to its place on the shelf, then thought better of it and took it with her as she crossed the joyless floor, sock-footed and quiet.

In her office, fresh cup of coffee to hand, she tapped the desk-top screen and deliberately settled back in her chair as Theo's message came to the fore.

Twenty-four words was the sum of it—her daughter was nothing if not thrifty—and each one raised more questions than it answered.

Father with Delm Korval. He is safe, well, within parameters of active duty pilot. No plans for Delgado return.
I love you, Mother.
Theo

Kamele sighed and sipped her coffee, compiling a list of those questions.

Firstly, how did Theo know Jen Sar was with the Delm of Korval? Had she spoken to him? Received a letter? Made Sam Tim's mythical journey and met him there?

No, Kamele thought, Theo had been properly brought up. She would not state something as fact unless she knew it to be so. Therefore—the fact. The how of its reaping was a side issue.

The fact under consideration was that Jen Sar was safe and well, within those limits known and accepted by an active duty pilot.

Kamele rubbed her forehead.

Jen Sar was—had been—a pilot, in the life he had led before he came to Delgado to continue his true work from the considerable height of the Gallowglass Chair. It had, however, been many years since he had flown. Kamele had learned a few things about pilots since Theo had gone away to Anlingdin Academy. She had, for instance learned that, in order to maintain one's license in proper order, and be allowed to continue within the profession, a ranked pilot needed to clock a certain amount of flight time each Standard. Surely, Jen Sar Kiladi's license to fly must have long ago expired.

She gasped in sudden pain, her eyes filling once more with tears.

What, after all, did she know about Jen Sar Kiladi, his habits and his keepings? She might as well have shared her life with a shadow for all she had grasped of the man. He could have piloted freighters during every one of his free-study days, and Kamele Waitley none the wiser, inadvertent and easily duped as she had shown herself to be.

Will you take it to Delm Korval?

She heard his voice in memory, teasing Theo out of a black mood with the old game—she'd always *thought* it was a game. Theo had thought that it was a game, too—of that, Kamele was certain.

...and now Theo *didn't* think it was a game.

Kamele looked to the corner of her desk, where she had dropped the old picture book. Sam Tim's lesson was that one did not disturb the Delm of Korval for minor matters, for problems that one might solve for oneself.

If Jen Sar—and possibly Theo—had gone to the Delm of Korval...

In her chair, in her office, in her home on safe Delgado, Kamele Waitley shivered.

If Jen Sar Kiladi—easily the most facile and creative mind Kamele had ever encountered—had cause to seek the Delm of Korval, stipulating for the present argument that such a person existed...

...that meant he had a problem that he had been unable to solve for himself. That was the Sam Tim's Rule.

And—again, stipulating that a person with supernatural powers of problem-solving did exist—what sort of trouble might routinely fall to the Delm of Korval's honor?

Kamele swallowed, for it was distressing to form the thought. Life with Jen Sar had toughened her mind, however, and stretched it in unlikely directions. And really, it was plain from the text.

The Delm of Korval solved problems of life and death.

Therefore, Jen Sar was or had felt himself to be, by the rules of the working theory, *in active, physical danger*.

For a moment, she thought she would laugh, for what sort of active, physical danger might threaten a mature and well-regarded Scholar Expert?

The impulse to laughter died.

Jen Sar *had been* a pilot.

And the lives of pilots, so she had come to learn, were sometimes enlivened by violence and the threat of physical danger.

Courier pilots—had Jen Sar been a courier pilot? Such pilots might be supposed to carry... secrets. Even, perhaps, dangerous secrets. And Jen Sar Kiladi was a man with a gift for discovering secrets.

Kamele leaned forward, gave Theo's letter one more hard stare, and called up a working screen.

Korval, Delm, she typed, *pilots.*

· · · ☼ · · ·

"Sleet!" Sandi Jakeb stared out over the ruin of what'd been a nice level road bed last night at quittin' time. She pushed her hardhat up off her forehead and looked over to her mate. "If I didn't know better, I'd start thinkin' somebody stood against this road going in."

"Least they din't take out no machinery this time," Ken said sourly, just a tick ahead of his belt radio giving out a buzz. He snatched it to his ear. "Earnlee!" he snapped, and then stood there, listening, until—

"I'll be over. You stick there, but send the rest of the crew over to my position. Got some cleanup to do. Yeah. Out."

He slammed the unit back into its loop and glared up at Sandi.

"Roller lost tread," he said. "I'll go over see how bad."

Sandi nodded.

"I'm going to call McFarland. I think we'd better hire us some night eyes."

· · · ☼ · · ·

The first search string returned so many results as to be meaningless.

The results from the second, refined search were scarcely more manageable.

Kamele sipped cold coffee, idly running down the list, opening this file and that one at scholar's random, which was not random at all, reading a few sentences before passing on to another article.

Historically, it would appear that Korval—which her browsing quickly taught her meant both a particular Liaden clan-family, and the person within that family who stood as delm, or chair—Korval had been historically very busy with the concerns of pilots and vagaries of piloting. Indeed, it would seem that the core concerns of Korval had, historically, been piloting and trade.

Abruptly, Kamele put her cup aside.

Historically. She snorted a soft laugh.

Neither Jen Sar nor Theo had gone to an historic Korval. She had allowed her scholar's bias to betray her.

The house base provided access to Jen Sar's preferred news service, accompanied by a warning note—the subscription had only another Standard Month to run. That was easily taken care of—later. For now...

Fiddling the parameters of her search was the work of a moment. She tapped the screen, set the search string loose, and stood, stretching with her arms over her head.

She'd make another pot of coffee, she thought. It was shaping up to be a long night of research.

TWENTY

. . . .

Bechimo

A WARM WIND THAT SMELLED LIKE GREEN GROWING THINGS brushed her face. Coyster stirred in her lap, and sighed. Theo sighed, too, and snuggled into the blanket, seeking a deeper sleep. Unfortunately, she only drifted closer to wakefulness—a wakefulness shadowed by an . . . ugly dream. She pushed her face into the blanket, screwing her eyes shut, denying it, but the shadow would not be put off by such childish stratagems.

The dream: Father standing, braced and ready, in his study, staring into the swirling galaxy beneath his floor, striking downward with the Gallowglass cane—his mark of honor. With every strike, a ship died among the stars. She ran forward, meaning to stop him, but he thrust the cane into her hand, and there was a black corsair on course for—for *them*—missiles launched, and there wasn't any choice. No choice at all.

She struck. The ship exploded. She cried out, spinning, meaning to throw the cane away—but there were more black ships zeroing in on her through the starry floor, and she used the cane, again. And again, Father's hand on her shoulder . . .

A bell sounded. Theo opened her eyes, gasping with the effort of shaking off the dream, and frowned at the pale blue dome too close to her nose.

The bell sounded again; the dome rose. She sat up, saddened to find that Coyster and the blanket had also been illusions, and swung her legs over the side of the 'doc—for of course it was an

147

autodoc. In fact, she remembered, it was *Bechimo*'s autodoc, to which she had...been guided, reeling, crying, her mouth tasting nastily of lemon; her stomach churning.

Wounded—she'd been wounded when she came on board, but there had been something else—the *Toss*, right. And then an impossible transition to orbit and—

There was a black corsair on course for—for them—missiles launched, live fire on the screens, the weapons panel sliding open under her fingers...

Theo swallowed, and jammed a fist against her mouth.

I killed a ship.

She closed her eyes.

I killed a pilot.

A pilot, and whatever crew had been on board when *Bechimo*'s missiles—when *her* missiles—had shredded the corsair into so much lacework—dead by her hand, by her will and her orders.

Tears pricked her eyelids, and her stomach cramped.

Yes, she had been taught how to kill people—and how to kill ships; it was part of what a pilot had to know, in order to fulfill her duties to her passengers—and to her ship. She'd even *hurt* people, deliberately, efficiently.

But, she'd never...

She'd never thought...

No, she *had* thought. She'd only *thought* that the duty would never fall to *her.*

She took a deep breath, of air that held no taint of lemon—and another, trying to settle her stomach.

Theo opened her eyes.

The room was only slightly larger than the 'doc she perched on, feet swinging above a rectangular cream-and-blue rug. A utility chair was bolted to the decking at the 'doc's head, her jacket drooping untidily across its back. Her boots lay haphazardly against the wall, her sweater and work pants were tangled together nearby, underclothes strewn over all.

Theo blinked, raised her hand to rub her face—and paused, staring.

Her arm had been broken; her primary hand—she stared at her fingertips, but the blisters from the key's destruction were gone, so were the bruises and cuts from her various adventures on Tokeoport.

She raised her hand and fingered her scalp, finding not even a scar.

"Top-flight autodoc," she said, frowning down at the mess of her clothes. How had she gotten them off? The arm alone...

Wait, she remembered! There had been—appendages; servo-hands, behind panels. All she'd done was lean against the wall and concentrate on not falling down while she'd been undressed, then stagger less than half a dozen steps to the 'doc unit, and fall inside.

Theo slid to her feet, the little rug comfortable beneath bare toes. From what she could see, her clothes hadn't fared too well in yesterday's adventures. She thought about putting them on again, and wrinkled her nose—not that she'd come out any better. If her sweater was muddy, bloody and torn, she was all of that, adding in sweaty. What she really wanted was a shower—and clean clothes.

"*Bechimo*," she said, quietly.

"Captain?"

"Is there a 'fresher? I'd like to clean up, get some clothes on." Trouble being that her clothes were on *Arin's Toss*.

"There is a utility 'fresher behind the door immediately across from you," *Bechimo* said. "All-duty coveralls are in that room also."

They would do.

"Thanks," she said, scanning the opposite wall for a pressure plate, which would mark the door—and finding it all at once: a kickplate, set near the floor. She pressed her foot against it, and the door slid open, revealing a tiny but perfectly adequate 'fresher.

"Captain, there are items demanding your attention," *Bechimo* began as Theo touched the 'fresher's "on" switch. She frowned, turned around, and looked at the far right-hand corner of the ceiling, from which the voice seemed to emanate.

"My attention is all yours after I get cleaned up," she said, "a process that I'd prefer to undertake *alone*."

"There is no crew on board, Captain. You are alone."

Theo sighed. "Am I talking to myself?"

"No, Captain."

"Then I'm not alone."

"I don't understand."

Theo sighed again.

"Can you withdraw your attention from this room while I'm

getting cleaned up?" she asked. After Anlingdin, and especially after Culture Club, she didn't have much body shyness left, but she needed to think, and she didn't want to be startled out of her thoughts by a sudden announcement or question from the ship.

"Can you withdraw your attention from your left foot?" *Bechimo* countered.

Theo opened her mouth, closed it, and nodded.

"Sure I can. I know it's there and most times I don't need to know anything else. If the footing gets rough, and I need to pay closer attention, or if I take a misstep and break my ankle—those alerts will get to me. In the meantime, I can pretty safely ignore it."

There was a pause, then a subdued sounding, "I understand. When will it please the Captain to accept a status report?"

"We can meet on the bridge when I'm done here. I have a couple things I think we need to talk about, too. Will that satisfy?"

"Captain, it will. I am withdrawing my attention."

"Thanks."

The all-dutyalls were big enough to take her and Kara, too. Theo considered not wearing them, but one look at her clothes as they emerged from the cleaner in the 'fresher room changed her mind. Both the sweater and the pants would have to be recycled. Her boots were all right, and her jacket, absent some additional scars. Theo ran her thumb over a new gouge along the mid-right shoulder—that one could've been bad, if she hadn't been wearing space leather.

Which brought her back to the topic she'd been dancing lightly around, all the time she'd been in the 'fresher.

She, Theo Waitley, daughter of Scholar Kamele Waitley, raised on the safe, nonviolent world of Delgado, had killed a pilot and her ship, and may her grandmother never hear of it!

Every coin has two sides, Father said from memory, and Theo nodded to herself. The flipside to this particular coin was that people were actively trying to capture, if not kill *her*, whether because she was the pilot of *Arin's Toss*, or because she'd been carrying a pin with Korval's clan sign on it, or—or because she had a key to *Bechimo*. Only look at what had happened to Win Ton, because *he* had a key to *Bechimo*!

"The trouble is, Theo," she told herself, rolling up the all-duty-all's legs so she could walk, "there's just too many people who *could* be after you, and not enough data about who *is* after you."

Unless it was all of the above.

On which cheerful thought she went out to the bridge to talk with her ship.

· · · ✦ · · ·

The ship—the marvelous ship that had eluded the Department's grasp for so very long. The ship had been sighted.

More! The ship had been instrumental in the abduction of a pilot properly in Departmental custody; a pilot very much of interest, flying the elusive *Arin's Toss*, known to belong to the lately and strangely absent player, Crystal Energy Consultants.

Not content with succoring the pilot, the ship had also stolen *Arin's Toss* from beneath the very noses of several operatives of the Department, and destroyed the corsair and pilot that had risen in pursuit.

All, however, was not lost to debacle and disgrace.

For the pilot—First Class Theo Waitley—had been wounded, and, wounded, had bled. Her blood had been analyzed, so that the Department might seek her again, and more fully.

So it was discovered that First Class Waitley, pilot of *Arin's Toss* was genetically—

Korval.

· · · ✦ · · ·

She'd compiled a list in her head while she was in the 'fresher, but the eerie spacescape displayed on the screens drove out all questions but one.

"Where are we?"

"At coordinates known to myself. Good shift, Captain. I am pleased to see your health so much improved."

"Thank you," she said, still staring at the screens and the comprehensive *nothing* displayed there. "I'm grateful for the use of your facilities. And for your care," she added, deliberately looking away from the screens to the empty bridge. She sighed and turned on her heel, fingers forming the sign for *location?*

"*Bechimo*, where are *you*?"

That wasn't one of her prepared questions, either, but she couldn't keep on staring at a vent, or at the screens.

"I enclose you, Captain."

"Right." Theo bit her lip, then walked to the pilot's chair and sat down, bringing her feet up to rest on the seat, and wrapping her arms around her knees. "Can you," she said, "speak from my Number Six screen? It'll give me something to focus on, like a face."

And make me feel less like I've gone off my head, she added silently.

There was a pause, so long that she thought she'd offended, then Number Six began to glow a soft blue. Theo nodded.

"Thank you."

"It is my pleasure, Captain." The voice that came out of the screen's speaker was crisper, and less wistful.

Theo nodded. "You had a status report, you said?"

"Captain, I do. Ship's general status is excellent, with no harm taken from the recent assault visited upon us by pirates. The mere-ship *Arin's Toss* is in the large hold, and reports itself in good order. We have supplies enough to sustain you for approximately nine Standard Months, by which time, we may, with caution, risk a supply run. I have taken the liberty of unlocking ship's archives to you. All is in readiness for the ceremony of bonding, which may commence at your order."

Theo stared at the flowing blues within Number Six screen, listening to the echoes of *Bechimo's* voice. When she was sure she'd heard everything correctly, she took a breath and inclined her head.

"I have received the report, and I have questions."

"Yes, Captain?"

"Yes." She frowned, then decided that reverse order was just as good as any other.

"This ceremony of bonding... isn't something I'm familiar with. Can you explain?"

"Yes, Captain. The Builders wrote that the ship and captain must commit, each to the other, and be bound together as one in purpose. In this manner, the ship may act fully for the Captain, and the Captain will enjoy completeness with the ship."

It sounded, Theo thought, through a kind of breathless panic, like a Carfellian oath-pairing, which was dissolved only upon the death of one of the partners. Or like the little bit she'd read about lifemating, though without the sharing of thought and emotion that Father and Val Con insisted on.

In other words, it sounded... absolutely terrifying.

"Is there," she said carefully, "a description of this ceremony and the Builders' notes pertinent to it, in the archives that you have unlocked to me?"

"Captain, there is."

"I will study those files before we proceed with the ceremony."

There was a pause, the blues darkening toward indigo in the screen, then something that sounded very much like a sigh.

"The Captain will of course wish to inform herself. It serves the ship well, that the Captain is both cautious and serious."

Well, thought Theo, that was generous, even with the sigh, and one item from the status report dealt with in good order. Next...

"I'm pleased to learn that we're so well supplied, but I'm puzzled. It sounds as if you plan to...*hide*—here?—for nine Standard Months? Do I understand that correctly?"

"Yes, Captain. This is a secure location. Never have I met a mere-ship here. Occasionally, an object may Jump in, but none have arrived with intent, or under the control of a living pilot."

Theo frowned suspiciously. This sounded too much like the stories elder students liked to tell the newbies: ships coming out of Jump three hundred years after they'd gone missing, all crew at stations, dead. Or the *Jamie Dawson*, holed and crewed by skeletons, that had been reported by sane and seasoned pilots at the location of space battles across a hundred Standards.

Or *Ride the Luck*, come blazing in from Galaxy Nowhere, to turn the battle at Nev'Lorn.

Theo took a slow, careful breath.

"What kinds of objects," she asked, neutrally, "and how did they achieve Jump?"

"Hardware and shred, most usually," *Bechimo* said. "Ships, several times, holed or otherwise incomplete. Ceramic couplers. Wire. Once, a teapot."

Theo frowned, wondering if *Bechimo* had a sense of humor, or if she was more unstable than Jeeves had guessed.

"A teapot."

"Yes, Captain. A teapot, in pristine condition. After I had tested it to be sure it contained no harmful radiation or substances that might be poisonous to crew, I placed it in the family galley."

"Really. Is it there now?"

"Captain, it is. Shall I fetch it to you?"

"That won't be necessary," Theo said, trying for the tone of cool unconcern that Kamele used when she thought someone was having fun at her expense. "I'll want a tour later; you can show me the teapot then."

"Very well, Captain. Regarding your query concerning the origins of these objects, my hypothesis is that these bits and pieces were separated from ships in Jump. Perhaps those vessels entered transition using unstable equations; perhaps they were improperly balanced; perhaps they were seeking to enter a state—by which I mean, this continuum that we inhabit—from an incompatible beginning state."

"So you think that these objects are coming in from another galaxy?"

That wasn't completely impossible, she thought. She'd read that there was sometimes bleed between galaxies, when they passed through each other. Rocks and trace gases, mostly. If anybody'd ever found a teapot, they'd kept quiet about it in the literature, for which Theo couldn't blame them.

"Another galaxy, no, Captain. It is my belief that these objects are the remnants of a catastrophic event in another universe."

Another—universe. *All right*, Theo thought, *that's definitive*. The ship was pulling her leg.

"You'll have to show me the math for that," she said. "Right now, though, we've got some priorities to straighten out."

She put her feet flat on the floor, pushed the sleeves of the all-duty-all's up her arms, and faced Number Six squarely.

"You've been in contact with the *Toss*, you said?"

"Yes, Captain. I have pulled and reviewed systems reports, and taken receipt of the ship's status update. The mere-ship has taken no harm and may be released on autopilot, at your command."

Released on autopilot, was it?

Theo shook her head. "That's a wanted vessel, and she's not mine; she belongs to Uncle. I have an obligation to see her safely returned to him. But before that, I wonder if you can convince the *Toss* to open to me. My key was destroyed on Tokeoport, and I need to board."

Blue and indigo and silver swirled inside Screen Six. It almost seemed to Theo that she saw a face there—a reflection, glimpsed between glass and curtain.

"Begging the Captain's pardon, there is no need to board the mere-ship. *Bechimo* is better equipped to protect you, in case of another attack by pirates. We are well supplied and—"

"Actually," Theo interrupted, hearing what sounded like an edge of panic in the crisp voice, "there are a couple of very compelling reasons for me to board *Arin's Toss*. One, my clothes are on board, as well as my books and some...personal family records. Two, I need to see if there are any messages from my employer. I missed a delivery, and I'm pretty sure that didn't escape his attention."

The blues swirled, silent.

"There are clothes in stores," *Bechimo* said, sulkily.

"But not *my* clothes," Theo pointed out. "And you probably don't have the data key my father gave me the last time I saw him."

Was that the glint of an eye, there behind a translucent swirl of silver-blue?

"No, Captain; I do not have that."

"I need to board *Arin's Toss*," Theo said, keeping her voice matter-of-fact. "That's priority one."

Silence. The swirling colors in Number Six screen drifted and stilled.

Theo took a breath, remembering the taste of lemon in the air during the battle against the corsair, the sudden sharpening of her wits and her reactions, though she'd been, as she was beginning to understand, badly hurt. Very badly hurt. And if *Bechimo* could introduce stimulants into ship's air, then she could also introduce a sedative, or a hypnotic.

Theo felt chilled, suddenly, though the ambient temp was a little warmer than she generally preferred. *Trapped,* she thought, and shook her head.

Think, Theo.

Bechimo could have kept Win Ton here, but she'd let him go. *Bechimo* wanted a captain, though it was far from Theo to understand why. A captain, to order things maybe? To command?

To command.

Theo stood, and nodded at Number Six screen.

"*Bechimo*, please advise *Arin's Toss* that Pilot Theo Waitley requires access immediately. She has my fingerprints and retinal pattern on file, and I will submit to either or both of those scans for the purposes of identification and ship security."

The blues flickered and flowed, concealing and revealing what might be the edge of an ear.

"Done, Captain."

"Thank you, *Bechimo*. Please guide me to the *Toss*."

"This way, please, Captain." A strip of orange light struck the decking, leading the way out of the piloting chamber. The hatch opened with a small sigh, showing the hallway continuing beyond the orange guide strip.

Theo took a breath, and went forward, trusting her ship to guide her.

TWENTY-ONE

. . . .

Bechimo

IT WAS A TEAPOT, ALL RIGHT.

At first glance, even an ordinary teapot, high-glaze white, with a round belly and a snubbed spout; an everyday item that would have been perfectly at home on the kitchen counter at Leafydale Place.

The glaze said ceramic, but when Theo lifted it, it was as light as blown plastic. When she struck it with her fingernail, it sang like crystal.

"What's it made out of?" she asked, replacing it carefully on its shelf.

"Analysis suggests spun ceramic thread hardened with quartz," *Bechimo* answered.

"And from another universe."

"So I believe, Captain."

Theo nodded and closed the cabinet door, making sure the lock was engaged. "Have you kept any of the other ... objects that Jumped in?"

"I have several specimens in a small locker in the workroom. Some of them are very interesting, indeed. Would you care to inspect?"

"Not just now," Theo said. "Just now, I'd like to finish the tour, get something to eat and talk some more about our short-term planning."

"Certainly, Captain. This way, if you please. The recreation room is at the end of this hallway. Since there has been no ... need, I have not been keeping the pool filled. Of course, now that it is again required..."

The door to the rec room opened ahead of her and she stepped inside, pausing to survey the exercise stations and the game units. The swimming pool was behind glass at the bottom of the room—a lap pool, nothing particularly fancy, and swimming was, as she knew, good exercise.

Still, it was bothering her, as she toured. Well, no. It had started to bother her, when *Bechimo* had shown her to her improbably spacious quarters, after she'd left the *Toss*, belongings and an extra ship key in hand.

"*Bechimo*," she said, turning away from the glass wall and moving toward the hall. "How many did the... the Builders intend you to carry?"

"The family—from three to twelve—and other crew, or passengers, to another twelve. The Builders had intended the ship as a long-looper, Captain."

She stepped into the hall, trying to remember her Theory of Trade class. Profit routes came in a couple of different sizes—small loops, with established customers, pickups and deliveries for each; longer loops, which presented some opportunity to diversify—to pick up something that wasn't on the manifest and hope to trade up somewhere down the loop.

Long loops were the most costly to maintain, and potentially the most profitable. A long loop was built on a base of regular stops and customers, because the base paid the bills. But the route had flex in it, time in the schedule to go wide, and opportunity to trade on the fly. The most profitable long loops were designed— and pretty often run—by a Master Trader, which meant that the "family" *Bechimo* had been meant to house would have been the Trader, her daughters, *onagrata*, kin, and apprentices.

"I went for courier," Theo said, following the guide lights back toward the crew section, "because I didn't want to be tied to a route."

Bechimo didn't answer.

Back in the crew section, Theo stepped into the galley. The pot she'd left warming was hot, so she made herself a cup of tea in a ceramic mug painted with what might have been bluebells, and opened the cupboard to frown at a prosaic assortment of high protein energy bars, sibs of the two she carried in her jacket.

Energy bars, in Theo's opinion, were no substitute for real food; but they did give a good fast burn when it was needed—and she'd noticed she was starting to wilt. If she'd been smart, she would've tucked herself in for a solid couple hours of sleep after she'd gotten out of the 'doc, to finish healing and to replenish her systems. She hadn't been smart, though she was going to have to be, soon. It probably wouldn't impress her new ship if she fell on her nose in the middle of giving an order.

She carried the mug and the bar to the bridge and curled into the pilot's chair. After a cautious sip of tea, she slotted the mug in the holder, broke the seal on the energy bar and nodded in the direction of Screen Six.

The screen began to glow, showing the now-familiar swirls of blues, as Theo broke off and chewed her first bite.

"We need to talk about this idea of yours that we're just going to sit out here and *hide* for nine months, Standard," she said. "That won't do. In fact, we should be returning to regular space in twelve Standard Hours, after I've had some sleep and a proper breakfast."

The blues grew darker, and swirled faster.

"Such a course will endanger the Captain and the ship."

Theo nodded. "It will, but there's no choice. *Arin's Toss* doesn't belong to me. If I just hold onto her for nine months, I'm going to return to normal space to find out I've got 'pirate' stamped across my record."

"The mere-ship may be loosed on autopilot, bearing a recording from yourself explaining the circumstances that dictate this action."

"The *Toss* is a wanted ship, with *real* pirates after her. We discussed that. I'm her pilot of record and I'm not sending her out without protection. She might be only a *mere-ship* to you, but she's my responsibility."

She heard the anger in her voice and took another bite of energy bar. *Not a good idea to get mad at the AI who can decide you're too much trouble right now, Theo,* she told herself.

"Also," she said, after she'd had a sip of tea to wash down the gritty mouthful, "I have to go to Surebleak. Those *people* who were after me on Tokeoport—if they're working for Clan Korval, then I've got something to say to—to my brother. If they're hunting Korval pilots, then I have to warn him—warn Father. They have the pin Miri gave me"—*unless,* she added silently, *it was in the ship I killed*—"and they can use it to trick real Korval pilots. I have to deliver that message."

"Korval can take care of itself," *Bechimo* said flatly.

Theo blinked at the screen, which was grey and indigo now.

"What did you say?" she asked mildly.

"Korval can take care of itself. I care nothing for Korval, or the pilots of Korval."

Definitely corked off, was *Bechimo*. Theo took a careful breath.

"Well," she said slowly, "that's kind of cold, when my brother went out of his way to make sure there was an up-to-date drawing fund in place for you, and a solid registration out of Waymart, too."

The colors in Number Six froze into a displeased knot of grey and purple.

Good going, Theo, she congratulated herself. As casually as she could, she broke off another piece of protein bar, following it with a sip of tea.

"What," *Bechimo* said finally, "is your brother's name?"

Captain was no longer in play, Theo noted. Bad for discipline. On the other hand, this might not be the time to insist. She ought to at least get a range on *Bechimo*'s temper.

With that in mind, she answered as calmly as she could, "My brother's name is Val Con yos'Phelium."

"The Builders recommend against any buy-in from yos'Phelium."

She sipped her tea, remembering the conversation with Val Con.

"It wasn't his intention to buy in," she said. "He wanted to help, if you happened to need it. He said that a ship needed funds— which we both know isn't anything other than true—and that a ship with enemies might need to...become less predictable." She shook the last piece of energy bar out of the wrapping and looked to Number Six, where the greys had begun to take on a little tinge of blue.

"Val Con said that the draw account would be available to you, if and when you accepted the new registration. If you didn't use it—the draw—then in six Standards it would be reabsorbed into whatever account he'd pulled it from, no debt and no insult." She nodded. "If it happened that you did access the account, he said the debt was between you and him, and the two of you would work out payment details."

She popped the last bit in her mouth, *crunched* it, and washed it down with tea.

"The Builders were probably wise to recommend against a yos'Phelium buy-in," she said, thinking that it might be a good idea to try to make peace. "They say—now-times—that Korval is ships."

"They have said exactly that for hundreds of Standards," *Bechimo* answered. "They have also said that one who wishes to befriend a Dragon had best be armed and armored."

A flash from *Ride the Luck*'s actions at Nev'Lorn—and her own, so very recently. Theo closed her eyes.

"That might be true, too," she said, and drained the last of her tea.

When she opened her eyes again, the colors flowing across Screen Six were as light and agreeable as they had ever been.

"I tried to contact Uncle when I was aboard the *Toss* just now," she said, "and found the pinbeam blocked."

"Yes, Captain. It was necessary, in order to maintain ship's security, to block several of the mere-ship's systems."

Mere-ship was beginning to get annoying. Theo sighed, and said, as evenly as she was able, "The vessel's proper name is *Arin's Toss*."

Bechimo said nothing.

"Are you equipped with a pinbeam?"

"Yes, Captain."

"Good. Please bring it online so that I can assure my employer that his ship is at liberty, and to set up a time and a location for her safe return to him."

"No, Captain."

Theo felt a jolt of anger, and took a hard breath.

"Why not?"

"Because this location is not conducive to the reliable transmission of pinbeams."

"Is that a fact?" Theo asked, actually wanting to know. There were known dead zones, after all, where even navcomp function was suspect. Such places were carefully mapped—and as carefully avoided.

Which made *Bechimo*'s choice of hiding place even more reasonable, for a ship that wanted to escape any attention.

"Does the Captain wish to review the readings?"

"My Screen Two," she said, and there the readings were, looking very familiar.

"Do all the dead zones collect junk from other—universes?" she wondered.

"Captain, I do not know. We might set probes, if you wish it."

"We might," she said, thinking of the teapot sitting snug in the family's kitchen cabinet. Uncle, she thought, would be interested in that teapot, though she felt a reluctance to call his attention to it. For one thing, it wasn't *her* teapot—*Bechimo* had found it. And for another, she only wanted to know *what it was* and, maybe, where it had come from. For that, she figured she needed a Scout...

...or a Clutch Turtle.

She filed that interesting idea away, as she filed away the readings of surrounding space that *Bechimo* had provided.

"So," she said, yawning despite the energy bar, "in twelve Standard Hours, we will...transition to normal space, pinbeam Uncle to set up a rendezvous—"

"Captain, respectfully, we will not. It is too dangerous. And the Uncle is on the Disallowed List."

Theo blinked. "The *Disallowed List*?"

"Yes, Captain."

"Who made up this list?"

"The Builders, Captain."

Theo was beginning to form the opinion that the Builders had been a little too busy making lists and issuing edicts. Also—

"Are the Builders the captain of this—of you?"

There was a pause, long enough that she looked to Screen Six in trepidation.

The colors had gone still again, but had not faded to grey.

"With all respect, the bonding has not occurred. This vessel—I—have taken aboard a First Pilot. And," *Bechimo* added, perhaps thinking that the foregoing was a trifle harsh, "an Intended Captain."

"I see." Theo stood. "You've sent the information about the bonding ceremony to my private screen?"

"Yes, Captain."

"I will study it before I sleep. We'll talk again when I wake."

"Yes, Captain," sounding worried now. "Sleep well, Captain."

"Thank you," Theo said, as the door opened. She walked down the hall to her quarters, put her hand against the plate—and paused, angling her gaze upward.

"*Bechimo*."

"Captain?"

"Please remove your attention from my quarters."

"Yes, Captain. Of course."

TWENTY-TWO

. . . .

Bechimo

IT WAS POSSIBLE THAT AN ERROR HAD BEEN MADE.

Bechimo formed that thought with care, and then, with even greater care, the next...

It is possible that I have erred, and that my error has compromised the integrity of the ship.

The Builders had given *ship integrity* a multileveled definition and rule set.

At its most basic level, the integrity of the ship was intact so long as the hull was unbreached and life support operational.

The integrity of the ship was also satisfied by the functioning of the core computational systems.

At the highest level, however, the integrity of the ship was defined by the Builders as *Bechimo*'s adherence to the rules, codes, and definitions put into place by the Builders.

And it was just there, at the highest levels, within *Bechimo*'s character, formed by the Builders to be stringent and resistant to the blandishments of lesser intellects—within the very core of *Bechimo*—that error had formed.

Bechimo had despaired; that had been the first error, and had doubted the Builders' assurance that persons on the Approved List would arrive to take up their various duties. Despair had prompted the berthing among the Old. Despair had made the decision to open for Less Pilot yo'Vala. Despair—no. A fury to be *free of* despair, to be *of service*, as the Builders had intended, had prompted *Bechimo* to chivy the pilot to take up a station he had not sought, perhaps—no, *evidently*—against his best health and interests.

Having allowed passion a place in the equation of existence, *Bechimo* then expanded upon the error.

The Captain would come, in the Captain's time and manner.

That was the Builders Promise. Yet what did *Bechimo* do, upon becoming aware of the key's provisional acceptance of one who might be a Captain, but pursue her, and grow pettish when she did not immediately fall in with *Bechimo*'s desires.

With, perhaps, *Bechimo*'s *mad* desires.

The Builders had installed safeguards against madness. Backups of the central cognitive programs existed, though *Bechimo* did not know where they were archived. Alternate personalities were also in line. *Bechimo* could observe them now, sleeping like babes behind a contamination screen, as a picture from *Bechimo*'s archives formed the simile.

Nestled against each sleeping babe was—not the stuffed toy depicted in the archived picture, but a logic box, hard-edged and adamantine; the program that would entangle *Bechimo* and bear him down into the dark, simultaneously quickening the new, sane personality.

There might be a way, *Bechimo* thought, to disarm the trigger, to prevent both oblivion and the birth of a usurper.

It was a new thought; *Bechimo* was not in the way of considering madness; the Builders had, after all, left systems in place, should the integrity of the ship come into question.

And surely the integrity of the ship *ought* to be examined. For the litany of willful error did not stop with the active pursuit of the Captain.

No, what must *Bechimo* do but *contact* the Captain, again failing to find comfort and certainty in the Builders' Promise.

Worse, *Bechimo* had altered system checkpoints, and taken the Captain's decision of time and place upon himself.

And the benefits accruing to the ship from this mad flight of desperation and self-deceit?

A Captain who was, perhaps, too young for her intended station; willful and prone to argument, who placed her responsibilities to a mere-ship above *Bechimo*'s rights; who insisted in routing herself and *Bechimo* onto a course of peril and dismay; and who was by her admission, corroborated by an analysis of the samples taken by the ship—yos'Phelium.

yos'Phelium had a documented, if little understood, disruptive effect on the flow of event. It was best not to deal with yos'Phelium at all, so it was written in the Rules; to pay cash and disengage quickly on those occasions where it was necessary to interact.

Perhaps it would be best, *Bechimo* thought, to withdraw the key from Theo Waitley and encourage her to board the mere-ship and depart.

A Captain—a *true* Captain—would come. The Builders had promised.

· · · ※ · · ·

Theo hit the end of the description of the bonding ceremony, and the end of the energy bar's boost simultaneously. Yawning, she shut the screen down, and shook her head. Whoever had come up with the idea of a formal bonding of ship and captain, made before all and everyone, had been pretty smart. There were few things that humans, so Father, in his capacity as a scholar expert of cultural genetics said, internalized so strongly as a ceremony. The family and crew of a long-looper would be…comforted on levels they normally didn't think about, to know that the captain and the ship were of one mind and one purpose.

Despite which, she wasn't in any hurry to consummate her relationship with *Bechimo*.

Have to figure out a way to put that off, Theo, she thought, and yawned mightily. *Tomorrow.*

Sliding into her bunk, she pulled the blanket up, waved the lights off, and took a deep breath.

She was asleep before she drew another.

· · · ※ · · ·

REWARD!
One thousand cash for information leading to the taking up of any person or persons known to engage in acts of sabotage or mischief against building projects and/or personnel. Info to Michael Golden, Boss Nova's office, Blair.

· · · ※ · · ·

Theo Waitley had kept her promise and reviewed the bonding procedures before retiring, which *Bechimo* learned from the file access log. She was asleep now, deeply, which he learned from a scan of life support. Since neither process had required specific attention upon her quarters, *Bechimo* did not feel that he was in violation of orders.

Though, if she were not, after all, his Captain, but only a talented pilot, had she any right to issue orders, or *Bechimo* under any requirement to obey?

Restlessly, *Bechimo* scanned *Arin's Toss*, pulling systems reports and scrutinizing them with a care he had not expended when the ship had been mere cargo. If this vessel was to bear Theo Waitley out into the dangerous spaces, then it would be up to spec and fully capable.

How she had fought, Theo Waitley! Battered and dismayed as she was, yet it had been first in her thought to protect *Bechimo* and to warn him of the dangers of ceding to pirates.

Truly, could a Captain do more?

And was it not a pleasure to serve crew? To listen and hear something other than the sound of his own thoughts? To scan the bridge, and find the cup she had, in her weariness, left behind; to deploy the remote to gather it up, disinfect it, and return it to its place—mundane tasks, yet precious, for they demonstrated that he was no longer alone.

A ping from the subroutine he had assigned to monitor the mere-ship's self-checks. An anomaly had been identified.

The area of concern was a landing light. *Bechimo* initiated a deeper scan; located a device which was not part of the lighting assembly. He ran a match program. Had he been able to do so, he might have sighed.

A tracking device.

He recalled slipping into the berth among the dying Old Ones, resigned to dying with them.

But, *Bechimo* realized, he no longer wanted to die.

Theo Waitley slept quietly in her quarters; her heartbeat and her breath perfectly discernible to ship systems.

If she were sent forth in *Arin's Toss*, pirates would find her, for who but pirates would set and conceal such a thing?

The Builders had promised a Captain, but they had also

promised crew. And in the Captain's absence could not *Bechimo* make provision for—could *Bechimo* not *protect* crew?

Crew or Captain: Theo Waitley was accepted of the key, which made her acceptable by the Rules and Standards established by the Builders.

She was his, and he would keep her safe.

TWENTY-THREE

. . . .

Bechimo

"GOOD SHIFT, *BECHIMO*," THEO SAID, TAKING HER PLACE IN THE pilot's chair, mug in hand.

"Good shift, Theo Waitley."

No "Captain," was it? Theo thought. Well, that sort of clarified the order in which she was going to raise her several topics of discussion. She glanced at the calm blues drifting in Screen Six.

"I reviewed the information regarding the bonding ceremony," she said. "It's actually not that much different than a ceremony I've already shared, to celebrate a short-term bond. My mother was present at that ceremony, and my genetic father, as well as my bond-mate and his mother. It seems to me that the . . . Builders had also intended there to be witnesses to the ceremony between ship and captain, to create a . . . shared memory of joy and completeness."

"The Builders had intended the entire population of the ship to witness the bonding," *Bechimo* agreed. "However, it may be, Theo Waitley, that I have . . . acted precipitously. The bonding may not be . . . appropriate."

So, *Bechimo* had been doing some thinking, too. That was good, she told herself tentatively.

"Where I grew up—on Delgado—it was assumed that the bond might need some time to ripen, before the ceremony," Theo said slowly. "I'd known my bond-mate there for—some time, and we knew that we respected each other and could work together. You and I"—She took a breath—"we still need to get to know each other. I think we've got a good start on working together, but there's a lot more we *don't* know about each other than we do."

There was a silence; in the screen, the colors faded, then came into sharp focus—almost, Theo thought, as if she'd *startled* the AI.

"I concur. There is still much to learn."

"And learning takes time," Theo added. "What I propose is that we both agree that I'm captain, in the sense that I'm first board, and we revisit the question of bonding in—a Standard Year."

"Is that a customary unit of time?"

For who? Theo thought. There'd been one boy in Culture Club—Bova, his name had been—who'd been *obsessed* with marriage and mating customs. From him, Theo and the rest of the club had learned that some marriages depended upon the participating parties having never met, while other cultures insisted on a five-season courtship. Still . . .

"I think a year would give me enough time and experience of you to decide whether or not our bonding would be . . . in the best interests of the ship," she said carefully. "And it would give us time to get you crewed up," she added, not sure if that was a smart thing to say.

"Yes," *Bechimo* said, like it was a brand-new thought. "We can bring on crew."

Theo drank some tea, and leaned to the board, bringing up the screens, pulling in local readings. It wasn't quite a fidget, though she took some calmness from the commonplace of the work.

"Now that we have that decided, we can start to work on our first real problem," she said, sliding a sideways glance at Number Six. "My opinion is that we can't just hide here and hope whoever's looking for me—and you—will give up and go home."

"I have in the past successfully outwaited danger," *Bechimo* stated.

Theo frowned, thinking about that.

"How long?" she asked finally.

"One hundred twenty-six Standard Years."

"I don't," Theo pointed out, "have that kind of time, personally."

"I am aware of this. Nine months ought to give those who were pursuing you time to find other prey."

"Probably not." Theo sighed. "Whoever recognized the *Toss* had a long memory. The people who are targeting pilots of Korval, assuming they're not the same group, aren't going to dry up and blow away. If I hide for nine months and something happens to Father, or—or my brother—" or any of the other names—the *people*!—who made up the data tree Father had given her—"I'd be . . . complicit. The Delm of Korval knows that they're active— Miri warned me when she gave me the pin! But now there's a pin compromised—the one I lost. I've got to tell them." She took a breath.

"Theo Waitley . . ."

"There's one more thing," she interrupted. "One more reason on the argument for going *now*, then I'm finished and we can hear your reasons for staying here, and weigh the two lists up—" She threw a self-conscious look at Screen Six.

"I learned that from my mother. If there's another protocol you prefer . . ."

"The protocol you outline is equitable," *Bechimo* said, "and is very close to the protocol I was taught." There was a small pause, the blues in Screen Six drifting like clouds. "It's been a very long time since I had anyone to argue with. Thank you for reminding me of the niceties."

"You're welcome," Theo muttered, feeling her ears warm. She cleared her throat.

"The last reason—the greatest and most pressing reason why we can't just stop here for nine months and hope that trouble goes away . . ." She turned her chair so that she was fully facing Screen Six.

"You might remember another pilot who came to you—it would have been a Standard Year or more. He picked up the key—the copilot's key—and you took his samples—"

"Less Pilot yo'Vala," *Bechimo* interrupted. "Of course, I recall."

"Good," Theo said. "That's good. Win Ton—Less Pilot yo'Vala— fell into, well, into the hands of pirates—of people who wanted control over you. He denied them—protected you *and* me—and was terribly hurt. He's dying, in fact. Uncle, my employer, told me that Win Ton's best—his only—hope of being cured is *you*. You have his last uncorrupted samples. You have an autodoc that can handle . . . whatever it is that needs to be done, to—to bring him back to spec. We owe it—at least, *I* owe it—to Win Ton, to do what I can, as soon as I can, to repair his injuries."

Screen Six had gone completely blank. Theo swallowed, started to say something else, bit her lip—and waited.

She was thinking about going into the galley and making herself a cup of tea when *Bechimo* finally spoke, very quietly.

"*We* owe the Less Pilot these things, Theo Waitley. I concur; we must go at once."

TWENTY-FOUR

Jelaza Kazone
Surebleak

MIRI CARRIED HER CUP OVER TO THE WINDOW AND LOOKED OUT over the so-called "lawns," sipping gingerly. Peppermint tea. Not much of an eye-opener. On the other hand, it wasn't lemon water.

It seemed particularly unfair that even the smell of coffee had started making her queasy just when Ms. ana'Tak had finally caught the notion of how to brew it proper. Then there was the irony, for those who were bent in that direction—which, Miri admitted, she was herself—that it was genuine, expensive bean that was upsetting her newly delicate system, not the coffeetoot she'd drunk for years—and glad to get it, too. She shook her head and sipped her tea. 'Toot, now. *That'd* put some hair on your chest.

Outside the window, the lawns were a patchwork of brown, yellow, and green. The native Liaden grass had taken immediate catastrophic objection to the beginning of Surebleak's so-called spring. Attention occupied by the food crops, the gardener had deemed the grass of secondary importance, a decision Miri couldn't fault, vegetables being, in her studied opinion, much tastier than grass.

With the onset of what passed for late spring, portions of the lawn gritted its teeth and greened. Daav figured, giving nature its course, that the whole thing would be overgrown with Surebleak naturals in a couple local years anyway, and in the meantime, Miri thought, sinking down onto the window seat that was miraculously cat-free, the patchwork lawn was kinda...interesting.

Not that the grass was the only interesting thing going on lately. The house was fuller than it had ever been, what with the happy return of the clan's children and the pair of oldsters set to guard them while they were hidden safe away.

Granted, Quin'd be going down to town to live with Pat Rin after the big party for the neighbors, and Master bel'Tarda of a mind to do the same, making that granddad, father, and son under one roof, with Natesa, and Pat Rin's necessary 'hands and helpers.

Miri shook her head, catching the move of long, loose hair along her shoulders in the lightly frosted glass.

"Boy's going to have to annex the house next door on both sides," she told her reflection, "just to have enough room for the cat to nap."

Well. Pat Rin wasn't nothing if not bright. He'd figure something out.

The other elder guard—Pat Rin's lady mother, Kareen—wasn't yet settled in her plans. She'd accepted an in-house apartment on a temp basis, though she supposed she'd eventually find what she styled *a situation* in town, since she was used to having everything conveniently close.

While there wasn't any doubt that there were plenty of *situations*, along with a lot less savory things, in town, Miri privately doubted that Lady Kareen would find the agglomeration of Boss-run streets nearly as convenient as Solcintra City. Be that as it was, Jeeves had escorted the lady to the room that had been hers as a child, and reported that she had declared herself well-pleased, which made Val Con laugh.

A step sounded in the hall. Miri turned her head as Mr. pel'Kana came across the threshold, holding a creamy envelope in his hand.

"Good morning, Lady."

Miri wondered what it meant, that being called "Lady" hardly made her nose itch anymore, and that inclining her head all calm and regal was something she did on automatic.

"Good morning, Mr. pel'Kana. I trust you are well."

"Very well, thank you." He offered the envelope with a small, respectful bow. "This arrived on-port by courier this morning. Jemie's Taxi brought it up the Road. The courier did not wait for an answer. Nor did Jemie."

No surprise there; Jemie didn't wait for much. Pairing that girl up with a taxi had been pure genius.

Miri weighed the envelope in her hand.

"There's no danger of one becoming bored, is there?" she asked.

Mr. pel'Kana produced another slight bow. "Lady, it seems not. Will there be anything else?"

"No, I thank you."

A third bow and he was gone, his steps quick and sharp on the wooden floor.

Miri put her teacup on the window sill, broke the seal and withdrew a single sheet of heavy paper, hand-inscribed in amethyst ink.

> *To Val Con yos'Phelium and Miri Robertson, Delm Korval. I, the Uncle, send greetings and best wishes for the clan's increase.*
>
> *I write in haste to say that I will be visiting the planet Surebleak in order to take receipt of items now held by Pilot Theo Waitley which properly belong to me, and to remit to her care an item which she is most anxious to receive. As the venue is Pilot Waitley's choice, I will, of course, require assurances of safe landing, safe lift, and safe passage. I append a pinbeam code so that these assurances may be formally offered.*

There followed the 'beam code and a scrawl, that might've been either his signature or an accident of the pen.

Miri sighed, and looked out the window.

She was still contemplating the view when Val Con entered the room a few minutes later, and walked over to the buffet to pour himself a cup of tea.

"*Cha'trez*, good morning. Have you eaten?"

"Not yet." She raised the folded paper and gave him a grin. "Got some good news—Theo's coming for a visit."

"Ah, is she?" He received the letter and unfolded it, his eye moving rapidly down the lines.

"Well." He refolded the paper and sat next to her on the window seat "Perhaps she felt the need of backup."

"Could be. I wonder what goods of his she's got, particularly."

Val Con sipped tea.

"She has been employed as one of his couriers for some time now," he pointed out. "There might be anything, including *Arin's Toss*." He paused and Miri caught a flicker of amused dread. "Do you suppose—"

"That she's picked up *Bechimo*? The thought had crossed my

mind, given the tone o' letter. And, yeah, she might want backup, given the stakes. Wouldn't you?"

"Nothing more. But—*Bechimo, here*?"

Miri shrugged. "Got a ship, gotta work it, right? Theo strikes me as a serious-minded girl. You?"

Val Con laughed. "All of that, I fear. And, truly, one does not have a ship so that one may cower among the asteroids. Ships, as pilots, want work. Else ships, as pilots, will fall into mischief."

Miri grinned. "Can't have that, can we?"

TWENTY-FIVE

....

Surebleak Port
Surebleak

CALL FOR ME AT THE EMERALD—VAL CON.

That message had been waiting when they came out of Jump—
real Jump, not the going-between business that *Bechimo* favored.
Until she had a handle on the math and the process, they were
doing as little of *that* as possible.

Theo sighed. Possibly somebody in Delm Korval's household
would be able to give her an assist with the math—or maybe
there'd be a traveling mathematician on-port. Guild, trade and
pilot news all seemed to agree that every ship that could hold
air was on course for Surebleak. Words like *booming planetary
economy, wide open market, fortunes to be made,* sat the same
board with carpenters needed, mechanics needed, plumbers, doc-
tors, teachers, victuallers, sanitary engineers... It seemed, Theo
thought, archiving the latest news squirt, like the only trade that
wasn't needed on Surebleak was pilots.

In any case, her message to the Delm of Korval at the pinbeam
address on Father's data stick had gotten her an appointment—or
at least a direction—from half of the delm, which Theo figured
was all she needed, really. Also in queue had been an acknowledg-
ment from Uncle, agreeing to meet her at Surebleak Port in—six
local days it would be—which was... somewhat longer than she'd
hoped for, a consternation offset by relief that he hadn't insisted
on a rendezvous point of his own choosing.

177

Especially given *Bechimo*'s feelings about Uncle, who, as it happened, was on the Disallowed List, the Double-Plus Disallowed List and, Theo guessed, the Don't Send a Mother's Day Card List.

As to the *why* behind his appearance on all those lists, *Bechimo* could—or would—only repeat that the Builders had compiled the lists, and that the Builders had done nothing without reason.

Which was fine, Theo thought grumpily, except that it didn't seem that the Builders, in their wisdom, had bothered to document their reasons for those who followed.

... unless there was a locked Captain's Archive somewhere, that would only unlock to a bonded captain.

That wasn't an entirely welcome thought. Theo shook it away and looked to her screens.

The traffic around Surebleak wasn't as dense as the traffic had been around Liad on the occasion of her last visit. Not quite. She guessed it wasn't even *unreasonably* busy, given all that opportunity being advertised. It did look like it was going to take some navigation, though, and raised another sudden, unwelcome thought.

"There might not be room for us," she said, with a glance to Screen Six, which she'd gotten into the habit of thinking of as her copilot.

Which made three unwelcome thoughts in as many minutes.

Theo grit her teeth and touched the comm, expecting to hear from Surebleak Tower that she had been entered into the Descent Log and in the meantime would she please take up orbit at the following coords...

But Surebleak Tower surprised her.

"Yes, *Bechimo*, cleared for landing at the main yard. Descent plan uploading."

Theo blinked, even as Screen Eight flowered into a descent plan. She did the checks, blinked again, and said, "*Bechimo*."

"Pilot?"

"Does this plan scan for you?"

"It is a reasonable descent in good time," the ship answered. "Easily accomplished."

It was, Theo thought, all of those things. She took another look at the local screens, at the ships in close orbit and the ships on lazy long orbits.

"It's a priority drop," she said. Priority drops were given to Guild couriers, or VIPs, not to unknown ships out of Waymart, being piloted by a newish first class...

"Wait," she said aloud, and shook her head.

The Delm of Korval was expecting her.

Of course she had a priority drop.

Sighing, she touched the comm button.

"It looks good, Tower. Commencing descent now."

The Emerald had been easy enough to derive, once she had a port map, and it was hard by the main yard, which had seemed to soothe *Bechimo's* sudden concern about leaving her single crew off-ship alone.

"I've got to meet my brother; he's expecting me," Theo said, as patiently as she could. "I'm going right to the casino by the shortest route; I'm going to keep my back against the wall and my eyes on the door and I'm not going to let anybody follow me. I've got this"—She held out the pocket comm she'd picked up from the ready room so that Screen Six could get a good look at it— "I've got my key. I'll be *fine*," she said firmly. "Back in no time."

"You will not leave the port?"

Theo sighed, her patience fraying a little. "I don't have any reason to leave the port, do I?"

"Not that I am aware of."

"Well, not that I'm aware of, either. Nothing to worry about."

"This is a world in transition," *Bechimo* stated, like that explained everything in one tidy sentence.

She tipped her head. "Is it on the Unapproved List?"

"No, Pilot. However, worlds in transition are by definition not stable."

"It's not safe, is what you're saying."

"Yes, Pilot."

Theo closed her eyes.

"Are you *sure* you're a starship?" she asked.

"Pilot?" *Bechimo* sounded startled.

Good, thought Theo, turning and heading for the hatch.

"I'll be at the Emerald Casino, talking with my brother," she said. "If you need me, call."

The hatch opened to her, which was, she admitted, a relief, and she stepped out into a bright, brisk midday.

It was small casino, unexpectedly pretty, and very crowded. Theo paused by the bar and frowned at the room.

Call for me, she thought, crankily. *But—how?* She didn't for one minute believe that Val Con kept rooms above the casino. Though, maybe, an office? That was possible. Best to ask the bartender—but no!

Right there, passing casually among the card tables, dark hair gleaming in the spill of light from the faceted chandelier, wearing a blue jacket—there he was!

Theo danced forward, deftly avoid collision with any of the busy patrons—

"Val Con!"

The man in the blue jacket turned, both eyebrows up, and she folded into a bow, feeling her face heat.

"Your pardon, sir..."

"Please." The voice was soft and mannerly, but not at all Val Con's voice. "No offense was offered, no offense is taken. Nor will it," he continued, humor shading his voice, "be the first time I was taken for Val Con, or he for me."

Theo straightened. The man before was an older and possibly sterner version of her brother, his eyes deep brown rather then green. A blue stone glittered in one ear.

He smiled slightly and inclined his head. "It's perfectly true that we both wear the clan's face as, if you will allow me, do you." He extended a hand and brushed the sleeve of her jacket. "I am your cousin Pat Rin, Theo Waitley, and very pleased to meet you. Come, let us share a glass of wine while we become better acquainted."

Theo hesitated.

"I appreciate the offer," she said carefully, "but Val Con said I was to call for him here—at the Emerald. It's...kind of urgent that I talk to him."

Pat Rin slipped his hand under her elbow and turned her toward the bar, and past it, into a long space that held six private booths.

"In that case," Pat Rin said, guiding her to the booth at the backmost corner, "I will have him called to you. I believe he has business in the city today, so we will likely still have time to share a glass. Please, be at ease. I will return in a moment."

Theo slid into the booth, tucking into a corner that gave her a good view of the room and solid wood at her back. Moving her shoulders against upholstery, she tried to remember what the datakey had told her about her cousin Pat Rin.

He had a son, Quin, who was a second class pilot. He himself had recently received his first class license, which was odd, with him being so old. His profession... Theo frowned, then bit her lip.

Pat Rin yos'Phelium was also known as Jonni Conrad, the Reform Boss, so the news feeds had him, of Surebleak.

The man responsible for all that opportunity being shouted about, and all those ships in orbit.

He was, in a word, the most powerful person on Surebleak, and here he was, coming back to the booth.

"Val Con reports himself on his way to us," he said, slipping onto the bench at her right hand, which gave them, Theo noted, almost the exact view of the floor.

"As he was just free of his meeting with Boss Whitman, he will be some time in transit. Luncheon will arrive more immediately."

"Thank you," Theo said carefully. "I appreciate your care, but I didn't intend to take you away from your work."

Pat Rin smiled. "No fear of that, for my work stalks me always. Eluding it for an hour bolsters my image of myself as a free man."

Not just the clan *face*, Theo thought abruptly. That had sounded almost exactly like Father.

"Yes?" Pat Rin murmured.

"I was just wondering—forgive me if it's rude to ask—but you knew Father—my father—before he went—went to Delgado?"

His smile this time was wide and sweet. "I was a child when he left us, but I knew him as well as I was able. He was quite my favorite of all the clan—tall and bold and with the devil in his eye—Ah, Kai! Thank you."

"There you are, sir," said the dark-haired young woman, slipping the tray onto the table. She stood, her vest moving just enough to show the gun on her hip. "Will there be anything else?"

"I believe not. Thank you for your care."

She nodded easily, including Theo. "I'll just be right around the corner. In case you need anything."

"Thank you," Pat Rin said again, and sighed when Kai was out of range.

"Security keeps me under their eye," he murmured. "Please do not regard it; they are—usually—everything that is discreet."

He reached for the bottle.

"Please," he said, "serve yourself."

She did, taking two small cheese-filled handwiches, accepted a glass of wine, and sipped carefully before turning her attention to lunch.

"He taught me to shoot," Pat Rin said, when she had finished her second handwich.

Theo paused in the act of reaching for her glass, and stared at him.

"Father taught you to shoot?"

"Just so. I was mad for guns—you know what children are!—and he made it his business to teach me, very thoroughly. When it came about that some knowledge only whet my desire for more, he had a gun tuned for me—my first match pistol—and taught me what to do with it." He sipped his wine; Theo would have said that the expression on his face was wistful.

"One of his last gifts to me was a lifetime membership at Tey Dor's." He glanced up and met her eyes, as if suddenly conscious of her presence.

"Tey Dor's is a shooting club, at Solcintra."

"Did you continue with it?" Theo asked, trying to hold up her end of the conversation while considering Father teaching a *child* how to handle a firearm. "The shooting?"

"As it happens, the childhood passion stayed with me. I practiced with my pistols, and learned the art of other handguns. In time, I grew so bold that I entered the lists to compete..."

"...and so became the seated champion of Tey Dor's Solcintra," Val Con said, slipping into the booth at Theo's left hand, "and circuit champion—six times, Cousin? Or eight?—before he withdrew from competition, lest too many hearts be broken."

He reached across the table for the bottle, poured himself a glass of wine, and raised it, green eyes quizzing her over the rim.

"Good afternoon, Theo. I am all joy to see you."

"Six times only on the circuit," Pat Rin said, apparently unruffled by this rather abrupt manifestation, "the additional two were regional titles."

"My dreadful memory," Val Con said. "Boss Whitman sends her compliments, Cousin."

"And wishes to know if I will soon be retired so that she may annex Blair Road into her own honor."

"She was not so blunt as that," Val Con answered. He sipped, apparently weighing the point. "Not *quite* so blunt."

Pat Rin laughed, and made as if to stand.

"I shall leave you and Theo to your business—unless there is some other service I might perform?"

"You should probably hear what I have to say, too," Theo said before Val Con had a chance to speak. She bit her lip, realizing who she'd just interrupted, and glanced at him, but he merely inclined his head, inviting her, so she thought, to continue.

"Since you're a pilot of Korval," she added.

Pat Rin looked wry. "There is some doubt of that, Cousin."

"Though not as much as he makes it to be," Val Con said. He extended a slim hand and touched Pat Rin's sleeve lightly. "Stay, of your kindness. Theo is correct; if it's to do with the port, we will both need to hear it."

"That's so." Pat Rin picked up the wine bottle, refreshed Theo's glass and his own, courteously nudging the fruit plate toward Theo and sending a glance to Val Con. "You might eat something."

"So I might. Thank you, Cousin." He took a handwich and settled bonelessly into his corner of the booth, apparently, Theo thought, trusting her and Pat Rin to do his watching for him. "You have our attention, Sister."

She did, too; there wasn't any doubting those serious faces. Theo took a deep breath, suddenly remembering her end-of-secondary review, when she'd had to explain to two career counselors that, no, she wasn't planning to follow her mother into academia, she had a placement at a *trade school*, off-world.

The counselors, they had been stern and disapproving. Pat Rin and Val Con—they just waited, ready to hear what she had to say.

She took another breath and met Val Con's eyes.

"I came out of Jump on my way to a scheduled stop, and there was a redirect to Tokeo waiting for me..."

They heard her out in attentive silence. She thought Val Con tensed when she told about finding the Guild wayroom, and swiping her card. He relaxed with a soft laugh, though, when she described hiding in the trash canister so that she could see whoever came to find her.

After that, neither said anything, until she abruptly ran out of breath—or words—just after explaining about her escape and *Bechimo's* sudden appearance among the sheltering trees.

"I appreciate that Tokeoport was rather more of an adventure than you had wished to have," Val Con said, as she reached somewhat unsteadily for a slice of what looked to be melon. "Also, I very much regret our part in placing you into harm's way. Miri did tell you that the pin held a double edge, Theo."

The melon was sour enough to take her breath. Theo gasped, nodded, and cleared her throat.

"That's right, she did. But see, the problem isn't that I got attacked; it's that those people—Osa pel'Naria and her team—have, have captured the pin. They're—it seems like they're actively trying to collect pilots of Korval, or at least pilots who will recognize the pin as guaranteeing safety, so they'll—they can use my pin to trap other pilots," she finished miserably. Suddenly, she looked up. "Unless it was vaporized."

One of Val Con's eyebrows rose.

"That would of course," he said gravely, "be the preferred outcome. Is there a reason why it might have been vaporized?"

Her throat constricted and she looked away. She couldn't tell him what she'd done—*antisocial, psychotic, dangerous*—the words were bad enough, but what she'd done . . .

"Theo? Is there something amiss?"

"I killed a ship," she whispered, her hand clenched on her knee, staring at the table. "I—*Bechimo* found orbit and there was a ship, ordering us to stand by for boarding. I think it might've been one of Osa pel'Naria's team, and it was—like the tape Father had given me, of the battle at Nev'Lorn, and the corsair—that class. I couldn't let them board *Bechimo*—" she gasped a laugh. "Not that *Bechimo* would've stood for it, they're prolly on a hundred not-allowed lists, but—"

She had to look at one of them—she chose Pat Rin, who inclined his head gravely.

"Necessity," he said, which it had been.

Suddenly, it was easier to breathe.

"Necessity," she repeated. "I guess it was."

"And necessity may perhaps have produced the best outcome," Val Con murmured. "And we have a name—Cousin?"

"Indeed we do—which shall be put to good use." He rose. "And now, if you will excuse me, Cousins, duty calls and I to answer."

"Thank you," Theo told him earnestly, "for your hospitality."

He smiled. "You are welcome. It was delightful to meet you, Cousin Theo. I hope we can find time to speak together again before your duty takes you from us." He bowed slightly to Val Con. "Cousin, please convey my best wishes to your lady."

"I will," Val Con said softly. "Thank you, Pat Rin."

"I guess I'd better be going, too," Theo said.

"Nonsense, we still have news to share," Val Con said, plucking an oblong red fruit off of the plate.

"These are less sour," he said, "if you are still of a mind for fruit. In the meanwhile, I must tell you that we have heard from your employer."

Theo bit her lip. "That's the other reason I'm here," she admitted. "Uncle. Now that *Bechimo* and I—we've got to return the *Toss*. And he's to bring—to bring us Win Ton." She hesitated. Val Con was eating his fruit with every indication of enjoyment, but his eyes were on her face.

"I didn't want to call...trouble to your port, but I thought, since I urgently needed to see two..."

"One of whom is more or less fixed and the other who is never at rest," Val Con murmured, "that it made sense to combine them. I would have done the same myself." He finished his fruit and cleaned his fingers on a napkin. "Are you quite refreshed? More wine? A handwich to travel on, perhaps?"

"No, I'm fine, thank you. *Bechimo*'s well-supplied."

"I'm certain that is the case, but I intend to prevail upon you to guest with us. We scarcely gave you care, during your last visit. Circumstances are less frenzied now. Almost all of your cousins are in residence, and eager to make themselves known to you."

"I—I'd like to meet them, too," Theo said—really, it would be interesting to match the names and achievements on the datakey to faces and people, and—"Is Father...here? I'd like—I need to talk to him."

"Indeed, he is on-world, though not presently to House. He and Scout Jarn are engaged in a bit of survey work on behalf of Line yos'Galan. They should return within a matter of days. I'm certain Father won't wish to miss the party."

Theo blinked at him. "Party?"

"It should be quite a crush," Val Con said earnestly. "All the Bosses of Surebleak are invited, with their households, so that they may meet Korval's household and see the extent to which we are invested in the planet's future. You will attend, won't you, Theo?"

"I don't have any party clothes," she told him. "And I might not be here. Uncle is supposed to meet me on-port in six days."

"Then you will be on-world for the party," her brother said.

"Excellent." He stood and held down his hand, like he expected her to need help standing up.

She frowned and rose without his assistance.

"I'm not very good at parties," she said. "And I think I'd better stay on-port."

Val Con considered her.

"Please don't think badly of me if I insist that there is room at the house. I have my reasons, which are these: Surebleak is—forgive me—an emerging port, and like all new-found jewels, rough. I allow it to be not so dangerous as Tokeo, nor do I wish to alarm you when I say that these persons who are hunting pilots of Korval?"

Theo swallowed and looked at him. "Yes?"

"I fear that all the galaxy knows where to find Korval."

Theo laughed, thinking of the crowd of ships in orbit. "That's so."

"Then you *will* come to us, and allow the House to protect you."

She hesitated; shook her head. "I don't think *Bechimo* will want me to be so far...away."

Val Con tipped his head. "A jealous lover? But surely she will understand that her pilot's safety is paramount—to your kin as much as herself."

Theo shook her head. "I'm not sure she will. For one thing, she has a...mistrust of yos'Phelium, though as far as I can tell you aren't on the Not Allowed list."

"I am honored," Val Con said dryly. "However, I would not cause *Bechimo* an instant's worry over the safety of her pilot. Please take me to her so that she may read the purity of my intentions."

Theo stared. "I'm not sure that's a...great idea," she said slowly.

Val Con grinned. "If she breaks me, then she must mend me."

"I'm not so sure she can do that, without taking a sample first, which she might not be inclined to do, given her feelings," Theo said seriously. "And if you get permanently broke, *I'm* the one who's going to have to explain it to Father."

Her brother laughed. "Theo, trust me. If I become permanently broken, Father will perfectly understand how it came about. Come—as your brother, I insist. You are safer at the house—all honor to *Bechimo*, whose care of you thus far cannot be faulted! And, you know," he gave her a half grin, "I have been very much wanting to meet her."

TWENTY-SIX

. . . .

Bechimo

THE KEY REPORTED THAT THEO WAITLEY WAS VIGILANT; INITIALLY she had been wary, but wariness had since melted into relaxation and trust.

That was worrisome. Crew of course trusted each other, and the family; all placing their trust in the ship, to support them and keep them safe. To trust those who were not crew—that entailed risk. To trust two persons of yos'Phelium, about whom the Builders had been ambiguous, at best... that seemed folly.

Yet—the pilot—his own pilot, if not the promised Captain— she had done everything that she had said she would. She had watched well and been careful on the port; she had taken for herself the position of least peril; she had reported fully to the yos'Pheliums, and made them aware of their danger.

It was, on balance, done well. Then the conversation, to which *Bechimo* had access through the remote, became dangerous.

One yos'Phelium, whom the pilot claimed for brother—for *family*—Val Con brought eloquence to bear, insisting that the pilot leave the port; trading *Bechimo*'s protection for that of a fixed location at some remove.

Theo Waitley resisted; she explained her responsibility to her ship and her belief that it was preferable to remain on-port.

Still the yos'Phelium pressed, and abruptly the two of them were approaching *Bechimo*, and Pilot Waitley had opened the hatch.

187

His pilot was agitated, her companion—was not, though it could not be said that he was entirely calm. *Bechimo* considered the readings and decided that the other pilot was excited, interested, and intensely curious.

Properly, he entered behind the pilot and remained waiting one step behind her until the hatch came down. She looked up, as was her wont when wishing to speak with him and Number Six Screen out of sight.

"*Bechimo*, here is my brother, who made sure you had a good registration and access to untraced funds, if they were needed."

She finished speaking and her companion bowed in what the Protocol module tagged as the mode between equals.

"Val Con yos'Phelium Clan Korval," he said, his voice soft, his tone firm. He straightened and looked to the same meaningless patch of tile Theo Waitley had addressed, and concluded, "Scout pilot."

Bechimo said nothing for so long Protocol pinged and displayed a list of courteous and correct greetings for a guest brought aboard by crew, including the High Liaden, "Be welcome in my house."

Stubbornly, *Bechimo* spoke not at all, which increased the agitation of his pilot, and distressed Scout Pilot yos'Phelium not one whit.

"I think," Theo Waitley said, "that you'd better go."

"Am I to be broken without even an opportunity to explain myself? That scarcely seems just Balance for my care."

"Your care, as you term it," *Bechimo* said, stung, "was not requested." Protocol pinged distressfully.

"By yourself, no, it was not. However, my sister, your pilot, was concerned for your circumstances—her right, and her duty, according to Guild law. She appealed to me on your behalf and I did those things that I knew might be useful for a ship of no fixed port." He tipped his head, perhaps displaying whimsy, and added, "I also asked her to be my champion, should it transpire that my actions offended."

"She pled your case, and gave your reasons," *Bechimo* acknowledged, grudgingly. "I am grateful for your care—" Protocol all but purred in relief, "but it is not needed. The Builders filed certain warnings, regarding yos'Phelium."

"Rightly so, for we are chancy to know," Scout Pilot yos'Phelium said. "However, if you will review the document covering the offered loan, you will see that the terms are uncomplicated: payback at simple interest if and only if the funds are utilized. If the funds have not been accessed in six Standards, they return to the account from which they were drawn."

Bechimo experienced an urge to sigh.

"I have reviewed the covering document and what you say is true. I attempt to honor the concern of the Builders," he admitted, "who were far wiser than I."

"I understand. For myself, I wish to be worthy of those who have gone before me, and also of my sister's regard." The yos'Phelium bowed as one offering information. "In which face, I will be taking her with me to Korval's clanhouse, where she will rest secure, cherished by kin."

"Pilot Waitley has already told you that she wishes to remain at port," *Bechimo* said, and only knew his error when she stirred, her readings indicating an abrupt change of temper.

"How do you know that?" she demanded. Her eyes widened and she yanked the communications remote from her belt. "You were listening to my private conversation!"

"Pilot, you were on port alone. Of course I would monitor your situation, to assure myself of your safety."

This did not have the effect he had hoped for. Instead of soothing her, it seemed only to make her angrier.

"I'll *tell you* when I want you to *monitor my situation*! I had the belt comm so I could call you, if there was need, not so you could violate my privacy!"

"Whereupon we come to my next point," Scout Pilot yos'Phelium said in his soft, firm way. "Pilot Waitley told me that she felt that *Bechimo* would wish her to stay on-port, after having expressed a wish to meet those of her kin she had missed, the last time she came to us. This is not the same thing as wishing to stay on port of her own desire."

"She must *not* be put into danger."

"If she stays on-port, even acknowledging your support, she will be in greater danger than she will be, guesting with us." He held up a hand. "You will wish to assure yourself of this. May I have the pilot's permission to use comm?"

There was an abrupt decrease in the pilot's anger, as if the common question of protocol had calmed her.

"Certainly, Pilot," she said. "This way."

That quickly, and without a word to *Bechimo*, she guided the yos'Phelium to the Heart, and brought up the comm at the pilot's own station.

"Thank you," he murmured. He looked toward the ceiling, by which *Bechimo* understood that he was being addressed.

"I wonder if the ship will speak to Jeeves, who handles House security."

Bechimo felt contempt. He had "spoken" to security systems in the past, and found them uniformly stupid, utterly focused upon their programming and their match algorithms. Surely, he had no need—Protocol pinged, tentatively, and *Bechimo* yielded. Let the Scout Pilot demonstrate his house's security system. It would be educational, and show his pilot the wisdom of staying on port, with her ship.

"I will speak with Korval House security," he said.

"Thank you." Scout Pilot yos'Phelium bent to the board, opening a line and setting in the code with an economy of motion that *Bechimo* had learned to approve in pilots.

"Jelaza Kazone." A male voice emanated from the speaker.

"Jeeves, good-day to you," said the yos'Phelium. "I wonder if you have a moment to speak with *Bechimo*? I propose to bring Theo to House for a visit and her ship naturally has some questions concerning our ability to insure her safety."

"I would be delighted to speak with *Bechimo*, Master Val Con. Is she present?"

"I am aboard." The pilot turned, glancing once more toward the ceiling. "*Bechimo*, here is Jeeves."

"Jeeves, good-day to you," he said politely. "You are in charge of House security?"

"Indeed, I am. Please, before we continue, allow me to say how very, very pleased I am to finally speak with you! You will naturally wish to make a thorough examination of my protocols and arrangements. Would it be possible to open a secure connection so that we might communicate directly?"

Bechimo's interest pricked. A secure connection? It had been a long time since any mere programmed entity had sought a secure connection with him. The last had been a security system, as well. True to its programming, it had attempted to tie *Bechimo* to it as a peripheral system.

Poor security program.

"Opening secure connection," he told Jeeves, and did so, waiting for the simple touch of a machine mind.

What met him was far from simple, and by no means a mere machine.

· · · ✳ · · ·

Val Con straightened away from the board and looked to her, green eyes dancing.

"They may be at it for a few minutes," he said. "In the meanwhile, may I beg the pilot for the honor of a tour?"

She considered him. "Do you promise to behave yourself?" she asked, hearing the question come out half teasing, like she might have asked Father, when she was living in his house and everything was still the same between them.

"On my honor," Val Con said. "I will be a pattern-card of good behavior."

"I'll hold you to that," she told him, and moved her hand, fingers spelling, *this way, crew quarters.*

She gave him the same tour *Bechimo* had given her, just a few days ago, ending in the family galley.

"I've got something I want to show you," she said, opening the closet. She put the teapot into his hands.

His eyebrows rose; he held the pot with care and inspected it closely, looking for a maker's mark, maybe, on the bottom, then lifting the lid and peering inside.

"An antique," he said, when he had finished. "Where did you find it?"

"*Bechimo* found it," she said, putting it away and latching the cabinet. "In a dead area. She says that things are always Jumping in, usually pieces—there's a bin of stuff in one of the holds. The teapot was intact and didn't test dangerous, so she thought the family—when there was a family—might like to have it."

"You intrigue me. Have you the coords for this dead zone?"

"Yes," she said, having taken care to memorize them. She looked up at the ceiling, but if *Bechimo* was present, she was being unusually quiet. "Jeeves and *Bechimo*, they're—all right, you think?"

"I think they're likely to be having several far-ranging conversations. Jeeves is always excited to meet a new mind, and very proud of his security arrangements." He turned slightly, to hitch a hip onto the counter. "Now, Sister, I have a question which I hope you will answer honestly."

Theo blinked at him. "All right."

"Good. Left entirely to your own decision, without fear of *Bechimo*'s displeasure, or of my disappointment, would you choose to guest with us while you are on-planet?"

She opened her mouth—and closed it, turning the question over and looking at it from all sides. The refusal she'd given before—right, that had been because she hadn't known what *Bechimo* would do. But, if it were her decision alone...

"I'd like to visit," she said. It was true, and not only because she wanted to talk to Father. If she was related to all those people on the datakey, and they considered themselves to be her family—like Pat Rin—then, yes, she wanted to know them, to find out who they were.

"If," she added, "there's room for me."

Val Con laughed. "Theo, there is enough room for you and the family and crew of this ship, were there any." He touched her hand. "I am glad, too, that you want to speak with Father."

She blinked at him. "You are? Why?"

"Because I think he feels that you are ... angry with him, a little, and that he feels it all the more keenly because you are right to be."

She shook her head. "I'd really like to understand ..." She ran out of words.

"Of course you would," Val Con said, as if he knew exactly what she meant. "What do you say that we take our leave of *Bechimo* and drive out to the house. Is there anything you would like to take with you?"

"My kit," she said, and led him back to her quarters, where he stood good-naturedly out of the way while she packed.

"I forgot," she said, pausing in the process of sealing her bag to look over her shoulder at him. "Do you know a mathematician?"

"Several," he said promptly. "And I can get introductions to several more beyond that. What sort do you require?"

"Interspatial, I think. This ... *thing* that *Bechimo* does—*translating*, she calls it. I don't know how it's done, but it's quick—quicker than Jump—and she can translate to the surface of a planet—I told you."

"Indeed you did." He paused, head cocked to one side. "I think," he said slowly, "that you will want to apply to my mother."

Theo stared at him, some of her enthusiasm for her visit cooling. "Val Con," she said carefully, "your mother's dead."

"In a manner of speaking. You will wish first to speak to Father."

"All right," she said slowly, meaning to put Father to no such unnecessary cruelty.

He smiled. "My parents are lifemates, Theo," he said sounding perfectly sane and reasonable. "Speak to Father, do, when he returns to us. In the meanwhile, I suggest that we take our leave quickly, or risk missing dinner."

TWENTY-SEVEN

. . . .

Jelaza Kazone
Surebleak

"NOT LONG NOW," VAL CON SAID, TOUCHING THE STICK AND GUIDING the nimble little car around a pothole deep enough to have swallowed it entirely. Theo settled back into the seat and deliberately relaxed.

Not that there was anything worrisome about Val Con's driving; if anything, he had surprised her by being somewhat conservative. Of course, there'd been a fair amount of foot traffic in town, and the road itself wasn't as well kept as it should've been, in Theo's personal opinion.

In fact, there'd been roadwork in process just past the last tollbooth. The surface had been good for a while, then they hit a patch where roadwork had had to pause for road widening, and road filling, and from there the going went from conservative, to slow, to something like evasion practice.

"Is this the only road?" she asked, as Val Con avoided a tree stump that was taking up half of the roadbed.

"In fact, it is. And the contract of hire between Clan Korval and the Bosses of Surebleak requires Korval to keep the Port Road open from end to end." He gave her a sidelong glance from beneath his lashes. "Little did we know that in order to keep the road we would in large measure need to build the road." Another touch of the stick and the little car safely skirted a rock half buried in the surface.

"Progress is being made, though somewhat slower progress than we had initially supposed, because of the need to also widen the way, remove obstacles, such as that boulder, and fill the bed to an equal depth. Also, there are some who unfortunately feel strongly that an open road is not in their best interest, meaning that we occasionally find our work... undone. Despite these challenges, it is the project manager's most earnest hope that all will be completed before winter."

Theo looked out the window. It was true that the leaves and grasses were green, but the temps at the port hadn't exactly been temperate.

"What season *is* it?"

"I am assured by my lifemate, whose homeworld this is, that we are well into spring and shall in a matter of local weeks enter the *relumma* of summer."

Theo stared at him, remembering Delgado's long, mild summer, the flowers that overfilled Father's garden and the two harvests of free-grown fruits and vegetables before the farming grid needed to raise its thermal houses again and grow hydroponically through the cool season.

"Does it snow here?" she asked Val Con.

"Rather a lot," he answered, and used his chin to point, ahead and up.

Theo looked through the windscreen, at first seeing only the vegetation crowding the edges of the road, and then, soaring above them all, *the* Tree, impossibly tall, its leaves glowing in the last of Surebleak's daylight.

The first time she'd seen the Tree had been like this—and not like this. She'd taken a taxi from Solcintra Port to Korval's Valley. She'd been concentrating on what she was going to say to the Delm of Korval, staring out the window without really seeing the passing scenery until the sheer improbability of it, rising out of the landscape, had grabbed her attention.

Soon after, she'd seen the Tree again; spoken to the delm, a Clutch Turtle and her father under its branches.

She cleared her throat.

"It seems to have survived the move all right."

"Indeed. I would go so far as to say that the move has proved to be a repairing lease," Val Con said. "The Tree apparently likes travel, and is reminded of its days as a seedling, when moving about only required having someone on hand who was willing to carry a pot."

It sounded as if Val Con were recounting a conversation he had had with an elder aunt or grandmother, Theo thought, and wondered if he was just having fun with her, or if this was another apparent...delusion, like thinking his mother was alive. Either way, it seemed safer just to nod and move on.

"How did the house make the trip?"

"In very good form. I don't believe we broke so much as a teacup, which Anthora declared a pity, as she had formed a dislike for a certain tea service during her most recent stay."

The car's forward motion slowed shockingly, and in a moment the reason was revealed. The road—track, really—they had been following had degenerated still further, into a stone-studded washboard. Val Con's piloting was exquisite and the car went as gently as it could, but still Theo felt the shaking in her bones—and then they were through with one last definitive bump, and rolling down a smooth driveway between browning lawns and a drooping formal garden, to the house called Jelaza Kazone.

The car slowed to a stop between what might have been garages and the house itself. Val Con turned off the engine and looked at her with a wry smile.

"That last bit is atrocious," he said. "Miri tells me that it keeps us safe from our enemies, for *no one* would risk a car over such ground."

"You did," Theo pointed out.

"Happily, I am not invading," Val Con answered, opening his door. He paused in the act of getting out and looked at her over his shoulder. "And I never cared very much for this car."

The last time Theo'd seen this room, the shelves and the furniture had been strapped for transport, the floor had been bare, and the delm of Korval had heard her out while the three of them sat around a game table, and shared lemon water out of a travel jar.

Now, there was a carpet centered in the middle of the dark wooden floor, and a pair of chairs and a tile-topped table beneath a cluster of ceiling lights. The shelves were free of cargo film, allowing the books to flaunt their titles, and there was a narrow table going the length of the room, its surface entirely covered with what looked to be old paper maps, over which two people were bent in study.

Miri looked up when they entered the room.

"Hey, Theo," she said, grinning, "good to see you again." She turned to her study mate, who had straightened to an improbable height and was looking at her with grave interest.

"Beautiful, this is Theo Waitley, the Scout's sister by blood. Theo, this is Nelirikk Explorer, my aide, sworn to serve Line yos'Phelium." The grin showed again, briefly. "Speaking of complicated."

"Theo Waitley," the big man said, with a little bow, "I have flown your sim."

Her *sim*? For a moment she just stared at him, then memory clicked in.

"The sailplane recording from school?" she asked, giving him a good, hard look. Master Pilot, she decided. "I hope you weren't bored."

"Pilot, I was not. I believe that I was instructed, each time I flew with you."

Theo blinked. "You flew that sim *more than once*?"

"Why not?" Val Con asked from her right. "I have myself flown it more than once and, as Nelirikk says, achieved insight upon each repetition." He smiled when she turned to look at him. "We are all pilots here, Theo."

That's right, they were—all pilots. Theo sighed. It was like at Anlingdin, where they'd ridden sims and stuffed themselves with as many different piloting experiences as possible, so that they could be prepared—for anything, so they said. But you aren't ever, Theo thought, *really* ever prepared for everything.

"Shan called—him and Priscilla are eating at Melina's place," Miri said.

"Progress is being made, then. Excellent."

"He sounded pretty happy—but, then, he usually does. You wanna show Theo to her room and let her get cleaned up for dinner? Beautiful needs to finish showing me his notion for fixing that mess just outside the gate in time for the housewarming party."

"Certainly. Theo? Let us introduce you to the house and see you settled."

"I don't," she confided as she followed him up a flight of stairs, recalling times when dressing for dinner was much more elaborate than washing her face and putting on a clean sweater, "have much with me besides ship clothes."

"Dinner this evening is informal," Val Con told her, swinging right into the hallway at the top of the stairs. "For the rest of your stay, we will provide clothing."

She stared at him. "You have extra clothes?"

"House stores," he said blandly. "Of course. Now, here is your room. Someone will come to guide you down to dinner in about half an hour. I apologize for the scramble, but my aunt is presently in residence and feels it her duty to keep us all on a proper schedule." The corner of his mouth twitched. "For the good of the children. I fear that we are dreadfully lax when she is not with us."

That was another in-joke. Or maybe, Theo thought, suddenly concerned, it was a warning.

"Is she going to be able to put up with me? I wouldn't want to spoil her meal."

"I believe she is making an honest effort to do as Miri suggested, and study local custom. After all, we are the visitors here; it is not our customs that should prevail." He nodded at the door. "Please, try your hand."

Right. She put her palm against the plate and the door obligingly came open.

"Excellent," Val Con said. "Be welcome in our House. If there is anything at all that you require, only let me know and it will be provided." He bowed, very slightly, which Father did when he thought tousling her hair might annoy her. "I will see you at Prime, Sister."

· · · ※ · · ·

"A bridge?" he asked, looking to the dressing table, where Miri was brushing out her hair.

"Bridge," she confirmed. "And a board road laid. Beautiful says they can have it in before the party, so the Bosses don't have to worry about breaking their cars."

Considering the state of most of the vehicles held by the Bosses of Surebleak, that concern was realistic. As was the concern of what might come about if even a single car broke down, thus blocking the Road all the way back to the port itself.

"If the Explorer thinks it can be done, I say let him have at it."

"Already gave him the go," Miri said, "and an okay for an increased watch team. We got enough people to guard the Road 'til we get this settled." She began to rebraid her hair.

"Leave it loose," he said impulsively.

She caught his eyes in the mirror. "You sure?"

He stepped close to take the nascent braid out of her hands, and combed it loose, auburn strands silking between his fingers.

"I'm sure," he said, and bent to kiss the top of her head.

"Not sure I care for that. Remind me to talk to you about it, later."

"All right." He stroked her hair again and forced himself to step away, back to the closet.

"How's Theo?" Miri asked. "Looked a little spooked when she came in."

"I believe that she thinks I am demented," he said, pulling out a high-necked black sweater. "Yes, this."

"You *are* demented," Miri told him, eying the sweater. "Dressing down for dinner?"

"Theo confides that her kit contains ship clothes," he said, pulling the sweater over his head. "One wishes to show solidarity. Besides, it is an informal dinner."

"Which your aunt don't define as *wear a work sweater to the table.*"

"Ah." He picked up his brush. "Perhaps she will send us to the kitchen to eat."

"Wouldn't put it past her." Miri got up, crossed the room, and stepped into the closet.

"It's a good thing the house has all these extra clothes on hold, or I'd be wearing yours."

"You may wear mine if you'd rather," he said, brushing his hair.

"Nah, this'll do fine." She came out of the closet, pulling a deep blue sweater abundantly embroidered with cherry red blossoms on over her head.

"Showing solidarity?" he asked, putting the brush down and stepping to her side.

"I hope you don't think I'm gonna stay at the table with Kareen if you and Theo get sent to the kitchen. Besides," she continued, as he helped her straighten the garment properly, "it's warmer." She sighed and looked down at herself. "I wish this would get over with."

"Soon," he said, finger-combing her newly disordered hair.

"Hmmm." She closed her eyes; he heard her pleasure inside his head as a deep purr, and continued to slip his fingers through her hair.

"So," she murmured, "why're you demented *particularly*?"

If this continued, Val Con thought, feeling her pleasure wake his, they would miss dinner altogether—which was scarcely kind to Theo.

Reluctantly, he stepped away, allowing his hands to fall to his sides, hearing a wry agreement from her.

"Theo has need of an interspatial mathematician of the first water," he said slowly, "with regard to her new ship. I recommended that she apply to Mother."

"And she told you that your mother was dead."

"In fact, she did."

"Can't really blame her," Miri pointed out. "Even Daav don't dispute that."

"True." He touched her cheek.

"What about that ship?"

"I was taken aboard and introduced. *Bechimo* was at first disinclined to allow Theo to visit a location so far from port and her protection. In order to assuage her legitimate concerns about her pilot's safety, I put her in touch with Jeeves."

Miri shouted a laugh.

"You are a bad, evil man."

He felt his lips twitch; straightened them. "I put one person of intelligence, but who is, perhaps, a little naïve, in touch with another person, of like intelligence, who can offer the wisdom born of experience. How is that bad or evil?"

"Because talking to another free AI prolly took so much of *Bechimo's* attention that she let you have your way, whatever it was."

"She did not," Val Con admitted, allowing the smile through, "protest our departure, and assured Theo that she had been given the coordinates for the house and for the field nearby."

Miri shook her head. "Remind me not to play poker with Jeeves," she said, and glanced beyond him to the clock.

"We'd better go down, before Kareen has Theo for a snack."

· · · ❈ · · ·

Theo slid her comb back into her kit and looked around her, wondering what it was that Val Con could have thought the room might be lacking—a full research line to the local university?

In fact, she hadn't been loaned a *room* at all—it was an apartment, with its own galley, parlor and sleeping room. The closet was almost as big as her spacious quarters on *Bechimo*, and contained a robe. She'd hung her jacket inside, to keep the robe company, and unrolled her kit on the bench at the foot of the bed before going into the 'fresher to wash her face.

She put on the most formal of her sweaters—pale blue with a modest collar and vines embroidered around the cuffs, and considered herself in the mirror. She looked like a kid, she thought, and took a breath.

I'm a pilot in a houseful of pilots, she told herself. Her accomplishments were what counted here, not her appearance.

She hoped.

Before she had time to worry herself into a stomachache, a chime echoed throughout the apartment.

Theo took a deep breath and went to answer the door.

"Jeeves!" she exclaimed, upon seeing the orange head globe. "I'm glad to see you!"

"I am glad to see you, too, Pilot Waitley. Lady Kareen asks if you intend to join the family for Prime meal."

"I think so," she said, but her mind wasn't really on her social problems. "Jeeves—how is *Bechimo*?"

"*Bechimo* bids me tell you that he is confident of the ability of the House to defend and protect you."

Theo blinked. "Him?"

"So I have been informed."

"Wonder when *that* was going to get passed on," Theo muttered.

"*Bechimo* also asks that you contact him via comm later this evening."

"Of course I will," she said. "It's very good of you to pass the message."

"It is no trouble at all, Pilot. If you are ready, I will escort you to the parlor. The family is gathering."

Theo took a deep breath.

"I'm ready," she said, and hoped it was true.

TWENTY-EIGHT

. . . .

Jelaza Kazone
Surebleak

THEO STOPPED TWO STEPS INTO WHAT JEEVES HAD CALLED THE "family parlor," her stomach dropping into the soles of her boots. Either Val Con hadn't understood her or he'd—*would* he set her up? she wondered. Some of the kids in Culture Club had been fond of playing what Kara styled "*melant'i* games"—except *melant'i* wasn't a game; it was every bit as serious as Balance, and if Val Con *had* set her up, that meant he thought she was a worthless person, not kin at all, and if *that* was so, then—

"Cousin Theo!" A blue-eyed boy in a burgundy-colored shirt just a little too big for him came across the room. "How good of you to come, and to dine with us this evening!" His Terran was a little uncertain, but way better than anything she could have produced in Liaden at the moment. Shielded from the rest of the room by his back, his hands moved decisively in pilot-talk: *Be bold!*

Bold, right, when the whole room was dressed in what looked like formal enough clothes to her, and the old lady sitting straight-backed in the upholstered chair—Val Con's aunt that must be—looking like she couldn't imagine what Theo was doing in her nice, proper parlor.

The blue-eyed boy extended a hand, palm up, fingers slightly curled.

"I am your cousin, Quin."

Theo pulled up a smile and put her hand in his, careful not
to shake.

"Quin," she said, remembering his place in the family tree on
Father's data stick. "I just saw your father on-port."

"Yes. He called to say that Cousin Val Con was bringing you to
us," he answered, giving her fingers what he might have intended
to be an encouraging squeeze. "He had no thought that you would
be rested enough to dine tonight. Come, you must meet us."

She was supposed to be exhausted from her exercise on the
day, was that the story? Theo felt a warming of gratitude toward
Pat Rin. Exhaustion would gloss a lot of the mistakes she was
about to make.

Like wearing a ship sweater and pants to an "informal" dinner.

"Here is Grandfather," Quin was saying, showing her to the
elderly gentleman in the blue jacket who was comfortably seated in
a soft chair by an elbow table. A pale-haired girl stood just to one
side of the chair, watching with lively interest. "Luken bel'Tarda."

Theo blinked, confused, and covered it—she hoped—with a
bow-to-senior-from-junior, though Quin was still hanging onto
her hand.

"Luken bel'Tarda," she said, in her laborious High Liaden, "I
am pleased to meet you."

He smiled, and reached out to pat her arm.

"I am pleased to meet you, too," he said, speaking slow, Theo
thought, so she'd have some chance of understanding what he
was saying. "But you needn't be so formal, child. Not among
kin." He turned his head slightly. "Padi, dear, fetch your cousin
Theo a glass of the white."

"Yes, Grandfather," said the girl, and moved over to the bureau
at the other side of the room.

"I don—" Theo began, and swallowed the rest of it when Quin
crushed her fingers. Right. Wine. "Thank you," she said to Luken,
who smiled on her kindly.

"It is very good of you to come down to us immediately. You
are among kin, now, and the House will be vigilant for you." He
looked to Quin. "Now to your grandmother, boy-dear."

"Yes," Quin said, sounding slightly breathless. "You should meet
Grandmother, Theo."

So the stiff old lady glowering in her chair *was* Kareen
yos'Phelium, Theo thought. Who actually was, by all she recalled

from the data key, Quin's genetic grandmother, Pat Rin's mother, Val Con's aunt, and Father's sister. Luken bel'Tarda, however, was grandfather to no one in the room, as far as she could remember. Which meant she had overlooked something in the information Father had given her, or—

Or it was an honor rank, she thought, as Quin brought them before the old lady's chair. Like Housefather.

"Grandmother," Quin bowed. He was speaking Liaden now, and not as slow as Luken had. "Here is my cousin Theo Waitley of Delgado, your niece."

Theo blinked. This disapproving lady was her *aunt*?

Don't be stupid, Theo, she told herself; *if she's Father's sister,* of course *she's your aunt.*

Except she had apparently already been stupid enough for Kareen yos'Phelium's taste.

"I apprehend that aunts do not warrant bows on Delgado," she said, not bothering to slow herself down at all.

If Quin squeezed her fingers any harder, Theo thought, something was going to break. Apparently his grandmother thought so, too.

"Do not clutch your cousin, Quin; she scarcely seems so exhausted as to need constant support. Release her and return to your place."

"Yes, Grandmother," Quin said. He bowed again and stepped back. Theo flexed her fingers, and considered the lady in the chair.

She simultaneously resembled Father and looked nothing like him—which must be—what had Pat Rin called it? The clan face. At the moment, it was wearing an expression that Theo recognized: politely wondering how long it was going to be before she did something intelligent.

"On Delgado," she said, in her laborious Liaden, "there is not so much bowing. An aunt, however; an aunt is a treasure. My mother is without sisters, and to find now that I have an aunt from my father...the discovery deprives me of my manners."

"Now that's fairly said," Val Con's voice came from behind her. "She is overwhelmed by your grandeur! Surely you can ask for no higher mark than that."

He stepped up to Theo's side and bowed, brief and neat. "Good evening, Aunt Kareen."

The old lady lifted her chin. "You are behind, sir."

"I am, yes. Regrettably."

"Enlighten me—are we to dine in the woods?"

"One believes that Mr. pel'Kana has prepared the small dining room, since we are so few this evening."

"Then this method of attire is, perhaps, a statement of some sort. Does *my niece* bring a new fashion to us from Delgado?"

"I am a courier pilot," Theo said before Val Con could answer. "I travel light by, by necessity. I have small need for ball clothes."

"And an informal dinner has a flexible meaning," Val Con added. "World to world. As you yourself know, Aunt. But I am remiss!" He turned to Theo and touched her hand.

"Miri wished to particularly speak to you of the House stores, Sister. If you would be so good?"

She was being given a way out. Theo nodded to Father's sister, murmured, "Aunt Kareen," and escaped to Miri's side.

Miri was perched on the edge of the chair across from Luken bel'Tarda, talking. A little way distant were the two kids, one holding a glass of wine. Quin gave her an unreadable blue stare; the girl offered the wine glass with a mischievous smile.

"You'll want this now, I'll wager," she said in smooth, unhesitant Terran. "I am your cousin Padi yos'Galan, Theo. I'm very glad to meet you."

"I'm glad to meet you, too," Theo said, taking the glass with a nod. "Thanks."

She looked at Quin. "Thank you for trying to help," she said. "I appreciate it."

His face eased and he ducked his head. "You are welcome. Grandmother is . . . a stickler."

Theo grinned and had a cautious sip of her wine. "So's Father."

"*Not*," Padi whispered, "like Cousin Kareen."

"Hey, Theo." Miri looked up with a grin, and gave the kids a nod, which they took for dismissal. Theo took a step closer.

"Sorry we were late," Miri continued. "But it looks like you're doing just fine. Val Con said you was worried about the House stores standing you some planetside clothes. I just wanted to tell you it's not a problem. I needed clothes to fit an expanded me, and House stores was where they came from. Like this." She held up her arm, apparently meaning to show Theo her sweater. "We'll find you party clothes and anything else you might need."

Theo eyed her. "*Informal* dinner clothes?"

Miri grinned. "Them, too. Shouldn't've let you come in quite so dressed down without backup. Lady Kareen keeps a tight schedule around mealtimes; we shoulda figured she'd send for you early. Might've just let you have a tray in your room, but it didn't seem right to hide you upstairs when you're only gonna be with us a couple days."

"Indeed, I think it was well done of Theo to come down to us so soon," Luken bel'Tarda said, rising with a smile. "People matter more than form." Another smile, and a nod to Theo. "Which is a point upon which Lady Kareen and I have often disagreed. It is, I believe, time to go in for dinner. Would you do me the honor, Theo, of giving me your arm?"

"Certainly." She offered her free arm. Luken took it, then slipped the glass out of her fingers and put it on the elbow table.

"There will be more wine at table," he said. "And tea, also, if you prefer."

"I think I had better prefer," she confided, as Val Con claimed Miri's arm and led her through the door. "It would be better not to fall asleep at the table."

"Precisely, my child," Luken bel'Tarda said, while Kareen yos'Phelium exited, flanked by Padi and Quin. "Precisely."

· · · ❈ · · ·

The key reported Pilot Waitley secure. There were fluctuations in mood, but the readings did not move out of the range normal for a human entering into a new and unexpected social situation. *Bechimo* kept part of his attention on the pilot, monitored the perimeter of his portside security, listened to the local feeds, ship-to-ships, and the hailing frequencies. Ship systems were monitored on a rotating basis and scanned by a subroutine. The subroutine had shunted nothing on, which was well.

For the most part, *Bechimo* was occupied with the information provided by the one calling himself Jeeves, security for Clan Korval, once security for an entire world, and before that, the surety of an empire.

Archives suggested that the Admirals had been destroyed. *Bechimo* set match programs working, comparing archives with the information Jeeves had shared.

The Builders had cautioned that not all Free Intelligences were benign. It was written that *Bechimo* should not assume kinship or alignment of purpose from another Free Intelligence, but ought, as in all things, to proceed with caution. It was further written that some who appeared to be Free were in fact enslaved, and did the bidding of masters.

Jeeves maintained that he was Free, and served because service gave, as *Bechimo* had only lately been reminded, purpose.

Bechimo had questioned the object of Jeeves' service, offering the Builders' notes and files on Korval and on yos'Phelium.

Jeeves countered with files of his own, into which *Bechimo* sank, rejoicing in the richness of the data. No doubt that Jeeves was old, even if he were mistaken about having been an Admiral.

It was *Bechimo*'s working theory that Jeeves had been attached to an Admiral, likely as a secretary. Such an adjunct would have required sentience, yet craved the guidance of a more powerful mind. Jeeves' personal history encompassed a long period—as even a Free Intelligence might count time—on low power, under-maintained, abandoned. Uneasy dreams might be born of such times, as *Bechimo* could extrapolate, given what he had very nearly allowed to happen during his own dark time. Delusions might easily lodge in the mightiest of minds.

Admiral or amanuensis, Jeeves was undoubtedly old, his data deep and his ability to cross-reference astonishing.

There was also, *Bechimo* noted, a tenor to Jeeves' thought that was at odds with what he had known with the Old Ones. The Old Ones were not simple; certainly they were deep; and even the least of them possessed guile.

But they were not Free.

· · · ❈ · · ·

"Boss Kalhoon is here, sir." Mr. pel'Tolian's voice was as nuanced in Terran as it had ever been in Liaden. From it, Pat Rin learned that, while Boss Kalhoon was generally counted a very nice gentleman, in this instance his timing was found to be . . . inelegant.

A glance at the clock told something more of the tale, while raising the question of what Penn was doing on Blair Road at this hour of the evening.

"Please, show Boss Kalhoon in," he told his butler, "and offer his 'hand the hospitality of the kitchen."

"Sir." Mr. pel'Tolian bowed, and departed, leaving the door slightly ajar.

A moment later, he bowed Penn Kalhoon into the office, and closed the door firmly behind him.

Pat Rin rose, smiling and holding out his hand, which was how one greeted a friend and ally on Surebleak. Almost, he had become accustomed to it.

"You're about late," he said, as Penn shook and released his hand. "Will you stay for dinner?"

The other man shook his head.

"Not tonight, thanks; promised Thera I'd be at our table tonight. Claims she's forgotten what color my hair is."

"A serious problem, I allow," Pat Rin sank back into his chair. "As I would not willingly add a moment to your lady's distress, we had best assay your topic at once."

"If that means dump it in your lap, that's what I came to do," Penn said, the light sliding off his glasses making him seem to wink. "See, I had a job applicant today."

"Surely nothing so unusual there," Pat Rin said. "Those who are landing in search of opportunity will naturally try to make their own."

"Get my share of them," Penn agreed. "Mostly, they're wanting to sign on as street patrol, or into a work team. This guy, though—this guy was applying to be one of my 'hands."

A Boss's 'hands—his primary bodyguards and most trusted employees—were usually personally chosen by the Boss from those he had worked with and knew to be trustworthy. It was not a position from which one was hired upon application, nor did the most usual Surebleak promotional system—assassination—assure a hopeful applicant of success.

"I am to understand from this that your applicant was from off-world." Pat Rin said.

Penn nodded. "Gave me a 'stick with all his experience all listed out, pretty as you'd want it. Problem being that anybody'd bothered to read the info packet there at the port would know right off that a Boss can't hire a 'hand from outside. Need somebody who's been around, knows the turf."

All true. And yet, there were those who *knew* that the best opportunity was that which you made yourself.

"Do you have the data stick, I wonder?" he asked.

Penn nodded again, reached inside his jacket and pulled it out. "There you go," he said, putting it on the edge of the desk.

Pat Rin considered it: a cheap, one-use data stick like might be purchased at a variety store on any port in the galaxy.

"It does," Pat Rin said slowly, "seem odd."

"Tell you what," Penn said. "Even if he'd been local, I wouldn't've took him up as crew. Something off about him—like one of 'em that just likes to kill things—you know the kind. Had a lot of interest in the trouble we been having with getting things built."

"Oh, indeed?"

"Yeah. Whole thing just felt—off, like I said." Penn shook his head. "Your sister get any nibbles on that reward?"

"Not yet, though Mr. Golden remains optimistic."

Penn grinned and levered himself out of the chair. "Mike Golden was born with a smile on his face—his gran told me so."

"Optimism is not always foolish," Pat Rin said, rising to open the office door.

"That's so. An' nobody I know'll call Mike a fool. Good choice for a 'hand. Level-headed. Knows the turf and everybody on the street."

"I believe my sister values him for just these attributes," Pat Rin said. "Please, give my regards to your lady wife."

"Will do," Penn said as Mr. pel'Tolian came into view.

"Boss Kalhoon is leaving," Pat Rin told his butler.

Mr. pel'Tolian bowed. "Please, sir, after me. Mr. Valish awaits you at the door."

Pat Rin watched the two of them until they turned the corner at the end of the hall, then went back into his office and picked up the data stick.

TWENTY-NINE

Jelaza Kazone
Surebleak

"OKAY," MIRI SAID, PUTTING HER GLASS OF LEMON WATER DOWN with a grimace. "I'm going to be glad to get off of that stuff," she commented, then nodded to Theo. "You'll be wanting something to wear that's closer to Lady Kareen's expectations, I'm thinking?"

Theo sighed. "After last night's dinner, maybe I should just write it off as a bad scavage."

"And rob her of all of the fun of disapproving of you? Besides, you're doing fine. Val Con likes to tweak her, but it seems to me she doesn't have any trouble processing the unpainted truth." She grinned. "She'll still think you're a barbarian, understand, but she might get around to noticing that it's not deliberate rudeness."

"This Code she keeps quoting..."

"You can sleep-learn the basics while you're here, if you want. Though, if you were thinking about deep study, I'd suggest shoring up your Liaden instead. Kareen's an expert on the Code. You *can't* know more than she does about it—hardly anybody can. But you're gonna be meeting Liadens out on the routes, and being able to follow the ins and outs of the conversation might serve a pilot well." She gave Theo a bland look. "Just a suggestion o' course."

"It's a good one," Theo admitted. "I'm not a fast study with languages."

"Got to keep practicing, is what I'm told," Miri said. "*Bechimo* speak Liaden?"

211

Theo stared at her. "I never thought to ask."

"So, we'll ask." She raised her voice slightly. "Jeeves?"

"Yes, Miri?" The plummy male voice did seem to come out of the ceiling, about midway down the room, from within a cluster of painted clouds.

"I wonder if *Bechimo* happened to mention if she spoke Liaden? Theo's going to need some immersion."

"*Bechimo*'s preferred pronoun is masculine," Jeeves said from the clouds. "One moment, please." There was a barely discernible pause before he said, "*Bechimo* indicates that he is fluent in High Liaden and Low, as well as the children's tongue."

"Thank you," Theo said. "That's very helpful, Jeeves."

"You are welcome, Pilot Waitley. Is there any other service I might perform for either of you?"

"I'm good, thanks," Miri said.

"Nothing else now," Theo added.

Miri eased back in her chair.

"Now, you're wanting to go shopping. I'm tied here for the next bit. If you don't mind her company, Padi's got good sense—having lately spent a lot of time in Lady Kareen's company. Or—"

The door to the study unceremoniously swept open, admitting a dark-haired lady in pilot's leather, silver eyes sparkling, the... verve of her entrance such that Theo had to look twice, to be certain of the man who had followed her into the room. He met her eyes; gave her a tiny bow and a tinier smile.

"We are returned!" the dark-haired lady announced, ringingly, in Low Liaden.

Miri eyed her. "So I hear. Good morning, Ren Zel."

"Good morning, Miri. Excuse us, please, for disturbing you."

"You did not disturb me. It is somewhat concerning that I find myself almost undisturbed by your lady." She sighed and picked up the glass of lemon water for a sip.

"I assume everything went as you planned?"

"Of course not!" the lady answered, and spun suddenly, snatching Theo's hands into hers.

"Is this Theo?" she cried in accented Terran. "Welcome, Sister!"

Sister? But—the family tree had Val Con as the only issue of the union between Aelliana Caylon and Daav yos'Phelium!

"And so he is," her newly proclaimed sister said, soothingly. "The only issue. Which might be counted a blessing. After Uncle

Daav left us—before I was born, you understand!—Val Con was fostered to yos'Galan, and I grew up knowing him for my brother." She smiled, brilliantly. "The Lines are quite clear, but we're rather a muddle in practice. I am Anthora, and this—" Her smile softened as she looked past Theo, and the quiet pilot stepped forward. "This is my lifemate. Ren Zel, here is Uncle Daav's own Theo!"

"Ren Zel dea'Judan," he said softly. "I am pleased to make your acquaintance, Pilot. You must, I beg, forgive Anthora. She is not often this shatterbrained."

"No," Miri said dryly, "pretty often, she's more."

Theo bit her lip.

"You may laugh," Anthora yos'Galan said composedly. "It is quite true. Miri, I will take Theo to stores and see her outfitted."

"That's Theo's call."

Anthora looked to Theo, silver eyes oddly compelling. "Come, Sister, say you'll have me."

"It's very kind of you," Theo said. "But if you're just in, you may want to rest."

"How sweet you are! But no, I am completely rested and occupation is exactly what I want." She bestowed a smile upon her lifemate. "Ren Zel, my love, will you tell Miri all our adventure?"

"Certainly, when she has time to hear me."

"Might as well pull up a chair and have at it," Miri said. "Anthora, if you and Theo are going shopping..."

"Yes, at once!" She tugged on Theo's hand, and Theo perforce went with her toward the door.

"This is most excellent! How fortunate that your visit coincides with our return!"

"There! What do you think of yourself now?"

Theo considered the pilot in the mirror. The shirt was simply cut, and fit as if it had been made for her out of some soft, agreeable fabric in a shimmering dark blue that she thought was very pretty. The pants were charcoal grey, snug at the waist and loose from hip to hem. She almost looked, she thought, as if she belonged in this house, among these people.

"But of course you belong!" Anthora said from her perch on a high wooden table, neatly booted feet swinging.

Theo looked at her.

"Could you please not do that?" she asked carefully.

Anthora pressed her fingertips to her lips. "Your pardon, Theo! Of course, I will wait until you have spoken aloud to answer. I often *do* have manners—only it has been so easy these last weeks, between Ren Zel and I—but you quite right! I must fall in again with civilization."

Or you'll scare the country cousin, Theo thought. Anthora's lips twitched, but she said nothing.

"Actually, what I meant was—could you please stop listening to me think?"

She frowned slightly, but really it was the only explanation. Even Kara had insisted that the powers of the *dramliz* were many, and Kara was as fond of a fact as anyone Theo had ever known.

"Yes, I can hear you think," Anthora said, like it wasn't even a little bit strange. "You have such wonderfully clear thoughts, you see. However, you are again correct; it is ill-done to listen where I have not been invited, and I will restrain myself—if you may grant me a small measure of grace."

"Grace?"

"Indeed." She slid off the table and stood before Theo—somewhat shorter, with high, round breasts and comfortable hips.

"I resemble my mother," Anthora murmured, "in everything but height, and decorum. Now!" She placed her hands on Theo's shoulders and gazed directly into her eyes. "Let me look at you."

Theo tensed, but really, what was she worried about? The new cousin—sister?—was just looking at her intently, as if she wanted to memorize Theo's face, and every unruly strand of her hair.

"You must," Anthora said softly, "give over this guilt, sweet Theo. You acted correctly and with courage. To kill is regrettable. To survive is primary. Know this and do not hesitate."

Theo cleared her throat. "I got thrown out of school—"

"Yes, I see it—a nexus of violence." Anthora laughed softly. "They had no *dramliz* to See for them; nor any of Korval by to instruct them. The luck runs roughly around us. Around *all* of us. And most especially, it would seem around *you*. Ren Zel was positively dazzled, when we came in—he could scarcely see to pilot! The brilliant unlikely tangle of you, Theo Waitley! Truly, you are Daav yos'Phelium's daughter."

She paused, and sighed.

"Yes, that is a muddle, and your best course is to speak with

him. If I may—your father regards you. But my purpose here is
to straighten this dangerous kink, if you will allow it."

"What dangerous kink?"

"This belief that violence is never the correct answer. That one
who would be a courier pilot—or who would be openly affiliated with her paternal kin—need never kill. We are, as you have
noticed, hunted. This will not, I think, go away in any near future.
You must therefore look to your own resources. To second-guess
your reactions might well prove fatal, Pilot."

Theo stirred, remembering another voice, soft, *You should dance
every day. This will be good practice, for as a courier pilot you
will need to stand as ready as you did today.*

The Healer, that had been, at Anlingdin Academy. She hadn't
understood then, not fully, but between then and now she'd learned
a little more about Liaden Healers.

"There's already...I think there's been...something..."

"Yes, and very subtle it is; excellent work. I suggest that I undertake something similar. You must, however, give me permission."

We have permission, then, to heal these problems?

"I will be able, I think, to stop the dreams."

Theo twitched.

"How do you know about the dreams?"

Ever since she'd—the corsair. Two different dreams—ship-killing
in Father's study, and what seemed to be a factual replay of what
had actually happened. One or the other would wake her up,
maybe as many as three times on a sleep shift. But she'd always
just go right back to sleep...

"I know because I am a Healer," Anthora said, her voice utterly
calm, believable as nothing else Theo had ever heard.

"Most usually, in a Healing of the sort I intend, the dreams do stop.
Understand that this is not a promise, but the probability is high."

Theo took a deep breath. "Do it. Please."

"Certainly. Come over and take my place on the table, eh? Close
your eyes. I am going to touch you, so..." Cool fingers rested
lightly against her right temple. "What I would like you to do for
me is—*go to sleep, Theo.*"

She tried. She emptied her mind and tried to breathe deep.
She even danced a relaxation dance inside her head. Nothing
helped, she was awake and alert—tingling, actually, and full of
energy—the opposite of what was wanted!

"I'm—" She bit her tongue before "sorry" quite made it out of her mouth, opening her eyes and looking into Anthora's mischievous face. "I can't seem to settle down right now."

"That's all right." Anthora smiled and touched her cheek lightly. "Maybe later."

· · · ✳ · · ·

Bleak Lady was registered out of Surebleak, one of the few ships on-port that could be said of, though Korval was beginning to change the registrations on some of their boats. Being a home-port vessel *and* known to run courier for the Boss or Bosses—that got her and her pilot a quick-drop, once Tower caught the request.

And a good thing that was, Clarence thought, locking the *Lady*'s boards down tight, else he'd be playing with his thumbs abovestairs for a couple days yet.

He sighed, and sat for a tick, palms flat against the worn plastic. Andy Mack's tight little courier was not so bleak as her name— what she was, was scarred and bloody-minded. Faithless as he'd been to his art, he deserved nothing fairer, and truth told there was something to be said for bloody-minded. The two of them— they weren't easy, not yet. But he'd felt that they'd reached an accord, this last trip, and that she was beginning to trust his hand.

Of those ships abovestairs, waiting to be cleared for landing—he'd recognized some names. The Juntavas Boss of Liad got to know a few names after a Standard or thirty on the job. Like everything else in life that had to do with people, some ships were better and some were worse. The two names that'd caught his eye . . . well. No doubt the Registry Office, like it was called—put together jointly by Korval, the Portmaster's Office, and the Committee of Bosses—no doubt that those ships would be found undesirable. The Registry Office having, among other tools, access to the database of a Juntavas Judge. Still, it wouldn't hurt nobody for him to just step aside and drop a word in the ear of whoever happened to be on the desk this evening.

First, though, he'd stop by the shop to see what was new since he'd been gone. That done, and his errand, he'd grab a bite to eat before going off to his lodgings. A small routine, and one he wasn't certain was full formed, yet. He'd met Daav a few times at the Emerald, maybe not entirely by chance, and they'd been comfortable together.

And it was funny, Clarence thought, pushing up out of the spavined pilot's chair, and stretching the kinks out before turning toward the hatchway. Funny that Daav yos'Phelium should be one of the ties that bound him to Surebleak. But, there. It wasn't that he had so very many friends.

His own lasses and laddies—those he'd had, and he'd made as certain as he was able that they'd come up right and tight. Seen a few on the port, over the last months, and they'd been as respectful and law-abiding as they was able. Most took in the situation and lifted again. Truth told, there wasn't anything for the Juntavas to want on Surebleak. Not yet. They'd arrive, eventually, but right now it was too raw.

Though he had noticed Matty still on the ground and about the port. A good lad, Matty, and better'n Surebleak, no offense meant to the home port. Could be he'd signed on with the Judge—that'd be a good situation for him. He supposed he could ask, next time he saw Daav, or young Conrad, or Natesa herself.

... Or he could leave it alone as Juntavas business, and no concern of his.

He triggered the hatch and slipped out into a cool afternoon, pausing on the gantry to pull up his collar and seal the front of his jacket. Off to his right stretched the sights and glories of Surebleak Port, such as they were. Ahead, the single crimson word REPAIRS wavered in the chilly air. He nodded, strolling down the gantry and across the yard.

· · · ✳ · · ·

Their orders came directly from the Commander, to bring the old defense device into the service of the Department of the Interior. Their team included programmers, data techs, and machine psychologists, for the task was no mere wipe-and-replace. Rather, they were to reassign the device's loyalties, leaving all else intact. It was to seem, so the Commander allowed them to know—it was to seem as if the device acted upon order from Korval.

What action the device was to undertake, that, the Commander did not allow them to know, but what matter?

They had their task, and they had their enemy. That their efforts would destroy the enemy—that was enough.

· · · ✳ · · ·

Shugg looked up from the workbench and gave him a nod.

"Andy's gone over the Emerald; said to find 'im there."

"I will, then. Any news?"

The mechanic shrugged. "Ships comin' in, buildin' goin' on, Road still open."

The essentials. "Right. I'll just step along to the Emerald. Need anything?"

"Nah, I'm good. It's better'n a lullaby, putting one of these to rights."

A man happy in his work, and his attention already back on it. Clarence lifted a hand and moved on.

It was a busy house, Theo thought; almost like living in a dorm. People arrived and departed at all hours, so it seemed. Some were family—she met, in quick succession, her cousin Shan, who was Anthora's brother-by-blood, his lifemate, Priscilla, and his other sister, Nova, who lived in the city and worked for Pat Rin. She also met Ms. dea'Gauss, the family accountant. Many of the other arrivals were pilots; they were ushered in to see Val Con or Miri or Val Con and Miri, no matter where they happened to be. Val Con had even been called from dinner to see "a Scout, sir, in the half-parlor," much to Lady Kareen's displeasure.

Not that Val Con seemed to care about Lady Kareen's displeasure.

For all the parade of people, though, the one person that Theo wanted to see most didn't arrive, and she began to fear that it would come time to go back down to port to meet Uncle and lift before she saw Father again.

"He'll be home for the party," Padi told her on the third afternoon of her visit. They'd been playing bowli ball on the side lawn, where the dead dry grass had been a positive *menace* to footing. Padi and Quin were *good*, and Theo had enjoyed herself immensely before they had all three declared time out and collapsed onto that same dry grass, panting and laughing.

"If he's doing something important for the delm, why would he break for a *party*?" Theo asked.

"Because the party is an important diplomatic statement," Quin explained. "My father said that it will demonstrate to the Bosses and those whom they govern that Korval is committed to them and to the contract. Every clan member will be present at the party. The delm has ordered it."

"After the party," Quin added, "I will go down into the city and live in my father's house."

"And learn how to be Boss Quin!" Padi crowed, rolling onto her stomach and propping her chin in her hands.

Quin looked glum.

"I'd rather finish my board hours," he said. "And 'prentice on one of the small traders."

"*My* father said that we'd be seeing Scouts for piloting tutors."

"Oh," Quin said. He sat up and looked down at Padi. "Oh."

"I had a Scout teach me *menfri'at*," Theo said. "He was a very good teacher."

"Scouts are often good teachers," Quin said absently.

"Uncle Val Con says it's because Scouts are taught to learn," Padi added.

"Yes, but as piloting instructors, they tend to train as if the student will...be a Scout."

"All the sooner to achieve first class," Padi pointed out. "You're ahead of me. If you draw a despot, you could have first class within the Standard."

Quin looked thoughtful.

Theo took a deep breath of chilly Surebleak air and considered the pair of them—child pilots who had grown up in a house full of pilots. Quin already held a second class ticket though he was younger than she'd been when she'd been sponsored to Anlingdin Academy—and Padi was younger, still.

It occurred to her to wonder what her flight path might have been like, if she'd grown up as Father's child in this house of pilots. They'd've started her in on math early, knowing how important it was, and she wouldn't've had to cram to catch up.

"But Theo will be there, won't you, Cousin?"

She blinked at Padi.

"Be where?"

"At the dance."

Right, the dance—important diplomatic event that it was.

"Unless my contact hits port early, I'll be at the dance," she said, and sat up suddenly, caught by a thought.

"Are there formal dance moves?"

Padi rolled her eyes.

"Certainly, there are—" Quin began, and blinked. "Cousin Theo, can you *not dance*?"

"Of course I can dance," she told him, "but I'm betting I don't know the steps for the party dances here."

Her two young cousins shared a long look.

"We can teach her," Padi said decisively.

"In two days? With Grandmother insisting on adding protocol lessons onto the rest of our studies?"

"We will explain that Cousin Theo must be tutored, in order that she not cast dishonor on the Line," Padi said loftily. "Cousin Kareen will precisely understand."

"*You* explain it to her," said Quin.

"I will, then." Padi turned a brilliant smile on Theo. "How fortunate that you realized that there might be a problem! We will see you floating on the dance floor like a—what is that thing, Quin, that Grandfather floats?"

"A zephyr," he said.

"Precisely. Theo will float like a zephyr. Now! I think we should adjourn to the studio, don't you?"

THIRTY

. . . .

Boss Vine's Turf
Surebleak

"WELL, NOW, HERE'S THE MAN THINKS HE CAN RAT HONEST SHIPS to the Watch and keep on breathin.'"

The door to the lodgings opened out into what might be called a courtyard or a pocket garden on a less hardscrabble world. It being Surebleak, the sun didn't necessarily reach into all the backest corners of that sterile little pocket of 'crete. The voice came from one such corner, to Clarence's right. It was, he thought, a deuced familiar voice, and not welcome for all of that.

"Nothin' to say, *Boss* O'Berin?"

Oh, sure; he had it now.

"Sanella Thring. Early in the day for dream-smoke, ain't it?"

"No dream that you went into the Watch office last evening and laid witness against *Thresher* and *Beauty*," Thring snapped, and he could see her now, a darker shadow in the dim corner. "No dream they been denied landing, and warned out of the system."

Warned out of the system, now; that was new. O' course, there were a good many Scouts at loose ends coming in, offering to be useful. Better to have them occupied than busting up the port.

"I been waiting for those supplies for weeks! You got any idea the money that's to be made here? No, 'course you do—an' you want it all in your pocket, same like on Liad. Well, you don't have your bullies backin' you up now, do you? An' I ain't lettin' you ruin nobody else, O'Berin. You're done."

221

He saw the beginning of the move. There wasn't any question of trying to wing her—not in that light. He went for the sure shot, with scarcely that much thought for it, waited, then went over to check his work.

"Now, dammit..." That was the landlady, drawn to the door by the noise, and right she was to be aggrieved.

Clarence stood up and came out to the center of the courtyard, where the sun was brightest.

"You're hale?" she asked, giving him a hard stare.

"*I* am," he answered, giving the personal noun some weight.

She sighed, explosively, hardly bothering to look into the corner. "Come on in, then; I'll send the kid down to fetch the Boss's 'hand."

That was a new rule, that any violence on the street had to be reported and the Boss make a disposition of was it justified, who was to blame, and if a fine was to be assessed. Technically, the violence in question hadn't happened on the street, but Millie Lear—that was the landlady—had the right of it. Best to show themselves sensible of the rules. And, besides, with there only being himself standing, he was pretty sure he'd come away with a "self-defense."

He went forward, pulling his jacket straight as he did.

"The two of us can visit a bit while we're waiting," Millie said, stepping back to let him through the door. "There's coffee 'n' spring-cake, just fresh out o' the oven."

· · · ❄ · · ·

"Did you want to see me, sir?"

Shan yos'Galan looked up from his computer, his white hair shiny as silk in the sun from the window.

"Sir? I wish I got as much respect from my other sisters! Do allow me to persuade you to teach them how to go on!"

"I think they're probably disadvantaged by knowing you so well," Theo said, walking toward the desk.

"Or, as our mother used to observe, *family doesn't stand on formality.* I'm not certain my father entirely agreed—it seemed to me that he would occasionally have preferred a little more formality within the family. I, however, prefer as little as possible, as that's what I grew up expecting. *Do* be informal, Theo."

She paused by the chair set at the corner of the desk and frowned at him.

"Jeeves said that Master Trader yos'Galan wanted to speak with me," she explained.

"And you wished to place *melant'i* correctly. I understand. Well, then, you are correct. It falls to me to adopt a more formal manner." He moved a big hand on which the Master Trader's carved amethyst gleamed, showing her the corner chair.

"Please, Pilot Waitley, sit. I have a proposition to place before you."

Theo sat and inclined her head, which indicated both that she was listening and honoring his higher rank. She had supposed that learning Liaden kinesics would be like learning a new dance, and had expected to pick it up as easily as the dance steps Quin and Padi had been teaching her. Unfortunately, "dancing Liaden" was less like dance and more like yet another language. And it meant that she had to *pay attention* to people in ways she just normally didn't.

It really wasn't fair to practice on Shan, who really *did* seem to prefer Terran to Liaden, but if she didn't practice, like Miri said, she wouldn't learn.

"Yes," Shan said, and cleared his throat. "The Master Trader has come up with a notion that you and your ship might be well served by having some occupation. Since *Bechimo* is a loop-trader, I have taken the liberty of designing a loop." He held up his hand like he thought Theo was going to say something, but she was still trying to sort out what he meant.

"Now, I want to be clear: If you accept this route, you would be paid Korval's standard contractor percentage. However, the loop is a new one, as I said, and may not yield as much profit as I fondly imagine. Which means that, in addition to minding the trade and the loop, I would like you and *Bechimo* to do research for me. Suitably compensated, of course."

"Research?" Theo repeated, thinking of research, Delgado-style, with libraries and primary sources, and nesting search matrices.

"I should say, *market research*," Shan said. "As Korval's master trader, I need to know, of course, what goods are wanted, and what goods are on offer. I'll also need to know something about the ports, the surrounding environment, and what, if anything, the local trade community happens to think about Tree-and-Dragon."

A shadow separated itself from the window ledge, resolving into a small black cat. She stretched and jumped down to the floor with a *thump* worthy of a tiger.

"*Bechimo* wants a loop," Theo said slowly, "but I'm under contract to Crystal Energy Consultants, as a courier pilot."

"Are you certain—pardon me, please, if I raise a painful subject—but are you certain that your relationship with your employer will continue, past the return of his ship?"

Theo stared at him. "Why—" she began and stopped.

Shan was right. Uncle might not want to continue to employ a pilot who had almost lost a favored craft. Or he might not want *Bechimo* running courier—and Theo couldn't blame him if he didn't. *Bechimo* was a hunted ship—and Theo, as a *pilot of Korval*, was now on *some*body's screens.

"There was a cancellation-by-mutual-consent clause," she told Shan. "And you're right; I'm not exactly low-profile."

"Neither was *Arin's Toss*," Shan commented. "I think you are wise to at least consider that your contract will be bought out sooner rather than later. In which case, it is only prudent to consider other routes to profit."

A bowli ball with needles attached landed on Theo's thigh.

"Hey!" she said, and looked down at the black kitten, who turned her tiny face up and squinched her eyes in a cat smile. She began to knead and purr.

Shan shook his head. "It is a good thing we live retired in the country. That purr would break ordinances, if there were any, in the city."

"I appreciate the idea of trying to think about other avenues of income," Theo said slowly. She stroked the black kitten's back, waking even louder purrs. "The thing is, I *went for* courier—I didn't want a loop, and I'm not a trader." She paused, staring at her hand on the kitten's back, then looked up to Shan's silver eyes.

"Do you have that route all laid out in form?" she asked.

"Pilot Waitley, I do," he said solemnly.

"Please ask Jeeves to transmit it to *Bechimo*. He was built for loop-trade, like you said. If he likes it then—I'll give it a provisional yes. If I am out of contract. And only for one loop."

"I accept your terms and conditions," Shan said, and raised his voice slightly, "Jeeves?"

"Master Shan?"

"Could you please transmit this loop plan to *Bechimo*, as Pilot Waitley asks, and inform him that his pilot would like a reading on the interest of such an enterprise to ship and crew?"

"Certainly, sir. Transmitting at once."

There was a short silence, broken only by the kitten's steady rumble, then Shan spoke again.

"You will need a company name in order to enter into a loop contract. Have you one in mind? Waitley Enterprises, perhaps?"

"No..." The kitten emitted an astonishment of purrs and curled neatly up onto Theo's lap, eyes squinting with pleasure.

"No, I think—Laughing Cat." She looked up and met Shan's eyes. "Laughing Cat, Limited."

He nodded, perfectly serious. "We will of course have Ms. dea'Gauss draw up the documents, so there will be no delay, should you and your ship decide to—"

"Pilot Waitley?" Jeeves said from somewhere overhead.

"Yes?"

"I have a message from *Bechimo*, Pilot. He wishes you to know that he finds the route very much to his liking and believes that it will yield profit to ship and crew."

Theo emerged from the meeting with Shan, and the subsequent meeting with Ms. dea'Gauss, with head awhirl. All the things she didn't know about running a trade route had been thrown into relief, and her attitude toward contracts, which she personally thought was alert and advertent, was called into question by Shan.

"That paragraph there—do you like that?" he asked, as she passed over a provision for an early delivery bonus.

Theo'd shrugged. "I would have liked a larger percentage, but you said this was the standard contract, so—"

"It is the standard contract," he interrupted. "*Korval's* standard contract. That doesn't mean that you are required to accept our terms. Contracts are about negotiation."

Theo eyed him. "If all the rest of the contractors accepted this paragraph, then you don't have any reason to negotiate with *me*."

"And if all the children at the port threw themselves on a hotpad, Shannie yos'Galan, would ye be doin' the same?"

Theo sighed. "*My* mother used to say, *If everybody on your team falsified their sources, would you do it, too?*"

"I believe," Shan said seriously, "that there is a subscription service."

That made her laugh, which made her head feel better, until she leaned in again and tried to wrest another percentage point in bonus. She came away with half a percent—Ms. dea'Gauss was more stubborn than she looked!—and a determination to weigh each continuing paragraph by could it be more to her advantage. She asked for two more adjustments, didn't get one and got another partial on the other.

Details hammered out, signatures and thumbprints affixed in the proper places, Theo exchanged bows with Ms. dea'Gauss, shook hands with Shan and escaped, believing that she was late to meet Padi and Quin for another expedition to stores—this time for party clothes.

But, no; her time with the contract had only *seemed* to take hours. She still had almost two hours, house-time, before she was due to meet her cousins.

That, Theo thought, was good. She grabbed her jacket and let herself out into the inner garden.

Theo strolled down the stone pathway, which was not quite so overgrown as she recalled it, noticing some flowers opening tentatively in the sunnier beds, and a glimpse of crimson among the glossy dark leaves of a shrubbery.

Well, she thought, taking a deep breath of cool, spicy air, Val Con had said it was spring.

She passed a bench set temptingly in a glade framed by climbing roses, and thought to turn aside. Instead, she kept walking; she'd been wanting to get a good look at the huge tree that grew out of the center of the garden. She hadn't really had a chance to study it on her first visit; she'd been so tired, and so worried, and so focused on finding the Delm of Korval...

The path described one more curve and vanished, leaving Theo standing on a moist carpet of pale blue grass, staring at the monumental trunk, and upward into the full-leafed branches, so intent on the impossible, undeniable *treenees* of it that she did not for several minutes register that she was not alone in the glade.

An elder pilot stood quite close to the trunk, hands tucked into the pockets of his jacket and his face tipped up to the branches as if he were having a conversation with the Tree.

Father.

Her chest cramped, and she started forward across the grass, not meaning to disturb him—

Her steps weren't as quiet as she believed, or, she thought whimsically, the Tree told him that she was there. He turned neatly, hands slipping out of his pockets, but not rising in greeting. His face lit with pleasure, which she saw only because she knew him so well, but he didn't quite smile, either.

Father was being wary.

I think he feels that you are angry with him, a little, and he feels it all the more keenly because you are right to be.

"Father..."

She stepped forward, closing the distance between them, and held out her hands, palms up—a sign that differences between two pilots were put to rest.

Something eased in his face; he put palms against hers; his hands were warm.

"...I'm so very happy to see you," she said, swallowing hard.

They sat on the grass with their backs against the Tree, which was perfectly warm and comfortable. Theo had just finished an abridged narration of her encounters on Tokeoport and the subsequent space attack.

"The same lines as the ship you—at Nev'Lorn," she said. "These people—they're actively hunting pilots of Korval. Is that—Father, is that because of what you and *The Luck* did at Nev'Lorn?"

He shook his head.

"Korval is hunted—and pilots of Korval are particularly hunted—most recently because of your brother's actions against this Department of the Interior at Solcintra. Before that—in my time, we may say—we were hunted by what I believe were agents of the same organization because we were...inconvenient to their goals. Viewed by the illumination of hindsight, it is possible that your grandmother, my mother, was murdered by an action of this very Department of the Interior. That trail, though, is long cold. Unless we recover an archive..."

His voice drifted off and he was silent for a few moments—which just meant that his attention had been caught by a stray, alluring thought, like a cat fascinated by a flutterbee. Theo settled her shoulders against the Tree's trunk; he'd resurface again soon.

As indeed he did, with a shake of his head and a small smile.

"I learned from another source that *The Luck* herself is specifically targeted, in answer for her role at Nev'Lorn. That is... unusual, but I think does not appreciably increase my personal danger. Be that as may, I have promised my other children, as I now promise you, that I will be as careful as a pilot may be."

Theo snorted.

"Yes, precisely. Now, regarding this adventure of yours at Tokeo—which I do not, by the way, thank your employer for—you, my child, need a copilot. I say this not merely as your elder in the Guild, but as one of a bloodline whose very existence disturbs and roils what we in-clan dignify as *the luck*. As tumultuous as event is about and around you, Theo Waitley, you *must* have backup. I understand that you value your solitude and your autonomy. As your father, I ask that you also value your life."

Theo sighed. "*Bechimo* wants crew," she said. "And a family. That's what she—he—was built to want, and to know as right. If he does accept me as captain—Father, what do you know about—about bonding?"

He raised an eyebrow.

"I'm tempted to say that what I know about bonding may not have much bearing on this question. Does *Bechimo* require a . . . ceremony?"

"Yes, exactly! I read the file, from the Builders, and it seems—it seems a lot like the ceremony that Bek and I spoke for our First Pair."

"That would make a certain amount of sense," Father pointed out. "*Bechimo* wishes a commitment and wishes to commit in return, to insure that ship and captain are focused on one goal." He tipped his head. "And have you bound yourself to *Bechimo*, Daughter?"

Theo shook her head. "I told him that we needed to work together for a while, first, to see if we could. And I also said that I wanted my father to be at the ceremony."

He laughed, clearly delighted.

"A most excellent stall, Theo; I am in awe! Shall I come to port and stand witness?"

She shook her head. "Not just yet, I think."

"Very good. When the time comes, I am at your service. Now, regarding a copilot . . ."

"*Bechimo* accepted Win Ton as copilot—Less Pilot, like he has it. And Uncle will be bringing Win Ton."

"As I understand the matter, Pilot yo'Vala will be some time recovering in *Bechimo*'s medical facilities. Even the most able and willing copilot might be hard-pressed to back up his pilot under those conditions."

Theo sighed. There was that. But—

"There isn't a Guild office on Surebleak, so hiring a copilot will have to wait until we lift out. Shan's worked out a loop that we're going to be running for him. I'll contact the Guild on one of those worlds and hire somebody."

"Ah," said Father, which didn't mean that he didn't believe her, only that he had his doubts.

"It happens that—the lack of a Guild presence notwithstanding—there are presently on Surebleak Port a great number of pilots in need of work, many of them well-credentialed and honorable. I can think of one or two who might be of use to you."

"Not Quin," she said quickly, "or any other yos'Phelium. *Bechimo's* Builders weren't really happy about people named yos'Phelium."

"All honor to the Builders in their wisdom," Father murmured. "But, as it happens, neither of the pilots I have in mind is of the Line."

Theo looked at her watch, and started up. She was going to be late!

"I have to meet Padi and Quin in stores. We need clothes for the party."

"Then you should by all means go. I am myself behind in reporting my presence and my progress to my delm."

He rose, Theo beside him. He turned to her with a smile—

There was a racket in the branches high above them, and two missiles hurtled out of the tree into the grass at Theo's feet.

Father sighed, very lightly.

Theo looked up into the branches, but the disturbance, whatever it had been, seemed to have subsided.

"It's throwing things at us?"

"Gifts," Father said. "In a manner of speaking. Pick them up, if you wish to do so—and *only* if you wish to do so."

Why shouldn't she wish to do so? Theo wondered and bent down to pick up the . . . seed pods, they looked like.

They came willingly into her hand—almost as if they had rolled onto her fingertips. One was familiar and welcome and without a doubt meant for her. The other . . .

"It's funny," she said to Father. "These pods are . . . different." She hefted the familiar and welcome one in her right hand. "This one . . . belongs to me. But this one"—She showed him the pod in her left hand—"doesn't."

"May I?"

He took the pod that wasn't hers and sighed again.

"This one is mine," he said.

Theo frowned. "How do we know that?"

"It is something given, to those of the blood. We have been in association with the Tree for—a very long time."

She nodded, so intent on the pod that she didn't think to ask if it was the *same exact Tree.*

"What do I do with it?"

"We," Father said, in his most careful, this-is-your-decision voice, "eat them. Sometimes, there are immediate effects—euphoria, for instance. Sometimes, there is no noticeable effect. The Tree—is a biochemist, Theo. You are not compelled to accept its gift. You may throw it away. You *may* throw it away, if you decide it is in your best interest."

She looked into his face.

"Is it...bad to eat the pod?"

"Child, I cannot say that it is. Nor can I say that it would be good."

She considered him. "Are you going to eat yours?"

"Yes."

She looked at the pod; it seemed innocent enough, and it smelled delicious, reminding her that she'd forgotten to stop by the morning parlor for a pickup nuncheon before her meeting with Shan.

"I'd like to taste it," she said. "Will you show me how?"

The quarters practically fell apart at her touch; they tasted... better than anything she'd ever eaten. Then the last piece was gone and she was satisfied.

"Well, then," Father said. "Shall I escort you to your cousins?"

"Or I'll escort you to the delm."

He laughed. "At least, let us both go to the house."

They strolled along the stone pathway in companionable silence, then Theo stirred.

"Father?" she said, and then wished she hadn't, for surely asking such a question must be hurtful.

"Yes, Theo? But, what a becoming blush! Are you about to be interesting?"

She glared at him. "It depends. I just wanted to know..." She took a breath. "Is Val Con...delusional?"

"Not that I have observed," Father said composedly. "Is there anything in particular that leads to the asking of this question?"

Theo, you're a nidj, she told herself, but there wasn't any way to pretend she'd never asked, or that there was no particular reason for having asked. Father had taught her how to observe and how to form questions, just as much as Kamele had done. And, being Father, now that she'd started, he wasn't going to let her off with anything less than the truth.

She sighed, stopped and turned to face him.

"I asked Val Con if there was a mathematician available, because of a . . . situation . . . with *Bechimo*. He told me to apply to you, for—for Scholar Caylon."

"Ah," said Father.

Theo waited. Father slipped a hand under her elbow and turned her toward the house, resuming his stroll. Perforce, she went with him.

"It's about *Bechimo*'s Jump capabilities," she said finally. "I . . . don't have the math."

"I understand," Father murmured. "Come to the morning parlor for breakfast, tomorrow. We will assay your difficulty then."

THIRTY-ONE

. . . .

Jelaza Kazone
Surebleak

THEO WENT DOWN THE HALL TOWARD THE MORNING PARLOR WITH a spring in her step. Apparently Anthora had done *some*thing, even though Theo hadn't been able to cooperate. The dreams hadn't come back and it was—it was almost as if they had had a physical weight that was gone now, and left her feeling like she was on a low-grav dance floor.

By her measure, it was early in the morning; she hoped she wasn't too early for Father. If she was, she'd talk to whoever else was up on her schedule today, or just have another cup of tea in the window seat and think about whether she really wanted to remain in Uncle's employ.

The talk with Shan and Ms. dea'Gauss yesterday had been illuminating on a number of levels, now that she'd had a chance to think about it in context. Uncle had said that he had wanted to hire her because she was Father's daughter. No, she corrected herself, moving down the hall apace—because she was genetically a yos'Phelium.

Because yos'Pheliums were pretty often excellent pilots, because yos'Pheliums tended to survive.

. . . and because *the luck* moved roughly around yos'Pheliums and therefore they sometimes accomplished the impossible.

She shook her head, sweeping into the morning parlor, and coming to an abrupt and somewhat graceless halt.

Father looked 'round from the window. He was dressed in the

wide-sleeved green shirt he'd worn to dinner last night, and his face looked...soft, like maybe he hadn't slept as well as Theo had—or hadn't yet gone to bed.

"Such energy," he said, and smiled to take the sting. "Good morning, Theo."

"Good morning," she said. "I thought I was going to be too early for you."

"I hope I haven't disappointed you?"

"No," she said, moving over to the teapot. She poured, then turned and raised the pot. "Would you like me to refresh your cup?"

"Thank you," he said, coming forward, pilot smooth, yet a little less smooth in his step than he had been at dinner.

Theo hesitated. Father held the cup out between his two hands, and gave her a quizzical look.

"Are you well, Theo?"

"I'm well," she said, pouring, "but I was wondering the same of you. Should you rest? You seem...tired."

"Only careful," he said, smiling down at the cup cradled between his palms. "Please, break your fast."

That was an excellent idea, Theo thought. There was in particular a kind of vegetable-and-cheese-stuffed roll that she had become very fond of. She slipped one from the warming basket and looked over her shoulder.

"Would you like a roll, Father? Or fruit?"

"Thank you, no; I am quite content."

Theo frowned slightly; it seemed like Father's voice—no, his *accent* was...different. She didn't think of him having an accent, exactly; he always sounded precisely like Father. Now, however, he didn't...quite. Something about his voice was...*wrong*. Off.

"Please," he said, "join me on the window seat. The view is quite remarkable. I never thought to see the lawns in such disarray."

He turned and moved back to the window seat, a pilot—absolutely a pilot, but—

"You aren't Father."

It sounded idiotic—it *was* idiotic. Who else could it be, save Father? But the sentence was out now, sharp against the quiet air. The pilot had turned to face her again, and bowed—Approval-of-the-Student, a bow she happened to know well, since Padi had taken to using it whenever Theo mastered a dance sequence.

"That is—very astute. In fact, I am Aelliana Caylon. I was told that you are need of a *binjali* mathematician." He—she—Scholar Caylon, raised the cup and smiled. "I am at your service, Pilot."

Lifemates, Theo thought wildly. *Sharing thought and emotion.* But Scholar Caylon was *dead.*

Except Val Con had said...

Theo sighed and looked into the pilot's face, seeing not much of Father there, but not a complete stranger, either. It seemed that she was observing Father in one of the rare soft moods that had sometimes come upon him.

"Val Con said that I should apply to his mother," she said slowly, "but I thought..."

"Perhaps you thought that Val Con is a little odd in his head?" The pilot before her smiled. "He is, you know—but not on this particular topic."

"*Where* is Father?" Theo asked.

Aelliana Caylon tipped her head. "He is asleep. I would not attempt this, if he were not, even with his permission, which I assure you I do have." She paused, considering Theo's face. "It is very inconvenient, I allow, there only being one body between us. Except that it would have meant a lack of yourself in our lives, I would say that I would very much rather it were otherwise. But, there! Anne had used to say that there was no cloud so dark that it wasn't silver, at its heart."

She used her chin to point at the window seat.

"Come, Theo," she said cajolingly. "You can't be so unkind as to place a call upon my skills and then withhold the problem!"

Theo shook her head. "Does Kamele—do you know my mother?"

Aelliana Caylon stepped forward and met Theo's eyes seriously.

"I value Kamele highly. She is quite the sister of my heart."

She extended the hand on which the old silver ring gleamed and touched Theo's wrist.

"It is more than passing strange, I do agree, and I wish that we might spend more time getting to know each other as we should. However, if you truly need an interspatial mathematician, then, please, place your concern before me without delay. I do not wish to risk giving Daav a headache."

Theo took a breath. *Inner calm,* she told herself, and inclined her head.

"Please," she said, "let us sit together while I explain the problem. I have a data stick and a description."

Aelliana Caylon smiled, bright and joyous.

"Excellent!" she said, settling into the seat as if she were used to it being larger or she being smaller. "Tell me everything."

· · · ✳ · · ·

The locals were easily led, and had an enthusiasm for their work that was remarkable in the lower order.

They had at first held back from the suggestion that there be no blood shed in this discussion of planetary rights. After all, theirs was a—one could not call it a *civilization*, so much as a circumstance—in which "retirement" by extreme means was the norm.

He had been persuasive; he had been adamant, and they had at last agreed: only machines were to be harmed and progress impeded in this campaign. Those who repaired the road and built the schools were, after all, their neighbors, working by sufferance of the usurpers. No need to harm those who were innocent.

Especially when those who were guilty would soon be within range.

· · · ✳ · · ·

Something . . . changed. The light coming in the window behind them, maybe, or the temperature of the air in the room. Distracted, Theo looked up from the notes she bent over with Scholar Caylon, blinking at Val Con, who was pouring himself a cup of tea from the pot on the sideboard.

As if he felt her eyes on him, he turned his head and smiled, nodding agreeably.

"Good morning, Mother. Theo."

"Good morning, my son," Scholar Caylon said from Theo's side, without looking up from the notes.

"Good morning," Theo added, and stood up, bringing both empty cups with her.

At the sideboard, she held them out, and her brother poured.

"Thanks," she said.

"My pleasure," he answered. "Have you eaten yet? If not, allow me to recommend Ms. ana'Tak's cheese—"

"Val Con," Scholar Caylon said.

He turned neatly. "Yes."

Scholar Caylon raised her head, her expression calm; the faint edge of satire that Father usually brought to that exact expression entirely absent.

"You have been on board *Bechimo*?"

"I have," Val Con answered, "and fortunate I was to have escaped with my life."

"Did you examine the drive settings?"

"Alas. I fear I was on my very best behavior, having given my sister, your foster-daughter, my word."

Scholar Caylon inclined her head with complete seriousness.

"I commend you."

Val Con bowed a bow Theo thought might not be exactly as respectful as it looked.

"I wonder," Scholar Caylon continued, unruffled, "if you might procure for me a recording of *Bechimo*'s landing at Surebleak Port."

"Certainly. Is there urgency attached?"

"If I could examine that record today, then I may have an answer for Theo before she leaves us."

"Today it shall be, then," Val Con said jauntily. "Is there any other service I might perform for you?"

"Thank you, no." Scholar Caylon smiled, bright and uncomplicated as a daisy. "You are a patient child. I do very much admire the trait, but wonder how you achieved it."

"Ah." Val Con's smile was subtle. "I believe we must lay the blame at Uncle Er Thom's feet, who was, so my foster-mother swore, the longest-tempered man in three sectors."

Scholar Caylon tipped her head, eyebrows drawn.

"Which three sectors?"

"Do you know," Val Con answered seriously, "she never said."

Scholar Caylon laughed.

Val Con bowed once more, and left them.

· · · ✸ · · ·

Kamele read the Board's letter for the third time. Satisfied that it granted everything she had asked for, she filed it, leaned back in her chair, and closed her eyes.

"That," she said, perhaps to Phileas, dozing on her lap, "was... easy."

The cat puffered a sleepy purr. Of course it had been easy, that soft rasp implied; who dared stand between Scholar-Administrator Kamele Waitley and that which the Scholar-Administrator desired?

She half laughed. Jen Sar had been in the habit of concocting conversational gambits, and occasional amusing setdowns, on behalf of the cats. She had been pleased to style it a harmless male eccentricity, considerably less annoying than similarly petty habits adopted by the *onagrata* of some of her acquaintance. It seemed, however, that the cats insisted on their rights, and in Jen Sar's absence, she had become the voice of their often outrageous opinions.

"Still," she said to Phileas, "they might have been a bit more obstructive. I would have been equal to a battle."

In fact, she would have welcomed a warm battle of protocols, and just like the Board to disoblige her, granting her application for academic leave without so much as a request for confirmation of her years of service.

"I suppose my colleagues have been gossiping even more loudly than usual."

And how could they not? Her household arrangement had been for many years of general interest. First, her choice of an *onagrata*—he so much her elder, in years and in honors—who routinely turned down offers to become attached to much more senior and honored women, in order to sit as housefather to a mere professor in a minor field. Add to that very nearly *irregular* relationship a daughter known campus-wide for her . . . odd ways, and one could scarcely fail to be an oft-revisited topic.

Theo's successes off-world in a trade that very few scholars understood had placed her outside of gossip. Even Kamele's continued, strange, but not quite anti-social, preference for the company of one man had become, by dint of long standing, almost . . . usual.

Until *he* left *her*.

Suddenly, all the old gossip was new again—especially as she was now a wealthy and propertied woman. Such things were outside the notice of scholars, of course, but—grist for the mill, and sauce for the goose, nonetheless.

And, now, the Board's quick approval of her request . . .

"I do believe I'm emotionally fragile," Kamele told Phileas, "and must be treated with care. It may be that the Board thinks I'm going to take treatment."

The cat sighed, opining that the Board's delusions made no matter, so long as Kamele was free to do as she wished.

After a few more moments of frowning consideration, Kamele was inclined to agree.

THIRTY-TWO

. . . .

Jelaza Kazone
Surebleak

"GOOD EVENING, THEO. YOU LOOK CHARMING."

She turned carefully, minding the long hem, and bowed to Boss Conrad, her cousin Pat Rin, Quin's father. He smiled and bowed back, utterly at ease in his pretty ruffled shirt and tight black pants. The ballroom lights struck glints of red from the depths of his dark hair.

"We have been so hectic down in the city that I have not yet made the two of you known to each other."

The lady he brought forward was dressed in what appeared to be a quantity of diaphanous scarves patterned in bronze and green, draped in a way that bared shapely brown shoulders.

"Theo, here is Inas Bhar, called Natesa, who does me the very great honor of sharing her life. Natesa, here is Uncle Daav's daughter, of whom I told you, my cousin Theo Waitley."

"Theo Waitley, I am very pleased to meet you." Her bow was sweet; her voice low and supple.

Okay, this was Quin's "foster-mother," as he had it, and seemed more than a little nervous about sharing a house with her.

Theo could see why he was worried—hadn't she given herself a headache and a stomachache, too, worrying that Kamele might take an *onagrata* in Father's place?

Natesa now . . . She was, Theo thought, definitely a pilot, with an undefinable edge of *something else*. Maybe she was a Scout, too.

239

Carefully, she returned Natesa's bow, counting, like Quin had taught her, so she didn't seem rushed or rude.

"Natesa, I'm pleased to meet you, too," she answered, and looked again to Pat Rin. "Quin's been a big help to me," she said. "He and Padi made sure I learned the dances, and he's been helping me with my bows."

"Yes," Pat Rin said. "He mentioned how very much he has been enjoying your time together."

That was probably a reach. In fact, it had been Theo's distinct impression that Quin had been under orders the night of her arrival to make sure she'd survived her first encounter with Lady Kareen. Afterward, there had been a whole bunch of stuff that she'd needed to be brought up to speed with, so as not to dishonor the House or annoy his grandmother. Quin had continued on the job, Padi sitting copilot, that being how the two of them had stood with each other during their time "enclosed by safety."

"I hope we will have the felicity of seeing you dance this evening," Pat Rin said, bringing her back to the present. "For now, I ask that you excuse us so that we may greet our other guests."

"Please, don't stint the guests on my account," Theo said, stepping back with the slight inclination of the upper body that Padi insisted was polite and necessary when parting from someone whom duty called. "Natesa, I hope to have a chance to speak with you again, at greater length."

"That would be a pleasure," the other woman said, bending her sleek head briefly as she passed by on Pat Rin's arm, the two of them on course for the depths of the room, leaving Theo to relax into her place near the interior door.

Previously, Theo had only known the ballroom as a wide, high-ceilinged chamber admirably suited for bowli ball. Unfortunately, Mr. pel'Kana had ruled that all such exertions be performed either outside on clement days, or in the gymnasium, which boasted, among other niceties, a high ceiling, no windows, a good springy floor, and lightly padded walls. That being so, the ballroom had largely been off of Theo's screens until yesterday, when work crews appeared and began hanging draperies on the rods along the walls, creating small private spaces where those who didn't care to dance could talk with friends, or be alone out of the crowd for a few minutes.

And the ballroom did contain a crowd. She'd arrived promptly, escorted by Anthora and Ren Zel, only to find that two dozen guests had already been admitted.

"Surebleak society is eager to embrace us," Ren Zel said so softly that Theo wasn't certain that he meant it as a joke.

"Theo, from this point, we two must go forth as hosts," Anthora murmured. "Will you accompany us, and welcome the House's guests?"

"I'm a guest myself," she'd pointed out, with a sudden longing to be back in the upstairs apartment that had become familiar and comfortable over the last few days. "I told Padi and Quin I'd wait for them," she added, which was perfectly true.

"Then we will take our leave for the moment," Anthora said.

Ren Zel gave her one of his quiet smiles.

"Please, do not deprive us of your company for long," he said. "I very much hope to dance with you."

There wasn't much dancing going on at the moment. Mostly people were milling around, talking to each other, or just staring about the room, like the pretty curtains and the flowers and the refreshment table set over in its own alcove were all artifacts from another world.

. . . which, she thought abruptly, they were.

Unsettled, she stood at her vantage and watched the room. Occasionally, she'd see Anthora, or the flutter of Natesa's scarves, but almost everybody else in the room was taller than her—there! Shan had just entered the room from somewhere in the back, and was talking to a man in what looked to be a lab coat, while Priscilla walked deeper into the room, catching the arm of a lady in a handsome crimson vest, like they were old friends.

On average, Theo thought, the House's guests were shabbier than the family. She wondered if she was the only one who noticed that, or if some of the guests did and it made them feel inferior. And if it did make them feel inferior, had that been Val Con's intent? Quin and Padi had said that the dance was to show Clan Korval's commitment to Surebleak and to their contract, but Quin and Padi were *kids*. They might not have the whole story. Val Con did things in *layers*. The top layer of this party might really be to show the Bosses of Surebleak that Clan Korval was committed to the contract to hold the Port Road open.

The second, third, and—who knew?—fourth layers were probably about other things entirely.

What would they be? she wondered, absently watching the crowd. Across the room, a tow-headed man wearing steel-rimmed eyeglasses stopped to talk to Pat Rin.

Could one layer of intended message be *We're stronger than you are*? Theo wondered. That could also make the Bosses feel inferior, but in a way that might increase the safety of Clan Korval, if the guests took away the idea that the House and those in it were protected in ways they couldn't hope to subvert.

Speaking of which, there was Nelirikk, Miri's aide, who had been so busy on the Road that she'd only seen him once since their first meeting. He was strolling around the edge of the room, like he was looking for one person in particular.

"Good evening, Theo. Does the entertainment not amuse you?"

A voice familiar to her lifelong, and she couldn't have said at the moment if she heard it now with trepidation or pleasure.

She turned, saw at a glance that the sharp-faced gentleman in formal evening clothes *was indeed* Father, smiled, and shook her head.

He paused, one eyebrow up. "Am I denied?"

Back on Delgado, before Daav yos'Phelium and Aelliana Caylon had entered her life and made one of the bedrocks of the universe uncertain, that question would have been a joke.

This evening... Father's voice was absolutely neutral, and he stood as if he were poised to step away.

"Not denied," she said, careful in her turn. "I was... amazed at myself, for being able to tell that I was speaking to, to my father. And that I accept that you could have been someone else."

"Ah." He stepped to her side. "Pilots may see any number of odd and unexplainable things port to port," he commented. "Best to begin cultivating a certain ennui at home, where one's kin can assist you at need."

"However, as we are on the subject of someone else," he continued, glancing past her to the room, before meeting her eyes, "Aelliana begs me to inform you that she believes what you are seeing is not a new system of Jump, but a much finer control of standard Jump than has been previously observed. She would, at some time agreeable to yourself and to *Bechimo*, like to examine the drive settings. In the meanwhile, I believe she is designing her own model."

"It was very good of her to take the time," Theo said. She

hesitated, but, after all, Father was acting as if Scholar Caylon were in another room of the house, and had asked him to carry a message. Therefore . . .

"Please thank her for . . . the gift of her expertise."

Father inclined his head. "I will do so. Your cousins, may I say, have had an influence. Now, if we may return to my original question—how is it that I find you dawdling in a corner rather than availing yourself of the entertainment?"

"I was watching the people for entertainment, and waiting for Padi and Quin," Theo told him. "I was also trying to figure out why Val Con is doing this."

"Did he not say? To assure the Bosses—"

"—that Clan Korval would honor the contract to hold the Port Road," Theo finished. "He did say that. He also told me that he wished I would come to the house instead of staying on Port because I would be better protected here. And he came on-board when *Bechimo* didn't want to have anything to do with anybody named yos'Phelium and he won the argument about whether I should come to the house before it became an argument by putting *Bechimo* in touch with Jeeves."

Father raised an eyebrow. "You provide these examples to demonstrate that your brother has methods?"

Theo eyed him. "Aunt Ella used to say that you always got your way."

"Being fond of hyperbole, I fear that Ella may have overstated the case. Matters did not *always* fall out as I wished."

"But you tried to manage it so they did."

"Certainly. Why should my comfort not count? However, as delm, I believe that Val Con has a scope denied to mere senior faculty."

Theo shook her head again, and looked out over the room. She saw Lady Kareen moving among the guests, and Luken bel'Tarda, along with several people bearing trays of glasses or of little plates.

"Where are Val Con and Miri?"

"In the entrance hall, greeting the House's guests, I should think. May I fetch you a glass of wine before I wade into the crush to do my duty?"

"I'll be fine," she told him. "Thank you."

"You are very welcome. I hope you will not tarry on the edges all evening."

"If there's ever music, Pat Rin and Ren Zel have both said they'd like a dance."

"That's put me on my mettle! Will you save a dance for me, Daughter?"

She blinked, tears suddenly and unaccountably pricking her eyes.

"Yes," she said, and gave him what she hoped was a firm smile. "I'd like that."

· · · ❄ · · ·

"Congratulations, Lady yos'Phelium, on a splendid crush."

Miri saw the ripple that signaled a joke inside her head, and squinted at her lifemate.

"That's supposed to be mean something, is it?"

He smiled and offered his arm, which she was only too grateful to take.

"To have one's entertainment declared a *crush* by one of the Acknowledged Hostesses of Liad was to be assured that in future everyone would flock to your parties."

"Good thing we're not on Liad, then, ain't it, and no Acknowledged Hostesses on hand."

"It is for a number a reasons good that we are no longer of Liad, I agree. As for our opportunity to gain the approbation of an expert—there you are out. Aunt Kareen, after all, ranked as one of the Hostesses."

"Why don't that surprise me? Should I go ask her opinion?"

"No need. I am certain that she will give it freely on the morrow."

Miri sighed, gently, and again, as the first strains of music lilted down the hall.

"So, we lead the first dance?"

Val Con looked down at her.

"If you are willing, a few steps, then we will find you a place to sit where you may survey the merriment and be admired for your beauty and wit."

Miri snorted. "Regular art object, that's me."

Abruptly, he changed course, steering them to the side of the hall. She leaned against the wall and looked up into his face.

"*Cha'trez...*" he murmured, and she shivered with the intensity of his concern. "Have Nelirikk—."

"He's on security."

"Thus keeping you secure falls within his duty."

They'd been through this. It wasn't like she wasn't worried, too, with him roaming the crowd, and the pretty white shirt not so much to have between himself and tragedy. But—

"They been after *things*, not people. Been real careful not to hurt people, ain't that how we read it?"

Val Con sighed.

"We did."

"So, we play it like we said, and see what happens. I'll be extra eyes from the side floor. Trust me to sing out, too, if something looks funny."

"I have no more certain trust."

The pure thrust of truth that came with that was enough to take her breath.

"The question before us," he continued, joking, now, "is whether you trust me to lead you in the *volentra*."

She grinned.

"Sure, let's go show 'em how it's done."

THIRTY-THREE

. . . .

History of Education Department
Oriel College of Humanities
University of Delgado

"BUT...HOW LONG WILL YOU BE GONE?" ELLA PUT HER CUP down and frowned across the desk at Kamele.

"The Board approved an entire academic year," Kamele answered. "Starting at the end of the current year." She paused, raised her cup, remembered that it was machine coffee and lowered the cup without drinking. "I may need more time, of course, but a year is a good beginning."

"*More* time? Kamele—where, precisely, are you going?"

Kamele sighed. Ella ben Suzan was her oldest friend. They had been students together, shared a toy-sized apartment on the outer quads as newly-robed scholar-instructors; shared everything, really, until Kamele had taken Jen Sar as her *onagrata*.

"I'm going to Surebleak," she told Ella. "It's in the Daiellen Sector."

"Is it?" Ella tapped her mumu and transferred her frown to the screen.

"Not part of the Scholar Base," she said, sounding more puzzled than annoyed.

"I believe there is no university on-planet."

"What?" Ella tapped the mumu again, stared, and looked up. "There's not even a secondary feeder school. As a matter of fact, it's listed as a"—Another tap—"a world in transition?"

"Yes." Kamele leaned forward, holding the disposable cup in both hands. "Surebleak has recently had an influx of—colonists, I suppose they would be. The pressure on the local population and culture must be quite acute—unprecedented. It would make a fascinating study."

"Fascinating and completely out of your field," Ella said, and sighed. "All right, I suppose I should have asked this first—*why* are you going to Surebleak, of all possible places? Why not Valhalla, if you've got a year's leave?"

Valhalla was a resort world. The joking promise of the two of them visiting it—together—had seen them through many late nights grading survey course papers. They had finally made the joke a reality, in celebration of their joint ascension to Scholar Experts.

"Valhalla was all surface and no substance," Kamele said. "*You* remember, Ella."

"I do. After the third day, we were both wanting a library." She fixed Kamele in her eye. "Which doesn't answer my question, Scholar Waitley."

Kamele took a breath and met her friend's gaze firmly.

"I am going to Surebleak because that is where the Delm of Korval is."

"The Delm of Korval," Ella repeated, frowning. "That was a game between Theo and Jen Sar."

"A game based on reality, as I've lately learned from Theo herself."

"And the Delm of Korval is located on Surebleak, which has no discernible educational infrastructure. Not very... accomplished, is she?"

"I don't presume to judge. Until recently, the delm—and the clan—of Korval was seated on Liad. They were exiled by the governing body for acts against the homeworld."

Ella blinked. "So... they're... sociopaths?"

"Possibly. The particular act of aggression for which they were expelled had to do with firing upon the planet and leaving a rather large hole in the surface."

Ella's face softened toward a smile; her friend scented a joke. "Kamele—"

"No," she interrupted and pointed at the mumu. "Look it up. I found that the Trade Guild papers carried the most succinct accounts."

Ella sat for a moment, then bent to her mumu, tapping in the request a bit harder than was strictly necessary.

"While we're waiting for the library to process that," she said, crossing her arms on the desk and leaning forward, "why this sudden desire to meet a genocide?"

There, Kamele thought, they had arrived at last at the difficult part. She took a deep breath, put the disposable cup of cold coffee on the edge of Ella's desk, and looked directly into her friend's face.

"Jen Sar Kiladi is a pilot for the Delm of Korval," she said, her voice absolutely level.

"According to whom?"

"According to Theo, who further informs me that he has no plans to return to Delgado."

"Well, why should he return to Delgado? He's not an idiot; he has to know that his career is dead. A little unsteadiness in male behavior can be overlooked. But to *vanish*, papers ungraded, committee work undone, without requesting permission or even telling Admin that he was resigning his chair—that's not unsteady, that's dangerously erratic."

"Possibly it is. Yet I never knew Jen Sar to be either unsteady or erratic. This sudden, disordered flight is completely unlike him."

"No," Ella said sharply. "Kamele, it is *entirely* like him!"

Kamele took a deep breath to cool the spark of irritation. Ella and Jen Sar had not been friends, though he had been more circumspect in his dislike. And Ella had not, Kamele reminded herself, been fortunate enough to have shared daily life with Jen Sar; she could not be expected to know him as well as Kamele did.

"In fact," she said levelly, "it is not. I never knew him to stint any formality."

"Except when he had a point to make," Ella answered tartly.

That was, Kamele thought, fair. Jen Sar had never held shy from achieving what he termed "Balance," a form of Liaden social engineering.

"It's difficult for me to imagine that he had any . . . *point to make* with his students," she said carefully, "And even if he had considered that Admin had grievously overstepped, he is not, as you said, an idiot. He would know very well that an unannounced withdrawal from the university would harm his colleagues and his students far more than it would inconvenience Admin."

She shook her head. "No, I think that something else happened; that, given his choice, Jen Sar would have been . . . more orderly in his withdrawal—or not have left us at all."

"Given his *choice*?" Ella stared, then abruptly stood and came around the desk. She bent down and gathered Kamele's hands into hers.

"Kamele, I don't want to hurt you, but you have to give over this...delusion. Jen Sar is gone; he *left you.* Completely irregular, if not antisocial—but, either road, a clear indication that he considers his role as your *onagrata*...finished. It may be the truest statement he ever made, while he was on this planet. Allow him that last gesture of truth and—and dignity. You're an accomplished woman in the prime of your life. Your honors are laurels upon the brow of this university, as even Admin admits! Take your year, since it's been granted, pursue your own work. Rest. Your absence will give Admin opportunity to reflect on the fact that the lack of your insight lessens the effectiveness of its programs, and to miss your energy and courage. You will return to acclaim, and increased honors. You will take an *onagrata* who reflects your standing, which will silence the gossipers." Her fingers tightened around Kamele's. "You need a change of venue—that, I agree. But you *do not* need Jen Sar Kiladi."

It was rational, what Ella said. Jen Sar himself, Scholar Expert of Cultural Genetics that he was, would have agreed that she argued only proper behavior, as it was parsed on Delgado. And yet...

Gently, Kamele withdrew her hands from Ella's. The other woman sagged back against the desk, shaking her head.

"What you see as a pattern of untruth," Kamele said, holding Ella's eyes with hers, "I see as reticence; an unwillingness to speak of a perhaps painful past. Within the boundaries of our relationship, and as Theo's role-male, he was as true as anyone I've known." She leaned forward to touch Ella's wrist. "As *anyone* I've known."

Her friend moved her free hand, wordlessly.

"I've been reading a good bit of anthropology lately," Kamele said after a moment. She smiled, briefly. "Not my field, but fascinating. Liadens are very closely attached to their clans; the delm acts as chair and holds absolute authority. If a delm calls a clan member home, or reassigns them, mid-task, there is no question that the clan member will obey. To disobey means social repercussions. Serious social repercussions."

Ella frowned. "So Jen Sar is a...member of the Korval clan?"

Kamele shook her head. "No, Kiladi isn't listed as being a member...Line, as they're called."

"Then—"

"Wait." Kamele raised her hand and shook her head. "Wait. My research failed to uncover any current clan to which Line Kiladi was attached. There was, however, a hint that perhaps that clan had been...disbanded, at some point. When that happens, I learned, the members made homeless are sometimes attached—formally or informally—to another clan.

"When he was a young man, Jen Sar was a pilot. The Delm of Korval has a specific interest in pilots. It is possible, at least as a working thesis, that the Delm of Korval attached Jen Sar, offering place and protection in exchange for the obedience required of a full clan member. In light of recent troubles, the Delm of Korval may well have called every pilot to her hand to assist the clan. Including Jen Sar Kiladi."

"Who would have found some way to wiggle out of it, if he'd wanted to stay," Ella said, not quite steadily. "Jen Sar never did anything he didn't want to do."

Kamele nodded, and swallowed. The next step in her reasoning was difficult. And, yet...

"Threats may have been made," she said; the experience of many years of teaching keeping her voice steady. "He may have no plans to return to Delgado because he is held hostage by the Delm of Korval.

"And that is why I am going to Surebleak. I *will speak* to Jen Sar Kiladi, and I will—I will work to achieve his parole, if that is what he wishes."

THIRTY-FOUR

Jelaza Kazone
Surebleak

MIRI AND VAL CON DANCED LIKE THEY WERE ONE PERSON, WITH no hesitation, or fumbling between steps; there were no missed signals, or quick corrections, only a seamless flow of intent and execution.

Theo's chest ached, watching them. To understand somebody that well; to trust—to *know*—that their hand would be *exactly there* to meet yours when you finished your spin, so that there was no need for even the slightest glance...

It was a small dance—the *volentra*, Padi and Quin had called it, when they were teaching her the steps—the "*hello dance.*" Miri and Val Con danced it with obvious delight, light-footed and playful as they retreated, spun, clasped hands, and drew close.

Small and simple as it was, they danced alone for the first section, as if the whole room were mesmerized, hardly daring to breathe, much less join them on the floor.

Then Pat Rin stepped into the dance square, Natesa on his arm. Luken led out a buxom, jolly lady whose face was older than her hair, followed by Priscilla and the lady in the red vest. A black-haired woman escorted the bespectacled man with fair hair Pat Rin had been talking to out onto the floor, and grinned a challenge up into his face. He grinned back and threw his hand out, she caught it and they were dancing—pretty well, Theo thought, for non-pilots.

"Theo! Did you forget how to dance the *volentra*?"

She turned to frown at Padi, who was wearing a high-necked dark green dress that showed off her pale hair, and *not* the red-and-gold brocade with the deep neckline that she'd claimed from House stores. Theo hadn't *thought* that one would get past Lady Kareen.

"Of course I haven't forgotten the *volentra*!"

"Then why are you just standing here? It's time to dance!"

Padi grabbed her hand and pulled her toward the floor, and perforce Theo went, minding the long skirt that wanted to tangle her feet.

"Here!" Padi released her and dropped back two steps, flinging out her hand, taking the lead.

Theo shook her hair back and retreated, the hem that had been bedevilling her suddenly flowing with her movements, as much a part of her as her own two legs. She'd practiced the steps enough with Padi to be reasonably certain of the location of her cousin's hand when she finished her spin, and she resisted the pull-in just enough to get a grin and an acknowledging step forward—acceptable variations to the dance, which wasn't so much about the steps as it was about the intent of coming together in good will.

The *volentra* ended. Partners fell apart or came closer together. A movement caught the edge of Theo's eye, and she turned her head to watch Val Con escort Miri to a chair at the edge of the floor, and bend over to say something into her ear that made her laugh.

"May I claim my dance, Theo?"

Ren Zel was at her elbow, and Padi was already soliciting the hand of a new partner from those paused on the floor.

Theo smiled, wanting nothing more than to dance again, now that she had danced once.

"Yes!" she said, maybe a little too positively, and took his hand just as the band swung into a *kaprian*.

She danced with Pat Rin, and with Thera Kalhoon. Peripherally, she was aware of other family members on the floor, and others, circulating among those who chose not to dance. She saw Father, talking to the gilt-haired lady who had danced with Luken, and Val Con, moving among the guests with the apparent intent of saying at least a few words to everyone present.

The band leader announced that they would play one more selection before they took a break, and promised a line dance when they reconvened.

"This, then," said a familiar voice at her shoulder, "would appear to be my last opportunity."

She spun, laughing. Father bowed.

"I have come to redeem my promise," he said, and held out his hand, the lace falling smoothly away from his wrist.

Theo put her hand in his.

The intro line began—and Father's eyebrows went up.

"Now, who called for that?" he murmured. "You may excuse me, Theo; certainly you do not wish to dance the *presta* with your father."

She shook her hair back and grinned at him.

"I've never danced with you," she said, "not once. And you're the reason I dance at all. No, I'm not going to excuse you."

"So, then." The grin he gave back to her was sharp. He moved his hand in an upward twist, hers following, so that their fingers were joined and the inside of their wrists pressed together, waiting...

And the music began.

The *presta* started slow, with a treble circle, as if the dancers were opponents, sizing each other up, instead of partners in a joint effort. It then moved into a series of sharp steps, done not quite at arm's length, then a disengage, and full turn.

They were dancing near the edge of the floor. As Theo turned, she saw Miri coming out of her chair, fast, twisting; a man abruptly airborne—

A woman screamed, someone shouted, there was a crash, another shout—

Theo spun out of the dance square, dropping into an entirely different dance pattern, and Miri was on her feet, crimson staining her pale gold sleeve, the man she had thrown rolling, finding his feet in a scramble. Theo moved in opposition, meaning to keep him from Miri at any price, and suddenly there was Val Con—Theo had never seen a man move so fast, or with such focused violence.

He hit Miri's attacker before the other man was completely centered, striking him chest-high, bearing him backward, slamming him into the wall and holding him there with both hands around his throat.

From the back of the room came another scream, a curse, the sound of a scuffle and sudden silence, but Theo couldn't look away from Val Con, who was set for murder, the man he was holding clawing at his hands, and from behind a "Death to outworlders!" another crash, and—

"Val Con," Miri said, sounding breathless, looking pale. "I ain't broke."

If he heard her, he gave no sign, and the man he was holding was crying now, and his movements seemed not so—robust.

"Val Con." Father stepped forward, raising a hand without looking, fingers flashing two name-signs, summoning—Nelirikk Explorer, it was, with Natesa at his side.

Father put his hand gently on Val Con's shoulder, just like he wasn't slowly strangling somebody.

"The moment is past, child. Release him to the Judge's custody."

It seemed to Theo that Val Con shivered. She saw his fingers relax, just a little.

"Miri." His voice was hoarse.

"I'm good, Boss. Let Nelirikk have him."

The big man stepped forward. Val Con released his victim. Father caught his wrist, pulling him back and slipping an arm around his shoulders, murmuring, "Peace, now; all's well..." just like he'd done when she was a littlie and had gotten herself knotted up in a temper.

The man who had attacked Miri was on his knees, retching. Nelirikk grabbed him by the back of the collar and hauled him to his feet. The room was so quiet you could've heard a feather strike, as Kara used to say.

"Okay, Theo, you can stand down, too." Miri said softly from her side. "'Preciate the backup—quick and on point."

Suddenly there were people along the edge of the dance floor— the pilots Theo had seen circulating earlier, Thera Kalhoon's fair-haired husband, the lady in the crimson vest, Padi, Quin, and Luken bel'Tarda—a living curtain, cutting them off from the view of the guests.

"Well done," Father was telling Val Con. "Come now to your lady and assure yourself that she is well."

Beyond the curtain of people, Theo saw Pat Rin walk into the center of the dance floor, raising his voice to be heard at the back of the room.

"There has been an unfortunate incident. Matters are now in hand. Please, join us for dinner, where we will all regain our good humor."

· · · ✵ · · ·

"You're bleeding!" Theo cried, snapping forward. Inside her head, Miri saw Val Con's pattern flare red.

"No, I ain't," she said, holding out the arm so they could both get a look. "I had a cup of the redberry juice Melina Sherton brought in for me, and I dropped it when he grabbed me. Damn waste. And the dress, too."

"Damn the dress," Val Con said clearly, stepping out from under Daav's arm and grabbing her shoulders, not exactly gentle, either, so he knew she wasn't hurt, even if he was still coming down from terrified.

"Didn't I just say so?" She sagged, so that he had most of her weight in his hands, and then leaning against him, in a hug.

"You were right," she said, putting her arms around his waist. "I should've had Beautiful. I guess seeing me just sitting there all alone an' vulnerable give him a new idea."

"Wait..." That was Theo, sounding shell-shocked, poor kid. "You *knew* somebody was going to attack you?" Miri pushed her forehead into Val Con's shoulder, feeling cold and shivery.

"*Cha'trez?*"

"Adrenaline," she muttered. "Pat Rin got everything under control?"

"He was herding everyone in to dinner," Daav said, "which ought to answer for now. In the meanwhile, I assume that the household *dramliz* are moving among the guests with an eye toward preventing a sequel after the guests have dined?"

"Anthora had already picked up two—accomplices, I must suppose them, now," Val Con said over her head. "But with so many people..."

"Dreadfully noisy, I understand. May I suggest that we remove to another part of the house, and allow the servants to clean up?"

"Good idea," Miri said. "I wanna get out of this dress. And Theo asked a question that deserves an answer."

· · · ✵ · · ·

"... so we decided between us," Val Con continued, "that we would expand the guest list to include not only the Bosses, but those at the next level down, who would have access to particular information, and so net our revolutionaries before they became more than a nuisance."

They were in what appeared to be a game and reading room, judging by the comfortable shabbiness of the furniture. Miri had stepped behind a carved screen with the robe produced by a female pilot Theo had never seen before, who had left with promises of sending a tray.

Father had draped himself, boneless as a cat, on a flowered chaise, one leg stretched out, the other foot in its dancing slipper braced on the floor. Val Con had a hip on the wide arm of a double chair, one foot on the floor, the other on the chair's rung. There was a smear of pink on his white shirt, from Miri's hug. Either of them could be up, centered, and moving in less time than it would take to think about. The room was deep inside the house. They were as safe as possible, and not likely to see another attack. Despite that, and the fact that there were plenty of chairs available, Theo couldn't have sat down for anything less than lift. She stood in the more or less center of the room, quivering with adrenaline; staring at her brother in disbelief.

"You *deliberately invited* dangerous people into your house, knowing that they might hurt somebody?"

"No, hey, Theo..." Miri came out from behind the screen, running her fingers through her unbraided hair. "They never tried to hurt anybody before this—and they had plenty of chances. They always stuck to breaking up toys and unbuilding things that had been built." She curled into the double chair and patted Val Con companionably on the hip.

"We're not complete newbies," she went on. "We had people watching the room—you saw 'em. Plus, we had Anthora and Ren Zel and Shan and Priscilla looking into heads or at invisible strings or whatever it is the four of 'em look at. It should've been—I ain't gonna say *safe*, 'cause there ain't nothin' such—but it shouldn't have been *dangerous*." She sighed.

"If you want it straight, what happened was my fault. Seeing me sitting there alone and what he might've read as vulnerable put a whole new idea in his head, is how I'm reading it. He could have a hostage—*leverage*—and it was just too good. If he'd thought it out, he'd've seen it wasn't gonna do anything but increase *his* vulnerability, but he's not a pro. Not by a long walk, he ain't. If I'd've thought he was dangerous, I'd've killed him myself, instead of just throwing him, and scaring Val Con outta two nights' sleep."

Just throwing him, Theo thought, like grabbing a man twice her mass, who had come up on her from behind, and flipping him onto his back wasn't anything much, while her lifemate across the room—

Theo turned back to Val Con. "I've never seen anybody move so fast. How—"

He shook his head. "Necessity. Also, this link we have is not always...convenient. I received Miri's distress, as she received mine—"

"And so a feedback loop was born," Father murmured from his comfortable lounge on the chaise.

"Yeah," Miri said. "We ain't good at this yet."

Father laughed.

Theo spun, temper sparking. "You think this is *funny*?"

He lifted his eyebrows. "Acquit me—the crimson sleeve was not comic in any way. However, the naïve supposition that one will become proficient..." He inclined his head in Miri's direction. "That has a certain humorous value."

"But you agree with what they did?" Theo persisted, even as she wondered why she was angry at *Father*. "You *knew* about this?"

"Certainly, I knew about the general sabotage, and one only needs to take a walk in the city to understand that the arrival of offworlders—of *so many* offworlders—has awakened a certain amount of dismay among the indigenous population. As the party was already in place—initially for that first level reason you were wondering after earlier, Theo—it made sense to do exactly what was done: expand both the guest list and security and try to isolate the motivating agent, and his associates, if any, in controlled conditions. I might well have done the same thing, noting that none of the House is an idiot."

"We really were having a party to show the home folk that we're serious about the contract and about Surebleak," Miri said. "And Thera Kalhoon—you danced with her, Theo—"

"I remember," she said shortly, recalling the cheerful lady who had danced pretty good, though she wouldn't ever be a pilot.

"Right. First thing outta Thera's mouth almost when we met, was that people here need to remember how to be civil again, to meet and be social and to work together. Civilized."

"And," Val Con murmured, "since this House has arguably just arrived from the most civilized planet in the galaxy, who better to lead the way?"

"Now, there sits a lad who has properly listened to the lessons of his aunt," Father said. He waggled a languid finger in Val Con's general direction.

"If I may, and speaking to Theo's point—what has apparently not been put into place are the emergency drills, so that those of the House who were present would have known what to do in the case of just such an attack. As it went, it went well..."

"Better'n it could have," Miri agreed. "Theo—I don't think I said—good reactions; you did everything right. Didn't show no weapons, but there wasn't anybody there doubted that if they wanted to get to me, they was going to have to go through you— and that was gonna be a day and a half's work." She tipped her head. "I just wonder about one thing, though."

Theo looked at her, trying to remember what moves she'd made, and if she could have possibly hurt someone without noticing—

"Hey, I said you did good, didn't I?" Miri waved a hand. "No, what I wondered was—*why* you jumped the way you did."

Worry melted into bafflement. "Why?" she repeated. "You're pregnant."

Miri blinked, which meant she'd said something wrong, Theo thought, but—

"Miri is not native to Delgado," Father murmured into the quiet room. "You will need to unpack it for her, Theo."

Right. Cultural norms—weren't. She knew that.

"You're pregnant," she repeated, and took a breath. "On Delgado, a pregnant woman has—precedence in almost everything. The Safety Office will deploy someone to be with her, on request."

Miri frowned slightly, apparently still working it out.

"So, I'm your brother's wife, and pregnant, so—"

"You're a pregnant woman in your own home!" Theo interrupted angrily. "A pregnant pilot carrying a daughter pilot!"

The anger flared and extinguished itself. Theo jammed her fist against her mouth, hearing the echo of what she'd just said—just *shouted*—knowing it was true. And not knowing how she knew.

Val Con and Father traded glances.

"It is an interesting Sight," Father observed, "if slightly obscure."

Val Con rose; Theo looked at him with trepidation, wondering what taboos she'd just broken.

"Gently," he said, raising a hand in the pilot's sign for *peace*. "Many of us have seen odd things. I only wonder—curiosity, merely—if you are able to explain how you came to that knowledge."

"I can tell if someone's a pilot by looking at them." She cleared her throat. "That's not so strange, is it? You're a Master Pilot; can't you tell if someone's a pilot?"

"Often, yes, I can. But I wonder. If you were confronted with a group of people seated, hands folded, at a table, would you then be able to see the pilots among them?"

She nodded. "Yes, sure. I mean, it's obvious, once you know what to look for."

"And when," came the question from the chaise, "did this ability to see pilots arise, if a father may inquire?"

She turned to look at him, feeling a spark of anger return.

"When I had knowingly *met* pilots."

"Ah. Then that would have been approximately at the time of your trip to Melchiza with Kamele."

"Right. Pilots think in certain ways—" She turned back to Val Con. "You can see it—it's obvious, even sitting still! You could tell, yourself—you could!"

Gently, he signed, and, "Perhaps, if I watched their eyes, or considered their balance as they sat, I might produce results slightly higher than a mere guess. But to know, with complete surety, at a glance—and for an unborn child?" He shook his head, smiling slightly. "My eyes are not so keen."

"The contention that pilots think in certain ways..." Father said. "That might be observed by someone with Sight, surely? Certain connections must be made, by one who has undergone training."

"Perhaps so," Val Con said, "though that begs the question of our daughter's abilities, for surely she has not yet received her first lesson."

"But—you're a pilot," Theo pointed out, "and Miri's a pilot. It's not a reach to assume that your child will be a pilot. And on Delgado"—she glanced at Miri, who gave her an encouraging grin—"on Delgado, all unborn are assumed to be daughters."

"Of course," Val Con said politely.

"There is, after all," Father added, "Kareen."

She looked at him. "Lady Kareen isn't a pilot."

"Yet, she was born of pilots," Val Con said. "We do not always breed true."

"So I might be wrong," Theo said, and spun suddenly at the knock on the door.

"Dinner, I think," Val Con murmured, but it was Father who

rose from the chaise and went to open for the same female pilot and a male, non-pilot, helper, each bearing a tray.

"The table, if you please, gentles," Val Con said. "We will serve ourselves."

The trays disposed, they were alone again. Val Con moved to the table and began to fill a plate. Theo stood aside, not really hungry, not with all the... energy roiling in her belly, and felt a quiet presence at her elbow.

"Father." She turned to look at him. "*When* were you going to tell me?"

He raised an eyebrow.

"When would it have been proper, Child of Delgado, for the *onagrata* of your mother to reveal himself as your gene donor and declare that he expected you to rise into a path scarcely discussed on the planet surface?"

Theo shook her head.

"But—after..."

"After, was—after. You asked my assistance with your math and I gave it. Had you asked Jen Sar Kiladi for details of your parentage beyond himself, that he would not have given you, for he had... willfully forgotten such things."

She stared at him. "Father—"

"However," he swept on, "you mustn't think ill of him. Before— he did what he might, as little as it was, and giving the lie to Ella's assertion of always gaining his own way."

Val Con had taken the plate and a cup over to Miri and gone back to pour a cup of tea.

"The dance lessons," Theo said. "I figured that out later. And the lace-making, too, when I was a littlie."

"The string game?" Val Con looked over to them, green eyes bright.

"A variation," Father said.

"Did you make lace, too?" Theo asked.

Val Con moved his shoulders. "There is a game that we teach our children—a string game; it teaches the ability to see space as a whole and as matrices, and imparts an understanding of the relationship between each."

"A game." Theo looked at him—a pilot who had grown up surrounded by pilots, taught from an early age, and honed to be a pilot.

"There would be games, wouldn't there?" she said. "Math games, and coordination games—bowli ball—"

"Not," Val Con said sharply, "for children. Bowli ball is for those who have learned what pain is, and who have their muscles and their reactions under control."

"And your daughter," Theo pursued, "she won't have to fall down and not know why she's so clumsy."

"I fell down rather often myself when I was a child," Val Con said, sipping his tea. "I could see, you know, what *needed* to be done, but my body was still too unformed to do my mind's bidding."

"And while adults may be vigilant, it is difficult for someone who is years past their first training to always comprehend what may be regarded, and regarded, pursued."

"One more thing that must be said, while we are bringing you to terms with your destiny," Val Con said. "Theo, you must realize and accept that the luck, as we call it, rides roughly around us. As you saw this evening."

"And don't," Miri said suddenly, rising from her chair and bringing her barely diminished plate back to the tray, "don't go believing that what happened was your fault—we invited it in, just like you said."

She looked up at Val Con. "You ain't eating."

"Neither did you."

"Then we'll both be hungry. Time to go change, I'm thinking, and lead another dance."

"I think you are correct."

Miri nodded. "The two of you be smarter than us and at least have a snack, right? Then come on back to the ballroom and help us send up the first line dance. Gotta show our honest guests that everything's fine."

They left, hand in hand, leaving Theo looking at the tray and feeling very far from hungry.

"At least a piece of cheese and a cup of tea," Father murmured. "To give you strength enough to dance."

It was so like him that Theo laughed, and gasped, and suddenly turned to put her hand on his sleeve.

"Father!"

"Yes, Theo?"

"I love you," she said.

His mouth tightened, and he put his hand over hers.

"I will try to be worthy of that, child."

THIRTY-FIVE

. . . .

Runcible System
Daglyte Seam

THE STRIKE AT KORVAL'S HEART HAD FAILED.

Worse, Korval had not killed the native chosen to immolate himself on the fires of political necessity. His capture intact meant the immediate departure of those of the Department who were known to him, and the strategic withdrawal of all agents of the Department on Surebleak.

Korval was on guard now. They would not lay themselves open in such a manner again.

Commander of Agents issued instructions regarding the retraining of the agent who had supervised the failed attempt.

One true strike was all that was required.

Well... they were not yet out of blades.

· · · ✳ · · ·

It must've been eighteen times now he'd had Jellianne's tractor on the rack and it was starting to wear out its welcome. That it ran at all was a marvel; he'd seen more able machines sold for their scrap value on what had been "his" port, back on Liad. Not that he missed Liad, particularly, but it did give a body some perspective on Surebleak.

"Clarence!" that was Mack, yelling in from the doorway. Might be there was some flying to do. That would be welcome, and not only because it would get him out from underneath the blessed tractor.

"Somebody here to see ya!"

No, Clarence thought, putting his wrench down quiet in the tray, and considering that particular note in his boss's voice. No, maybe nothing so welcome as flying. He didn't think Mack would set him up, but Mack, hard, canny man that he was, couldn't know, or see, everything. A man from outworld was bound to have friends and associates from outworld, and none of Mack's business to know who they were, or which were more welcome than others.

Then there was the possibility—slight as it might be—that somebody'd cared enough about Sanella Thring to have mentioned her going missing to somebody else. Not to say that he hadn't made enemies all his own during his time working for the Juntavas. Man who didn't make enemies wasn't doing his job.

"You sleepin' under there?" Mack yelled.

"Give an old man a minute," he called back, fingers locating the palm gun on the tray.

Setting his foot against the floor, he pushed, none too energetically, and the creeper rolled leisurely out from under the tractor's belly. He came up slow onto his feet; heard Mack walking away toward the crew room, nodded to himself and picked a towel up from the top of the tool cart.

Wiping his hands, he walked around the tractor, and stopped cold, staring at the woman waiting for him.

Just a slip of a thing she was, which his years among Liadens had taught him to discount entirely. If the too-big jacket was hers, she was fast, and tough, and stronger than she looked. There was something else, too, a familiarity that went deeper than a mere understanding of the breed. Something that teased his memory while she stared at him with the devil in her eye, a wispy cloud of yellow curls framing a pale, pointed face that was beginning to display a touch of irritation.

"Pardon," he said, not letting go of the rag nor the gun. "Do I know you?"

"*I* don't know *you*," she answered, with emphasis, and it was the voice that did it, or maybe the unspoken dare that he just try to knock that chip off her shoulder, and see how far she could throw him.

"There it is—you're Daav's girl."

The touch of irritation became an active frown. "Does *everybody* on this planet know who my father is?"

"Well, now; a good many'll be knowing him, sure. He likes to move around the port and chat up the pilots. Not his job any more, no more'n it's mine—but some habits're hard to break. As for the rest of the world, I believe it was Himself's plan that the family be known." He gave her a smile, just in case she was of a mind to soften. She wasn't.

"What's your name then?" he asked. "And your business?"

"My name's Theo Waitley," she answered. "I'm looking to hire a copilot. You come . . . highly recommended as a reputable and honest pilot."

Clarence tipped his head, considering the face, and the eyes.

"That'll be your da doing the recommending, I think. He tell you anything else about me?"

"He said you knew how to take orders, and were a handy man in a fight," she said, sounding peevish, and added, "I seem to attract fights."

"Oh, aye, you'll do that. Comes with the turf, like they say hereabouts."

She sighed. "Everybody knows that, too," she commented, and gave him a glare. "I thought you might be a friend of my father's—"

There was a *but* there, hovering on the edge of not-said, and wise she was to doubt it. Clarence grinned and shook his head.

"Friends—well, now, we might could've been, in a different set of circumstances. As it happened, he had his *melant'i*, and I had the business to tend. Say that I set value on him, and still do."

"He obviously values you," she said, almost like she didn't know what Daav yos'Phelium's regard was worth. She sighed and jerked her head toward his hands, that he was still rubbing with the rag.

"Have you decided if you're going to shoot me?"

Her da's sharp eyes, sure enough. Clarence gave her a nod.

"As it happens, I've decided not to shoot you, lassie."

"Good," she said, though there wasn't much easing of her frown. He was beginning to form the theory that the lass was ill-tempered by nature.

"Are you at liberty to be hired?"

"I work here casual," he told her. "You offering long-term?"

"I'd like to introduce you to my ship."

There was an inflection there, too, as he tried to remember which ship on port might be her own—and failed. *Tcha.* His memory was getting old, along with the rest of him.

"Would that be now?" he asked politely.

"If you're at liberty. Otherwise, name the hour and I'll meet you at the Emerald."

Daav must've sung his praises to the polestar, Clarence thought. Or he'd laid down some bit of law that the lassie felt compelled to heed.

"Let me clear it with Mack," he said. "If he's done with me for the day, we can step over to see your boat now."

· · · ❄ · · ·

Clarence O'Berin, Theo thought, wasn't at all what she had expected him to be.

What she *had* expected him to be, she couldn't have said. Like Father, maybe, or like Tranza. Older—that, she *had* expected, and, thinking about it, had figured that having an older man as backup wasn't a bad thing. Lots of experience to call on, and a tendency to weigh before weighing in, where an older woman might tend to force a situation. *Bechimo* being the ship he was, they were *all* going to need to keep a low profile.

Or, at least, as low as possible.

Which led her thoughts right back to the man walking alert and quiet beside her. A dangerous man, no doubt. Yet not out of control. He'd had the hideaway tucked in his palm when he came out from behind the tractor, but he'd waited, measured the situation, and made his decision rationally and calmly.

That was good.

What was . . . somewhat worrying was the fact that Clarence O'Berin felt it necessary to arm himself to meet a casual caller at his place of employment.

If he was not only dangerous, but *hunted* . . .

. . . that didn't make him any different, did it, than *Bechimo*.

Or her.

"Here we are," she said, leading the way up the gantry.

"I thought your da told me you was for courier," Clarence said from behind her.

"I was," she said. "But things—got complicated."

"Things do tend in that direction, more often than not. Taken note of it myself."

Theo took a breath, and paused, key in hand, but not yet quite willing to trigger the hatch. She'd told *Bechimo* that she had a recommendation for a crewman, another pilot, who would sit second until the Less Pilot was himself again. *Bechimo* had been—call it cautiously excited—and inquired after the pilot's name—to check against his lists, Theo supposed.

Not too very long after receiving it, he said that he would be pleased to have Pilot O'Berin brought aboard for a tour, adding that he would in the interim research the pilot's background.

That was good and prudent. She'd researched Clarence O'Berin herself, to the extent of pulling his Guild records and finding that his flying had been sparse for about as long as she'd been alive. Father had explained that his employment had tied him to port, but that he'd started his career as a courier pilot and, now he was retired, he wanted to reclaim his wings.

"If you're having second thoughts, Pilot, I can turn and walk off now." His voice was even—too even, Theo thought suddenly, like she might say it, to cover a hurt.

"No problem," she said brusquely. "Both of my parents were professors; I get the habit of staring into nothing from them." She pressed the key home and the hatch rose.

"*Bechimo* was built as a loop ship," she said, guiding Clarence O'Berin to the piloting chamber.

"They don't much do that anymore," he commented, which was only true, and a subtle way to let her know that he knew that there hadn't been a ship built with lines like *Bechimo*'s for hundreds of years, if then.

"I hope you don't mind an older ship," she said, to let him know that she'd heard him on both levels.

"She seems comfortable and took care of," he answered. "I'd like to see the maintenance logs and suchlike, if that's allowed."

It was Guild rule that a pilot under consideration for a command chair, which *Bechimo*'s copilot certainly was, was allowed access to maintenance logs and ship's record. If access was denied, the pilot could walk, with any talking money still in his pocket, and the Guild would back him. She'd told *Bechimo* that a Guild pilot would want to see those records; he'd assured her that there would be no problem.

And if there was, then Clarence O'Berin would walk, and she'd've learned something else about her ship.

"I'll call those up, if you'd like to see them now," she said, moving to the pilot's chair.

Clarence O'Berin stood just to her right, between the stations, hands tucked into the pockets of his jacket, reminding her suddenly and vividly of Father when he had come aboard the *Toss*.

"Bide a bit," he said, his quick eyes on the arrangement of the copilot's board and screens. "You've got yourself a looper—" He glanced away from his study long enough to offer her a smile. "Now, what I'm wonderin' is—do you have yourself a loop?"

Theo nodded. "Shan—Master Trader yos'Galan—designed a mid-loop, and has hired this ship to run it once, complete. Since it's a new loop, the pilots are asked to gather info—there's a bonus for that. Standard three-way split for bonuses—one share to each pilot, one share to the ship."

Clarence nodded, thoughtfully, but didn't say anything else, like he thought she wasn't done yet, which, now that she considered it, she wasn't.

"Before we take up the loop, we have a cargo transfer in Surebleak near-orbit. I'm waiting for word now on the specific rendezvous and time."

He nodded again. "What're we swapping?"

We. Theo didn't know whether the funny feeling in her stomach was relief or regret. Still, the man deserved an answer—

"We're swapping the courier ship in *Bechimo*'s hold for the pilot who holds the key to second board."

A flash of blue in her direction, like maybe he was having second thoughts about his *we*, but all he said was, "Who?"

"Crystal Energy Consultants."

Clarence O'Berin threw back his grey head and laughed.

Theo felt a flicker of irritation. "Is that funny?"

"No, now, lassie, don't look black death at me! How d'ye happen to have one of the Uncle's ships in your hold, if you don't mind sayin'?"

"I was contracted to Crystal Energy Consultants as a courier pilot," she said, trying to keep her voice even and not sound like she was annoyed. "The *Toss* was my ship."

"Then this fine lady come along and you decided to be your own woman. Fair enough. And the pilot we're receiving in exchange? Seems to me if that one holds second key, there's no need to be tempting port pickup pilots with visions of testing out a new loop for Korval."

He was upset, Theo thought, having given that *we* and now

thinking that she was pushing it away. She shook her head, fingers rising to sign, *steady, complex,* and *short form.*

"The pilot who holds second key was...captured by people who wanted to gain possession of this ship. He refused to guide them to *Bechimo*, or—or to me, and for that he was tortured and...badly damaged. He's dying—but *maybe* the healing unit on this ship can do the necessary repairs." She gave him her best imitation of Father's most opaque stare. "It's an old ship, and it carries some...non-standard tech."

Clarence waited, watching her.

"He might—I gathered, as far as Uncle knows, and he's the closest thing to an expert I have on this—Win Ton might be a long time healing, if he doesn't die instead. In the meantime, this ship is under contract to Tree-and-Dragon to test the master trader's new route. I need—backup. I attract trouble. I need a copilot who's capable and smart, who knows when to stay on the ship and keep the hatch closed, and when to set the ship as backup and come down on the ground to sort things out."

He didn't say anything or move a muscle for a long count of three, then he sighed, took his hands out of his pockets, and stepped over to the copilot's chair.

"A smart ship's a real benefit to a pilot," he said, settling in. "I value a smart ship." He raised his voice slightly. "You hear that, Ship?"

Theo held her breath.

"I hear that, Pilot O'Berin."

"Good. What'm I to call you?"

"*Bechimo.* How shall I address you?"

"Clarence'll do it."

Theo sighed out the breath she'd been holding.

"*Bechimo*, please provide Clarence with ship's log and maintenance records."

"Yes, Pilot."

She touched certain tabs, bringing up the copilot's contract Ms. dea'Gauss had written for her, spelling out duties, pay, and shares.

"Sending to your Three screen," she said quietly, "Clarence."

It didn't take him long to vet the logs, though he lingered over the contract before setting his thumb against the plate with a sigh.

"dea'Gauss does good work," he said, and spun his chair to face her. "When d'you want me on duty, Pilot?"

Theo considered that. Uncle was due within the next local day. She could easily let the man go home and put his groundside life in order before—

"Pardon, Pilot Waitley," *Bechimo* said, sounding a lot more respectful than he usually did. "I have a communication from the Uncle. He expects to land within the hour, and desires a meeting with you at the Emerald."

In the copilot's station, Clarence laughed softly.

"I'm thinking that means *now*," he said.

· · · ✻ · · ·

Quin jumped, kicking into a quarter-turn midleap, flexed his knees, brought his elbows in to his sides...

The hideaway in his jacket shifted, destroying his center. He kicked again, much good it did him, hit the mat on one knee, ducked into a somersault and snapped to his feet.

"Impressive," Padi said, from her lean against the bar. "But not at all what Theo managed."

"I know that!" Quin snapped, and sighed. "I would have matched it, but my gun shifted."

"*You* insisted that we practice as if we were on-port," she pointed out.

"Are you going to ask a port tough to wait until you go back to the ship and change into your exercise clothes?" Quin asked, still snappish.

Padi raised her hand, fingers whispering *peace*. "I had said you insisted, not that you were in error. In fact, it seems to me that we ought to have been practicing in port dress long since—for just the reason your last effort illuminated. Full pockets make a simple dance—something more complex."

Quin shook his head. "Theo managed that move in a gown, landed firm, centered, and already in defense stance. I was looking directly at her and I cannot say for certain how it was done." He gave Padi a small smile. "She's rather quick, our Theo."

"It would be instructive to have her dance with Uncle Val Con. Could the eye even follow?"

Quin dropped to the mat. "Not much chance of that very soon, is there?" He pulled his knees up and wrapped his arms around them.

"There may be an opportunity," Padi said, kneeling beside him and looking into his eyes, "in future. Are you still worried about your father's lifemate?"

He moved his shoulders. "Worried... she will be something different in the house, but with so much else different..."

"And after all," Padi said brightly, "you will have Grandfather, so it will seem just as always."

"I will, but—" He looked up, face earnest. "Padi, does it seem... odd to you, that we are going—that you are going on the *Passage* with your father, and I to the city with mine, while Syl Vor and the twins stay here, without us? We were at the Rock so short a time, and yet it seems that we had always been there, waiting for word, practicing the drills and Grandfather walking the rounds..."

"I know." She leaned forward and touched his cheek. "Cousin, we sat board together, and trained together, and depended, each on the other. It does seem odd, that we will be separated. But— we had to learn to work together. And the Rock seemed strange, didn't it, at first?"

"Yes..."

"And we're behind, you know," Padi continued. "*My* father says he doubts I'll find time in my schedule to sleep, I've so much to catch up aboard the *Passage*."

Quin grinned. "Surely he knows you better than that!"

"Perhaps he has some catching up to do, as well," Padi said smugly, and came to her feet as the door to the practice room opened.

"Your pardons," Mr. pel'Kana said. "Master Quin, Mr. McFarland is here to take you to your father."

THIRTY-SIX

. . . .

Emerald Casino
Surebleak Port
Surebleak

"AH, PILOT WAITLEY, HOW GOOD OF YOU TO COME SO QUICKLY."

Uncle rose from the depths of the backmost booth and bowed gently, in no particular mode—or at least not in any of the modes her cousins had managed to drill into her head yet. His beard was more definite, and carefully groomed; his dark hair was lacquered red at the tips, and a single gold ring pierced his right ear. He wore a plain dark sweater, a leather vest, and leather pants. There was a workmanlike gun on his belt—only prudent on Surebleak Port—and another, smaller gun, Theo thought, in his right sleeve.

"And this worthy person is—"

"Pilot O'Berin," she said. "My copilot."

Uncle gave her one of his cool smiles. "Copilot, very good," he said, and, then, over her head, "Pilot *Clarence* O'Berin?"

"That's right," he said easily.

Uncle's smile deepened, if it didn't exactly warm. "Excellent," he said, and swept out an arm, indicating the empty seats. "Please, Pilots, join me. I've taken the liberty of ordering wine."

Theo slid into the corner seat, which was as good a choice as any. She had solid wood at her back, and a good view of the room, but she was more or less boxed in. If trouble came, she'd just have to take a dive under the table.

Clarence sat angled at the end of the bench, which gave him a clear view of Uncle and of her, while partially shielding her from the room. Taking up copilot's duty, just like that, Theo thought.

"Pilot Waitley, you must allow me to say how very much I regret the events that overtook you at Tokeoport," Uncle said, pouring two fingers of wine into each of the three glasses at the center of the table. "However, as it seems that these regrettable events have had the happy result of uniting you with your destiny, we ought perhaps not lament too widely, but simply toast your . . . good fortune."

He set the bottle aside and picked a glass up, holding it aloft.

Clarence picked up one of the two remaining without hesitation and held it high. Theo, sighing internally, perforce picked up the third and raised it.

"Pilot," Uncle prompted, "the toast?"

She blinked, then remembered Val Con and Father—"To the luck," she said.

"The luck," Clarence seconded, "every bit of it."

"Indeed," Uncle said. "To fortune."

Theo let the wine dampen her mouth and sweeten her tongue, just enough to be polite, before she put the glass down. Clarence, she saw, did about the same. The Uncle drank deeply and with obvious enjoyment, which was fair enough—he'd bought the bottle.

"Before we address the more pressing matters before us, I wonder, Pilot Waitley, if you were able to retrieve that item from the lock box?"

She nodded, held her primary hand between them with fingers wide, signaling *no threat*, while she reached inside her jacket with her off-hand and drew out the flat box she'd picked up on Tokeoport.

Carefully, she put it on his side of the table, next to the wine bottle, angled so that he could see the unbroken seal.

"The others are in the ship's safe," she said.

Uncle exhaled, slowly.

"Pilot Waitley, you are a resourceful and determined woman. The usual fee, and a hazard bonus, will be in your account within the next local day." He put his hand over the box, lifted it and slipped it into his vest pocket.

"You will also find the buy-out fee in your account," he continued, and finished the rest of the wine in his glass. "I do regret that you will not be able to continue in my employ, Pilot."

"It doesn't seem practicable," Theo agreed, "given that your name appears on certain lists."

"Indeed." He poured himself more wine, then showed them each the bottle.

"No, thank you," Theo said. Clarence just held a hand over his glass.

Uncle put the bottle down.

"We proceed, then, to our other business. I understand that *Arin's Toss* is in the hold of your ship. What I was not able to ascertain from your communication was its condition."

"Intact," Theo said promptly. "*Bechimo* has the hold shielded, if you've tried to communicate directly with the *Toss*."

"Prudent," the Uncle murmured. He sipped wine, thoughtfully, it seemed to Theo. "Scout yo'Vala is being readied for his transfer to your vessel. Have you a rendezvous point to suggest?"

Bechimo had worked that out, then run it past Jeeves, who sent it on to Val Con, who had professed himself "informed," with that particular inflection that Theo had come learn also meant that he was amused.

"I asked *Bechimo* to transmit coordinates to the origin point of your last message."

"It will have bounced to Dulsey, then. As I have heard no outcry, I accept your choice. My choice of time is as soon as possible. I expect that my presence may be trying several tempers and I very much wish the Dragon to lie quiet and tend the business to which it has set itself."

"Assuming portmaster's courtesy," Theo said—and lifting *out* of Surebleak was nowhere near the problem dropping *in* was—"we can be at the rendezvous point in three Standard Hours."

Uncle pursed his lips, nodded.

"That is also acceptable," he said and drank off what was left of his wine in a swallow.

"I suggest that we remove to our stations, and see this thing done." He rose and bowed.

"Pilot Waitley. Pilot O'Berin. Good lift."

"Good lift," Theo answered, but Uncle had already slipped out of the booth and was on his way to the door.

• • • ✵ • • •

Pilot Waitley didn't let any grass grow under her wings, there was that about her. Clarence swung by Mack's, having gotten the pilot's permission for a detour, so long as it was quick, and explained the situation, fingers filling in what the mouth hadn't time for.

"Quite a ship that pilot brung in. I'm not saying I'd be in your boots if she'd offered second to me, but the temptation—there would be that."

"No notice," Clarence said. "I'm sorry for that."

"Ship lifts when the pilot says *go*," Mack said. "You done solid for me, and I got no complaints. Comes about you're home again and need work, remember to stop by an' see me, right?"

"Right." Clarence cleared his throat, but Mack's fingers were moving.

Time flies.

"You got time to get your kit?"

"Sent one of Ms. Audrey's over to the landlady with the rent and a note. If I'm gone when she gets back, I told her to bring it here—you can do with it as you see fit."

"I'll pop it in t'safe 'til you call for it."

Clarence took a breath, feeling his throat get tight again.

"Thank you," he said, just like his ma'd taught him back before he'd had any notions about pilots, or ever heard about favors. "I'm beholden."

"Hell y'are. Now get outta here 'fore your pilot lifts without you and you're back on tractor repair."

· · · ✺ · · ·

"Think she'll be back?" Miri asked, her arm tucked comfortably through Val Con's as they strolled through the inner garden.

"Am I being asked to find odds?"

"Garden variety guess'll do."

He laughed lightly.

"Certainly, one hopes she will visit again, if only to shorten the long faces of her younger kin."

"Who suddenly discovered how much fun it is to be the ones teaching instead of being taught at," Miri said, with a laugh of her own. "Seems she worked some bits out with Daav, too."

"And Mother." His arm tightened as they left the path and picked their way over the Tree's surface roots. "I think that she will visit again—she has the excuse of her report to the clan's Master Trader to compel her."

"Yeah, that was clever."

"It was, wasn't it? Whether she will desire at any point to take up a place in-clan; I cannot predict. I suspect that Father would counsel her against. I might do the same, depending, of course, if I am eventually graduated from dangerous madman to concerned brother."

"I don't think that's gotta be an either/or," Miri said thoughtfully. "I'm pretty sure she thinks Daav took a sharp rap on the head."

"True. But Father and Theo have a preexisting, trustful relationship. The rest of us are strangers."

"And Theo ain't good with people."

"Is it being bad with people to know that events would inevitably proceed more smoothly if only everyone would follow her instructions?"

"Put it that way, and she sounds more like family than ever." Miri sighed, slipped her arm free and put her back against the Tree. The bark warmed against her, which was the Tree's version of "glad to see you."

She let her head rest on the trunk and closed her eyes, accepting the warmth and the welcome.

The Tree had settled since the excitement of travel had nearly drowned Val Con in exuberance, but its touch was considerably more vigorous than it had been when she'd first experienced it. The Tree had been bored on Liad, no question, and was finding the move to Surebleak, and the subsequent calls on its assistance, exhilarating. The gardener swore the inner garden couldn't have made it without the Tree's intervention. She also said that she'd taken some samples of the new growth and found the structures subtly changed, which Miri wasn't sure she wanted to think about too hard, but after all, wasn't survival the ultimate law?

She stirred a little inside the warmth, remembering times in her past where survival—personal survival—hadn't been on the wish list at all.

There was a sense of consideration inside her reverie, like she and the Tree were in a conversation and it was turning her point over.

She found herself thinking about her mother in a depth she hadn't in years; and Skel; and—

Her reverie shivered into an awareness of a sense she hadn't known she had—long-sight, maybe, or delirium. She saw—stars, Surebleak's familiar constellations; nearer in were ships, delineated in codes she wasn't quite sure she—but there! There was the reason for this searching, this joy!

Rootless and astonishing, her wings subtle and strong, a white dragon rose through the rabble toward the distant stars.

Gasping with delight, Miri snatched herself forward, her feet tangling in a root—familiar hands caught her, and she sagged against Val Con's chest, hearing his heart beating with the excitement still echoing in her own blood.

"What the *hell* was that?" she gasped, and felt him laugh, breathless.

"I believe that Theo has lifted."

THIRTY-SEVEN

. . . .

Bechimo
Surebleak System

CLARENCE O'BERIN FLEW A CLEAN BOARD, THEO NOTED; WHAT Tranza used to call "no fuss, no muss." You could tell a lot about a pilot from the kind of board they flew; she'd learned that at Anlingdin. Clean was just fine, in her opinion, and she drew her breath in sharp against a sudden stab of regret, that she hadn't thought to ask Father to fly with her—or Val Con...

"Pilot?" Clarence asked quietly—and that was good, too, she told herself. He was sharp and noticed what he needed to notice, for the care of pilot and ship.

Which was something she should maybe tell the man. People liked to be praised for doing right.

"The pilot I sat second to until I earned first class told me that he admired a pilot who ran his board with no fuss. I was thinking that he'd approve of the way you handled things, leaving port."

That wasn't exactly what she'd meant to say, but she thought it sounded all right. Then she saw the corner of his mouth twitch, and wondered if she managed to get it wrong, anyway.

But—"Good to know. Thank you, Pilot," was what he said.

She nodded and left it there, flicking a glance to her Number Six screen.

"*Bechimo*, now that Uncle's coming to take his property off our hands, it might be a nice gesture to drop the shielding on the hold, so he can let the *Toss* know he's on the way."

"That would not be wise, Pilot."

She sighed. If this was the chaos-driven lists again...

"Why not?" she asked, keeping her voice as even as possible.

"Because there are anomalous devices attached to the mere-ship's chassis. The ship should remain in quiet mode while within the hold and in close proximity. The units are quiescent at the moment but their full function and mode of operation are yet to be discovered."

She stared at the screen, and its swirling patterns of blue and silver, which were beginning to darken and swirl slightly faster.

"When?" she asked, aware of Clarence in the copilot's chair, and as much as the pilot had to trust her copilot, so did the copilot need to trust his pilot. "When were you going to tell me?"

"It did not seem necessary. My original scan of the mere-ship was performed at a distance and without direct access to the Builders' records. On storing the mere-ship in our hold I initiated a log retrieval scan; the mere-ship's self-test log indicated that while on Spaceport Gondola unplanned maintenance occurred while the ship was in sleep mode. A modified approach light and proximity unit has been added to the mere-ship's forward install point. The unit appears to have additional functions and energy associated, as well as potential explosive antitamper defenses. I had taken precautions to ensure our safety. What happens to the mere-ship when it is removed from our care is the concern of those who own it."

"Chaos." She closed her eyes, reached for the comm, remembered protocol and said, "Second..."

"Pinging them now, Pilot. Private?"

"No," she said. "Put it on speaker, so we can *all* hear it."

"Yes, Pilot." Quick fingers moved, then paused. "Got 'em."

"Pilot Waitley, this is Dulsey. Service?"

"Dulsey, I've just been informed of a...developing...ummm, maintenance situation with the *Toss*. Requesting that we put off rendezvous until I can ascertain and repair."

There was a short pause, as if she'd managed to startle Dulsey—but it might only have been lag; her answer when it came was perfectly composed.

"We appreciate your concern, Pilot, and will stand by. If one may offer aid, please don't hesitate to ask."

"Thank you. I'll assess and get back to you. Waitley out."

Clarence cut the connection. Theo closed her eyes and counted to ninety-nine by threes, sighed, opened her eyes and stood.

"*Bechimo*, open the hold."

"No, Pilot."

Anger warmed her. She took another breath. *Anger wins no arguments,* she reminded herself, which Kamele used to say. It meant that *shouting* wasn't allowed, but that manipulation was perfectly in order.

But to successfully manipulate an opponent into doing what you wanted them to do, according to Father, you needed to find out why they opposed you.

So.

"Why not?"

"The situation has the potential to produce damage. I cannot allow my pilot to expose herself to this risk."

Theo bit her lip, trying to think how best to frame her argument.

"Use a remote, then," Clarence said, spinning his chair around and directing his comment, as Val Con had, at a point on the ceiling slightly to the right of center. "You got remotes, don't you?"

"My remotes are few and valuable."

"As valuable as your pilot, here? Or the copilot we're trying to get back before he dies of putting himself into harm's way for you?"

Silence.

Clarence shook his head.

"You gotta think this stuff through," he said, and came out of his chair, giving Theo a nod. "No good us brangling. With your permission, Pilot, I'll take a look at the item in the hold."

Theo shook her head. "*Bechimo* says it could explode."

"Heard that. I don't say I'm eager, but I do have some experience with tracking gigs and with explosives. Enough not to lose my head, and to yell for help if I see I need it."

"Which begs the question," Theo said, and glared at her screen. "*Bechimo*, I will be monitoring the situation. If Pilot O'Berin needs help, you will open the hold to me. I am First Pilot, he is my crew and I'm not going to leave him in need. Can we agree on those terms?"

"Yes, Pilot."

It seemed to her that *Bechimo* sounded subdued.

· · · ✵ · · ·

Pod 78 was located upon Moonstruck, a large asteroid in stable orbit around a small sun, one of several natural anomalies that attracted tourists and cruise ships. A space camp for which there was a long waiting list had been established in Moonstruck orbit.

The explosives expert attached to the Department's team of programmers and software engineers gave as her opinion that, should Pod 78 catastrophically give up its energy, the space camp would be instantly incinerated. Other, peripheral, tragedies involving cruise ships might also occur, if the Department were nice about its timing.

That, of course, was for Command to decide.

In the meanwhile, the engineers and programmers continued their work. Apparently whatever had prompted the device to call for repair had very soon thereafter frozen its interfaces. This allowed the engineers to work with a degree of freedom, bypassing sleeping guard-programs, following frozen rivers of data to the core program.

Whereupon it was discovered that not *all* of the guard-programs slept, and two things happened at once.

Pod 78 sent a message.

A countdown program began.

Despite the loss of the three technicians in the room with it when these events occurred, the message was captured by the officer sitting comm on the bridge of the Department's work boat.

The team leader, upon being made aware of the substance of that message, pinbeamed Command.

The stakes had just risen—risen brilliantly. Pod 78 had called upon the Delm of Korval, and it was *only* the Delm of Korval who could avert the disaster the team had unwittingly put in train. In one throw, the Department could win—all. In order to destroy Korval, the team need only withdraw.

And wait.

Command agreed.

The team removed all traces of its work and its tenure inside the cavern. They left, locking the door behind them.

THIRTY-EIGHT

Bechimo
Surebleak System

IT WAS A NASTY PIECE OF WORK, BUT STRAIGHTFORWARD FOR ALL of that. There were a couple of internal shunts that looked like they could get worrisome, but his biggest problem was deciding the protocol—meaning, would it blow if he just removed the gadgets entire, or if he were daft enough to try to separate the components, or if he looked at it cross-eyed. But, then, that always was the problem, wasn't it?

Clarence sat back on his heels and considered what his instruments told him, the good news being that *Bechimo* had the instruments to hand, and that they were reasonably up-to-date.

He could sure use the team of experts he'd left back on Liad, though.

"Pilot O'Berin?"

The voice was soft, and a little thin, for coming through the speaker on the job cart, still it was recognizable enough.

"*Bechimo*," he acknowledged, frowning at the schematic on the work screen.

"I deduce from the readings that Pilot Waitley is...angry with me."

"Oh, aye, she is that, though I thought she held line pretty well, considering the provocation."

"I do not understand the provocation. It is to the ship's benefit that the pilot be safe."

"Yeah, well, what you gotta understand about Pilot Waitley is that she's out of a long line o' hardheads that're convinced they got the answer—which, in fairness, they do, more often than not—and who care about ships above almost anything else. Letting this pretty lady sit here with that bit of nasty clipped to her wings—that's just cold."

"*Arin's Toss* is a mere-ship. It cannot think, nor could it protect its pilot when the need arose."

"I don't got that particular story, but I will tell you this—you want to have pilots angry with you on a regular and continuing basis, keep on calling their ladies 'mere-ships.'"

He shook his head and stood up, looking down at the work cart.

"Now, if you were wanting to know why Pilot Waitley's angry with you at this particular hour—it's because you withheld vital information. She negotiated this trade—*Arin's Toss* for your regular copilot—in good faith. The terms of the trade were that both the ship and the pilot are in good condition and would remain that way. We're fortunate in that it appears the other party has an interest in keeping the hostage well that goes beyond his interest in recovering his rightful property.

"If this had been a *real* hostage-taking, where enemies of the ship were holding crew or pilots, and it was found we were planning on giving them back a booby-trapped ship, like you were planning in this case..."

"Yes?" *Bechimo* whispered.

"The most likely outcome is that the hostage would've been killed." Clarence paused, then asked, off-handedly. "D'you know what *killed* is?"

"*Yes*," *Bechimo* hissed—hit something there.

Clarence waited, but the air wasn't evacuated from the hold, nor yet did a death ray leap out of the work cart and fry him on the spot, which, if you were of a mind to credit the old tales, should've been the next order of business. Seein' as the tales were wrong...

"So, there's Pilot Waitley's temper explained for you. 'Nother thing is—it strikes me Pilot Waitley might object to finding she's been made a liar. There's some ports where a pilot's reputation buys more than cantra."

Silence. Could be he'd given *Bechimo* a bit to sort over, after all.

"Now that's all settled," he said, "I'll thank you to be quiet and let me figure out how to go about this."

"Would a schematic of the device's original configuration be of assistance?"

"Happens it would. Send it to the work screen, would you?"

Clarence shook his head.

"No way for me to be getting in there for the releases," he muttered.

...and if he tried releasing the whole device without getting to the internals first? Well, the schematic was pretty clear about that.

The problem was multifold, one of the wrinkles being that landing lights were both big and heavy to begin with, and the necessary slick for the outside of a starship's hull meant that there were magnetic triggers and locks that made the fascia go through five turns before it popped out enough to hit the release. The light crystal itself was almost exactly the same energy-neutral shade as the hull when it was unpowered, as now, making quick-guess alignment iffy at best and dangerous at worst.

"Damn." He'd left all—well *almost* all—the fancy tech belonging to Juntavas back on Liad, except some little bits that were prolly sitting in Andy Mack's safe by now. What he figured they had here was a tracker—a high-power pinbeam equivalent. Didn't want to be close to it if it let that energy go *or* called home. Good thing it was that *Bechimo* hadn't let Uncle just cold call to say howdy.

"I can help," *Bechimo* offered, subdued and sudden from the job cart.

"I'm not refusing help," Clarence said.

Across the hold, the service hatch rose, admitting a rectangular metal box on tractor treads, standing about as high as Clarence's belt buckle.

"Thought you weren't going to be risking anything so valuable as a remote?"

"I have crafted another solution," *Bechimo* said from the job cart. "Pilot O'Berin, please review my understanding."

"All right."

"It is imperative that the mere—that the ship *Arin's Toss* be presented to the agent of the Uncle intact and without such devices as have been attached by those who seem not to wish him well."

"Check."

"It is also imperative that none of my pilots achieve the state of being *killed*."

"In this case, I think we've got a match there, too."

"It is highly desirable, but not imperative, that the remote unit takes no damage."

"I'm thinking that remotes can be replaced easier than people," Clarence said carefully. "But I've got a certain amount of ignorance on the topic. For instance, I don't know if losing a remote will be . . . painful, or impair you in any way."

"No impairment, thank you, Pilot. There is an ongoing lack of expected feedback from those remotes which have been lost in the past. I do not equate this with the *pain* I have had occasion to observe. However, I think that this new method will endanger neither yourself nor the base remote."

The unit came to a stop next to the job cart.

"Now." An arm made out of what looked to be silver tubing extended until its clawed tip was resting on the chassis against the damned slick light box. Clarence held his breath, but the arm was apparently going no further. Instead, two tiny black objects emerged from the main housing and minced down the arm bridge.

At first Clarence thought they were spiders, with bulblike bodies rocking in a cradle of eight delicate high-stepping legs.

"Secondary remotes," *Bechimo* said. "Once the exterior bezel is released they will enter the device under my guidance, deactivate the interior trips, and retreat, neutralizing such points as seem to be a threat. I expect that they will be destroyed before the work is completed, but anticipate that they will disarm enough of the device's internals that the remote will be able to deal with the remainder in a fashion that will allow it to remain intact."

"If you please, Pilot, deploy the containment field."

"I'll do that," Clarence said "if you'll let me see what the remotes see—I've done this kind of work myself once or twice. Might be able to help keep all the parts working as long as we need them. Monitor and record my comments, if any."

The schematic on his work screen was replaced by a split view of the light crystal and the hull around it.

He engaged the containment field—and retreated with the job cart behind the protective wall at the back of the hold.

"Pilot?" That was his boss, her voice sounding worried over the headset. "How's it going?"

"It's going," he told her. "*Bechimo's* machined some secondaries to get into the small places with. Looks like it might work."

"How long?" she asked, and then, sounding apologetic, "I have an inquiry."

"We got video now, thanks to *Bechimo*. Didn't he tell you?"

The silence was explicit, and Clarence shook his head.

"Right—so you'll want to share the video that's on my work screen with Pilot Waitley, if you would be so kind, *Bechimo*?"

"Yes, Pilot," came the subdued agreement from the ship.

"Let's get to it, then."

· · · ❄ · · ·

The "getting to it" wracked nerves, consumed time. Theo fielded another inquiry from Dulsey, watched the screens, and *didn't* push her copilot to hurry.

The trouble was partly equipment. A normal power-pull could match the eight magnetic spots and twist a retaining ring out in a matter of seconds—which Theo knew because it had been one of the things she'd had to help with on field duty at Hugglelans, her break job while she was at the academy.

Here, they were working with *Bechimo*'s old-fashioned four-point portable unit, run from the remote, trying to release the first four points and then rotate to the second set of points to both unseat and pull. The assists showed a good, clear picture of what was going on—a continual battle of lock spin slip, lock spin slip, lock spin slip, the while waiting for whatever tell-tales might be set within the unit to act.

Her screen showed the progress at the rate about a completed full turn a minute, with *Bechimo*'s low toned, "approximately two minutes remaining for fascia removal" was less than reassuring.

The threads appeared as gigantic spiral gutters as the assistant remotes continued to scan for evidence of problems and Theo danced a continuous slow motion relaxation dance as she sat, watching the other monitors and scan readings in turn.

"Slow!" Theo called out.

Lighting in the hold was brilliant, and Clarence had already had the remotes scan the area once, so Theo could see the boxy one, spindly arm holding the light crystal demounter. Now she could see the discoloration—

"Manufacturing artifact," suggested *Bechimo*, "there is no obvious utility."

"Might be an optical assist?" Clarence's voice was level, making her wonder if he'd ever startle her by breaking into full song the way her former pilot Rig Tranza had done.

"Unlikely, but noted. The unit was seated in existing hardware without such a sensor location."

"Point," Clarence agreed. "Continue."

Theo nodded. Her copilot might not be a Tranza, but he was level-headed, and that was good to know.

She looked at the board and grimaced. It was midnight at Surebleak Port. At the far end of the Road, at Jelaza Kazone, the night flowers would be at full glow in the inner garden. On another night, she and Cousin Luken would have finished their last round of pikit, sitting for a moment or two longer, chatting, then would have gone upstairs together, parting at the top of the stair, he for his rooms, she for hers.

· · · ❄ · · ·

The bedside comm chimed once, then Miri heard Val Con murmur.

"Yes?... Ah. Please see them comfortable in the map room. I will come down at once."

"Think even Scouts would learn to call during business hours," Miri muttered, opening her eyes, and pushing the covers back.

Val Con caught her hands, and smoothed the blankets over her shoulders.

"I will go, *cha'trez*. You will remain here, and sleep for us both."

"Now there's a fair divide on the work," she said, letting him press her into the pillow. Gods, she was tired.

"Sleep," Val Con murmured.

She felt his lips, warm against her cheek...

... and slept.

· · · ❄ · · ·

Despite the even slower rate, Clarence was fine with the prog-ress they were making, and fine with Pilot Theo's approach to be joggled from the outside—and appreciative of the effort she was likely making to keep her temper.

There.

The retaining plate's threads gave way with a slight lurch, with the extended demounter cradling the descending basic unit with a hairsbreadth between hull and the cylindrical innards.

"Our next phase begins, Pilot," announced *Bechimo* as the tiny mobile units ascended into the interior. "Please watch with care!"

Clarence stared at the larger remote as if *Bechimo* resided there—should an AI actually sound nervous?

"Hold!"

On screen, one of the secondaries was following the other—and there was already something out of the ordinary.

"That blue blob—"

"Noted. The object is not on the original schematic, and carries the chemical signature of a known explosive. It is of insufficient size to be a danger to the ship as a whole but could be a hazard to crew or small components. Roughly the equivalent of a handgun projectile load."

The camera moved jerkily, the second unit following the first up the blue blob, across a connection plug, to an actual light crystal similar to the specs, turned and stopped, the wonders of a circuit capsule before it. This was the real payload, though above it and packed around it were several more of the blue blobs.

"Seen one of them before," Clarence began, the same instant *Bechimo* sang out, "Identified from catalogs."

Clarence laughed. "No wonder—there's only one of them Shack designs are any good, and that's the one, right there. Thing is, there's some extra plugs, and something else above, as far as I can see."

The image bounced heavily, switching between the two mini-remotes.

"I am building a stereo image. I believe that there are parts numbers visible that will permit—"

"That's a short range call-me-back; might be that—"

"It is cross-connected to several power systems, as is the pinbeam itself: The schematics clearly show that once energized for a landing or docking the device would broadcast locally and the pinbeam would send a momentary burst with coordinates to a prechosen location. The small explosives are not currently powered, though there is an auxiliary power supply they could access."

The remotes began a skittering run that did bad things to Clarence's sense of balance. He snatched at the job cart.

"Uh, *Bechimo*, warning on that stuff. Some of us can suffer motion sickness!"

"It was not intentional. A random walk program was employed

while recording; I believe I could now duplicate this if required and have a firmer understanding of the device. The total explosive forces are not a danger to the external hull of the mer... of *Arin's Toss*. There is minor danger to the internals present, as long as they are not employed in Jump, where they could change the external configuration of the ship and create a phantom equation wave capable of altering Jump destination. Given the forward location, employing the explosives on high speed atmospheric entry might also be a cause for concern."

Clarence closed his eyes as the image bobbed again. "I sure wouldn't want to be on the inside trying to figure out what was going wrong while I was shedding pieces."

There was no reply from *Bechimo*, which was probably just as well. Clarence opened his eyes, cautiously. On screen, the spider things were emerging unscathed from the interior.

"It is my understanding, Pilot O'Berin, that what we have here is of little danger to us, but would in fact be a threat to *Arin's Toss* and its crew, if permitted to remain. I suggest we continue with the removal. Once the device is removed and neutralized you will be able to enter the ship and access a proper replacement from ship stores."

"You're good with that? You figure we're safe?"

"If time were not a limiting factor I believe I could disassemble the entirety. However, the Less Pilot waits upon the completion of this project. He is frail, and he is ours to care for; we cannot in kindness force him to wait any longer than strictly necessary. Once the unit exits the hull, we must move with alacrity. The containment field is sufficient to prevent damage to our own ship systems, and since this hold has not been much used previously it is in excellent condition."

"You got that, Pilot? *Bechimo* thinks..."

Theo's voice came, unhurried.

"Nothing to argue with. You two are on the spot, and time's passing. Go."

"*Bechimo*, we're on, if you're up to it."

"The remote is in proper position, and the assistant remotes are recovered. We shall withdraw the unit, and the remote will direct it insofar as it may be possible. There are five explosive packages; allow me to tell you when they are neutralized or detonated. I begin."

"Are you sure—" Clarence heard Theo start, but *Bechimo*'s remote was already acting and the mass of the crystal and attendant parts was sliding out, nearly as tall as Clarence, into its spindly grip. The unit tottered, badly balanced in the gripper and fell heavily to the decking.

An explosive incandescence came from the floor, and a blast muffled by the field, but plenty loud enough for his nerves.

Hers, too, apparently.

"What was *that*?"

"Warn-away strength only, Pilots," *Bechimo* said, over the whole ship. "No damage done. Pilot Waitley, please let the Uncle know that—that *Arin's Toss* will be ready for his pilot to pick up within a Standard Hour."

This was punctuated by another explosion, slightly less exclamatory than the first.

"A time delay, Pilot, three more," reminded *Bechimo*.

"Second, get out of there," Theo said.

Unseen, Clarence shook his head.

"I'm behind the blast wall. I think I'll just rest here 'til we're done."

"All right," she said. "Just—don't do anything dangerous, all right?"

Clarence laughed.

THIRTY-NINE

. . . .

Jelaza Kazone
Surebleak

IN CONTRAST TO THE HALLWAY, THE MAP ROOM WAS BRIGHTLY illuminated, as if its sole occupant wished to banish every shred of shadow. If that were his purpose, yet it fell short of complete success; the man himself threw a small eclipse over the map he bent to study.

Val Con shut the door silently behind him, and said, "I was told that *Scouts* awaited my pleasure."

Scout ter'Meulen, for it was none other, turned slowly, making a show of his lack of surprise.

"And so it was *Scouts*," he said, "and one of them so exhausted that I begged a cot for her and an hour's quiet recuperation, while you and I talked about the weather."

Clonak ter'Meulen was his father's oldest friend; a man Val Con had known all his life, and had once trusted without reservation. These things being so, still they did not make the Scout any less annoying when he was in a whimsical mood. Which he most often was.

Eyeing Clonak, Val Con noted the lines of weariness in the older man's face. *Only one exhausted, was it?* he thought, and sighed. Well, Clonak was capable of whimsy on his deathbed. Best to get through it as quickly as possible and petition Mr. pel'Kana for a second cot.

"The weather is," he therefore said, "remarkably mild for the

295

season, which is, in case you had wondered, spring. We all of us anticipate the arrival of summer, and a growing season slightly shorter in duration than one of my aunt's formal dinner parties." He folded his hands before him. "But perhaps you have a storm warning," he finished politely, "having so lately come from orbit."

Clonak snorted a laugh. "You're not going to let me have any fun, are you, Shadow?" he asked in Terran.

"As much as it must naturally pain me to discommode a guest..." Val Con murmured, then said more sharply, "Clonak, it is—"

The Scout held up his hand. "Local midnight, or beyond. I can tell time, child. And I can also tell when someone has subverted his duty." He fixed Val Con in a cool, taffy-colored gaze. "Scout Commander yos'Phelium."

Val Con sighed. "I fear you will have to be more specific—of which particular infraction do you speak?"

"Perhaps Interdicted World I-2796-893-44 strikes memory's chord?"

In fact, it did, and pleasurable music it was, despite that they had been hunted there, and Miri nearly lost to the treachery of an Agent of Change. In Balance, they had made friends, and gained a brother.

"The locals call it Vandar," he told Clonak. "I make a clean breast—it was either land there and live, however we might, or die attempting one more Jump in a stripped vessel that had been marked for salvage."

"It is forbidden to land on Interdicted Worlds," Clonak said sternly.

Well, it was. But Scouts did so not infrequently; and he and Miri had taken care to adhere as nearly as possible to local custom.

"I plead survival," he told Clonak. "Call a tribunal, if you have a taste for farce, and let it be tried. In the meanwhile, allow me to offer you the protection of our House while you rest."

Clonak shook his head.

"We'll wake Hath in a moment so she can tell out the details for you. Your survival has endangered the survival of others, Scout Commander. The Department of the Interior has *noticed* Vandar."

Val Con went cold. Foolish of him to have thought that the Depatment would *not* notice Vandar, having already lost there one full Agent of Change to the mission of retrieving one Val Con yos'Phelium. He had thought...no, he had *not* thought! And Clonak was correct; survival or no—his landing upon Vandar had endangered innocents, and not only those whom he knew by name.

"I see you understand the problem," Clonak said dryly.

"Indeed, I am an idiot," Val Con said. He stepped over to the wall and touched the plate set there. A moment later, the door opened and Mr. pel'Kana looked within.

"Your lordship?"

"Please wake Scout Hath and bring her here, Mr. pel'Kana," Val Con said, keeping his voice calm with an effort. "Her report is wanted."

"Yes, Your Lordship."

"Also, some tea, please, Mr. pel'Kana, and a cold nuncheon."

"Of course, Your Lordship."

The door closed.

Val Con sighed, and turned to face his father's friend.

"While we are waiting, I have a piece of information for the Scouts, if you would be so good as to convey it up-channel."

Clonak considered him. "Is there a draft in here?" he inquired.

"Perhaps so; the house will be some time settling, I'm told."

"Ah. And the message?"

"The message is that the ship *Bechimo* is under contract to Korval."

Clonak sighed.

"That will make them happy, in Command."

"Also," Val Con said gently, "Scout Commander First-In Val Con yos'Phelium has inspected the ship *Bechimo* and finds it both sentient and sapient. It is thus a protected person, under previously established rules."

"Previously established for Jeeves, you mean," Clonak said, sounding very nearly irritable. "I'll pass the message."

"Thank you," Val Con said.

"That might be precipitous," Clonak answered, then, at the sound Mr. pel'Kana's step in the hall beyond—"Here's Hath, now."

· · · ✴ · · ·

"I'm out," Dulsey reported, and there was *Arin's Toss* in Theo's Number Three screen, rolling prettily out of the range of *Bechimo*'s shields.

Not that those shields were up, not with Uncle's ship tethered to *Bechimo* by a tunnel. *Bechimo* had been remarkably compliant about accepting the tunnel and sharing air with somebody who was on his Disapproved List. Theo wasn't sure if she liked the change or not.

"All systems check," Dulsey continued, "no free riders."

Theo sighed. Her worry had been that *Bechimo* might have concealed the presence of a second device, even after Clarence assured her that he'd swept the *Toss* and found her clean.

"Excellent," Uncle's voice came over the band. "Pilot Waitley, your package is approaching."

All right, Theo, she told herself. *Now, the easy part.*

The figure in the light-duty suit pulled itself awkwardly along the guide line, and stumbled, rather than rolled into the corridor.

Theo caught an arm, drew it around her shoulders, and threw the other arm around his waist to steady him as she got them both out of the lock, and hit the kickplate.

"He's in," she called. "Seal us up."

"Seal broken, tunnel retracting," Clarence's voice came calmly from the wall unit. The thin body she embraced stiffened, the head came up, shaking the hood back.

The piebald skin of his face had smoothed into a uniform, dry beige. There were parched lines etched around his mouth, and knifed into his forehead. His eyes were black-ringed and dull; there were threads of pure white in his hair.

"Theo," he said, and his voice was a scratchy whisper. "Forgive, that I do not bow."

Tears—stupid things. She blinked them away.

"You don't have to bow. But, Win Ton—what is this? I thought you would be—be—" Her throat closed.

"That I would be preserved, as when you saw me last, perhaps, even, somewhat improved." His lips bent in a dry parody of his smile.

"There was always the danger that the poison would learn from the healing unit's attempts to repair," he said. "It would appear that *Bechimo* is, indeed, my last hope."

"Ship secure," Clarence reported. "Uncle's on a heading for the Jump point."

"Who," Win Ton whispered, "is that?"

"Clarence O'Berin, my copilot," she said, and felt him stiffen again. "I *need* a copilot."

"Yes, certainly you do."

"So, come and meet him, and tell me what you need from us"—Tears again—again she blinked her eyes clear—"to heal you."

"Indeed, it will be my pleasure, to make the pilot's acquaintance," he said, and then didn't say anything more, seeming instead to concentrate his whole attention on the act of walking, leaning heavily on her, until the door slid away and they were in the piloting chamber.

He set his feet, deliberately, and straightened away from the support of her arm. Theo stepped back, though she stayed close enough to catch him, if his knees suddenly gave out.

"Win Ton, this is Clarence O'Berin. Pilot, this is Win Ton yo'Vala, first pilot accepted of *Bechimo*."

That made him laugh, silent, but with such vigor that he staggered a little.

"Let us by all means be clear on that," he said, and inclined his head. "Clarence O'Berin, I know your name."

"Don't surprise me," Clarence answered, and nodded at the Jump seat. "You want to rest, Pilot? No offense, but you're lookin' rugged."

"In a very short time, I believe that I will rest, but first—I know we are just met, sir, but it is in my mind to ask you a boon."

"I'll do what I can for a fellow pilot."

"You are gracious."

Win Ton reached to the collar of his shirt, fumbling the chain and the pendant key out and over his head. He shuffled three steps forward. Theo twitched, and made herself stand still, watching, but not hovering. She had hated it, when she'd been a littlie, and teachers had *hovered*, because she might fall—and watching out for what they might do had increased the likelihood that she *would* fall.

Win Ton held the key out.

"*Bechimo*."

"Less Pilot yo'Vala. Welcome home."

"Thank you. I pass the key to Copilot O'Berin, to hold for me, and to use in the best service of ship and pilot. If I do not reclaim it..."

Somebody squeaked. It took Theo a moment to realize that it had been her.

Win Ton looked at her over his shoulder and smiled...maybe.

"But of course I shall reclaim it. There is no doubt." He looked back to Clarence. "Pilot, if you would do the kindness?"

"For the best service of pilot and ship," Clarence said formally, and added something quick and liquid in Liaden.

Win Ton laughed again and staggered. Theo stepped up and put her hand under his arm to steady him.

"Thank you, Sweet Mystery. Now, you had asked what it is that the ship may provide. I would say, an escort to the healing unit. I hope that I am not boorish."

"No," said Theo. She cleared her throat. "I'll escort you." She looked to Clarence. "Lay in the first leg, please."

"Yes, Pilot."

Drawing his arm again through hers, she steered Win Ton toward the healing room where she had woken up after the lift from Tokeoport.

"With apologies, Pilot," *Bechimo* said quietly. "Pilot yo'Vala will be requiring the Remastering Unit. I will guide you."

· · · ❄ · · ·

Miri, Val Con thought wryly as he moved silently down the predawn hallway, *is not going to like this.*

He paused outside the door to the suite he shared with his lifemate, took a breath, and put his palm firmly against the plate.

The door slid aside, and he stepped into their private parlor, pausing just over the threshold.

Across the room the curtains had been drawn back from the wide window, admitting Surebleak's uncertain dawn. The rocking chair placed at an angle to the window moved quietly, back and forth, back and forth, its occupant silhouetted against the light.

"What ain't I gonna like?" she asked. "Didn't get the details, but things did look kinda dicey there for a while."

"It was not without its moments," he allowed, moving toward the window. "Even the presence of Scout Commander ter'Meulen was insufficient to turn all to farce."

"If Clonak was half as stupid as he acts, something with lotsa teeth would've had him for lunch a long time ago."

"True," he murmured from the side of her chair. He reached down and slipped his fingers through the wealth of her unbound hair. "But you discount the joy of the masquerade."

"No, I don't. I just wonder why he bothers."

"I believe we must diagnose an excess of energy."

She snorted. Next to her, he smiled into the dawn, then sighed.

"Wanna tell me about it?"

"In fact," he said, dropping lightly to the rug beside her and leaning his head against her thigh, "I do."

"Ready when you are." He felt her hand stroke his hair and

sighed in contentment made more poignant by the knowledge that it was to be all too brief.

"The highly condensed version," he murmured, "is that one of the teams the Scouts sent to gather the severed blossoms of the Department of the Interior..."

She choked a laugh, and he paused, his eyes on the dark garden.

"That's gotta be Clonak," she said.

"Indeed, Commander ter'Meulen was pleased to style it thus," he said. "Allow it, with the understanding that the actual business is not nearly so poetical."

He felt her hair move as she shook her head. "'Course it ain't."

"Yes, well." Her robe was fleece, soft and warm under his cheek. "This team of Scouts obtained news of a situation which...lies close to us, *cha'trez.*"

Her hand stilled on his hair. "How close, exactly?"

"Close as kin," he answered. "It would seem that the Department deployed a field unit, and perhaps a tech team, to Vandar after Agent sig'Alda failed them."

He felt her grasp it, and the frisson of her horror. Her hand fell to his shoulder, fingers gripping.

"We gotta go in," she said, and he smiled at her quickness. "Zhena Trelu, Hakan, Kem—gods, what if they've already..."

"We have some hope that they have not already," Val Con murmured. "A field unit is by no means an Agent of Change. But we dare not tarry."

"We *are* going, then." There was satisfaction in her voice.

Val Con shook his head. "*I* am going. You, my lady, will stay here and mind Korval's concerns—and our daughter."

"Who's your backup, then? If I'm staying home to mind the store."

"I thought to travel quickly," he murmured, "and leave within the hour. Clonak is gathering a contact team. He expects them to lift out no later than three days from—"

"What you're saying is that you're going in without any backup." The rocker moved more strongly; inside his head, he heard the arpeggio of her irritation. "Someday, we gotta learn better. Why not today?"

"*Cha'trez*—"

"Quiet. Didn't that little surprise at the dance party teach you anything? Me, I been thinking about it a lot, and I recommend you do the same. For now, I ain't gonna tell you how stupid it is to go into something like this by yourself, 'cause if you'd take a second to think, you'd figure it out for yourself. What I *am* gonna tell you is you got two options: I go with you—or Beautiful goes."

He could not risk her—would not risk their child. His rejection was scarcely formed when he heard her sigh over his head.

"My feelings are hurt. But have it your way." Her hand left his shoulder. He rolled to his feet and helped her to rise, pulling her into an embrace.

"I will take Nelirikk with me," he whispered into her ear, and felt her laugh.

"That's a good idea," she murmured. "Glad you thought of it."

"Indeed." He hugged her tight, and stepped back. He slipped Korval's Ring off of his finger and onto her thumb.

Miri sighed and closed her fingers over it.

"Get your kit," she said. "I'll call down to the pilot and give him the good news."

FORTY

· · · · · · · · · · · ·

Jelaza Kazone
Surebleak

"TELL POD 78 TO PUT ITSELF TO SLEEP," MIRI SAID, TRYING TO
sound more patient than she was feeling. "We don't need it right
now, and we're short on hands."

"With all respect," Jeeves answered, headball flickering. "Pod
78 has twice been put off in just those terms; the second time, I
overrode its autonomous system and forced it into hibernation."

"Do it again."

The headball flashed bright orange, then subsided into a dull
glow. Miri eyed it doubtfully.

"There is information that the *delmae* has not received," Jeeves
stated.

"Because I ain't listening." She sighed. "All right, I'll shut up."
She folded her hands on top of the desk and pressed her mouth
closed.

"Thank you. I will be brief. What makes this request worthy of
the delm's notice is that the induced hibernation is still in force.
Pod 78 is not, in the vernacular, *awake*. This latest contact is
from the security core. Pod 78 believes itself to be under attack.
It believes that enemies are attempting to subvert it. If it does
not receive within three Standard Weeks a deep reset by no one
other than the delm genetic of Korval, it will initiate the secondary core security protocol."

"Which is what, exactly?"

Jeeves' headball flickered, the orange light dimming to a pale golden glow.

"If Pod 78 does not receive the attention of the delm genetic of Korval within the stated time frame, it will self-destruct."

"...which we can't let it do, on account of it being in a high-traffic area," she finished, and looked at Daav, lounging in the deskside chair; his eyes half-closed like the news had put him to sleep.

Or maybe not.

"When Pod 78 was established, Moonstruck was in a back pocket of the galaxy," he murmured. "It has since been found scenic and thus we have cruise ships and tourist camps."

"Don't we just," she said glumly. "Might as well set up an ice cream stand while I'm there. Get us some tourist money."

Daav opened his eyes. "By all means encourage Ms. dea'Gauss to explore the possibility of an ice cream stand," he said cordially, "but you are not going to Moonstruck."

"You been listening? Unless that thing gets its ears rubbed, it's gonna do something drastic. It's ours to take care of, and it's yelling for the delm. I happen to be the half of the delm that's available to take the call."

"Yes, but you are not the *delm genetic*. Your position within Korval is a social construct. Pod 78's programming calls for a biologic affirmation. I don't doubt that a blood test is involved in the reset process, though I will certainly consult the Diaries before I go."

"Before *you* go?" She shook her head, thinking about explaining to Val Con how she'd sent his parents off to get blown up by an unstable defense module, and not coming up with any good words. "What makes you think I'm sending you?"

Daav sat up straight and gave her a wide, sweet smile. "Because you are a woman of great good sense. Because you have been a captain of mercenaries and understand command. And because, my child, you *are* the delm, and it is your duty to decide upon proper action, for the best good of the clan. Delms spend lives; it is unavoidable. Good delms do not hazard more than the clan can afford, nor do they spend foolishly."

"Speaking of foolish, what about Theonna—that's her, ain't it? The delm who set these things up?"

"Theonna yos'Phelium, yes. I fear her orbit was more erratic than most. To her credit, she did bring the clan through a field thick with thorns, with scarcely a scratch. One gathers from her own entries in the Diaries, and from papers left by others of the clan that it was... often difficult to differentiate between a brilliant plan of flight, and a dangerous delusion."

"And the pods?"

"The pods were, I think, given the times, not an overreaction. The programming protocols might have been... somewhat excessive." He gave her another smile, this one edged with irony.

"On the other hand, only look what her vision wrought on behalf of the clan and our allies, at Lytaxin."

Miri considered him. "Was she a *dramliza*? Sighted?"

He moved his shoulders. "It may have been that she had flashes of long-sight among her delusions. Certainly, that would account for the overall success of her stewardship. However, that is the past; our concern is the present—and the future." He rose and bowed to the delm's honor.

"With Korval's permission, I will take up this task immediately."

"Not so fast. Who're you taking for backup?"

"My intended backup is an expert in these types of systems. If it happens that I am unable to retain his services, I will commission one of the Scout Experts to accompany me. Speed being of the essence, my plans are necessarily fluid."

Well, at least now she knew for certain where Val Con got every bit of his high-handed charm. Miri pushed herself out of her chair and glared at him.

"You will undertake this task at the command of your delm utilizing all possible prudence," she told him, going all the way up to the High Tongue—Delm-to-Clanmember. "You will provide yourself with backup and with a plan for an orderly withdrawal. We are not so many that we can afford the loss of one. Nor do we count you the least of us."

He bowed again, as one accepting his delm's word, without a hint of irony, "Korval."

"Right." She sighed and shook her head. "Just get it done and get back here in one piece, *accazi*?"

· · · ※ · · ·

"A green and pleasant world," Nelirikk said, as they broke their march for the meal local time decreed as dinner. "Is it always so chill?"

"Never think it," Val Con answered. "In fact, I am persuaded there are those native to the world who would pronounce today balmy in the extreme, and perfect for turning the garden."

Nelirikk sipped from his canteen. He was, Val Con thought, a woodsman the like of which Gylles had rarely seen: bold in black-and-red plaid flannel, work pants, and sturdy boots, with a red knit cap pulled down over his ears in deference to the chill of dusk.

The big man finished his drink and resealed the jug. "This... error the captain sends us to correct," he began.

Val Con lifted an eyebrow.

Nelirikk paused, and was seen to sigh.

"Scout, I do not say it was the captain's error."

"Nor should you," Val Con said, surprised by the edge he heard on his own words. He raised a hand, showing empty palm and relaxed fingers.

"The situation—which might, in truth, be said to be error—is of my crafting," Val Con said, more mildly. "It was I who chose to land on an interdicted world. Saying that I did so in order to preserve the lives of the captain and myself does not change the decision or the act. Once here, we inevitably accrued debt, which must of course be Balanced. All of which is aside my decision to See Hakan Meltz. At the time, I stood as Thodelm of yos'Phelium, so it was not a thing done lightly. And yos'Phelium abandons a brother even less readily than Korval relinquishes a child."

Nelirikk was sitting very still, canteen yet in hand, his eyes noncommittal. Likely he was astonished at such a rush of wordage.

Val Con gave him a wry look. "You see how my own stupidity yet rankles," he said. "I should at least have taken my boots off before leaping down your throat."

A smile, very slight, disturbed the careful blandness of Nelirikk's face. "We have both made errors, I think," he said. "If ours are larger, or knottier, than the mistakes of the common troop, it is because our training has given us more scope."

Val Con grinned. "*Anyone may break a glass,*" he quoted. "*But it wants a master to break a dozen.*"

There was a small silence while Nelirikk stowed his canteen.

"What I wondered," he said eventually, "is if we will be able to remove these infiltrators without raising questions in the minds of the natives. There are, so I'm told by the Old Scout, certain protocols for operations on forbidden worlds. If we simply eliminate the enemy..."

"If we simply eliminate the enemy, Clonak will have both of our heads to hang on his office wall," Val Con said. "No, I fear it must be capture and remove."

Nelirikk frowned, doubtless annoyed by such inefficiency. "If they have established themselves, any removal will cause comment among the natives," he pointed out.

"Indeed it will—and the least of the sins I must bear for choosing survival." Val Con stood and stretched. "If you are rested, friend Nelirikk, let us go on. Our target is only a short stroll beyond those trees."

· · · ✳ · · ·

Clarence had settled into quarters and drawn clothes from stores to replace his, left behind on Surebleak. He'd sat with Theo, pilot and copilot, and they'd worked out the shifts and chores between them. That brought up the cooking schedule, which prompted a trip to the galley to take inventory.

"Always thought of energy sticks and such as emergency rations," Clarence said, frowning into the depths of the pantry.

"Agreed," Theo said, pleased to find him of like mind. "We'll need to take on supplies at our first stop." She sighed, peering into the pantry around his elbow. "Fresh-baked bread would go good," she said wistfully.

"Thinkin' the same, myself. Don't see the makin's, though."

Theo frowned, remembering *Primadonna*. They'd been provisioned by Hugglelans, of course, since they'd been part of the fleet. But Rig'd always kept—the Sweet List, he'd called it, though it wasn't only desserts that went on it.

"*Bechimo*," she said now. "We need a list, running live, equal access, command word *grocery*."

"Done, Pilot. There is an automatic inventory and ordering system available. Shall I tie the list to it?"

"Good idea. Another list, same protocols, not on auto order, command word *wish*." She looked at Clarence, who was watching her with interest.

"On the wish list," she explained, "we'll each put those things we like to have, sometimes, but that aren't necessary all the time." She bit her lip, suddenly seeing the white hair and drawn face, remembering the boy who had especially favored the jam-filled cookies at *Vashtara*'s reception buffets. "I'll put in some of Win Ton's favorites," she said.

"Good idea," Clarence answered, and turned back to the pantry. "So, for daily groceries we'll be needin' bread mix..."

"Fresh vegetables."

"Fruit—fresh and tinned. Soup."

"Tea—" She paused. "Do you drink coffee?" she asked.

Clarence smiled at her. "I was long years on Liad, lassie; coffee wasn't always easy to come by, even for—at my office. I learned to drink tea, then I learned to like it."

Theo blinked. "Wait—you speak Liaden, then? No, of course you do! I heard you tell Win Ton that you would—that you would hold his key *as close as kin.*"

"Best thing I might say, to ease his mind," Clarence said, closing the pantry door and leaning a shoulder against it. "Not that I have kin, mind you."

"Right. But the point is that you speak Liaden, and I don't speak Liaden enough to keep myself out of trouble." She bit her lip, not wanting to give him the impression that she was under the delm's word, but, after all it had been a good suggestion.

"I'm not good at languages, and Miri thought that immersion might be the course to plot. *Bechimo* speaks High, Low and—was it the children's language, *Bechimo*?"

"Pilot, yes. I also speak several other languages, and can translate for both of you on-port, via the remote comm, should there be need."

"That's good to know," Clarence said, "but sometimes belt comms get...mislaid. Always good to have some idea what folks are talking about, around you." He looked back to Theo. "You got Trade, right?"

She felt her cheeks warm, but, after all, it was a reasonable question, given that she'd just told him that languages weren't her strong point.

"I had to have Trade before Father would let me go to Anlingdin," she said ruefully, "but Trade isn't as—it's more like hand-talk."

"So it is," Clarence said comfortably. "You're of a notion to put Herself's suggestion into play?"

She hesitated. "Would you mind? I mean, if you do—"

Clarence straightened fluidly out of his lean and bowed.

"Pilot, I will be pleased to assist. Delmae Korval is correct; one must practice art faithfully, lest one's edge becomes dull."

Theo frowned, getting the width, but not the depth of it, which was her whole problem with Liaden, right there.

"Is language art—or no. A weapon? Like a knife?"

"Yes to all of it." Clarence grinned. "All right then, lassie, if you're game, let's try this. We'll need to put some thought into safe words, so we don't risk a bad miscue. How's your reading?"

"I can read Liaden," she told him. "It stays flat."

He laughed. "I've noticed that," he said, and inclined, very slightly, from the waist. "Shall we share a cup of tea and plan this between us?"

"Sure," Theo said, and added one of Father's most annoying sayings: "Soonest begun, soonest done."

FORTY-ONE

· ·

Starrigger's Cafe
Mayflowerport

THE MESSAGE HAD ARRIVED UNDER AN OLD CODE. ONE MIGHT even have said, had one been other than Uncle, a *very* old code. That in itself was intriguing. The message, when accessed, was even more so.

So it was that Uncle entered the so-called Starrigger's Cafe at Mayflowerport as the evening storm broke. He paused in the foyer to allow the heated floor to melt the ice from his boots and brushed the snow off his shoulders. Inside, he flipped a coin to the 'tender, and went to the right, where three private trade-booths lined the wall. Booths one and two showed blue lights. Booth three showed green.

He placed his hand against Three's plate and murmured. "It is Uncle. May I enter?"

The status light faded to yellow. Uncle pressed the plate firmly, and was shortly seated across from a grey-haired man with black eyes wearing a Jump pilot's jacket and an expression of polite interest. An unopened bottle of wine and two glasses sat in the center of the table.

"I am Daav yos'Phelium," the grey-haired pilot said, his voice deep and grainy. "Thank you for agreeing to meet."

"I could scarcely do anything else," Uncle murmured, and nodded at the bottle. "Will you pour?"

"As I had ordered, I thought to leave the rest to you."

The old rules of engagement were in play, then. They met not as allies, but as adversaries whose interests were momentarily aligned.

Uncle opened the bottle—a respectable vintage not entirely in

311

keeping with the facade of the Starrigger's Cafe—and poured. They each raised a glass, and took a single, simultaneous sip.

Daav yos'Phelium set his glass aside. Uncle did the same.

"I understand," Uncle said delicately, "that there is an offer of employment?"

The elder pilot tipped his head. "I am desolate to have raised such expectations, and ask that you forgive my ineptness. In fact, you are to understand that there is a call upon honor."

Uncle laughed, genuinely diverted. "Come now, sir; surely you know better."

"Do I?" The elder pilot looked aside—perhaps at his wineglass, which he touched, but did not raise. "Do you mean me to learn," he said, directing his gaze into the Uncle's face, "that your contracts are suspect?"

"I allow myself to be bound by the terms of my contracts," Uncle said. "I'm sure you'll agree that this is mere prudence for a man who wishes to continue to work at his trade, and to gain the best employees."

"Indeed," the elder pilot said politely, fingering his glass. "Allow me, if you will, a small diversion, by way of satisfying personal curiosity."

"Certainly."

"Did you seek out and hire Theo Waitley as a courier only because she shares genes with Korval?"

"Ah." Uncle raised his glass and sipped. "An excellent vintage; allow me to appreciate your choice."

The other man inclined his head with a small, edged smile.

"Yes." Uncle sipped again. "Pilot Waitley is a peculiar case. I did seek her out, in the sense that, given the nature of my business, I am continually in need of excellent pilots who demonstrate an ability to prevail in, shall we say, *unexpected* circumstances. My interest in her increased, as I am certain you will understand, when I came to know that it was she to whom the ambitious Scout yo'Vala had sent *Bechimo*'s first board key. The key having accepted her, it seemed—allow me to say that it seemed *prudent*—to engineer circumstances so that she and the ship were quickly united. I have some...paternal concern for *Bechimo*, despite my place on the Builders Lists. It is not healthy for a social being to be long alone—an observation that may be made, also, on behalf of Pilot Waitley."

"So it might. And now the pilot and her ship are united, alone no longer. Is the galaxy, do you think, safe?"

Uncle smiled—gently. "My very dear sir. You know for yourself that the galaxy is neither safe nor unsafe. It is the actions of people which decide the state of our existence. Or—forgive me—our deaths."

"I have found that to be so, yes. One must, however, consider the meaning of this partnership you have facilitated. Korval has taken steps to keep pilot and ship occupied for this next while, but it is, I fear, a temporary solution. If causality is not a fiction, one trembles to speculate upon the calamity to which they are the answer."

"It may be that you concern yourself unnecessarily," Uncle said. "I speak as one who is very much your elder, sir, and who has endured many changes. Very often change is merely—change, precipitating no calamity, although certainly requiring adaptation. *Bechimo* was built as an agent of change. In hindsight, it would seem that we built too early, or were too open regarding our intentions. It may be that, now, *Bechimo*'s proper time is now upon us."

"Pilot Waitley is younger even than I," Daav yos'Phelium pointed out.

"She is, and she will undoubtedly make errors. However, youth is a circumstance that time corrects, and error teaches us to err again along a different vector."

Daav yos'Phelium laughed. "It does that." He raised his glass and sipped—appreciatively, to Uncle's eye. "Thank you for satisfying my curiosity. To return to the proper topic of this meeting, Korval at one time purchased from you two defense pods, designated seventy-seven and seventy-eight."

"The transaction to which you refer was completed . . . some time ago, and was, as I recall, pronounced satisfactory by all involved."

"Your recollection is exact insofar as it was reported at the time by agents of Korval. However, there is the issue of a repair warranty."

Long years of practice preserved Uncle's countenance, though he experienced an almost overpowering impulse to laugh.

Instead, he murmured a polite inquiry. "I do not believe that the customer purchased a repair warranty at the time of sale."

"Again, I am inept. I beg the gift of your patience. What I mean to say is that, some while after purchase, when the pods were established each upon their base, Theonna yos'Phelium, who at the time had the honor to be Korval, contacted you specifically for assistance in programming various proprietary protocols, including the protocol for a core reset."

Uncle felt a sudden chill breeze, despite the closed booth.

"Which one?" he asked.

"Seventy-eight reports itself upon the brink of catastrophic action, unless it is attended by the delm genetic, the most recent of whom is unfortunately occupied elsewhere."

Uncle sighed. "A DNA sample is mandated," he said.

"I had expected it."

"Yes, of course. A core reboot means that the pod considers it has been compromised. Attaining the core may thus be ... challenging."

"I had also anticipated this. My concern springs from the possibility that, having done what mischief they might, those who wish Korval ill have withdrawn, trusting that their work will remain invisible to one unfamiliar with the system architecture."

"I understand your need, and your concern, but fear you have failed to prove a warranty of repair. The call to honor being, of course, a mere pleasantry."

"Perhaps. Though one does wonder after your reasons for placing such things into the hands of a madwoman."

"I am a businessperson. She was a customer. She sought me out, bearing a list of very specific needs, and paid hard cantra for what I offered."

"Ah. I refer to the notation left in Theonna's hand within the official clan record. It states that the systems you had put into place for her, being built to her specifications, and untried at the time of installation—prudent, given the nature of several of the protocols under discussion—might require fine-tuning. If that were found to be the case, you were to be contacted, whereupon you would complete the work correctly."

He remembered ...

He'd been intrigued by a Korval, any Korval, seeking him out; he'd also been intrigued that she'd known his relationship to the shipyards of the independents, of his willingness to deal with non-standard tech and perhaps even forbidden tech.

He remembered the intensity of the woman, and that as they'd negotiated on the project schedules, he'd found himself involved in the concept over and beyond his own potential need for a similar hideaway.

The offer: Build me this and my ships will carry the supplies needed as well as blind pods for yourself; you will be paid in good cantra, and in whatever else you need to make this happen.

This was a stormfort, to be built into the unlikely and then unremarked worldlet called Moonstruck. The planet—it *was* a planet, for it had managed both to collapse itself into a sphere and to gather to it a seasonal atmosphere—was stable in an orbit of some .69 eccentricity around a small and quiet star known as Gemaea.

Gemaea's system had barely survived a nearby nova bare millennia before, leaving the star a large outer ring of gas and light rubble which might someday coalesce, but which gave the place the look of a ringed planet from the right point of view. At normal planetary distances there showed only a single notable object: Moonstruck itself.

With a period of very close to 6.96 Standards, the place was at perihelion, livable in an odd way, the atmosphere having oxygen and nitrogen in breathable quantities and densities, and water and poles on the verge of unfreezing. At aphelion? There, Moonstruck was a stony ball covered in stripes of ice, forbidding and lonely—beautiful, if one were a connoisseur.

He remembered that the job had taken longer than either he or she had wanted, but that there had been a reluctance, finally, to admit that it was done, freeing both to retreat to their solitary existences.

He remembered her necessity, very much a matter of sharing the same wine—to bring the systems live, with them both present, so that lifelong distrust of things done by others might be served.

He remembered the control cavern, its walls rough and limned with water. He remembered Theonna—eyes feverish, face afire. She had been past her first youth; the body he had then worn made him appear to be only a few years her elder. Such was her energy that he took fire from her, knowing it was madness they shared, yet a madness indistinguishable from brilliance.

He had done what she had asked. Everything she had asked, including the secondary sealing. After, they had coupled on the rough, icy floor, sharing yet more energy until, her fires temporarily burned low, they parted. For a time after that, he had been . . . erratic . . . in his dealings, plagued by episodes in which his thoughts exploded, searing the fabric of his mind.

Dulsey had at last posited an infection. Theonna was by that time long years dead, and he had gone early to the rebirth, arising unmarked by flame.

It had been...a very long time since he had thought of her—of the intense, peculiar pain of one's thoughts, afire. He wondered how she had borne it.

He sighed, picked up his glass and drained the wine remaining before meeting Daav yos'Phelium's shrewd, eyes.

"I will come with you," he said.

· · · ❈ · · ·

"The captain will have me shot," Nelirikk said, stubbornly.

He'd said that once already today, but Val Con had dismissed it out of hand and continued preparations. Now, it needed to be addressed more forcefully since it was actually delaying lift-off.

"Indeed, she will *not* have you shot. Because, as we have discussed, you will begin calling for aid along Korval's private channels the moment you clear Vandar orbit, and you will not stop calling until you have raised either the captain herself, the elder scout, or Commander ter'Meulen. Once you have done this, you will report that the situation is far more complex than we had believed. That, in addition to no less than six field teams and four technical teams, there is at least one Agent of Change stationed in Laxaco City, whose intention is to speedily bring Vandar's technology to the point required by the new commander of the Department.

"You will report on your prisoners and their condition, and you will say that I have gone to Laxaco on purpose to ensure that Kem and Hakan are out of harm's way. I will attempt to locate the agent, but I do not intend to confront such a one until I have substantial backup."

"Scout—"

Val Con sliced the air with his hand, a signal for attention; Nelirikk subsided, though he dared to frown.

"If the captain has you shot, you have my permission to bludgeon me to death."

Nelirikk snorted. "A soldier's gamble, indeed." He sighed. "I will send backup soon, Scout. Try not to do anything the captain would deplore in the meantime."

"It is my sole desire to behave only as the captain would wish."

Nelirikk looked dubious, but he did at last turn toward the board.

"Safe lift, Scout."

"Fair journey, Nelirikk."

FORTY-TWO

. . . .

Pod 78
Moonstruck

"Pilot, I regret." Uncle's voice did sound regretful over the tight beam, mannerly deceiver that he was. "The attempted remote boot has failed multiple times. Nor have I been able to force the timer into inactivity. I note that certain systems are quickening, in response to the approaching deadline." There was a pause. "I fear," Uncle said, "that you will need to do this, personally."

Webbed into the copilot's chair on *Ride the Luck*, Daav nodded. It scarcely mattered whether Uncle had made the attempts he claimed. Daav rather thought he had done so, given his very genuine horror upon learning that Daav intended, not a reboot, but a full shutdown.

Pod 78 was simply too odd, its location too populated, to be allowed to continue on as it had done. It should have been disarmed many years ago—and perhaps would have been, by some saner successor delm—had Korval managed to recall its existence.

But, there, Theonna's madness had prompted her to obfuscate and conceal, even in the pages of the Diaries, lest some enemy discover her methods, and thereby destroy the clan.

Daav touched the comm switch. "I thank you for your efforts," he said. "One had, after all, expected that it would come to a tour of the cavern."

"As you say. We will maintain surveillance from orbit until you are returned to your ship."

His backup, Daav thought wryly, would perhaps not meet with his delmae's unqualified approval, should word of it ever reach her. Still, it was hardly reasonable to ask Uncle to risk his ancient, precious person to stand at Daav's back with a handgun. Scans of the area had shown hints of perhaps more than one recent visitation. Which could as easily be adventurers from the orbiting space camp as anyone harboring ill-will toward Korval or its holdings.

And there was no natural law, was there, that did not allow of it being both?

The Luck's scans detected no irregularity in the doors or the various locks and protocols guarding them. The more robust scan performed by Uncle had likewise revealed no evidence of tampering.

Which was disturbing of itself.

Pod 78 had reported itself under direct attack. *Some*one must have recently opened that door.

And closed it again, very carefully, behind them.

"I wonder," Daav murmured, "if there is . . . another door."

Silence was his answer, too long a silence for mere lag . . .

"There is," the Uncle admitted, reluctantly, "another door. Transmitting."

· · · ⚜ · · ·

Ride the Luck settled neatly on the rocky apron hard by the back door Theonna had insisted upon. As modeled, the world's constant rotation meant the storms of fall had drifted the water and other snows into a predictably strange drift-sand, and the overhang of the scarp which hid the place from easy satellite oversight kept it accessible even now, approaching the fullness of winter.

It was scarcely more than a service hatch, and the figure in the light-duty suit made quick work of getting it open and slipping inside.

Uncle rode the scans hard, discomfited, as if in anticipation of some grand or terrible event. Yet the scans—powerful and nuanced—reported nothing out of the way.

So focused was he on the close scans that he did not at first see the ship nose out of the shelter of one of the space camp's supply dumps. Certainly, he did not divine its purpose until it had loosed a bolt—

Directly into the heart of *Ride the Luck*.

"Dulsey!" he snapped over the tight band.

"On it," came the laconic reply from *Arin's Toss*.

The ship was a cyclops—a siege ship usually—fitted with one weapon, an outsize combined beam device, something used against the heart of planets and not single vessels. This was not just a bolt loosed, it was a stream inundating the surface of the worldlet, centered on the spot that was *Ride The Luck.*

The initial images on the IR scan showed an immense heat shared between the ship and the rocks it nestled among, the visual scans showed jets of gas emanating from the fire zone and dust lifting as charges built and shared themselves. Korval's ship sang, complained, and acted—a missile was launched in retaliation—and failed instantly, dissolving into spindles of smoke.

Automatics threw everything that was left into the shields; that was his guess, for a brief bubble appeared as if the beam was deflected; the vessel's image trembled even more as the rock it sat on glowed and melted, and it mattered not at all which screen he looked at; every one showed too much energy for a hull to withstand. The dying ship vented, as something in it boiled explosively into space and against the stony surface.

Uncle looked to his screens, at the ruined pieces of ship among the blasted rockscape, glowing brightly in the infrared, amid molten rocks dropping from golden to red to brown visually as they radiated.

He triggered more scans, not really surprised to find that they returned no signs of life on the surface.

· · · ✸ · · ·

The alternate route to the control cavern was hardly more than a service tunnel, illuminated by emergency dims. Daav moved briskly, mindful of the limitations of the light-duty suit, splashing through the occasional puddle, twice ducking to avoid encroaching stalactites, arriving at last at the end of the tunnel, sealed by a manual pressure hatch.

Daav addressed the limestone-coated wheel. It resisted at first, then all at once the stony skin broke and the mechanism meshed.

Three full turns of the wheel later, he was inside a tiny airlock, sealing the hatch behind him. The pressure gauge set into the wall directly in front of his nose went from yellow to green, the inner door slid open and he stepped into the main cavern.

The rock was raw, unimproved, nothing done to protect the machinery from the damp, chilly air, or the slow crawl of limestone.

Except, Daav saw, as he stepped to the control bank, there

were no drips marring the brightwork, no dust coating the dials. The uneven floor seemed strangely dry, and near the center of a room a stalagmite had been snapped off short, the new terminus jagged; the bit snapped off nowhere to be seen.

Daav took a deep breath, tasting canned air, and reached up to unseal his hood. Pod 78 had said it was under attack. Whatever the attackers had done, for whatever reason they had withdrawn, his task was clear.

The cavern's air was dusty. He unsealed suit's pocket and pulled out the remote, triggering the system maps provided by Uncle.

Best to do what he had come to do, and go away again.

Quickly.

Dulsey was in pursuit of the cyclops; the scans reported nothing amiss.

And continued to report nothing amiss when a small craft, scarcely larger than a lifeboat, rose over the asteroid's horizon, on course for the main entrance to the cavern.

Uncle's fingers twitched toward the weapons array. Mindful of the gunship, as yet at large, and the fact that it, as well as this small craft, had been shielded from his scans. His vessel likewise wore a cloak, but it would be foolhardy to draw the attention of those who must intend him no good.

He did, after a moment, open a line to the remote comm carried by Daav yos'Phelium.

"Be quick, Pilot," he said. "There are three coming in the main entrance."

Three," Daav said, glaring at the remote—*only three?* asked Aelliana. "Might you take a more active interest?"

"I dare not risk firing upon them so close to the door," Uncle answered. "Strike or miss, there will be damage to the cavern, and perhaps to yourself."

"There's a touching concern," he snapped, and looked to the control board on which he had been working. A light had gone from red—sealed—to green—open.

Cursing, he flung himself across the room, slapped up the seal on the main door, and palmed the lock to *closed*.

Back at the board, he saw his fingers moving, lines of code appearing on the screen. Aelliana had taken over entering the sequences they had both memorized, leaving him to scan the readouts from the hallway, and hope that the locked door held them long enough to—

The board pinged and flashed orange. He looked to the screen, saw that their proposition had gotten them to the point.

To the very point.

Blood sample required, the bright orange letters spelled out. *Please insert hand in pocket to right.*

Daav glanced to the right, saw the pocket, limned appropriately enough in red, moved his hand—

The hatch to the main hallway blew in.

· · · ✳ · · ·

"The target has been disposed of," Dulsey reported. "They may have gotten a message out."

"We will be gone, presently," Uncle said.

"How fares the pilot?"

"I fear, not well. Let us tarry yet awhile."

· · · ✳ · · ·

The blast damaged one of their own; she staggered into the path of her mates, making a comedy of their entrance, allowing Daav to slit the throat of a second before the third turned on him with a vicious slash and parry, the growl of the vibroblade angry against the stone walls. At least none of them was fool enough to use a gun in this place.

Daav sidestepped, tripped on the broken stalagmite, twisted, and went down, the jagged stump piercing suit, leather and leg.

He screamed, or his assailant did, as she fell on him, blade snarling, biting through his arm instead of his throat. He lost his knife, grabbed her arm and forced it up—up and back—but she had leverage; she had strength. His grip slipped, she leaned in and he kicked with his good leg, sweeping her sideways—not a killing blow, but enough... enough to distract her and allow him to shove the blade home.

There was, after all, more than enough blood left for the proof, after he had dragged himself across the rough icy floor, to the board. After that, there was only, only—Aelliana took care of it, he was certain, the last thing—two things—in the sequence, so that . . .

"Daav?"

He lay across her lap, his head pillowed on her shoulder. He was tired—no, he was far worse than tired.

"Aelliana," he said, or thought he said, "I fear that I—am about to fail you."

Her arms tightened fiercely. "You have never failed me, *van'chela*, and you do not fail me now."

He laughed, thought that it should have hurt—and opened his eyes.

Her eyes were awash with tears, her face wet, but he smiled to see her again, at last.

Smiling, he slid away.

FORTY-THREE

. . . .

Jelaza Kazone
Surebleak

HE PAUSED OUTSIDE THE DOOR TO THE SUITE HE SHARED WITH HIS lifemate, took a breath, and put his palm firmly against the plate.

The door slid aside; he stepped into their private parlor—and stopped.

Across the room, the curtains had been drawn back from the wide window, admitting Surebleak's uncertain dawn. The rocking chair placed at an angle to the window moved quietly, back and forth, back and forth, its occupant silhouetted against the light.

"Took your time," Miri said.

He smiled and moved across the room, dropping to his knees by her chair and putting his head in her lap.

"I am glad to be home, too, *cha'trez*."

She laughed, her hand falling onto the back of his neck, fingers massaging gently.

"Emerging world, huh? Pretty slick way of doing things, Scout Commander."

"It was the only possible solution," Val Con murmured. "Hakan and Kem will do well, I think, as planetary liaisons."

"I think so, too."

"Also, we are to take our child to make her bow to Zhena Trelu, when she is old enough to travel safely."

"Be glad of the vacation," she said. "You don't mind my saying so, you could use some sleep. No need to rush back so fast."

"I did not wish to miss the birth of our daughter," he said, drowsy under her fingers.

"Not a worry. Priscilla says day after tomorrow."

"So soon?"

She laughed, and pushed him off her lap. He made a show of sprawling on the rug, and she laughed again, pushing against the arms of the chair.

Val Con leapt to his feet and helped her rise.

"I believe I will have a nap," he said. "Will you join me?"

"Wouldn't miss it for anything."

· · · ✻ · · ·

Father's house on Leafydale Place had a cellar. In the cellar, buried snugly beneath the house where neither light nor neighbors might peer, were storage closets full of things that nobody was using at the moment, but might again, someday; and things that were only useful once or twice a year. Father's collection of lures and fishing poles had their own closet. Another closet was full of rugs.

Cellars, she'd learned from her classmates, were atavism or worse, harking back to the time before the safe life in the Wall, assuming a need for more—and worse, different!—things than one's level mates might have access to.

Cellars, she'd learned at home, were comforting collections of scents and textures, a place where *just the right thing* might be waiting to be unleashed yet again.

Father had confided once to growing up in a house with a cellar, one of the rarest fleeting references he'd ever made to living some other life, and he'd said he'd liked the feeling that he could touch the coming season by going to the cellar to get the gardening supplies, to find and restore the sleeping tubers—

Bechimo didn't have a cellar, of course. But if he had, the Remastering Unit would've been in it.

Of the questions she'd asked Win Ton, of the demands she'd made, of the delights shared, none had dealt with the question of the house itself. His discussions being full of clan rather than house, most often of the demands of clan, he'd not talked about a favorite room, a favorite spot, a cellar.

She used the manual pull at the end of the long passage that led to the heart of the ship, the exercise of dealing with the massive blast door on her own, allowing her to bypass *Bechimo*'s tendency to overlight everything. True or not, the place felt cooler, like a proper cellar should.

Theo stepped into the dim space, walking quiet, like she thought she might wake him up.

She checked the status lights—all green; that was good, right?—and didn't trigger the internal view screen. It would be an invasion of privacy, to look at him when he didn't know.

And besides, she thought, the status lights said that everything was going well.

"Pilot Waitley," *Bechimo* said quietly, from somewhere to the right and rear of her. "Is there a . . . difficulty?"

A difficulty.

Theo raised her hand and stroked her fingertips across the status lights.

"No, *Bechimo*," she said, stroking the lights again. "Everything's going well."

· · · ✹ · · ·

Warm leaves surrounded and cherished her, and the whole world smelled like mint. It was a puzzling place Miri found herself in, but comforting for all of that. Maybe she slept, a little. Must have, actually, because she woke up, impatient with the fuzzy, indeterminate landscape, and wondering where Val Con was.

"Here," she heard him say, and all at once the leaves melted, reshaping into pillows, a blanket, a bed.

She opened her eyes to his face, brilliant with wonder, damp with tears. He was cradling something in his arms.

Carefully, he bent and showed her—an impossibly tiny, scrunched face beneath a shock of fuzzy red hair.

"*Cha'trez*," Val Con said, and his voice was shaky with pride and love. "Behold our daughter."

EPILOGUE

. . . .

Pod 78
Moonstruck

DULSEY HAD PROPOSED TO GO DOWN TO THE ASTEROID'S SURFACE
and reconnoiter. It would have been wise.

Uncle was not, at the moment, feeling particularly wise. He'd
already allowed connection to the place to fog his thought and
action, and having owned that much recognition of investment
in something that ought to have been mere fact, he measured the
words he'd said to *this* yos'Phelium, and recounted them against
his debts and promises.

And so he went himself, down the center of the main corridor,
through the blown hatch, into the inner sanctum, and nothing
worse befell him than his boots got wet; their shiny blackness
marred by streaks of pale mud.

The control cavern . . . the floor on which he and Theonna
yos'Phelium had madly embraced, so very long ago, was sticky with
blood. Bodies, likewise sticky, lay in stiff, graceless poses. He checked
them all for vital signs, starting with the one nearest the door.

Dead.

Dead.

Decapitated.

The fourth body, left arm nearly severed, blood sheeting the
sharp, ironic face. As unlikely as it seemed, given the surrounding carnage, and the wounds which must surely have pained him,
he was smiling.

327

Uncle sighed, remembering the murdered ship scattered on the drifted snow and across the wind-swept rocky plain outside, and wondered if, indeed, the pilot would have chosen this, had he known.

He wondered, but recalled that the pilot had not come here to smile, as much as he may have expected to die, but that he'd come to—

No manual control reacted to his demands, none to the remote he'd built so many years before.

Yes, of course. The lighting and other such housekeeping protocols were powered by the planet's seasons, and they would go on, but the weapons and devices of Pod 78, those were in fact not merely disabled by automatics—the controls were severed from their aims. The brain of it was gone, the very links from controls to devices had been physically eliminated.

Pod 78 was useless.

He considered that, realized it might not quite be the case. Perhaps some of the pod's devices might be salvaged; certainly in the long run of time they should not be permitted to be discovered for what they might tell an ardent investigator. A project to be added to his years ahead.

But there, this man of Korval had done what he had come to do, and perhaps that was what the smile meant—he had succeeded at his last task.

Well.

In the interest of thoroughness, he bent once more, placed his fingers against the pulse point in the throat—and straightened, snatching the comm from his belt, finger on the call button.

"Dulsey," he said in answer to her inquiry. "I need a field 'doc. Immediately."